The
INNOCENT

By Bertrice Small

The
INNOCENT

BERTRICE SMALL

FAWCETT BOOKS

THE BALLANTINE PUBLISHING GROUP

NEW YORK

A Fawcett Book
Published by The Ballantine Publishing Group

Copyright © 1999 by Bertrice Small

All rights reserved under International and Pan-American Copyright
Conventions. Published in the United States by The Ballantine Publishing
Group, a division of Random House, Inc., New York, and simultaneously in
Canada by Random House of Canada Limited, Toronto.

ISBN 0-7394-0290-0

Jacket design by Carlos Beltrán
Jacket illustration by Franco Accornero
Manufactured in the United States of America

For my neighbors,
Emily and Jim Gundersen, who rock!
This is no April Fool, guys!

PROLOGUE
THE CHILD
England 1143

"*I want my mama!*" The little girl struggled within the firm clasp of the young nun's arms. "*Mama! I want my mama!*"

"Hush, Elf," her elder brother said gently. He was already having his doubts about this course of action, but the de Warennes were right. He could not raise his five-year-old sister alone, and it was unfair to Isleen to saddle her with Eleanore, although God knew other brides took on greater responsibilities.

"Dickon," the child sobbed piteously, "*I want to go home!* I want Mama and Ida!" Her small heart-shaped face was woebegone. Her fine gray-blue eyes brimmed over with tears that rolled down her rosy cheeks.

Richard de Montfort felt his heart twist within his chest once again, but swallowing back his own emotions he said sternly to his younger sibling, "Now, Elf, you know Mama is dead. There is war all around us, and I cannot raise you myself. We spoke on this, you and I. You will be safe here at St. Frideswide's. This is your home now."

"Say farewell to your brother, Eleanore." Reverend Mother Eunice patted the child. Then, turning to a young nun, she instructed, "Take her to meet her new companions, Sister Cuthbert. Quickly! The longer you linger, the harder it is for the girl."

"Adieu, little sister," Richard de Montfort said, and he kissed the top of her pale red-gold hair.

Elf looked at him just once. She could not speak. Then she burst into a fit of renewed sobbing, and as Sister Cuthbert hurried through the gates of the convent with the weeping child, Elf cried out but once, *"Dickon!"*

Richard de Montfort looked as if he would cry himself, and so Mother Eunice put a comforting hand on his arm. "It is always hard for the little ones the first time," she said. "We will take very good care of the demoiselle Eleanore, my lord."

"Elf," he said. "We call her Elf. Perhaps if you could call her that for a short time, it would help her to adjust. With Mother gone, I could not take care of her, Reverend Mother. *I could not!*"

"Of course you could not, my lord. Do not fret yourself. We have several young girls in our care at this time. One is your sister's age. She came to us when she was three. Another maiden is a year older than Eleanore . . . *Elf.*" She smiled at him. "I understand that congratulations are in order, my lord, and that you will soon take a wife." She had reassured him, and then neatly turned the subject.

"The demoiselle Isleen is not quite fit to be a wife, but her mother assures me it will be within a year at the most," he answered. How anyone could believe that a girl as sensuous as Isleen was not yet ready for marriage baffled him, but he could hardly question Lady de Warenne.

The nun, too, was equally surprised, but her face showed nothing. Isleen de Warenne had been at St. Frideswide's for a year, and a more carnal girl the Reverend Mother Eunice had never met. The convent had been most relieved her stay was a short one, however it had had its benefits. The de Warennes had been generous, and on their recommendation the convent had little Eleanore de Montfort and her dowry. "I am certain that Lady de Warenne knows what is best for her daughter, my lord de Montfort. Now, however, I must bid you farewell. I would suggest that you wait several months before visiting your sister. It will give her the time she will need to acclimate herself to her new life. Come at Martinmas, if you can. You will be most welcome." Then with a nod the Reverend Mother Eunice turned and glided serenely through the convent gates, which closed slowly behind her with a very firm thunk as the bar was set in place.

Richard de Montfort mounted his dappled gray stallion, and turned the beast's head to begin the eight-mile ride back to his manor of Ashlin. He was unaccompanied, which was dangerous in these troubled times, but of late the countryside about Ashlin had been quiet, so he had taken the chance of riding alone. He had wanted his last moments with Elf to be between the two of them. How very much he loved his little sister. When their father had died four years ago in the fighting between King Stephen and the late King Henry's daughter, the Empress Matilda, he had been eleven years of age. Guided by his mother, he had assumed control of their family's manor. Elf, still at their mother's breast, had just begun to toddle; she would never know the fine man who had sired her.

Fortunately Ashlin was not a large, important manor, or it might have been taken over by a stronger baron. Their small wealth was in sheep; they had enough serfs, along with a few freedmen, to do the work that needed to be done. Survival was the chief occupation at Ashlin. Their house sat upon a hill. It was stone, and surrounded by a small moat. About it clustered the barns, the outbuildings, and the huts for the serfs. There was a mill by a swiftly flowing stream near the barns. The little stone church, however, lay half ruined. A wall enclosed it all to protect them from the marauding Welsh. The sheep grazed upon the surrounding hills beneath which lay the arable fields, where they grew hay, oats, marrows, barley, and wheat, in rotation.

But his mother had suffered greatly the loss of her husband, for their marriage had been a love match, and without him she was lost. Isolated as Ashlin was, and with England at war with itself, they saw no one but an occasional passing religious brave enough to dare the road in hopes his devout vocation would protect him. Adeliza de Montfort had clung to life as long as she could, teaching her son everything he needed to know about running his manor. His father's old sergeant at arms, Fulk, had continued his lessons in the art of warfare. *And Elf.* His baby sister had been the joy of his life. She was sweet-natured and extremely intuitive. At the end of the day when he would sit exhausted before the fire in the hall, she would crawl into his lap and stroke his face with her fat baby hand, chattering away in her infant babble at him. How he loved her!

But then last autumn their mother had sickened. By now he was a man, and he had Ashlin under his control. Adeliza de Montfort knew it, and while she worried about the fate of her daughter, she could no longer hold on to her empty place in life. They had found her in her bed one morning, a smile upon her face. By chance a passing friar had taken shelter at Ashlin the night before. He blessed Adeliza de Montfort's soul, and helped to bury her before going his way. The next house in which he sheltered, two days later, was that of Hugh de Warenne. Baron Hugh was most interested to learn that Richard de Montfort and his sister were now alone in the world.

Hugh de Warenne had quickly approached Richard de Montfort, and proposed a marriage between the two families. The young lord of Ashlin agreed to consider Baron Hugh's proposal. He was invited to visit the de Warenne manor, and leaving Elf in the charge of her old nurse, Ida, he went. One look at Isleen de Warenne, and he was lost. She was the most beautiful creature he had ever seen, with long silken hair the color of purest gold, and limpid blue eyes. But it was not merely her perfect beauty. There was something about Isleen that aroused savage lust in him. She had a way of moving, of speaking, none of it too obviously suggestive, that made him desire her so much he would have gone to hell and back to possess her.

The match was agreed upon. Richard de Montfort would marry Isleen de Warenne when the bride's womanhood flowered. In the meantime there were other things to consider. Isleen could hardly come a bride into a house where another and younger female of her station resided, her family said. Nor could she be either asked or expected to raise a tiny girl, not her own child, although such a thing was hardly unusual. Richard de Montfort explained that his sister would be little trouble, being cared for by her nursemaid, Ida. But the de Warennes were adamant that another home be found for Elf, although they did not offer to foster her themselves to facilitate their daughter's marriage. Richard suggested a match between his little sister and one of the de Warenne sons, but, according to Baron Hugh, his sons were all spoken for, alas.

It was Maude de Warenne who suggested Elf be placed at the convent of St. Frideswide's. "You cannot raise her," she told her future son-in-law smiling, her tone kindly. "And she cannot be there when you wed Isleen. St. Frideswide's is home to the Order of St. Mary the Virgin. They take in young girls as a means of support. Some are there to be educated and prepared for marriage. Why, Isleen spent time there herself. Other maidens are there to be prepared for a religious life. Do you not think that would be a good choice for your little sister, Richard? Place her at St. Frideswide's, and her future is assured. She will be happy and safe there, I am certain."

"And," Baron Hugh said, "they will take but half the dowry you would have to expend on a husband for her. It's a practical solution, my boy, as well as a good one. What say you?"

"I loved St. Frideswide's," Isleen chimed in with a tinkling laugh. "We maids had such fun, and the nuns there are really quite kindly, Richard . . . *m'amour.*" Her voice seemed to purr at him. She put her elegant hand upon his sleeve. "Your sister will be as happy there, Richard, as I will be as your wife, *if, of course, all the terms can be settled between you and Papa.*" Her little pearl teeth gleamed as she smiled at him, her dark gold lashes brushed her pale cheeks, even as her fingers tightened a moment upon his arm. *"Please, Richard,"* she murmured low.

He had agreed because, of course, he had to have her. Having seen Isleen, he could not be happy with any other woman. He had not, however, as his future father-in-law suggested, offered the convent only half of Elf's dower portion. His father had set aside a specific sum for Elf when she had been born, and Richard de Montfort would have felt his parents' disapproval from the grave had he cheapened his sister's worth. As neither Isleen nor her family knew the amount, there would be no quarrel over the matter.

Elf had turned five on the first of May, and now a month later as he rode home alone, Richard de Montfort felt a deep sadness at having left her at St. Frideswide's. Old Ida had wept when he had told her his decision. She had gone down on her knees and begged him not to send Elf away, demanding to know what kind of creature the lord was wedding, that she would send a baby from her home. At first he had been comforting to the elderly woman who had nursed his father, and had nursed him and his sister as well. But Ida would not be pacified, and he had finally, in anger, reminded her of her status as a serf. The old lady had pulled herself to her feet, ignoring his hand, and with a fierce look at him, had stalked away. She had not spoken to him since, and while he felt sorrow about it, he would allow no one to criticize his Isleen. When his bride-to-be gave him a son, old Ida would recover and be happy to care for his child. She would soon forget her anger over Elf. She had no choice. None of them did. Isleen must be happy at Ashlin, and Richard de Montfort would do all in his power to assure his future wife's contentment.

PART I

THE NOVICE,

England 1152

CHAPTER ONE

St. Frideswide's Convent sat atop a hillock with a fine view of the surrounding countryside of Hereford, and across the hills into Wales. Its high stone walls enclosed themselves about a quadrangle on the south side of which was a church. From the church four sheltered walks went around the quadrangle connecting with the refectory, where the nuns and their female guests ate, the chapter house, where they met guests or did the business of the house, and the dormitories. There were special places for the students and nuns to study, and a kitchen, a bakery, a brewery. St. Frideswide's, though small, had a storehouse, a barn for its farm animals, a hen-house and dovecote, not to mention an infirmary to treat the sick, several workshops for metalwork and illuminating manuscripts, and an herbarium.

Within the convent each day was carefully ordered. At midnight, Matins, the first holy office of the day was said, followed shortly thereafter by Lauds. The nuns would then go to their sleeping quarters. Prime was said at six during the summer months, and seven in the dark months of winter. It was then that the young girls in the convent's charge joined the nuns for the first Mass, which was followed by a breakfast of oat porridge, a slice of buttered bread, and a small cup of cider, or ale for the nuns. The children then returned to their dormitory to make their beds and sweep the rooms. They emptied the common night jar, and opened the windows to air the space.

It was during this time the nuns met together in the chapter house. Convent business was discussed, announcements, if any, were made, letters read, and finally discipline was dispensed to those miscreants who had earned it. Terce was the next office said at nine o'clock of the morning. A High Mass was sung. It was then the nuns went to their daily tasks, which might involve personal study, teaching, household duties, the workshops where skilled illuminations and simple, beautiful metalwork were done. Some of the nuns did heavy farmwork, caring for the convent's flock of sheep, its smaller herd of cattle, or its milk cows, pigs, or poultry. At noon the office of Sext, at three, Nones, and at four, Vespers, were conducted, and attended by those nuns whose other duties did not prevent it.

From midmorning until five in the afternoon, the young girls in the convent's care were taught. All of them learned how to read and write and keep simple accounts. They learned Latin, French, and English, for both of the latter languages were spoken in England, but not all the convent's students could speak them when they came to St. Frideswide's. The girls who were eventually to become nuns were taught to do needlework and fine tapestry work. Those who showed a talent for it were taught the art of illumination and scribing. When a girl showed her competence in administration, she was taught the work of supervising the convent and its lands so that should Mother Eunice, the convent's abbess, be away, or too ill to do her duty, there would be someone able to pick up her burden. Maidens prepared for the church were also taught the arts of healing.

The young girls destined for marriage took a slightly different path, learning how to play on some instrument, do pretty needlework, oversee the kitchens; which meant they must learn to cook, make conserves, and salt foods to be stored for a time. They must know how to make soap for bathing, and soaps for cleaning. They learned how to manage an estate in the event their husbands should be away, how to manage their own households, care for the sick, and tend the wounded.

Frightened and lonely as she was, Elf quickly adjusted to life at St. Frideswide's. Sister Cuthbert, the nun who had carried her away from her brother and into the convent, was enormously kind. It was she who was in charge of the six young girls currently boarding in the cloister. She was plump beneath her robes, and had a round face with rosy cheeks and warm brown eyes that twinkled more often than not. She was sympathetic over her newest charge's sadness, but she would not allow the child to wallow in her misery. Bustling into the girl's dormitory, she set Elf down upon the floor.

"This is where you will live with your new companions," she said brightly. "Come now, maidens, and meet Eleanore de Montfort, who is called Elf. She is five."

"She doesn't look five," the biggest of the girls said. "She is very petite. Matilda FitzWilliam is five, and she's far bigger."

"I am bigger than Isabeaux St. Simon, and she's six," Matilda said, glaring at the older girl, who was ten and an earl's daughter. "Nature makes each of us differently." She held out her hand to Elf. "You may call me Matti, for we are going to be friends, little Elf." She had round blue eyes and yellow braids.

Elf looked shyly at the other girl from the safety of Sister Cuthbert's robes. "I was five on Mary's Day," she said as if to reinforce the fact. "I am called Elf because I am so small. My brother named me."

"I have six brothers," Matti said, "which is why I was sent here to St. Frideswide's to be a nun. There wasn't enough monies to dower me into marriage. I came when I was three, and my mother died birthing the last of my brothers. You'll like it here. Are you going to be a nun, too?"

"I don't know," Elf said.

"Yes, she is," Sister Cuthbert said. "Now, Matti, you will have someone to go to your special studies with, my child."

"She's going to be way behind us," the earl's daughter said.

"Of course she is," Sister Cuthbert said with a cheery smile. "She is the youngest and the newest of you, but I believe Elf will like her studies, and quickly catch on. You cannot expect her to know as much as you do, Irmagarde. After all, you have been with us four years now. As I recall you had no knowledge at all when you were six, and Elf is just five."

What the good sister didn't say was that she believed Elf would far outstrip Irmagarde.

Irmagarde Bouvier had departed St. Frideswide's three years after Elf's arrival to be prepared for her marriage to a knight some years her senior. She was to be his third wife, and he had children older than she. By that time Elf had indeed surpassed the earl's daughter in her abilities.

"She was not the brightest of girls," Sister Cuthbert noted shortly after Irmagarde had departed in pubescent triumph for her wedding.

Outside the convent's walls, the war raged on. In 1139 the Empress Matilda had landed in England. King Stephen was captured by her forces in 1141, and the daughter of Henry I, the granddaughter of William the Conqueror, entered London. But the empress was arrogant, and immediately imposed exorbitant taxes on the populace. Stephen's wife, another Matilda, drove the empress from London. Finally in 1147 Henry's daughter departed England forever. Her cause was taken up by her son, Henry Plantagenet, Lord of Anjou and Poitou in his own right, and Lord of Acquitane by virtue of his marriage to Alienor, its heiress.

In 1152 Elf was fourteen, and a novice at St. Frideswide's. It was planned she would take her final vows on the twenty-second day of June that year. This was the feast day of England's first martyr, and Elf had decided to take his name for her own. She would be known as Sister Alban. Her best friend, Matti, would also take her vows that day and become Sister Columba. As for Isabeaux St. Simon, their other friend, she would be married in the autumn and would leave St. Frideswide's in late summer for her own home near Worcester.

On a late spring afternoon the three girls sat out on a hillside watching over the convent's sheep. Two were dressed alike in the gray gown all the convent novices wore. Isa, however, wore a red tunic over her deep blue skirts.

"I can't believe," she said, "that they're going to cut your hair, Elf. Mary's blood, I've always envied it." She stroked Elf's long pale red-gold hair. "What a sin!"

"Vanity has no place in a bride of Christ," Elf said softly.

"But you're not vain!" Isa protested. "It is a great pity you cannot be wed, Elf. I'll wager there would be men of rank who would take you even with your small dowry. You are far more beautiful than either Matti or me." She sighed. "I hate it that we're being separated in a few months. I know I grumble a lot about the convent, but the truth is it has been a lot of fun for us over the years, hasn't it?"

Matti giggled mischievously. "We've had a few small adventures."

"Misadventures is more like it," Elf said with a smile. "Keeping you two out of difficulties has been a full-time occupation. You are really going to have to change your ways, Matti."

"Reverend Mother knows how impossible that will be for me," Matti replied. "That is why I am going to remain with Sister Cuthbert, taking care of the little girls. Reverend Mother says that will help me to use up all my energies until I am too old to have any. She says we all serve God in our own way. Sister Agnes says if my voice continues to improve, I shall be a head cantrix one day. I would like that, for you both know how I love music!"

"But once Matilda FitzWilliam becomes Sister Columba," Isa said wickedly, "there can be no more visits to the dairy barn to see Father Anselm swiving the dairymaid with his big poker."

Matti chuckled. "It's a shame you would never come with us, Elf. You can't possibly know what you're going to miss unless you can see it. I think I am making a big sacrifice now that I have seen a man and a woman together in the throes of passion. I am filled with regret that my family has not the means to marry me off to a big healthy fellow. Still, I have accepted my fate, and am the better for knowing the forfeit I make for our good Lord's sake."

"I can't wait until Sir Martin and I can be joined in the marriage bed," Isa said. "They say it hurts to lose your virginity, but afterward it doesn't hurt at all. When Father Anselm puts his big, thick manhood into Hilda, the dairymaid, how she squeals with delight!"

"And waves her legs about until she wraps them tight about our good priest," Matti noted with relish. "Then they bump up and down until the crisis comes. I like it when he pillows himself on her nice big breasts, and sometimes, Elf, he even suckles on her like a babe at its mother's breast. It's very exciting to watch."

Elf put her hands over her ears. "Matti! Matti! You know I don't want to hear such things. You are very, very wicked to gossip so salaciously. If you do not cease, I shall have to tell Reverend Mother, and I don't want to tell. How I fear for your soul, Matti."

Matti reached out and patted her friend with a plump hand. "Do not fret yourself about me, Elf. Once I have taken my vows, there will be no more visits to the dairy barn, alas. One cannot serve two masters, and my master is our good Lord, not the lord of lust and darkness."

"I am relieved to hear you say it, Matti," Elf replied, mollified. She loved both these girls with whom she had been raised. It did not matter that Isabeaux St. Simon was worldly, for she would be a wife soon; but Matilda FitzWilliam was another matter, particularly as she was to help Sister Cuthbert with the little girls in the convent's care. She had uneasily broached the subject with the nun who had raised them just a few months ago; however, Sister Cuthbert did not seem to take the matter very seriously. "But some of the girls sneak into the dairy barn to hide and watch Hilda when she sports with a lover," Elf told the nun, a worried look upon her face. *"Even girls who are to take holy orders,"* she finished in an unhappy and shocked whisper.

Sister Cuthbert had said almost what Matti said. "But they are not nuns yet, little Elf, and they are curious as to what they will miss, if anything. Having seen the carnal act, they will either find it unpleasant and be glad to be free of such things, or they will finally understand the loss they must forgo if they are to serve God properly. There is no harm in *seeing* as long as they remain chaste. Most of the girls in our care go to the dairy barn at one time or another. Even I did when I was very young," she told the surprised Elf. "Do not worry, my child. Matilda FitzWilliam will be a good nun."

"But I didn't say—" Elf began.

"No," Sister Cuthbert said, *"you didn't."* Then she smiled. "Perhaps you should go to the dairy barn one day, Elf, before you take your final vows."

But Elf shook her head violently. *"Never!"* she told the nun. "I want to be as pure an offering as I can be, a totally innocent bride of Christ. That is the only way for me."

"Each of us knows the best way for herself," Sister Cuthbert said soothingly. Then she turned the conversation. "Sister Winifred tells me you are the best student she has ever had. She has asked Reverend Mother if she may have you for her assistant in the herbarium. She is not young anymore, my child, and you may one day take her place, but do not say I told you until Reverend Mother tells you it is so."

Elf had learned of her appointment to the herbarium a few days later, and was very pleased. She liked the old nun whom she would assist, and who had taught her all manner of healing, physicking, and tending of wounds. She liked the herbarium because it was quiet and peaceful. In the summer they had a garden in bloom all around the little building housing the herbarium. Elf was content knowing her place in the orderliness of the convent.

"Look!" Isa, pointing, broke into her thoughts. "A mounted rider is approaching the convent. I wonder what news he brings. Mary's blood! Look how the sun shines on his hair! It's like beaten gold, I vow."

"My hair is gold," Matti said.

"Your hair is yellow like straw, and when it's all cut off that's just what it will look like." Isa giggled. "It's a good thing your head will be covered by your wimple, Matti. Still, you have a very pretty face. No one will miss your hair."

"I hope you'll send your first daughter here to St. Frideswide's in a few years so I can tell her what a troublesome wench her mother was as a girl," Matti said sweetly.

"You are terrible, the pair of you," Elf chided them, but then she joined in their shared laughter. "Oh, Isa! I shall miss your honesty

and your wickedly sharp tongue. I will pray God that Sir Martin
appreciates what a wonderful wife he has been blessed with, even if
she is a bit of a naughty baggage."

"Men like naughty women," Isa responded.

"But not *wives*," Matti said wisely. "Even I know that. When my
father sought a match for my eldest brother, Simon was mad for the
daughter of a neighbor, but father had heard she was a bit wild. He
sought elsewhere for a more modest girl. The neighbor's daughter
was twenty before a husband was found to take her; and that bridegroom was mightily surprised to find the neighbor's daughter a virgin, for all had believed her not. A reputation must be guarded as
carefully as a maidenhood, my father always said."

"I was betrothed to Martin of Langley when I was five, and then
immediately sent here to St. Frideswide's," Isa said. "I will go
home some time after Lammastide, and be married immediately. *I
have no reputation!*" she complained bitterly.

"What does he look like?" Matti asked curiously.

"As I remember, and I have not seen him since our betrothal,"
Isa replied, "he had brown eyes and brown hair. He was fifteen, and
had just been knighted, but as I recall he had no pockmarks on his
face. I can't remember his face except that it was pleasant. He shall
be a complete surprise to me, and I hope a nice one. I shall be a total surprise to him from the runny-nosed little maid I was on our
betrothal day. I had a cold, as I remember, and wanted to stay warm
in my cot, but I was dragged up, and dressed in my finest, and taken
to the church to stand by his side while the betrothal ceremony was
performed. I don't think he ever even looked at me more than
once, and I suppose then to ascertain that I didn't have a squint," Isa
concluded.

The three girls giggled, but then they turned their heads at the
sound of a voice calling them. It was the convent gatekeeper, Sister
Perpetua, and she was waving her apron at them.

"Eleanore de Montfort, come down at once," she shouted up
the hill at them. "Reverend Mother wants to see you."

Elf arose, and waved back. "I am coming, sister," she called. She put on her wimple, tucking her long braids beneath it, brushed the grass from her dove gray skirts, and looked to her two friends. "Am I all right?" They nodded, and Elf hurried off down the hill to the convent.

"You are to go right to the chapter house, my child," Sister Perpetua said. "You will find Reverend Mother in the hall with a guest."

"Who is it?" Elf asked curiously. "Is it the rider we saw coming through the gate a few minutes ago, sister?"

"Yes," the nun answered, "but I do not know who he is. Hurry, child! Do not keep Reverend Mother waiting now."

Elf walked quickly through the gates, and across the cloister courtyard to the stone chapter house. Entering it she went directly to the great hall. At one end of the chamber was the abbess's chair of office, flanked by a row of stall seats where the nuns sat each morning. Mother Eunice sat in her place, a booted gentleman by her side. Elf came forward, and prostrated herself before the abbess.

"You may arise, my daughter" came the permission, and when Elf stood before Mother Eunice, head bowed respectfully, her gray-blue eyes modestly lowered, the abbess said quietly, "This is Sir Saer de Bude, Eleanore. He has come to escort you home to Ashlin."

Elf raised startled eyes to the abbess.

"Your brother, Richard, is ill, my daughter, and he wishes to see you" came the answer to Elf's unspoken question. "Sir Saer is the cousin of your sister-in-law, the lady Isleen. It is not a very long journey, and if you leave within the hour, you will be home before twilight this very day. Sister Cuthbert will help you to pack what you must have. You are to remain as long as you are needed. When your brother releases you, you will return to us." Seeing that Elf was desperate to speak, the abbess said, "What is it, my daughter?"

"My vows, Reverend Mother. Matilda FitzWilliam and I are to take our vows together on the twenty-second day of June. That is less than three weeks away. What if I am not back by then?" Elf could feel tears pricking at her eyelids.

"Then, my child, you will take your vows at a later time. Remember, all of this is God's will, not ours. You must obediently follow the path our gracious Lord Christ has set out for you."

"Yes, Reverend Mother," Elf replied, disheartened. If Richard had sent for her, then the matter was serious. She had seen him only once in the nine years she had been at St. Frideswide's. That had been six months after her arrival when he had come with his new bride, Isleen, who was the most beautiful creature Elf had ever seen, but did not seem particularly interested in the small child who was now her sister-in-law. And Dickon had changed. He was distracted, and had eyes only for his wife. They had not stayed long, and Elf had had no contact with them since but for a letter from her brother that came each year on her birthday. This year, however, there had been no letter.

The abbess's voice cut into Elf's thoughts. "Go now, my daughter, and prepare for your journey. Sir Saer will await you outside the gates of the convent. When you are ready, take yourself to Sister Joseph, who will see that you have a proper mount. Go with God, my daughter."

Elf bowed to Reverend Mother Eunice, turned, and hurried out.

"The demoiselle Eleanore is of good family," the abbess said to her guest, "and of gentle disposition. She came to us when she was five, and has not left the environs of St. Frideswide's since. Be certain you treat her gently and with respect. Above all, do not speak harshly to her. She is not used to men as you will surely understand. Father Anselm is the only man she knows."

"Of course, Reverend Mother," Saer de Bude answered the abbess. "My cousin would be angered with me if I were thoughtless of the demoiselle." He bowed to the nun. "I shall take my leave of you, then, my lady abbess, and await the demoiselle outside your gates." He turned quickly to go.

"A moment, sir," Mother Eunice said sharply. "What is Richard de Montfort's true condition? I shall not tell Eleanore."

"He is dying," Saer de Bude replied sanguinely.

The abbess merely nodded. Then, after a long pause, she said, "You may go." She had been certain that nothing short of impending death would have elicited a call for Eleanore de Montfort. She well remembered Isleen de Warenne. A proud, selfish girl with little care for anyone but herself. *And Isleen was childless after nine years of marriage.* Even here in her convent the abbess had heard the gossip about that. If Richard de Montfort did die, the manor of Ashlin would devolve upon Eleanore de Montfort. And that sweet child was shortly to take her vows of poverty, chastity, and obedience. As a nun she could possess nothing, not even her immortal soul, which belonged to God. Therefore Ashlin would come to St. Frideswide's.

The abbess considered this conclusion. There was a piece of property that matched the convent's lands, which she had coveted for some time now. If Ashlin were sold, this excellent grazing land could be purchased. The Reverend Mother Eunice smiled. God always answered her prayers, even if He sometimes took a bit longer than she thought was entirely necessary.

And while the abbess considered the rich grazing land soon to belong to the convent, Elf was standing in the center of her dormitory with Sister Cuthbert looking completely confused. "I don't know what to take with me," she wailed. "Do you know what I will need?"

"Take your other skirt, two tunics, all three of your camisas, your stockings not with the laundress, your hairbrush and comb. You will need a pair of gloves for riding. I will give you mine. Our hands are almost the same size. You will wear your cloak, of course." As she spoke, Sister Cuthbert gathered up Elf's possessions and wrapped them neatly in a piece of dark cloth. When she had finished, she said, "Go and pee, child. You have eight miles to traverse today. Then wash your face and hands. You'll need a clean wimple. That one looks as if you had been sitting on it in the grass, which I suppose you were. I'll fetch you a new one."

Elf pulled off the offending headdress, and did as she had been bid. When she returned to the nun, there was a fresh wimple on her bed. She put it on and slipped her cloak about her shoulders, fastening it with a closure in the shape of the cross. The garment was a darker gray than her skirt. "Will you tell Matti and Isa where

I have gone, Sister Cuthbert? And that I will be back as quickly as I can?"

Sister Cuthbert nodded, gently adjusting Elf's wimple as she said, "It will be a grand adventure, little one, and you should have one small adventure before you pledge your life to our good Lord. We will pray for your brother, Elf. Do not fear for him, for he is in God's hands. Come, I will take you to Sister Joseph, to make certain she mounts you decently. She always wants to give us that wretched mule who will only go where he is minded to go, and not necessarily where you need him to go. You are too young and innocent to defy Sister Joseph. I am not."

Together the two of them walked to the convent stable, a small building on the cloister's west side. And indeed Sister Joseph was of a mind to mount Elf on her favorite mule, but Sister Cuthbert would not have it.

"She must have the white mare," the older nun said.

"That is reserved for Reverend Mother," Sister Joseph protested.

"Reverend Mother is not going anywhere, but Eleanore de Montfort is. That mule is impossible with everyone but you, and you know it."

"But we don't know how long the mare will be away, and if Reverend Mother needs her, what am I to say?" Sister Joseph persisted.

Sister Cuthbert turned to Elf. "Can you have your brother's serfs return the mare in a day or two? I am sure he will mount you decently when you return. That way should Reverend Mother need her mare, the beast will be here in its stable."

Elf nodded.

"Oh, very well," Sister Joseph acquiesced, "but that mare had best be back in two days' time, Eleanore de Montfort."

"It will, sister, I promise," Elf said softly. "And hopefully I will be the one to ride her back." She stroked the mare's soft nose.

The mare was saddled. The bundle with Elf's possessions was strapped into place, and she was helped to mount. All the girls in the convent school were taught how to sit a mare in the event they had to do so. Elf had not expected she would ever ride outside of the convent courtyard, but as she gathered the reins in her gloved hands, she felt a little tremor of excitement. She was going back to Ashlin. She would see Dickon, and using her own skills she would make him well, she was quite certain. She would see old Ida, if indeed Ida was still alive. Then she would return to St. Frideswide's, take her vows, and spend the remainder of her life serving God. Still, she wished she could speak with Isa and Matti herself before her departure.

Sister Cuthbert led the mare and its rider from the stable. Sister Perpetua opened the gates of the convent, and Elf was led outside. Sister Cuthbert put the lead rein into Saer de Bude's outstretched hand. "Go carefully," Sister Cuthbert told the young man sternly. "The lady is not used to being astride. Go with God, my child," she told Elf.

They set off at a staid pace. Elf could see Isa and Matti still upon the hillside with the sheep. She wanted to wave to them, but she was too shy to do so, and afraid of causing a scene. Saer de Bude kept the mare beside his own mount, and to his right. For a time the animals moved in silence, and then the young man spoke.

"Are you permitted to speak with me, lady?" he asked her.

"Aye," she replied. "We are not a cloistered order."

"You have not been home to Ashlin since you were brought to the convent," he said. It was not a question.

"No," Elf replied. "Tell me of my brother, sir. How ill is he, and what has been done for him?"

"Richard is dying" came the blunt answer.

"*Mon Dieu!*" the girl exclaimed, and then blushed with the knowledge that she had sworn an oath.

"The lady Isleen cares for her husband with the devotion of an angel," Saer de Bude continued. "He is a fortunate man, your brother."

"Why is he dying?" Elf demanded of her companion. "What is the matter with him, good sir? Surely a physician was sent for and a diagnosis made."

"There has been no physician at Ashlin," Saer de Bude replied. "We would have had to send to Worcester for one. At first your brother's illness was not thought to be serious."

"I assist the infirmarian at the convent," Elf told him. "I will want to examine my brother, although I am certainly no expert. Still, Sister Winifred says I am the best assistant she has ever had. I am certain there is something I can do to help my brother."

"The lady Isleen will be most grateful," Saer de Bude replied.

"How came you to Ashlin?" Elf asked him.

"My mother was a de Warenne" was the reply. "The lady Isleen is my cousin. Her family thought I could be of help to your brother."

"I am certain Richard is grateful," Elf answered him primly. Then she grew silent again. She had, of course, only met her sister-in-law once, and perhaps she had judged her through the eyes of a small child, ripped from her home, and put in a strange place. This was the person who had taken her beloved Dickon from her. That Isleen was extravagantly beautiful had not helped. Her hair had been like golden thistledown touched by the moonlight. Her eyes were a deep blue, and her skin was as pure as cream, her cheeks touched with just the faintest hint of rose. She had smelled of roses, too. A delicious, heady scent that bespoke elegance. It was difficult for a little girl just five and a half years of age, in a dull gray gown, to like such a woman. And Isleen had made no effort herself to draw her bridegroom's little sister to her heart. That one visit had been brief, with Isleen staring out the window of the visitor's chamber while Dickon spoke briefly, his eyes always going to his bride until he could seemingly not bear it any longer, and they had taken their leave of Elf.

But now her brother and his wife, childless after all their years of marriage, had sent for her. *I must not judge Isleen by that one visit,* Elf chided herself silently. Still, they could have surely afforded the expense of a physician. *Yet she loves my brother, and has taken good care of him. It must break her heart that God has not blessed them with sons and daughters. I must greet her as my sister, and as if it were the first time*

we met. I will love her because she loves Dickon. Has not our dear Lord said
we must love one another as we love Him?

"You have not yet taken your vows?" Saer de Bude spoke again.
"Do you really wish to be a nun, and do you never consider the
joys of marriage, lady?"

"I have never wanted to be anything but a nun," Elf answered
him honestly. "I bless the day my brother brought me to St. Frideswide's, although at the time, I was frightened, and confused. I had
just lost my mother and never knew my sire, you see. All I had were
Dickon and my old nurse, Ida. The nuns, however, mothered me
and taught me. And one day I realized how happy I was in their
company, how happy I was that I should join their ranks and have
the privilege of serving God forever."

"I can understand," he told her. "I always wanted to be a knight,
and fight in the king's service. I am happiest when doing it."

They rode on in silence for a time.

"Do you think you could go a bit faster?" he finally asked her.

"I think so," Elf responded, "but if I become frightened, will
you stop, sir?"

"Aye." He grunted, and kicked his own animal into a gentle
canter.

The mare followed, with Elf leaning forward just slightly into
the faster gait. She was quite surprised that she could do it, for she
had only cantered a few times, but it was not unpleasant at all. She
could feel a light wind on her face, and there was a freedom about
it that was positively exhilarating. Sister Cuthbert was always teasing Elf that joy was not forbidden within the order, for Elf had a
great tendency to be quite serious. Finally after a time she began to
grow tired and called to him to stop.

"Forgive me, lady, you are so quiet I almost forgot you are here.
Of course you will want to stop and rest a bit. It is not far once
we begin to ride again. Let me help you down." Reaching up Saer
de Bude lifted Elf from her saddle, setting her upon the ground.
"There is a stream just down the slope there. Would you like a
drink?"

"No, thank you," Elf said. "I only wish to stretch my legs a moment before we travel onward." She looked about her. "Are we on Ashlin land? It has been many years, but it does seem familiar."

"Indeed, lady, your memory is a good one. Aye, we are on your brother's lands. We have just about two more miles to go, and you will be home again." Then he smiled toothily at her.

He made her uncomfortable, Elf thought. Was it because he was a man and she was not used to men; or was it something particular to him? She glanced casually at him. He was a pleasant enough looking man. Stocky, of medium height with gold hair and dark eyes. His face was just slightly pockmarked, but not enough to spoil his good looks. His round face was edged with a beard and mustache that connected about his mouth. The beard was barbered and short. He was well dressed, but not ostentatiously so, in medium brown and green garments, and Elf noted that his boots, though well used, were of the best leather.

Saer de Bude drank from a small flask he carried. Wiping his mouth with his hand, he went off into the bushes, and she blushed to hear him relieving himself. When he returned, he said, "If you are certain you want nothing to drink, then let us be on our way again."

Elf nodded in the negative. She was thirsty, but terrified to drink anything lest she should have to pee. How could she while in the company of this man? "Let us go, sir," she said. "I am as anxious as you to reach Ashlin." Then she looked past his shoulder as his hands lifted her up into the saddle again. "Thank you, sir," she told him. "I am well settled now."

He gave her a curt acknowledgment and after climbing upon his own horse, led her off again. Finally they came through a dense wood, and on the hill beyond, Elf saw her childhood home, the small stone manor house lit by the late afternoon sun. Her heart stirred within her, and unaware of her actions, she kicked the little mare into a gallop, racing across a meadow, scattering the sheep as she went. Her companion, startled at first, followed after her, rather surprised by the little nun's show of enthusiasm. He hadn't expected it in one so meek and mild. He chuckled. The next few days would certainly prove interesting indeed. He wondered if this bit of spirit was unusual, or if beneath her mouse gray robes, and prim little white wimple, Eleanore de Montfort was perhaps intelligent and lively. Isleen was not expecting that, nor would she like it one bit, but his cousin, he knew, would wait to see the lay of the land before making any move. What had begun as a simple mission to bring Richard de Montfort's sister from her convent was now appearing to become a most fascinating and intriguing matter. Saer de Bude chuckled again.

CHAPTER TWO

A young serf helped Elf from her mount. "Welcome home, lady," he said. She did not recognize him at first, but thanked him. "Please see the mare is treated kindly," she told the boy. "She is the abbess's personal mount, and must be returned to St. Frideswide's in two days' time."

He nodded. "I shall care for her myself, lady. I am Arthur, Ida's grandson. I did not expect you to remember me."

"*But I do!*" Elf exclaimed. "We played together as children, and when my mother died you brought me daisies you had picked in the meadow. You cried when I went away. I remember you standing by your grandmother's side, sniffling, and wiping your eyes with your sleeve. May God bless you, Arthur, and always keep you from harm."

Arthur nodded his head in acknowledgment, a smile on his face, and then he led the mare away toward the stables.

Saer de Bude cantered in through the gates of the manor then, and called out to Elf, "Lady, wait, and I will escort you to your brother." He slid from his horse. Grabbing Arthur by the neck of his smock, he said, "Here, lad, take my horse with you, too."

"You are kind, sir, but I remember my way," Elf called to her escort.

"Lady," he said, walking over and taking a firm grip on her arm. "I was sent to bring you to Ashlin, and I would not be doing my duty in full if I did not escort you directly to my cousin and your brother." He led her into the house and to the manor hall. "Cousin, I have returned!"

Isleen de Montfort turned quickly, a smile upon her face. Then she hurried forward. "Welcome home to Ashlin, my dear Eleanore," she purred. "I am so sorry your visit must be a sad one."

It suddenly crossed Elf's mind to say that her sister-in-law might have asked her sooner, and in happier times, but she pushed the uncharitable thought away. Holding out her hands, she went to Isleen and kissed her on both cheeks. "May God bless you for calling me, Isleen. Your cousin has told me how devoted your care of Dickon has been, but now I am here, and I shall help you. Where is my brother?"

"He is there." Isleen pointed to the cot that was set by the fireplace. "He sleeps now, but he will awaken when you call him. I shall leave you alone for your reunion. Come, cousin. You must escort me while I walk about my gardens and take the air."

Elf did not even notice her sister-in-law and the knight depart. She was staring, horrified, at her brother as he slept. Richard was practically a skeleton, and his skin tone was an unhealthy yellow gray. He had been a handsome man, but now his cheeks were sunken, his nose prominent, and his cheekbones quite visible. The skin was stretched tightly over his skull, and his once fine russet hair was so thin he was almost bald in places. Elf knelt by her brother's cot, her eyes tear-filled. "Dickon," she said softly to him. "Dickon, I have come home to make you well again."

Richard de Montfort's gray eyes opened slowly. A bony hand gripped her arm. "Who are you?" he rasped.

"It is I, Dickon. It is Elf," she said. "Your sister." Undoing the chin strap that held her wimple in place, she pulled the covering from her head so that he might see her hair. Then she smiled.

"*Elf*," he said softly. "Is it really you? You have grown."

"I would hope so, brother." She laughed. "It has been nine years since we last saw each other. I was but a little girl of five years, Dickon. I am now fourteen, and soon to take my vows, but Isleen sent for me, as you are gravely ill. I am the assistant infirmarian at the convent. Perhaps I can help you."

He smiled back at her. "I am dying, Elf, and there is no help for me," he said. "When I am gone, sister, Ashlin will be yours."

"But what of Isleen?" Elf asked him, astounded. "Isleen is your wife, Dickon. Ashlin should be hers, not mine."

"Isleen's dower portion will be restored, and she will be returned to the de Warennes," he told Elf. "Ashlin, by law, is yours. You have not taken your final vows yet, Elf. If you decide to, you may take a husband instead. Ashlin is small, but it is a respectable dower portion. Allow St. Frideswide's to have the dowry I paid them when you went there. It is only fair. They have cared for and educated you all these years."

"But I don't want a husband," Elf told her brother. "I am content to take my final vows, Dickon. Besides, I do not intend to allow you to die on me. I am an excellent herbalist. Tell me your symptoms. When did you begin to grow ill?"

"Well over a year ago," he replied. "At first it was just my belly. It would take offense at some food or other, but in a day or so I would be well. Then, however, I became sick more and more. My guts began to burn with an unquenchable fire. I began to have bouts of weakness. I could not walk, or ride, or even stand. Then the sickness would go, and I would recover only to grow ill again. Now I can keep nothing on my belly, and as you can see, my hair and teeth have begun to fall out. Even I can tell that I am dying, Elf. I do not believe that you can help me, little sister."

"I can try," she told him fervently. *"I can try, Dickon!"*

"I cannot feel worse than I already do," he said with a wry smile.

"Why do you have no children?" Elf asked him frankly.

"It is Isleen," he replied, "although I dare not tell her, for it would break her heart. I have two sons and a daughter among the serfs, but you must not say I told you so. She believes because I am ill, it is my fault, but it is not. You will keep my secret, Elf, will you not? I have confessed my fault to you, and are you not bound by your vocation to keep the knowledge of my sins to yourself? God will judge me." He smiled weakly at her.

She wondered why he had felt it necessary to seek among the

serf girls. Still, it was not her business, she decided, pushing the thoughts from her head. "I will keep your secret, brother," she promised. "Now, you must sleep again while I ask Isleen to find me a place to set up my herbarium. If I am to help you, I cannot delay. Where is old Ida?"

"She has not spoken to me since the day I took you away, nor has she set foot in this house."

"I will find her," Elf told him, "and she will help me to get you well, Dickon." She arose from his side, and calling to a servant, asked, "Where is the lady of the manor?"

"She is in her gardens, lady," the servant answered.

"Take me to her," Elf said, "and then go find old Ida. Tell her I am home, and I need her aid."

Elf followed the servant to the manor garden, where the roses were already in bloom. The garden was not as well kept as it had been in her mother's day, she noted. At first she did not see her sister-in-law, but then she spied Isleen with her cousin, their heads together, seated on a wooden bench at the far end of the garden. Elf called to her as the servant accompanying her hurried off in the opposite direction.

Isleen seemed to leap from her seat and, turning about, came toward Elf. "Gracious, you startled me, Eleanore," she said. Her cheeks were flushed, and the color made her look all the more beautiful.

"I do not mean to disturb you, sister, but I need a place where I may set up my little herbarium. I have seen Dickon now, and he is indeed seriously ill. I pray God I can help him."

"As do I, dear sister," Isleen said sweetly. "There is a small shed at the end of the garden that I believe would be perfect for your purposes. Come, and see it." She was pointedly ignoring Saer de Bude now as if he did not even exist. Isleen's pale blue skirts swayed gracefully as she moved through the rosebushes.

The fragrance of the pink, white, and red blooms was heady. Large bumblebees floated about the flower heads, dipping into the blossoms to gather their nectar, the hum of their wings just barely audible. Elf followed in her sister-in-law's perfumed wake to the edge of the garden, where a small, rather ramshackle building stood.

"Will this do?" Isleen inquired in dulcet tones.

"It will have to," Elf told her. "It's really in the best place for my herbarium. Will you permit me to requisition some serfs to make any necessary repairs, Isleen?"

"Of course" came the reply. "This is, after all, your home." The last was said a bit tartly, and Elf heard the change in tone in her companion's voice.

Isleen knows if Dickon dies that Ashlin is mine. She is bitter about it, Elf thought. "Thank you," she told Isleen.

Isleen shrugged. "I will leave you to your work, then, Eleanore," she said, and hurried back up the garden path.

"My baby! Is it really you?" An old woman hobbled into view.

"Ida!" Elf's face broke into a smile, and she enfolded the elderly nursemaid in her embrace. "Oh, Ida! How good it is to see you once again. Dickon tells me you have not spoken to him since I went to St. Frideswide's. That was really very bad of you, and now my poor brother lies ill unto death, I fear. I need your help, Ida."

"Now that you are here, my baby, I will enter that house again, and make my peace with the lord Richard. I swore I would not do it until you returned, and I have kept my promise." The old lady's jaw was set firmly with her resolve, and her hazel eyes were sharp.

"But what if I had not come home, Ida?" Elf gently said. "Surely you could not have allowed Dickon to go to his grave without your forgiveness?"

"How could I forgive him when he chose *her* over his own blood?" Ida said fiercely. "It was her duty as lady of the manor to raise her husband's younger sister as your mother was dead, God as-soil the lady Adeliza's good and pure soul! Great heiresses have gone into their husband's homes and raised their younger brothers and sisters, and even their children from earlier marriages. *But not that one!*"

"You do not like her," Elf said quietly. "Why? Surely not just because Dickon sent me away, Ida?"

"It began with that," Ida told her former charge. "But then I have watched these nine years while she lorded it over your poor, benighted brother. He thinks the sun rises and sets on her, he does. When she came to this house, not a servant did she bring from her father's house, though he could have easily afforded to give her several. We quickly learned why, my child. She is a bad-tempered mistress, though never before your brother does she show her evil nature. She beats the servants at the slightest provocation, or complains to the lord Richard of some fault or slight in a servant that brings punishment. She is a wicked creature, my lady Elf, and you must beware of her!"

"But her cousin tells me she has nursed my brother with utter devotion," Elf protested.

"Hah!" Ida exclaimed. "If he is indeed her cousin. He came to Ashlin a year ago. Shortly before that your brother fell ill for the first time, although he had been the picture of health until then."

Elf felt a shiver race down her spine, but she shook off the feeling, saying, "I am certain that is just coincidence, Ida. We must not think ill of Isleen because Dickon is ill. I can only judge her on my own experience with her, and to date it has been a good one. She has welcomed me warmly and given me leave to take this little shed for an herbarium so I may help Dickon."

"Of course she is pleasant to you," Ida said. "You are her brother's only living relative, and Ashlin will be yours if he dies."

"I know that," Elf replied, "but my brother is not going to die, Ida. I have learned a great deal from Sister Winifred, and she says I am the best student she has ever taught. I am told I shall be her assistant when I take my final vows, and one day, God willing, I shall serve the convent as its infirmarian. That is the life God has planned for me, and it is the life I want. Now, let us find some brooms, old friend, and clean this little shed so it is a suitable place for me to set up my herbarium and make my medicines."

"You are too innocent, and your heart is far too good," Ida said, then rushed to obey her young mistress.

Several young strong serfs came, and removed the clutter of many years from the shed. A fire was built nearby to heat the water that would be necessary to clean the shed properly, while two well-muscled men dug a new well and enclosed it with a waist-high stone wall. A post was pounded into the ground from which a wooden arm could be swung over the well to lower the bucket into the water, drawn up, and swung back over the well wall for the water-drawer's convenience. A sturdy door was hung. Two windows with rounded tops were set, covered with very thin sheets of animal membrane, which served a dual purpose—to allow the light in and keep the wind out. The shed was swept clean of dust and vermin. It was whitewashed inside to aid in lighting it. Shelves were built to store Elf's jars and materials. A table and a chair were built. Within seven days Elf had an excellent workshop.

In that time she had done her best for Dickon, making him a sweetened barley water, which she fed him in an effort to purge his system of whatever was harming it. Elf quickly noticed that while her sister-in-law hovered about making sympathetic noises, she did little to aid her husband. It was Ida who saw that her master's bedding, linen, and person were kept clean and fresh. It was she who tended the terrible bedsores Dickon had, using a salve of lamb fat and acorn paste Elf had made after first smoothing beaten egg whites on the sores to ease their pain. Still, Isleen was kind to her husband's sister, the manor hall was kept neat, and meals were served on time. Yet in the evening Isleen would sit on the far side of the fireplace with her cousin, the two of them speaking in whispers while the manor's lord dozed on the other side. Elf, sitting next to her brother, worked on a tapestry to while away the time. Was there something wrong as Ida was constantly hinting, given the opportunity; or was poor, beautiful Isleen simply taking comfort in the company of her relative?

I must not think idle and evil thoughts, Elf chided herself. Isleen and Saer de Bude do nothing wrong, and they are in full sight of everyone in the hall. *God forgive me,* Elf prayed, *for sitting in judgment of my brother's wife. Ida is querulous and bitter. She has no children to care for, and children are her very life.* "Ave, Maria, gratia plenia," Elf murmured, and afterward thought she did not like being kept away from St. Frideswide's, where her days were peaceful and her hours ordered.

Ida's son, John, and his son, Arthur, took it upon themselves to build a small fireplace in the herbarium. It was a small raised half hearth, constructed upon a base of stones with a slate flooring, and set above floor level in a wall. Its shape was a half round, and when the two men had finished it, they drilled holes in the side of the hearth and affixed a swinging iron arm from the smithy that would hold a pot. A little chimney ran up the outside of the shed, which was now quite habitable. Both men were delighted when Elf thanked them profusely.

" 'Twere nothing, lady," John said quietly. "I know little of your skills, but I did not think you should have to go outside each time you needed hot water. Especially if the weather were foul."

"I hope I have not taken you from your manor chores," Elf replied. "I would not want the lady to be angry with you on my account."

"The manor is well looked after by your serfs, my lady Eleanore. We do not need the likes of that knight telling us what to do. He is not a man of the land, and knows less than nothing. You will forgive my frank speech, lady, but my mother says you are too good, and I would have no harm come to you, or yours." John then gave a little bow, saying, "We are your serfs to command, lady, and will protect you if we must." Then he turned from her, leaving Elf quite puzzled in her new domain.

During the week the shed was being made useful again, Elf had enlisted the company of several young female serfs to go searching in the fields and woods for many of the things she needed to make her remedies. Pinecones had been gathered, for they were useful in healing problems of the kidneys and bladder, although if not used properly were known to excite lustful desires. She had found a small store of acorns in a storage room beneath the hall, and was grateful for them. There would be no more acorns until the autumn. There was some wheat and barley remaining in the granary from the previous harvest. Elf took a basket of each. She roasted the latter grain, for otherwise it was mildly laxative. Mixed and cooked with dried figs in a sweetened water, it was a cure for abscesses. She found a host of capers growing on some rough ground near the granary, and gathered them, for they were most valuable for any number of complaints from a toothache to sciatica and cramps. A beehive in a half-rotted log in the nearby wood gave her a large cache of honey. The kitchen gardens yielded cabbages, marrows, cucumbers, leeks, onions, and garlic, as well as asparagus, spinach, lettuces, parsnips, and beets. There were mustard greens, mint, sage, parsley, and fennel. In a nearby meadow Elf discovered horehound growing, and behind her shed, elecampane.

Very soon sheaves of herbs were drying within the little building. Jars were filled with violets, dandelion roots, crocus bulbs, as well as figs and dates that Elf had taken from the kitchen. She had been surprised to find them there, for they were items not easily come by, but, the cook told her, the lady Isleen likes a sweet dessert occasionally. Albert had opened a small garden for Elf next to her shed. She planted all manner of herbs not grown in the kitchen's gardens, including chamomile.

Dickon seemed to be growing weaker every day despite her efforts, but she found herself with a growing number of patients from among the serfs. When she questioned Ida about it, the old woman told her that Isleen was not particularly skilled at healing, and disliked such labor.

"But it is the lady's duty to care for her people," Elf said, shocked. "Do you mean in all the years she has been married to my brother, she has not healed those who came to her for aid?"

"Not once," Ida said. "She does not give your brother an heir, although he has children among the serfs. She will not bind up her people's wounds, or prescribe for an ague, or flux. She is useless."

"But Dickon loves her," Elf said softly.

Ida made a rude sound. Then she muttered, "A lot of good it does him to love so useless a female. When my poor lord Richard is dead, you will be a better mistress for Ashlin, my dear lady."

Elf said nothing more. It was foolish to argue with Ida. Her mind had been set against Isleen from the very moment she had arrived at Ashlin. Still, Elf was concerned about her sister-in-law. Just last night she had caught her feeding Dickon a sweetmeat that Elf knew he loved, but should not have. It was not the first time, either. Elf was hard put not to scold her sister-in-law severely. Instead she had protested gently while Isleen had looked properly contrite at first, then made a face at her.

"Isleen, you must not feed Dickon anything of which I do not approve, for it is difficult enough getting his belly under control. The sweets but upset him, although I know you do not mean to harm him. You spoil him because you love him, but you cannot."

"If I were ill, would you care for me so tenderly, my lady Eleanore?" Saer de Bude asked her. She found his smile unpleasant.

"It is my duty as an infirmarian, and a servant of our God, to use what skills I have to ease suffering, sir," Elf answered him primly.

"It would be easy to recover if I were tended by you" was the silken reply. "You are most fair."

Elf flushed, ignoring him, for his words were quite inappropriate, and he well knew it. A gentleman did not speak to a bride of Christ in such a suggestive manner. She bent low over her tapestry frame, but she did not miss the angry hiss of her sister-in-law's voice, although she could not hear her words.

"How dare you flirt with the pious little bitch!" Isleen whispered to Saer de Bude. "If Richard were well, he would kill you for your words to her. Are you mad?"

"No, I but think of our future, as should you, my pretty cousin. Have you and I not planned all this? And is this not why the little nun was called from her convent? You have played your part well so far, Isleen. Do not allow your jealousy and envy of her to ruin everything. It is you I love, and not the little nun. It has always been you. Had I been a man of property, we might have convinced your father to give you to me instead of Richard de Montfort."

"But you are not a man of property," Isleen murmured cuttingly.

"No, I am not, but I will be once I wed your sister-in-law," Saer de Bude answered his cousin. "Then Ashlin will belong to me.

When I suddenly find myself a widower, it is you who will be my bride." His eyes, so deep a blue that they were almost black, looked into hers passionately. A lock of his golden blond hair fell lazily over his forehead. Isleen wanted to reach out and push it back, but she knew she dared show no sign of intimacy toward her cousin.

"She will not marry you, or anyone else," Isleen said almost spitefully. "I saw her only once, before she came to Ashlin, when Richard and I were first married. He took me to her convent so I might meet her. I think he hoped I would offer to bring her back to Ashlin. The fool! She was but a child then, and knew nothing. Now, however, she is grown enough to know what she wants, and 'tis a nunnery, although I cannot understand why. She is certainly pretty enough, and with Ashlin for her dowry, can easily attract a flesh-and-blood husband, but she wants none but her Lord Christ. How can you compete with that, cousin?"

"If we cannot bring her around reasonably, there is but one way, Isleen. I will rape her. Her convent will not have her if she is despoiled. Believe me, her virginity will be gone, and the little nun well used before I release her to prayerfully reconsider her decision."

"You are very wicked," Isleen murmured in appreciative tones. "I think you hope she will resist you so you may violate her."

He chuckled darkly. "Perhaps I do," he said. "Would you like to help me, Isleen? Would you like to rape the little nun, too?"

Isleen's blue eyes widened. *"How?"* she whispered half fearfully. This was dangerous territory. Sometimes Saer frightened even her, but she had to admit to herself that she was intrigued by his words.

"I have among my possessions an object called a dildo, which I purchased at the Moor's shop in Hereford. It is a forbidden object, not easily obtainable, but the Moor knows my tastes. It is shaped like a manhood, and fashioned of polished ash wood." He smiled wickedly at her. "After I have taken the little nun's virginity through her temple of Venus; perhaps you should like to take her other virginity through her temple of Sodom. The dildo can be used by its hand grip, or you might enjoy attaching it to yourself with the leather straps I have for it, and playing the boy, cousin. Would you like that, Isleen?"

Her cheeks were flushed with the lewd thoughts racing through her mind as he had spoken. The depravity of his suggestion was absolutely mind-boggling. *"Yes!"* she said. "Oh, yes, Saer!"

"Then, stop being such a jealous little fool," he said quietly to her.

Across the hall Ida watched the pair suspiciously. "Do you see how flushed *she* is, my lady," she murmured to Elf. "What could he say that would make her flush so? It cannot be anything fit for a decent woman's ears. They are poisoning Lord Richard, I am certain."

"Do not say such a thing! 'Tis wicked, Ida! What would make you voice such a suspicion?"

"Lady, you have been too sheltered!" Ida told her. "You must see things as they truly are. Your sister-in-law is a wicked woman. Perhaps she has been sweet to you, but that does not change the fact that she is wicked. We fear for you when the lord dies, left with that woman and her cousin. It is very likely that they are lovers, my lady. He has been seen on several occasions coming out of her chamber. We could not tell the lord in his helpless position, *but you must know."*

"I do not understand," Elf said softly. "Does she not love Dickon, Ida? How can she betray her husband if she loves him?"

Ida's weathered face was kind, and her eyes were tender with concern. She patted her mistress's hand gently. "I do not believe the lord's wife ever loved anyone but herself. All she wants to do is take. She knows not how to give of herself, or of anything else. You have been taught to sacrifice your all for the world as did our dear Lord Christ. The lady Isleen does not know the meaning of the word sacrifice. She wants her cousin, and she wants Ashlin."

Elf was extremely disturbed by Ida's words. Sheltered and innocent she might be, but she was no fool. She had frankly wondered about the apparent intimacy between Isleen and Saer de Bude. It had begun to concern her that Dickon would rally only to grow sicker, and always after Isleen had tempted him with his favorite sweetmeats, sugared almonds. Was he, as Ida suggested, being poisoned? It was unthinkable! But it was also very possible. She sighed. She wished Isa and Matti were here to talk to, or Sister Cuthbert, who was a font of common sense. She was alone, though, and as helpless as her brother's serfs, unable to prove her suspicions and forced to stand by and watch as Richard de Montfort slowly faded away.

Her thoughts were interrupted by the entry of a knight ushered into the hall by Cedric, the manor steward. He introduced himself as Sir Ranulf de Glandeville, returning from Wales on the king's business. He was a large man with a deep voice.

"Will you give me shelter this night, my lord?" he asked Richard, who was now awake and alert as he lay upon his cot.

"You are most welcome, my lord," Richard said graciously, albeit in a weak voice. He looked to Isleen, who smiled vapidly, but made no move to see to the comfort of their guest. "This is my wife, the lady Isleen," Richard said in an effort to encourage her to courteous action.

Isleen smiled again at the knight, but remained in her place. Ranulf de Glandeville was but a momentary distraction from Saer's licentious words. "And my younger sister, the lady Eleanore, *who will be mistress of Ashlin when I am dead,*" Richard finished, his anger aroused by his wife's open lack of hospitality.

Elf arose, prodded gently by Ida. "You are most welcome to Ashlin, good sir," she said. "Ida, please fetch our guest a plate and some wine. Come, sir, sit by the fire and warm yourself while our good Ida brings food. It has been a rainy, chill day for June." Taking his cloak, she said, "We will see it is dried for your departure tomorrow."

"Thank you, lady," Ranulf de Glandeville answered her. "You are kind, and I am grateful for your hospitality." He sat, observing those of consequence in the hall. Another man who was familiar. The lord's beautiful wife and his equally beautiful sister. By her simple gray garb he recognized the sister as a religious. Her long pale red-gold braid, however, told him she had not yet taken her final vows. The heart-shaped face was sweet, and he thought it a shame that her calling was to God and not a husband. His thoughts were interrupted by the other man who was approaching him.

"I am Sir Saer de Bude. We have fought together for the king," the man said. "The lady of this manor is my cousin. I have been here this past year aiding her husband, who is ill to death as you surely see."

Ranulf de Glandeville stood, and held out his hand. "I thought you familiar, Sir Saer," he replied. The man was officious and tactless. He almost behaved as if he were lord here, and not Richard de Montfort.

"Wine!" Saer de Bude called loudly. "Why have we no wine?" He swaggered with a proprietorial air toward the high board. "Come, sir, and join me. The servants will bring your food quickly."

Not knowing the situation, and not wishing to appear rude, the king's messenger sat himself at the high board. The fair lady Eleanore herself set down a plate laden with food and a fresh trencher of bread. There were slices of well-hung venison, a generous spoonful of rabbit stew, several juicy prawns, a thick slice of ham, an artichoke, and a wedge of cheese. With a small smile she handed him a polished wooden spoon. He flushed beneath his ruddy wind-tanned cheeks, realizing his appetite had been showing. Crossing himself, he bowed his head a long moment, then crossing himself again, he began to eat. When he had mopped the last bit of gravy from his pewter plate with the last scrap of bread, and swallowed a final gulp from his cup, he sat back with a grin of contentment.

"Lady, you set a fine table," he said appreciatively.

"This is my brother's house," Elf said modestly.

"You have, I would imagine, returned home from your convent to help," Ranulf de Glandeville observed. "Have you been able to aid your brother, lady? Is there anything I can do to aid you?"

"Dickon will die," Elf said, voicing for the first time what she had all along known in her heart. This knight had kind eyes, and for a brief moment she didn't feel quite so alone. "I am the assistant to our herbalist and infirmarian. It is said I am skilled in these arts, but just when I think I am making progress, my brother has a relapse. It has happened thrice now in the few weeks I have been back at Ashlin. If I cannot overcome the mystery of whatever it is that plagues him, I cannot make him well, sir. It is but a matter of time, and he will indeed surely die." There were tears in her gray-blue eyes as she spoke.

"You cannot determine what ails him?" the knight probed gently.

"It is a complaint of the belly first and foremost," Elf told her companion. "Pains, sometimes so severe his body folds itself in half. A continuous flux in the bowels. He has lost most of his hair, and a good many of his teeth. His skin is sallow, and tinged with gray. He is but ten years my senior, but he appears an ancient man now. All I can do," she concluded, "is keep him comfortable, sir. I feel so terribly helpless that I cannot make him well again."

"Was he always of a weakened disposition?" Ranulf de Glandeville asked Elf. Sometimes this was unfortunately so.

"Oh, no!" Elf replied. "Until about a year ago, according to old Ida, who was our nursemaid, Dickon was in the best of health." Then the young girl blushed. "I have almost forgotten, sir. My brother wanted me to ask you if you will come and speak with him before you retire. I have had a comfortable place made up for you in the bed space next to the fire. You will be quite snug there."

He arose from the high board, giving her a small bow. "I will see to your brother immediately," he said. "Again, I thank you for your hospitality, my lady Eleanore."

"God grant you good rest, sir," she answered him.

"I did not know you were so skilled in the arts of flirting, my pretty," Saer de Bude said suggestively. "Did the good nuns teach you that amorous art, Elf? You do not flirt with me, and I am quite overcome by your loveliness." He reached out to take her hand in his, but Elf snatched it away before he might do so.

"Why do you mistake simple courtesy for something else?" she asked him sharply. Then more boldly, "And why do you remain here at Ashlin, sir? You are not really needed by anyone. Dickon will die soon. It is not fitting that you be here in this house with two women and no older relation. Surely you do not wish to damage your cousin's reputation?" Suddenly, Elf was more angry than she had ever been.

"You do not fear for your own reputation?" he mocked her.

"Why? All who know me know I am chaste, for I am a bride of Christ. My reputation is safe, but what of Isleen's, sir?" Elf countered, then turned and came down from the high board. After seeking out Ida, Elf crawled with the old woman into a bed space at the end of the hall. The space Elf had allocated to Ranulf de Glandeville had actually been hers, but as it was the best one in the hall, she gave it to their guest. Ida and Elf preferred being near Richard de Montfort, who spent all his time in the hall now. Isleen slept in the small bedchamber off the solar, which was located behind the hall, while Saer de Bude found his rest in a little attic room.

Richard de Montfort greeted the king's messenger, and invited him to sit by his side. "I have a commission for you, if you can take it, sir," he said softly. "My wife and I are childless. Under the laws of inheritance Ashlin must go to my sister, Eleanore. My wife's dowry, of course, will be returned to her family, the de Warennes, as will Isleen. She is still young and beautiful. Another husband can be found for her, I am certain. In the morning I will ask my sister to write my will, for she has been most excellently educated at St. Frideswide's. She will make three copies. One I shall keep. The second I would have you deliver to the Bishop of Worcester; the third take to the king. I do this so that there is no mistake in my intentions for my wife and my sister. A serf has already been delegated to ride to the bishop when I die, and inform him of my demise. The bishop is to notify the king. I entrust Eleanore's safety to King Stephen. Will you do this for me, sir?" the lord of Ashlin finished weakly.

"I will, and gladly," Ranulf de Glandeville said quietly.

Richard nodded, openly relieved. "Thank you, sir. I do not like my wife's cousin. He presumes too much, but I have tolerated him for Isleen's sake because she seems so fond of him. Of late, however, I have seen this Saer de Bude looking at my young sister when he thought no one was noticing him. His gaze is too predatory to suit me. Elf is an innocent. She would not know how to defend herself against such a man."

Elf, Ranulf thought. It was a charming nickname. "How long has your sister been at St. Frideswide's? I know it, for a young relative of mine is there. The girl's name is Isabeaux St. Simon, but she is to marry soon, this autumn, I think."

"Isa is one of Elf's two best friends," Richard answered. "You must tell my sister that you know her. I took Elf to the convent shortly after her fifth birthday. Our father had died, and then our mother. I had contracted a marriage with the de Warennes, and they did not think it fair that Isleen should have to raise my sister. It was they who suggested St. Frideswide's. Knowing my sister's dower was a small one, they also suggested that she become a nun when she was old enough. It was a good decision. Elf has been safe in these troubled times. Her gentle disposition is perfect for the life she will lead. I should fear for her otherwise after I am gone." He coughed, his face paler than usual.

"Perhaps now she is to inherit your manor," Ranulf de Glandeville said, "she might decide she prefers to marry."

Richard shook his head. "I think it more likely she will give Ashlin to her order. They will do with it what is best for them. Marriage is not for Elf. Now, if you will excuse me, I shall sleep. I am very weary despite the fact all I do is lie here day after day."

Ranulf de Glandeville sought his own bed space, nodding to the young serf who had come to sit by his master. To the knight's surprise there was a small stool by the bed space with a basin of warm water. He washed the grease of his supper from his hands and face gratefully, drying them on the small linen cloth with the ewer. What a shame his young hostess had chosen the church over marriage. She would make a fine chatelaine of any man's manor. Pulling off his dalmatica, he laid it aside, and unlaced his corselet, a tight-fitting leather jupe, and set it out of the way, too. Then he removed his boots. He would sleep in the rest of his clothing. He needed to pee, and so walking across the hall, he let himself outside to complete the task, then returned inside, carefully barring the door again.

A serf awoke him shortly after dawn. There was hot oat stirabout, fresh bread, cheese, butter, and brown ale to break his fast. Having eaten his fill, he went to Richard de Montfort's side, where Elf was even now copying out a second parchment of her brother's will. She looked up at his approach, the expression on her young face serious. He sat silently by the lord's side. Richard's eyes were closed, his breathing labored. Ranulf de Glandeville crossed himself, and folded his big hands in prayer. They were hands more used to battle than supplication, and his hazel eyes could not help but stray to the earnestly bent head of the girl as she wrote.

"There, only one more to copy," she finally said. "It is not a long document, sir. I will try not to keep you. You must be eager to be on your way as your business is for the king." Then she bent her head again over her task.

He picked up one of the parchments. It had been dictated in a straightforward manner. Richard de Montfort, right lord of the manor of Ashlin, being childless after nine years of marriage to his lawful wife, Isleen de Warenne, leaves said manor with its lands, its serfs, its buildings, its livestock, and all of his possessions to his only heir, his sister, Eleanore de Montfort. The will went on to note that Isleen's dowry portion should be returned immediately to her family. Here Ranulf de Glandeville raised an interested eyebrow. The de Warennes had been most generous, perhaps a bit over-generous. They had obviously been quite eager to rid themselves of this daughter. Curious, he could not help but wonder why. The lady was quite beautiful and from an excellent family. The will went on to commend Richard de Montfort's wishes to His Majesty, King Stephen, and to his lordship, the Bishop of Worces-ter. The bishop was awarded six ewe lambs and a young ram for his trouble.

"I have finished, sir," Elf's voice broke into his thoughts.

The knight looked up to see Richard de Montfort signing each document, and sealing them with his seal both by his signature and on the rolled-up document's exterior. The lord of Ashlin had to be braced by a servant so he might sit up enough to scrawl his signature and press his seal into the hot wax. Before he did so, however, Ranulf de Glandeville signed each will in witness.

"What is it you are doing?" Isleen had entered the hall, Saer at her side.

They were a beautiful couple, Ranulf thought, fascinated by their appearance.

"I have dictated my will to Elf," Richard said softly. "Ranulf de Glandeville has witnessed it, Elf has made copies, and now our good guest will deliver a copy each to the bishop in Worcester, and the king, so my wishes will be carried out with expedience. Elf will inherit Ashlin as she is my heir."

"Of course she will," Isleen said, and her voice was almost angry. "I know that, but what a little nun will do with a manor is beyond me. Will she use these lands to found a new convent, perhaps?"

"I am not allowed to own any personal possessions once I have taken my final vows," Elf said, speaking up. "When I return to St. Frideswide's, I shall sign my rights in Ashlin over to my order. Ashlin will belong to the sisters of St. Mary, Isleen."

For the tiniest moment, so brief that Ranulf de Glandeville wasn't even certain, an ugly look touched Isleen's face, but then it was gone as swiftly as it had come. Why, she hates her sister-in-law, the knight thought. Well, the woman was human. Her childless condition was costing her a comfortable living, and her very home. She would get over it, but who could blame her in the meantime? He took the two rolled documents Elf handed him and arose.

"I will see these are delivered properly," he told Richard de Montfort, "and I will pray for your soul, my lord." He bowed.

"Thank you" was Richard's simple reply.

"Your cloak, my lord," Ida said, handing the garment to him.

"Why, it looks like new!" he exclaimed, surprised.

"Nothing a good brushing couldn't accomplish, my lord," the old lady said sharply. "That is why God made women. Men need taking care of, it is obvious. Godspeed, lord."

He put the garment about his broad shoulders, and then made his farewells, saving his last good-bye for Elf. "I shall not forget your hospitality, lady," he told her softly. "Your kindness lifted the weariness from my shoulders last night, and I am grateful. I have a long way to go yet. Thank you."

"May you go with God, then, Sir Ranulf," Elf told him. "I shall remember you in my prayers."

He bowed to her, then turned and left the hall.

CHAPTER THREE

"Will you remember me in your prayers also, lady?" Saer de Bude queried when the king's messenger was out of hearing.

"I remember all here in my prayers, sir," Elf said, and then added more tartly, "I expect you need praying for more than that good knight, sir." She turned to Ida. "We will need fresh linen for my brother's cot. I will go and fetch it if you and Isleen will bathe Dickon, please." Without waiting for an answer she hurried off to the linen cupboard, where she drew forth clean bedding for her brother's comfort. The cupboard smelled of lavender and damask roses. Hearing a footstep behind her, Elf turned about and found herself face-to-face with Saer de Bude.

"You are even more beautiful than my cousin, Isleen," he began.

"Your words and your obvious thoughts are inappropriate, sir," Elf said. She was irritated by this man's proximity, but her voice did not quaver, nor did she shrink from him.

The deep blue eyes fixed her fiercely. "I find you ultimately desirable, Eleanore de Montfort, and as you have not taken your final vows as a nun yet, I feel I may tell you so." He moved closer, pressing her back into the cupboard.

"In my mind and in my heart, sir, I am a nun. I do not welcome your attentions. I find them distasteful, extremely offensive. Now, step aside so I may pass! These linens are needed in the hall."

He laughed, and she saw his teeth were slightly yellowed. It spoiled the illusion of his overall handsomeness. Reaching out, he caught a tendril of her pale red-gold hair between his fingers, rubbed it, and then brought it to his lips to kiss. "Your hair is soft."

Elf was instantly repelled. Now she understood why a nun cut off her hair when she took her final vows. A woman's hair was a terrible and sensuous provocation even when she didn't want it to be. *"Let me pass!"*

His answer was to run a slender finger over her lips. "You have the most kissable mouth," he murmured seductively.

Elf was nauseated. Unable to help herself, she disgorged the contents of her morning meal on him. The vomit spilled down his sky blue tunic. Horrified, he stepped back with an oath. It was then Elf took the opportunity to shove past him, clutching the linens, which had somehow managed to remain free of her spew. She was dizzy, but she didn't stop in her flight, handing off the fragrant linens to a young servant woman, saying, "Take these to the hall. I must have some air." Then she ran from the house into the sunny summer morning.

She ran through the gates, and kept running until she found herself in a meadow filled with ewe sheep and their lambs. Sitting down beneath a large oak tree, she clutched her knees to her chest and wept. Dickon was going to die, and there was nothing she could do about it. All of her skills were useless, and worse, she wished Dickon had never sent for her. She wanted to be back at St. Frideswide's. It was almost the end of June. Midsummer's Eve was upon them. Matti would probably take her vows alone while she was stuck here at Ashlin with a dying brother, his wife, and Saer de Bude. Dickon had visited her only that one time in all the years since he had placed her in the convent. Why now this need to have her by his side? He could have died, and she could have inherited Ashlin without all of this fuss. Her presence had made absolutely no difference at all.

Or did her brother, perhaps, feel guilty for sending her away to please his bride-to-be? He needn't have, Elf thought. After the first month she had grown used to her convent, and enjoyed the company of the other little girls. Or maybe Dickon had realized all along that he was dying, and felt a deep need to have his sister with him. There seemed little love between him and Isleen now. Had he given in to her every whim in the past to try to make her love him? If only Isleen had borne Dickon children . . . but she had not.

Elf started, terrified, as a body plunked itself down next to her. Then her eyes met Arthur's, and she sagged, visibly relieved. "It's you, praise God!" she said, and wiped her eyes with her sleeve.

"I saw you tear out of the hall like the devil himself was after you," Arthur said.

"He was," Elf answered her old playmate, "but he calls himself Saer de Bude. He followed me to the linen cupboard and tried to kiss me," Elf told Arthur. "He has spoken to me several times in a most unsuitable manner. It is almost as if he were trying to woo me."

"Maybe he is," Arthur suggested quietly. "I wouldn't put it past him, Elf." Then he flushed, realizing he had used her nickname as he had always done when they were children.

Elf put a hand on his arm. "It's still Elf to you, Arthur," she told him. "Why would that awful man attempt to woo me? I am a nun. I have voiced no indication that I have changed my mind about taking my final vows. Indeed, I cannot wait to return to St. Frideswide's!"

"But shortly you will be an heiress with a fine, small manor in your possession. Saer de Bude is a younger son. He has nothing. I believe if the lord's wife were to inherit Ashlin instead of you, Elf, he would wed her, but the lady Isleen is not the heiress. You are. What will you do with Ashlin, and what will become of us?"

"The manor will belong to my order," Elf said. "I do not know what the Reverend Mother will decide. Perhaps she will rent the manor to some knight seeking a place of his own. Perhaps she will sell it off, but it doesn't matter. You and the others belong to Ashlin. You will be secure, Arthur."

"But without our family," he said. "The de Montforts have been part of Ashlin forever."

"Not really," Elf told him. "Ashlin was a Saxon manor in the

Conqueror's time. Its daughter wed a de Montfort, and Ashlin was her dowry. My ancestress, Rowena, did what was expedient for Ashlin, and for herself. The story goes that her brothers were killed at Hastings, and her old father wounded seriously, but his bravery had attracted King William. He ordered one of his knights, the first Richard de Montfort, to bring Sir Edmund home to Ashlin. And when he did and met the lady Rowena, it was love at first sight. She had hair my color. It is said that at least one child in each generation since has had hair this color," Elf concluded, then she giggled, for two lambs, curious, had come over to investigate beneath the tree, and were nibbling on her soft shoes. Reaching out, she stroked them. "They are so pretty," she said. Then she sighed. "I suppose I have to go back now."

"What of the lady's cousin, Elf?" Arthur asked her.

"I vomited on him when he attempted to kiss me," she said. "I hope he will now keep his distance for fear of a recurrence."

Arthur laughed heartily. "I know I should certainly steer clear of a girl who threw up on me." He chortled, then stood and, giving her a hand, pulled her up. "Elf, I know I am only a serf," Arthur told her, "but if that man approaches you again, I want you to tell me."

"Arthur, a serf who strikes out at a nobleman is accorded death without exception. I should not want your death on my conscience, heaven forfend!"

"There are ways other than open defiance or violence to right a wrong between serf and noble," Arthur told her with a wink. "We cannot have you harassed in your own home by that rude fellow, Elf. Don't worry. We shall not endanger ourselves by our actions."

"Thank you, Arthur," she told him, and then she walked back to the house, her heart a bit lighter.

"Where have you been?" Isleen demanded as she reentered the hall. "I have had to change Richard's bedding myself as that wretched old woman disappeared just when I needed her. She said she was fetching water for my husband's bath, but she has not yet returned."

"Do you want me to remain here with you, or find Ida?" Elf asked her. Isleen's tone was whiny, and frankly annoying. It was about time she did something for her husband.

"Oh, go and find her! Richard is asleep again. Where is my cousin? If I must sit here, I want some company at least," Isleen complained.

"I will find Ida," Elf said.

"I am here," Ida said, coming into the hall with a large basin. "I am not as young as I once was, lady, and cannot be hurried."

Isleen jumped up. "I cannot bear to sit here and watch my husband die!" she said. Then she hastened from the hall.

"You are not *that* slow," Elf said. "What on earth kept you, or did you mean for her to be alone with Dickon?"

"Her cousin came upon me howling and covered in vomit," Ida said. "He insisted I take his tunic from him to wash, and then he demanded a bath be brought for him. Imagine, a man who cannot hold his wine this early in the day," Ida concluded. "Come, let us bathe the lord."

Reaching out, Elf gently shook her brother. "Dickon, dearest, wake up. Ida and I would wash you."

Richard de Montfort's eyes opened slowly. "Elf," he said, "I am sorry I sent you away. I should not have. *I should not have.*" Then his body gave a long shudder, and his head fell to one side.

"Lord God and his blessed Mother have mercy on his soul!" Ida cried out, crossing herself as she began to weep.

Shocked, Eleanore de Montfort stared at her brother's limp body, his sightless eyes. *"He is dead,"* she said, stating the obvious and crossing herself. Then she fell to her knees. "Dear God, forgive me that I could not save him, for I truly tried to do so, but I had not the skills despite all I have learned." Then she began to cry.

"She poisoned him!" Ida said in venomous tones. "She has killed my baby, and I curse her for it! He called for you to come months ago, but she would not do it until she was certain nothing could save him, the wicked bitch! God curse her! God curse her!"

Hearing her old nurse's lament, Elf stifled her own grief. Putting her arms about Ida, she said, "You cannot say such things, for you have no proof of it. Like you, I have become suspicious, but there is no real evidence. You can be killed for slandering Isleen. We must keep such doubts to ourselves, Ida. *We must!* Do you understand me, old woman? You cannot voice your concerns in this matter."

"Is she then to be allowed to escape judgment for the lord's murder, my sweet lady?" Ida demanded angrily.

"Unless we can show the sheriff proof positive, we cannot accuse Isleen," Elf said quietly. "God knows the truth of this matter, and God will render his judgment and his punishment in his own time, Ida. We must trust in God." She hugged her nursemaid hard.

"For you," Ida said, "and for you alone will I be silent. You are now the lady of Ashlin, and I will obey you. Now, release me, child. We must bathe the lord's body, and lay him out for his burial."

"Should we tell Isleen?" Elf wondered aloud.

"Not until he is ready and looking his best," Ida said. "I will go and fetch his shroud."

Elf sat by her brother's side praying. Anyone entering the hall would assume that Richard de Montfort was sleeping. When the old woman returned, they stripped Richard's body and tenderly bathed it. Elf was horrified at his skeletal look. She carefully kept her eyes averted from his private parts and let Ida attend to them. As he was washed, they wrapped him in his shroud, leaving his head uncovered so his mourners might gaze upon his face a final time. When he was buried it would then be covered over.

Elf looked at her brother's once handsome face, now peaceful. She touched his cheek, and felt it was cool and waxlike. Tears rolled down her cheeks. What had brought her poor brother to this fate? Was it indeed poison as Ida insisted? It was odd that Dickon had sickened so suddenly when he had been robust all of his life. Bending, she kissed his forehead, then said to Ida, "Send Arthur for a priest. Dickon must be shrived before he is buried. And tell the carpenters to make the lord a fine coffin. My brother will lie in the hall for all his serfs to see and pay their respects."

"The coffin is already made, lady," Ida said. "I shall call for it to be brought in, and the lord laid in it. Arthur will go for the priest.

He will have to bring him from the convent, I fear. There is none nearer."

"Very well," Elf said. "I shall tell Isleen now." She turned and made her way to the solar, which was behind the hall. Opening the door, she spied Isleen and Saer by the fireplace in a heated discussion.

Hearing the door creak, Isleen spun about. "What do you want?" she demanded angrily of Elf. Her face was flushed with her ire.

"Your husband is dead," Elf said.

"Oh, my God!" Her eyes went to Saer de Bude. "It is too soon!" she said. "He cannot be dead yet! *He cannot!*" Now her glance took in her sister-in-law. "Could you not have done *something,* Eleanore?"

"I am only human, Isleen. I cannot hold back death," Elf said tartly. "You knew Dickon was near his end."

"But now?" Isleen wailed.

"It is God's will," Elf answered her.

"Oh, cease your pious mouthings at me," Isleen cried, and she stamped her foot. "Now you have what you wanted all along, Ashlin! I hate you! *I hate you!*" And she burst into tears.

Saer de Bude gathered his cousin into the shelter of his arms. "She does not mean it, Eleanore," he said. "I am certain she doesn't mean it. She is just distraught with Richard's death."

"I was sent from Ashlin at your behest when I was only five years old," Elf said, unable to control the sudden anger she felt welling up. "Great ladies raise their husband's siblings, children from earlier marriages, and their bastards, Isleen, but you could not be bothered by one small girl. I was fortunate, however, for I found a real home at St. Frideswide's, and I found a wonderful life. I never aspired to possess Ashlin. If you had given my brother children, we should not have come to this point. I should have probably never seen this place again. Your children would have inherited, and if I were lucky, you might have taken a moment to send me word of my brother's passing. But you did not do your duty by Dickon. You had no children, so under the law Ashlin is mine, *but I never wanted it!*"

Isleen looked up from Saer's shoulders. "I wanted children," she sobbed, "but your brother was not man enough to give them to me."

"Nay, lady, you were not a fertile field. My brother has fathered three children among the serfs since he wed you." Elf heard the words spill unchecked from her mouth, and was unable to stop them.

"*What?*" Isleen's tears were suddenly gone.

"My brother has fathered children on other women," Elf said fiercely. She would not allow this woman to slander Dickon's name, and if that was a sin she would confess it to Father Anselm when she returned to her convent. For now, however, she would defend her brother.

"*Liar! Liar!*" Isleen screamed. Her face was blotched with her fury. "You are a nasty little liar, and I hate you!"

"I am a nun, Isleen, and I do not lie," Elf said quietly. "The fault for the childlessness in your marriage rests with you, and not with my brother."

"Where are these little bastards?" Isleen demanded furiously. "I will have them slain along with their whoring mothers! *Where are they?*"

"You will kill no one, Isleen," Elf told her sister-in-law with devastating effect. "You are no longer the lady of Ashlin. I am, and those children, *my blood,* are under *my* protection. Attempt to seek them out, and I will have the church on you, lady." Then Elf turned on her heel and departed the solar.

"Oh, my God," Isleen gasped. She sagged against her cousin.

"You are truly a fool, Isleen," Saer said grimly. "You have made an enemy of Eleanore just when we need you to be her friend."

"Did you hear what she said, Saer? *Did you hear?* I am barren! Richard fathered three children, and none of them mine." She looked at him panic-stricken. "Now you will not want me!" And she burst into fresh tears, clinging desperately to him.

"Do not be absurd, Isleen. Of course I want you. I have always wanted you, and that has not changed. We will follow our plan with but one change. I will force the little nun into marriage, and after she has given me a son, then we shall dispose of her, and you will raise my heir as your own. She might even die in childbirth,

but if not, soon thereafter. The boy will never know you are not
his real mother. What difference does it make who births him? He
will be my son, Isleen . . . *and yours*."

Isleen sniveled. "I hate it that you must couple with her."

"I know, I know," he replied, smoothing her hair in a soothing
gesture, "but there is no help for it. If you cannot have a child for
me, I must take a wife who can. It is better this way. There will be
less suspicion if I marry another, and have a child first. After the little nun has returned to her God, we will be together."

"How do we know she has not lied?" Isleen said softly. "Perhaps
I can have a child for you, Saer. I am sure she has lied!"

"No," Saer de Bude replied. "She did not lie. She would not.
There is no deception in her, Isleen. She is a true innocent. I suspect she never meant to tell you of Richard's bastards, but that you
actually drove her to anger with your lack of sympathy regarding
your husband's death. She will say a hundred Aves to expiate that
sin." He chuckled. "Now, you must go into the hall and show your
respect for your husband. We have waited long for this day, my
pretty cousin."

"Do you think they suspect anything?"

"They are peasants," Saer de Bude said, "and Eleanore has not
been here long enough to realize something was wrong. No. I am
certain no one knows that we have killed your husband, Isleen. *No
one.*" He smiled warmly at her. "Did I not promise you when your
father gave you to Richard de Montfort that you and I would be
together one day? I have kept my promise, Isleen. Now you must
be patient just awhile longer, *and you must trust me.* If you do, we
will have each other, an heir, and Ashlin for ourselves. Promise
me, Isleen. Promise me you will resign yourself to waiting a bit
longer. If you should lose your composure now, we could lose
everything, including our lives. Do you understand me, Isleen?
You must make your peace with Eleanore this very day, my pretty.
Give me your bond, cousin."

"*But what if I could give you a child?*" she persisted.

"If you could, you already would have done so, Isleen," he told
her. "I have bedded you practically every night since I arrived at

Ashlin, even during some of your unclean periods. Never have you conceived of my seed, and like your husband, I have my smattering of bastards, including a little girl born several months ago here at Ashlin."

"*Ohhh,* villian!" she shrieked, pulling away from him and striking out at him with both of her fists.

"Cease your caterwauling, bitch!" Saer de Bude said. "It is a man's right to amuse himself among his serfs. Now, go and behave as a proper grieving widow would, Isleen. Our future is secure if you can manage to keep your head and your temper in check." He released her wrists, which he had caught when she began beating him, and gave her a push toward the door of the solar.

Isleen moved away from him. Her look was scathing. "When will you force the little nun?" she asked. "The sooner we begin this charade, the sooner it is played out."

"Let me try and woo her first," he responded.

"Like you did this morning? You have not so many tunics, my love, that you can allow another one to be spoiled."

"My error in judgment was approaching a virtuous young maiden too quickly. I meant to help her with the linens. She misunderstood."

Isleen snorted in derision. "You allowed your lust to gain the upper hand, Saer. Do not lie to me, *my love,* for I above all people know you best. Now, I will go and humble myself before Ashlin's new lady, claiming shock and grief were responsible for my temper. I will beg her forgiveness, and she will give it to me because it would not occur to her that I was lying, or had any other motive."

"Eleanore is not a fool, Isleen," he warned her. "Pure of heart and innocent of the world she may be, but she is no simpleton. Make certain you are sincere. Remember, there is none among the serfs or house servants who love you. You have not been an easy mistress. They will seek to find fault with you at every turn and complain to Ashlin's new lady of the manor. They knew her from birth until you convinced Richard to send her away. Old Ida in particular bears you malice for that selfish deed."

"Why should I have had to raise someone else's brat?" Isleen snapped. Then she smoothered her veil, making certain that her fillet was neatly in place. "Leave my chamber after I have gone," she said, and departed.

In the hall Isleen found her husband already laid out in his coffin upon an oaken bier. At each corner of the bier, a tall footed candlestick had been placed, and from each stick a tall beeswax candle burned. Roses from the garden and field flowers were arranged in large stone jars by his head and his feet. His hands had been folded neatly upon his chest beneath his shroud. A crucifix had been placed on his chest. His hair, or what was left of it, was neatly combed. A snug binding was wrapped about his head and under his chin, preventing his mouth from sagging open. A little copper penny had been placed upon each of his eyelids to keep them closed. He looked quite peaceful.

Isleen gave a shriek, and then flung herself dramatically upon her dead spouse's coffin. "Richard, my love! Oh, why have you left me?" she wailed, and began to sob in a most convincing manner.

"Hypocritical trull," Ida muttered beneath her breath. "She sends him to his grave, then weeps her insincere tears. If there is any justice, God will strike her down dead now and raise our good lord Richard back to life, healed and in his full vigor!"

"God has already raised Dickon up," Elf said softly.

It was at that very moment Father Anselm entered the hall. "My lady Eleanore," he greeted her, hurrying to her side.

Elf turned and came forward, holding out her hands in greeting to the convent priest. "Thank you for coming, good father, but how quickly you arrived. I am grateful. Will you shrive my brother, and bury him tomorrow for us?"

"I was but three miles away on another matter when your young Arthur found me," the priest said. "Yes, I will remain. I am glad I may be of service to you and the grieving widow."

Isleen, for all her weeping, nonetheless heard the exchange. She turned and fell on her knees before Elf. "Sister, forgive me for my harsh words earlier. I knew my poor Richard was dying, and yet when the moment came, I could not believe it. In my shock and pain, I struck out at the one person who came to aid my dearest husband and nurse him these weeks with such devotion. Forgive me, Eleanore, I beg you! I cannot bear the thought that you and I have quarreled!" She held out her hands in supplication to Elf.

Elf bent and drew her sister-in-law up. "Of course I forgive you, Isleen, but I must also ask your pardon for my harsh words earlier. Like you, my grief overcame me, I fear." She kissed Isleen on both cheeks.

"And I forgive you," Isleen replied sweetly, kissing Elf in return. "We must never quarrel again, *sister*."

Father Anselm smiled at the two young women, pleased by their public display of affection. Then he greeted the young widow with kindness as Elf introduced them.

"And this is my cousin, Saer de Bude," Isleen told the priest. "My father sent him to help us when Richard fell ill. He will escort me home to my parents with my dower portion after we have buried my poor husband. Ashlin now belongs to Eleanore to do with as she pleases."

"I shall give it to our order," Elf said.

The priest nodded his approval. "Reverend Mother would be quite delighted by such a gift."

"Has Matilda FitzWilliam taken her vows yet, Father Anselm?" Elf asked him. "We were to do so on St. Alban's Day in June."

"Sister Columba became a bride of Christ forever on that day, Eleanore. She sends you her prayers, and looks forward to your return," the priest said. "Reverend Mother says you may take your final vows on St. Frideswide's Day itself in October if your business here at Ashlin is completed by then. It is quite an honor, my daughter, as you well know."

Elf's face was alight with joy.

The priest and the young novice prayed the night through by Richard de Montfort's bier. Isleen cried off from exhaustion in midevening, and disappeared into the solar. Throughout the long hours and into the early morning, the serfs came into the hall to pay their last respects and to pray with the two religious. Finally in the hour after dawn Isleen appeared again, asking for time alone with her departed spouse. Ida came, clucking and fussing that Elf must break her fast, and afterward escorting her to her bed space for a nap before Richard de Montfort's funeral. They buried the lord of the manor in the early afternoon of a summer's day. The air was heavy with the promise of rain, and the skies a dull gray above them. Elf had declared a half holiday, and provided her people with a small feast afterward. The rains held off until dusk when a thunderstorm rolled in from beyond the hills that separated Hereford from Wales.

"I will say Mass in the morning here in the hall," the priest said, "and then return to St. Frideswide's. When shall I tell Reverend Mother to expect your return, my daughter?"

"I shall come with you tomorrow," Elf said. "I am no longer needed at Ashlin, and I am anxious to resume my own life."

"Oh, please remain until I am ready to depart Ashlin, and rejoin my family," Isleen said prettily. "It is unlikely we shall see each other again. Do a few days really matter, dear Eleanore?"

"I am certain that Reverend Mother would approve," Father Anselm said helpfully. "The lady Isleen has told me of your devotion to your late brother, my daughter. You are entitled to a few days of rest before you must resume your life at St. Frideswide's. I shall tell Reverend Mother myself. Return when you can."

"Well," Elf reasoned, "I should really appoint a bailiff until Reverend Mother decides what to do with Ashlin; and I must separate Isleen's dowry portion from Ashlin's other assets so she may carry it home to her family. After you have mourned a proper time, Isleen, your father will undoubtedly want to arrange another marriage for you."

"Then, you will remain?" Isleen clapped her hands together in a childish gesture of delight. "*Ohhh,* I am so glad!" Her glance flicked to Saer de Bude for the briefest moment, but old Ida saw it.

What mischief were those two up to, Ida wondered. She had best watch carefully over her sweet child lest they do her some harm. They were a wicked pair, and she would put nothing past them.

Shortly after Father Anselm departed for St. Frideswide's the following morning, Isleen sought out her sister-in-law.

"You are now the lady of Ashlin," she said. "I will move my things from the solar so you may take your rightful place."

"No! No!" Elf replied. "We will be here but a few more days, sister. Do not go to the bother of removing your possessions for me. I am not used to having a chamber to myself. I have always slept in the dormitory with the other girls. When I take my final vows, I will be assigned a tiny cell for myself. I would be uncomfortable in the solar, Isleen. I have not slept there since I was a child."

"At least share it with me, then," Isleen cajoled. "It is not proper for the lady of the manor to be taking her nightly rest in a bed space in the hall. We will share our memories of Richard before we must part forever." She gave Elf a winning smile.

Now, what is that vixen about? Ida wondered.

"Very well," Elf agreed. "As long as I do not discommode you, Isleen. It is just for a few days after all."

"*Ohhh,* good!" Isleen purred. "Let us move your belongings right now, *sister.*"

"I will do it for you, my lady," Ida said quickly. She was anxious to learn if there was anything she should be concerned about in the solar, for she had not been inside that chamber since Elf had been taken away as a child.

"Be certain you do not touch any of my belongings," Isleen said meanly. "I will know if you do."

Ida glared at the young woman, but said nothing. Her thoughts were racing, however. *Nay, I'll not touch your things, lady, but I'll be certain to make sure that nothing belonging to Ashlin has been taken by you for transport back to your home.* The old lady gathered up Elf's few possessions, and wended her way to the solar. She found the chamber dirty and in terrible disarray. Not even setting down her small burden, Ida stamped back out into the hall and marched right up to Elf.

"My lady, you cannot stay in the solar. It is filthy and in such disorder that there is no room for you. Until it is cleaned, it is better you remain in your bed space in the hall."

"Why has the solar not been kept in order?" Elf asked her sister-in-law. Cleanliness was a watchward at the convent.

"Since Richard died, the servants will do nothing I ask," Isleen whined piteously. "Even the girl who served me has disappeared."

"I'm not surprised, but that clutter has been there longer than a day or two," Ida muttered low to her mistress.

If Elf heard, she gave no sign of it, instead saying, "Who served the lady Isleen? She is to return to her duties until my brother's widow departs Ashlin for her own home. Only then is she freed from her obligations. She is to come at once and put the lady's possessions in their proper places. Then the room is to be thoroughly cleaned. When that is done, I shall join my sister in the solar, and I expect to sleep there this very night. Am I understood?"

Cedric, the household steward came forward. "It will be done at once, my lady. Your word is our command."

"Very good, Cedric. The lady Isleen and I shall leave the solar to you and your minions." She smiled sweetly.

Isleen could not help but be annoyed as the servants hurried to oblige their new mistress. They had never toiled as diligently for her, but, she decided, they were simply trying to get on the innocent Elf's good side for the brief time they thought she would remain with them. When Saer was lord here, and Elf had her brief tenure as lady, they would reveal their true colors, for they were lazy and slothful creatures at heart. She was therefore astonished when she and Elf entered the solar in late afternoon to find it cleaner than she had ever known it since she came to Ashlin.

The stone floors had been scrubbed thoroughly, as had the walls. The fireplace was clean, its small chimney drawing perfectly. The two narrow and arched windows had been washed! The sunlight was shining brightly through them. The two tapestries hanging on the walls had quite obviously been beaten and brushed, for they no longer looked dusty, nor were there cobwebs hanging from them. The bed she had once shared with Richard had clean hangings, fresh, lavender-scented linens, and plump new pillows. Its feather bed had been well lofted. The two wooden chests that belonged to her had been rearranged, and were open to display her belongings all neatly set inside. A smaller painted chest that she had never seen had been placed at the foot of the bed, and Elf's few belongings were visible.

Elf clapped her hands and laughed. "It is my mother's chest!" she said, delighted. "I have not seen it since I left Ashlin. I always loved it because of all the animals and birds painted upon it. The chest originally belonged to my ancestress, Rowena." Her silvery glance swept the chamber. "They have done well, Isleen, haven't they? The room is well ordered now. Come, and let us tell Cedric how pleased we are." She took her sister-in-law's soft hand.

Isleen pulled her hand away from Elf's gentle grip. "*Tell Cedric we are pleased?* Because the servants have done their duty? It is past time they did their duty! I shall thank no one."

"Well, I shall," Elf told her. "Do you think the servants are not as distressed over Dickon's death as we are? He was the last de Montfort who will rule here; the last of his Saxon ancestress's long line. Ashlin's serfs and their families have belonged to this land for hundreds of years, Isleen. They fear the future."

"This ancient line you speak of would not be broken," Isleen replied, "if you would consider marrying a man instead of locking yourself away in a convent for the rest of your days, Eleanore. Now that Richard is gone and I have no child to inherit this land, it is your duty to give up the nunnery and accept the responsibility of your inheritance. Instead, you selfishly pursue your own desires rather than accepting the obligations that God has given you."

Elf looked suddenly stricken. She had not even considered such a thing. *She would not!* "I am already a nun, Isleen."

"You have not yet taken your final vows, Eleanore. When Richard placed you at St. Frideswide's, it was because the small dowry your father had apportioned for you would not gain you a proper husband of stature who possessed his own properties. Richard discussed the matter quite thoroughly with my parents, and it was then the decision was made to put you in the convent. The nuns would take your little pittance, and be glad for it; and you would have a life of safety and contentment serving our dear Lord. Now, however, you are an heiress of respectable means. You have a small manor with livestock, a house, and serfs. This makes you a most desirable commodity for a knight of good name."

"My course in life has already been determined," Elf replied in firm tones. "I pledged myself to our Lord at the age of ten years. It was then I became a postulant. At twelve I advanced to the blessed rank of novice. In October, on St. Frideswide's Day, I shall take my final vows and become Sister Alban. This is what *I* want. *It is what God wants.* You are wrong, Isleen, to try and tempt me from my chosen path. I shall not be enticed, no matter your argument."

"Very well," Isleen said. "I think you very wrong." *But, your intransigence suits me well,* Isleen thought. *I shall enjoy seeing Saer despoil your virtue, and force you to his will. You will be taught how to use your lips for more than just prayers. You will be taught how to kiss, to lick, to suck, and how to give your husband pleasure in ways you cannot even imagine, little nun. You will be taught obedience as you never learned it in your convent. And when you have given Saer a strong son and heir, I will kill you myself.*

CHAPTER FOUR

"I shall sleep on the trundle," Elf said as they prepared for bed. "First we must have a bath," Isleen replied. "There is the tub all ready for us by the fire. You may go first, dear sister."

Elf looked nervously at the large oaken tub. It appeared to be big enough for two people, not at all like the small modest tub they bathed in at the convent. Bending, she undid her garters, which were fastened at her knees, and rolled down her stockings, kicking off her shoes first. She drew her round-necked gray tunica off, and laid it aside, placing her long skirt atop it. Then she pinned up her braid and started to mount the steps of the tub.

Isleen shrieked. "Do you mean to bathe still clothed?" she cried to Elf. "You still have your camisa on, Eleanore."

"I was taught to bathe like this in the convent," Elf answered. "It is more modest. It is not good to flaunt one's body shamelessly."

"You are not in the convent now," Isleen said. "Take it off so you may bathe fully. There is no one here to see you. I shall not look, I promise you, if you are so modest that you fear my gaze."

"Turn your back, then," Elf said, not of a mind to argue, and frankly curious to learn what the water would feel like on her bare skin. When Isleen had turned away from her, Elf drew the long garment off, dropping it on the floor, and stepped down into the tub. The water was scented, and hot. It felt wonderful. She sighed with the decadent pleasure of it. She would not know such luxury once she returned to the convent. Then she silently chided herself. She had lived her life very well without such delights. She would readjust perfectly well.

From his hiding place behind a tapestry, Saer de Bude had let his eyes wander over the young girl's body as she stood naked for that brief moment. She had not the lushness of his cousin, Isleen, but she was perfectly formed for her size. He was sorely tempted to step from behind his shield and violate her now, but he restrained himself, remembering her violent reaction to his nearness the day before. No. He had to attempt to win her over, at least a little before he seduced her.

Isleen moved next to his hiding place. "Well," she whispered, "what do you think, cousin?"

"She will prove an amusing tumble," he murmured back so softly, she could barely hear him.

"Go!" she said low, and was relieved to hear the soft click of the little door behind the tapestry open and close as he departed. She turned, saying, "Are you enjoying your bath, Eleanore?"

"Oh, yes!" Elf admitted. "It is ever so much better without my camisa, but of course at the convent we must be more modest, sister."

"Oh, Eleanore, you should at least consider my earlier words," Isleen said, her tone kindly. "You are a lovely young girl, and there would be at least a dozen offers for your hand if you would but say so. My father, Baron Hugh, would be delighted to act as your guardian in such a matter. Ashlin needs you."

"God has called me," Elf said, "and to disobey his call would be wrong. Do not peck at me so, Isleen. You knew marriage was for you. I know the convent is for me, and that is an end to it."

Isleen clamped her lips together. Saer thought he could breach the girl's defenses, but he was wrong. In the end he would have to rape her to have his way, and to have Ashlin. "Here is a warm drying cloth for you," she said. "Come forth from the tub while the water still has some warmth so I may bathe, too."

"Turn your back, then," Elf commanded her, standing, although the tub concealed her nakedness from Isleen. Taking the toweling she climbed out, wrapping the cloth about her, blushing as Isleen turned, pulled off her own camisa, and moved to encase her voluptuous nakedness in the warmth of the water. Elf dried herself, put her camisa back on, and lay down upon the trundle. When Isleen had bathed and exited the tub, she protested Elf's decision to sleep upon the trundle.

"You are the mistress of Ashlin. The bed is yours," she insisted.

"It is a bed for a man and a woman," Elf replied. "It was my parents' marriage bed, and your marriage bed. I would be uncomfortable sleeping in it, I fear."

"Then, we will share it, silly," Isleen said.

"Nay," Elf responded. "I am content on the trundle, Isleen. God give you a good rest. Good night." And Elf quietly, but audibly began to say her prayers.

Little prude, Isleen thought to herself, and rolled onto her side, drawing the feather coverlet over her shoulders. She would have to sleep alone tonight, and the notion did not please her at all. When the little nun was fast asleep, Isleen decided, she would creep from the solar and up into the attic room, where Saer was now residing. Would he have some ripe little serf girl in his bed tonight? She hoped so! She always enjoyed it when there were three of them. She had often longed to bring one of the young, well-muscled serf lads into their bed, but Saer did not fancy that kind of a game. There were times when she thought him very difficult, but it never caused her to cease her affections. She had loved him since they were children together, for he had been in fosterage with her parents since he had been six. As the youngest of her parents' children, she had not been sent off as had her three sisters and her brother. Isleen closed her eyes, and dozed. She would awaken when she needed to, and she would go to Saer.

When Elf awoke, the sun was well up. At first she wasn't certain where she was, and then she realized she was in the solar. Stretching, she arose from the trundle and reached for the rest of her clothing. She was fully dressed when Ida bustled into the chamber.

"You are awake at last, child," the old woman said. "I did not awaken you because you needed your sleep. You have hardly had any proper rest since you returned home, so busy were you with your poor brother, may God assoil his good and noble soul! Come into the hall now, and break your fast, my dear lady."

"What time is it?" Elf asked, following Ida into the hall.

"Half the morning is gone," Ida said.

"*Ohhh!*" Then realizing she felt much better than she had in many a day, Elf said, "Where is the lady Isleen?"

"Out riding with that cousin of hers," Ida answered. "She wanted me to awaken you so you might go with them, but I would not let them disturb your rest. You needed it more than you needed to ride with the likes of those two."

"Where is Cedric?" She sat down at the high board. "I must see to the business of restoring Isleen's dower portion so she may return to her father's house. He will want to arrange another marriage for her."

"You must first eat and renew your strength," Ida told her mistress in no uncertain terms. "What you put into your mouth would not satisfy a bird, lady! Have they been starving you at that convent?" She signaled the servants to bring Elf her morning meal.

"Gluttony is a grave sin, Ida," Elf replied. "We eat just what is necessary to sustain the body. I have never gone hungry at St. Frideswide's, I promise you. We cook too much food and then waste it, I fear." She bowed her head a moment in prayer, crossing herself. A round trencher of bread filled with hot oatmeal was put before her, and Elf began to spoon it up. A plate with a hard-boiled egg and a small wedge of cheese was set at her elbow, and a goblet of watered wine spiced with herbs put by her hand.

"The servants eat the leftovers, lady, for how else would they be fed but from your table, as is their right; and that which remains is

given to the beggars, who frequently come to our door. These
wars have not been easy on anyone, I fear, lady. Safe and secure in
your convent, you do not know these things, but this is the way of
the world."

"And our blessed Lord himself preached charity," Elf replied. "I
stand corrected, Ida."

"Eat your breakfast," Ida said, pouring a dollop of heavy cream
on her mistress's oatmeal.

Elf laughed, but discovered she had an excellent appetite this
morning. She finished her cereal, and then ate some of the bread
trencher with the cheese and egg. When she had finished, draining
the last drop of wine from her cup, Cedric came and stood before
her, awaiting her sign to speak. She nodded at him.

He bowed politely, then said, "I have gone back over the manor
records to determine the exact amount of the lady Isleen's dower
portion, and of how it was paid. It was mostly in coin, which your
brother, may God assoil his good and noble soul, wisely set aside.
He never touched it, and it still remains in the bag in which it
came. The lady brought certain household goods and a palfrey as
well. They are all carefully listed, and can be separated from that
which belongs to Ashlin manor."

"How quickly can it be done, Cedric? I am certain the lady
Isleen is eager to return to her own family, and I wish to rejoin my
sisters at St. Frideswide's," Elf told her steward.

Cedric smiled knowingly at his young mistress. "It can be done
by day's end, lady, so that you may all depart Ashlin on the morrow.
Will that be suitable, my lady?"

"That," Elf answered him with a small grin, "will be perfect,
Cedric. You are a good servant, but then my mother and brother
always said it was so. You have not changed over the years."

"Lady, if I may ask a question?"

She nodded.

"What is to happen to us if you return to your convent?"

"As a nun I am not permitted to own personal property," Elf
told him. "I shall give Ashlin to my order. There are any number

of ways in which they might make use of it. They might found another convent here; or they might lease the manor to a tenant; or they might sell the manor. That will not be my decision, but the one thing I can guarantee you is that the serfs and freedmen who have lived on these lands for centuries, and are as much a part of Ashlin as the lands itself, they will remain here. The Reverend Mother is a wise and good lady. She will allow no harm to befall any of you. On that you have my word, the pledge of Eleanore de Montfort, and you know, Cedric, that the word of a de Montfort is as good as gold."

"Thank you, my lady," the steward said. "I needed to know in order to reassure our people that no ill would befall them with your departure. But we truly wish you would stay with us."

"I cannot. It is not my fate. You may go now, Cedric, and see to the departure of my brother's widow."

He bowed, and left her. Elf looked about the hall. There was nothing for her to accomplish. Her packing, which Ida would do, would take but a few minutes, and could be done in the morning before she departed her childhood home. *I'll go to my herbarium,* she finally decided. There were things there for her to do, and the little side garden had grown nicely since it was planted. It would be wasteful not to harvest what she could now, and take it back with her to the convent. Sister Winifred would be delighted. Elf hurried from the hall and down the garden path, waving to Arthur, who was weeding among the roses. She saw two riders coming toward the house, probably Isleen and her obnoxious cousin.

Elf chuckled. Saer de Bude had certainly given her a wide berth since their encounter by the linen cupboard. As she thought back on it, she had no idea why she had vomited her breakfast on him, for she hadn't been afraid of him. He simply revolted her, and, after all, it had been the time of the month when her link with the moon had been broken. Still, it had certainly put him off, for which she was grateful. Her tears had been those of frustration and relief. And Arthur had cheered her up as he often had when they were children and she had been frightened. She realized now that his friendship was one of the few things she had missed about Ashlin, and it would be very sorely missed again. She was giving up a great deal, she realized.

But was not sacrifice a part of the religious life? Still, was there any truth in Isleen's contention that she was pursuing her own desires instead of accepting her obligations? After all, did not all things come of God? Eleanore de Montfort shook her head. Her very thoughts were the most disturbing she had ever known. There had never been any doubt in her mind that she was one of God's chosen brides. Why was she even considering the possibility now that she wasn't? *The devil!* It was surely Satan tempting her! She crossed herself and entered the herbarium, noting the hearth was cold.

I will make some elixirs and salves today that I may carry with me, Elf decided. She called to Arthur, "Go up to the house, and bring me some coals from the fire so I may start my own. Cedric will give you a pan in which you may carry them."

"At once, lady," Arthur called back, dashing off.

Elf went to her well, drew up a bucket of cool water, and brought it into her shed. She used some of it to wipe off the slate-topped table upon which she worked, then placed the bucket on the floor beneath her table, and took down from a shelf several mortars and pestles. After going out into her garden, she picked the biggest greenish yellow leaves of her lettuce plants, and brought them back into the herbarium to wash.

Elf filled a kettle and added the lettuce leaves. Boiled down and made into a syrup with honey to both thicken and sweeten it, it could be reconstituted into a soothing tea that would cure spider bites, but was also useful for bringing sleep in a manner very much like poppies.

Next she took down a sheaf of horehound leaves that had been drying for some weeks. She crumbled the leaves slightly, then added them to a mortar, and began to pestle them into a fine powder that she transferred into a stone jar. The powder would make an excellent tea, or a syrup. Horehound was known to cure jaundice, bad coughs, and was also beneficial for fading eyesight, always a problem among the convent's elderly nuns.

"I've brought the coals, Elf. Do you want me to make the fire? I see you have one kettle ready to boil up," Arthur said as he entered the herbarium with the pan of live coals from the hall fireplace.

"Syrup of lettuce," she told him. "Yes, start the fire for me, Arthur, and then you can go back to your work. Thank you. I'll be in my garden." Outside again, Elf took up a basket. First she gathered leaves of sage, which was good for the nerves; mint, an excellent remedy for retching, stopping hiccups, and for maladies of the stomach in general; mustard greens, which were a sure cure for gout, particularly in the toes; and anise, which was used to rid a body of flatulence.

"I'm off, then," Arthur said. "The hearth is drawing nicely, and your kettle is coming to a boil, Elf. Can I carry your basket?"

"Nay, I'm fine," she replied with a wave as she reentered her little shed. She placed her basket upon a small wooden table and began to separate the plants she had just cut. She had about finished when the door to the shed opened. Elf looked up. "What," she demanded, "are *you* doing here?"

"I have wanted to apologize to you, Eleanore, for the other day. My behavior was most unchivalrous. Still," Saer de Bude said, "no man who saw you would blame me. Despite your drab robes, you are a lovely young woman, lady."

"I will accept your apology, for to refuse it would be most un-Christian of me," Elf told him.

"What is it you do here?" he asked her.

"I make medicines, elixirs, and salves," Elf replied, wishing he would go away.

"Like a good chatelaine," he said, smiling at her.

"I assist our infirmarian, Sister Winifred," Elf told him.

"What is that kettle boiling on your hearth now?" He moved into the small shed, closing the door behind him, and peered into the pot. "The smell is familiar."

"I am making a syrup of lettuce," Elf told him. Why would he not go?

"I have heard lettuce dulls desire," he remarked.

"You obviously do not eat it," Elf replied tartly.

Saer de Bude laughed aloud. There was more to the little nun than they had realized. She could be humorous. Something he had not expected. And she was not as vapid as she appeared. No, not at all. "Lady," he said, "I will be frank with you." He had decided in that instant that to dissemble with the girl was not wise. "I am a younger son. I want my own manor. If you would reconsider your decision to return to your convent to take your final vows, I should make you a good husband. My mother was a de Warenne, and my father's family is a respected one in Normandy. I have always been a man of honor."

"Nay, sir, you are not honorable at all, for you have committed adultery with my brother's wife. I am not so great a fool that I did not realize it, although I prayed it not be so. I hope Dickon never knew, although I think he did, for he was no fool, either. There is talk among the serfs that you and Isleen poisoned my brother. No formal accusations can be made for nothing can be proven. In that you are safe. As for me, I am God's chosen, and will wed with no man. If you want Ashlin, then speak with the Reverend Mother Eunice at the convent. It will be her decision as to how Ashlin is disposed of, and she may be seeking a tenant."

"I will be no one's tenant," he said grimly. Then reaching out, he pulled her into his arms. "Lady, I will have Ashlin, and I will have you whether you will, or no."

Elf attempted to squirm from his grasp, but he held her too tightly. "Let me go this instant, sir!" she said in her firmest voice.

Laughing mockingly he kissed her, his lips smashing hard on her soft mouth. One arm pinioned her to his broad chest while his other hand reached up, hooked itself into the round neckline of her tunica, and yanked the fabric of both her gown and her camisa asunder. The marauding hand pushed the materials aside and captured a round breast, squeezing it hard.

His sudden attack both astounded and terrified her. She couldn't breathe, and his grasp on her person was like iron. Desperately she tore her mouth away from his, and tried to scream, but her throat

muscles seemed constricted and nothing but a small squeak came
forth. She grew faint, and struggled to maintain consciousness even
as she fell back against his arm.

"There is a river of passion within you, Eleanore," Saer de Bude
growled. "I will awaken it." His mouth pressed kisses against her
white throat while his hand fondled her breast hungrily. "By the
time I am through with you this day, no convent on earth will have
you, my pretty. You will be a very despoiled dove, Eleanore." Then
he kicked her legs from beneath her.

She fell to the floor with an *"Offff,"* the wind temporarily knocked
out of her. He stood above her, straddling her as he loosened his
garments, then pulled forth his swollen manhood. "This, my pretty, is
all for you!" Then he lowered himself, covering her body with his.

The sight, her first sight, of an engorged manhood restored Elf's
voice, and she began to scream at the top of her lungs. Strength
flowed back into her body, and she fought him as if she were fighting for her very life, and in a sense she was. If he violated her, her
life as a nun was finished. She would be forced into marriage with
him, and that was the last thing on earth that Eleanore de Montfort
wanted. Her hands reached out, clawing at his handsome face as he
pushed her skirts up and began to push her resisting thighs apart
with his knee. Her shrieks grew louder, frantic peal after frantic
peal rending the quiet afternoon air.

Saer de Bude slapped the girl beneath him, hard. "Shut up, you
little bitch!" he shouted at her, and he slapped her again and again
to silence her cries, but Elf would not be silenced.

"Help! Help!" she shouted as loudly as she could.

"You wanted this," he snarled. "Admit it, you little bitch! *You
wanted it!"*

"No! No!" Elf screamed.

"You'll like it," he promised thickly. Her resistance was the most
exciting he had ever encountered.

God save me! Elf thought as her strength began to give out, and
as if in answer to that prayer, the door to the herbarium burst open.
Elf heard Arthur's voice swearing a string of extremely colorful

oaths as he grabbed Saer de Bude by his neck and dragged him off the resisting girl. Immediately the boy's fist made contact with the man's chin, and Saer de Bude fell back to the floor, his head striking the edge of the slate table. Elf scrambled up, pulling her skirts down, clutching the torn fabric of her upper garment across her chest.

"Come on," Arthur said, grabbing her other hand.

"But he's injured," Elf protested. "I must see to him."

Arthur pulled her from the shed. "We'll send someone from the house to tend to him. By the rood, Elf, you are either a saint or a fool! The slimy bastard tried to rape you, and you would tend to his wounds?" He dragged her up the path to the manor house and into the hall. "Cedric! Grandmother!" he shouted as he entered.

"Holy Mary, and all the saints in heaven," Ida said as she saw Elf. "What has happened to my baby?"

"The knight tried to rape her," Arthur answered bluntly.

"I'm all right, thanks to Arthur," Elf said, "but the knight lies wounded in the herbarium. Arthur hit him, and Saer de Bude hit his head when he fell. Send someone for the sheriff! I will press charges against the man for his attack on me."

"Nay," Cedric the steward said grimly. " 'Tis our Arthur who would be arrested, lady, for he is a serf, and he has hit a noble. The punishment for that crime is death. We will take care of the knight, but you must return immediately to your convent, and Arthur must go with you to beg sanctuary. He will be safe there until you can explain to the sheriff what has happened. It will be a far more effective story told within your convent walls than here at Ashlin. Go to the stable, boy, and saddle two horses. Lady, we will see to the knight, I promise."

"I must know before I go if we have killed him," Elf said.

"I will check myself," Cedric answered, and hurried from the hall.

When he returned several minutes later, Ida had managed to pack up Elf's small belongings, and Elf had changed into a fresh camisa and tunica. Isleen had been napping, and had not heard the two women creeping about.

"The knight will live, worse luck," Cedric said. "He was already trying to sit up. I told him we would send aid. Now, lady, you must go! We will take the other horses in the stable out to the far pasture to make it difficult to follow you, but I do not believe the knight will be in any condition to chase after you for a day or two. He is injured enough, but sadly not mortally."

"I want them both out of Ashlin as soon as Saer de Bude can travel, Cedric. Send to Baron Hugh in my name for an escort for his daughter and her cousin. By the time they arrive, that wretched man should be ready to travel, even if he has to go in a litter!"

"Yes, my lady," the steward answered her, with a small smile. "Godspeed you."

"And God bless all here at Ashlin," Elf answered. Then with Ida at her side, she hurried from the hall to where Arthur was waiting with two horses for them.

The boy helped his mistress onto her horse, then mounted his own. "Good-bye, Grandmother," he said, and Ida began to weep.

"Now, Ida," Elf told her old nursemaid, "I will let nothing happen to Arthur. He did nothing wrong. If worse comes to worst, I will send him into Wales, where Norman law cannot touch him." She drew the old lady's hand up to her lips, and kissed it. "Farewell, my old dearie. God bless you."

"The Holy Virgin keep you safe, my baby," Ida sobbed. Then she whirled and ran back into the house.

"Can you go faster than a walk?" Arthur asked her.

"Can you?" Elf teased back, and kicked her mount into a canter.

They rode straight through the eight miles to St. Frideswide's, reaching it at sunset.

"Welcome back, Eleanore de Montfort," Sister Perpetua, the convent portress, greeted her as they came through the gates.

"Thank you, good sister," Elf replied. "This is my serf, Arthur. He asks us for sanctuary, and when Reverend Mother hears my tale, I believe she will give it to him."

"Elf!" Isabeaux St. Simon ran forward as Elf dismounted her horse. "I didn't know you were coming today!"

"Neither did I," Elf said. "Isa, will you go find Reverend Mother, and ask her if she will see me on a most urgent matter."

Isa nodded and hurried off. Several minutes later she returned. "She'll see you in the chapter house." Her eyes flicked to Arthur. "Who is this?" she asked.

"My serf," Elf said with no further explanation.

"Oh," Isa said, her interest waning. The handsome young man was only a serf. For a moment she thought that perhaps Elf had decided not to take her final vows now that she was an heiress; that mayhap she would marry, and that her companion was her chosen.

"Come with me," Elf said to Arthur, and hurried off across the cloister toward the chapter house. Moving quickly through the door, Arthur in her wake, Elf headed directly to the hall, where Reverend Mother Eunice awaited. She made obeisance to the abbess, flattening herself upon the floor before her.

"Rise, my daughter, and tell me why you have arrived so precipitously, and in this young man's company," Reverend Mother Eunice said.

"This is Arthur, my serf, Reverend Mother, and he would beg sanctuary of us. You must give it to him, for he saved me this day from a fate worse than death," Elf began, arising to stand before the abbess. She then went on to explain, telling the Reverend Mother all that had happened since her arrival home at Ashlin: her brother's subsequent death, her sister-in-law's insistence that she give up her calling and marry, Saer de Bude's attack on her person this very day. "If Arthur had not been nearby and heard my cries, I should have surely been ravished and despoiled." She began to weep softly. "I should not have been able to return to St. Frideswide's, and been forced into marriage with that horrible man! And poor Arthur! Because he came to my aid, he will now be condemned to death unless you will give him sanctuary."

"Arthur of Ashlin, I grant you sanctuary here at St. Frideswide's for a year and a day. If we cannot straighten this matter out by then, I shall grant you sanctuary for as long as it takes," the abbess said. "Now, go to the stables, my lad, where Sister Joseph is in charge. Tell her I said she is to house you and find work for you to do."

Arthur knelt before the abbess, and taking up the hem of her robe, kissed it. "I thank you, my lady abbess, for your mercy." Then he stood and left the hall.

"Oh, thank you, Reverend Mother! Arthur was my childhood playmate, and one of the first to greet me warmly on my return to Ashlin. Ida, his grandmother, was my nursemaid. I would not want to be the cause of his death. . . ." She was sobbing now.

The abbess recognized that Elf was suffering from shock, but there were questions she had to ask. "I must know exactly what it is this man did to you, my daughter. Come, and sit with me," she said, leading the girl to a bench set against the wall. "Now, speak honestly to me, Eleanore de Montfort. Your immortal soul stands in peril if you lie to me. Do you understand, my daughter?"

"Yes, Reverend Mother," Elf replied, and she shuddered. "He grabbed me, and kissed me. He fondled my breast. Then he threw me to the floor of the shed, and exposed his male member to me. He was saying horrible things to me, about how I should like what he would do." She shuddered again, but swallowing hard as she relived the attack, she bravely continued on. "Then he laid his body on mine. I was screaming, and screaming, and thank God, Arthur came. He pulled my attacker from me, hitting him on the jaw. It was when he fell back that Saer de Bude's head grazed the edge of the table.

"I saw the blood gush from the wound, and wanted to remain to aid him, but Arthur would not let me. We ran back to the manor, and Cedric, my steward, went back to the shed. My attacker was alive and moving. Cedric told him to remain where he was, and he would fetch help. In the meantime Ida gathered my belongings together, and Arthur and I fled here to St. Frideswide's," Elf concluded.

"Did your attacker's male member touch your private parts, or penetrate you at any time, my daughter?" the abbess probed.

"*No!* Never, Reverend Mother!" The shocked look on Elf's face told the nun that the girl was telling the truth.

"Are you wearing the same clothing as you wore when you were accosted?" the abbess asked. She had to make certain, as painful as it was.

"All but my tunica and camisa," Elf said. "He tore those from me when he sought to fondle me." Her face was pale. "May I have a bath, Reverend Mother? I can yet smell that man's body on me."

"Of course, my daughter, and you may bathe this night only without your camisa. Tell Sister Cuthbert I said so. Nay, I will tell her so myself." She arose from the bench. "Come, my poor Eleanore, let us go and find Sister Cuthbert, and get you settled safely."

They left the chapter house and walked across the cloister to the dormitory where the girls were housed. Both Sister Cuthbert and Matti, now Sister Columba, hurried forward to hug Elf.

"Go inside with Sister Columba, my daughter, and take the tub from its cabinet. Then begin filling it with water warmed from the fire. Use the small tub. It will be easier for you. Come and tell us when you are ready," the abbess instructed the two girls. When they had gone off, she spoke seriously to Sister Cuthbert, telling her what had happened. "I am certain Eleanore has told me the truth as she knows it, but sometimes the shock of such a terrible experience, the fright— Well, just be certain there is no blood on her skirts or her thighs. The man ripped her camisa and tunica so they were changed, but we must be sure she is still a virgin, and pure, Cuthbert."

The younger nun's face was stricken with sorrow. "What a terrible time the poor girl has had, but I will make certain as you have asked me, Reverend Mother. Still, I am sure Eleanore told you the truth. Her calling means too much to her that she would lie. Who was the lad who escorted her?"

"The serf who rescued her. His name is Arthur, and we have given him sanctuary because his brave and noble actions have put him in jeopardy. You well know the punishment for a serf who hits a master."

Sister Cuthbert nodded. "But it would be an injustice for them to punish the boy for defending his mistress, wouldn't it?"

"We will wait to see if this knight files charges," the abbess said. "If he does, and they come here for the boy, we shall tell them he has sanctuary and speak for him in the courts. Knowing what has happened, it would not be right for us to do otherwise."

CHAPTER FIVE

Hugh de Warenne looked at his youngest daughter with annoyance and distaste. She was still beautiful, and certainly young enough to make a second marriage. Yet he was extremely irritated at her. "If you had given Richard a child, even a daughter, you would have been a very eligible widow. As it is, I shall have to find some old man, desperate for a child, who will overlook your small dowry."

"She is barren," Saer de Bude told his uncle. "Both Richard de Montfort and I fathered bastards at Ashlin, but your daughter could not conceive by either of us."

"You were at her again, then?" his uncle replied wearily. "Well, if what you have told me is true, then at least we will have no bastards from her. Yes, an old man with gold is just what we shall find for you, Isleen. We shall blame your childlessness on him, and when he dies you will be a wealthy widow, ready for another rich old man's bed, eh? You'll like that, won't you, you greedy little bitch?" He chuckled, then turned to his nephew. "As for you, Saer de Bude, what am I to do with you? You are my sister's son, and I feel an obligation toward you, but how can I settle a man with nothing to offer?"

"Richard de Monfort's sister is Ashlin's heiress. Arrange a match for me with her, and I shall have my own lands. She's a pretty creature, and I want her."

"*The nun?* Are you mad, boy?" his uncle snapped.

"She has not yet taken her final vows, and will not until October, Uncle. I have already had her, Uncle, but in a burst of remorse she fled back to her convent. She was aided by one of her serfs, a lad who was her childhood playmate. I am certain he has dallied with her, too, for she was no real virgin, Uncle. I have filed charges with the local sheriff. The boy will be hanged when he is caught."

"If the girl is loose, why take her, then?" his uncle demanded.

"I forced it from her that he had only used his fingers on her, and not his male member. I ploughed her furrow well, Uncle. She may already be with child. *My child.* The next rightful heir to Ashlin if I can but wed her. Give me your aid, Uncle."

The baron considered his nephew's request thoughtfully. He was the youngest of his sister's brood, and had always been a mercurial fellow. Still, he was a good soldier, but Saer had a weakness for women. *Any woman.* Baron Hugh had given Richard de Montfort a larger dowry for Isleen than he otherwise might have, for he had caught his daughter and her randy cousin in flagrante delicto, their bodies intertwined, sweating and groaning as they serviced each other. From the look of it, he had known it was not the first time. His wife, when told, had beaten Isleen thoroughly, then taught her daughter how to feign her long-gone virginity. If Richard de Montfort had realized the deception played upon him, he had never complained, for he was madly in love with her. Now Isleen was back like a bad penny, and he discovered that Saer had been at Ashlin for almost a year.

Hugh de Warenne did not want to know the truth. He had his suspicions, for Richard de Montfort had been an exceptionally healthy man until a year ago. These two bad pennies would bring ruin upon them all if he did not separate them for good and all. A young wife, children, the responsibility of a manor would certainly keep Saer's thoughts from Isleen. As for his daughter, the sooner he could find a husband for her, the better. In the meantime, his wife must handle the problem. Isleen was, after all, in mourning for her husband. Or at least it must appear to be so. *The bitch,* he thought irritably.

"I'll dispatch two messengers in the morning. The first to the Bishop of Worcester, telling him what you have told me. The second to the king asking that he appoint me the lady Eleanore's guardian. When I have that authority, I will arrange your marriage, nephew. Will that suit you, Saer?"

"Very much, Uncle," Saer du Bude replied.

In her father's garden that evening, having escaped her mother's vigilant eyes, Isleen excoriated her lover. "Why did you not help me when my father said he would find a husband for me? We will never be together, Saer. I do not think you love me at all."

Backing her against a stout oak, Saer de Bude raised Isleen's skirts and lifted her up to slowly push his member into her. "Do not love you, my pretty? Is this the cock of a man who does not love you?"

"It is the cock of a lustful man," Isleen murmured, putting her arms about him as she locked her legs about his waist.

He smiled into her face. "You are the only woman I have ever loved or will love. Your father's plan is perfect, Isleen. You will wed a rich man who will expect you to give him a child, which you cannot, but he will not know that. When he begins to become impatient with you, you will slowly poison him as you did Richard. In the meantime I will wed the little nun, and she will give me a son. Then she, too, will die, and lord Saer of Ashlin will marry the wealthy widow, the lady Isleen. With our wealth we will buy more land until we become a great power in the area. It is so perfect, Isleen, and all we need is to be patient, my pretty."

"Why did you tell my father you had had her already?" Isleen demanded. "I thought you said she escaped, thanks to her serf."

"She did, but I knew your father would be reluctant to take any action unless I claimed to have despoiled the girl. I knew if I told him that it was a fait accompli, he would send to the bishop. The bishop, until he can prove the truth of my charges one way or another, will not allow Eleanore de Montfort to take her final vows. My claim alone may be enough to have her exiled from the safety of her convent. But if it is not, certainly the king will rule in my favor based on my testimony. Remember, I have watched her bathe. I can describe in detail the flaws and perfections of her body if I am called upon to do so. Only a lover would know such a thing, my pretty." He thrust against her.

"You have puzzled this all out quite carefully," Isleen said thoughtfully.

"I want Eleanore de Montfort, and I want Ashlin," Saer de Bude said. *"And I shall have them!"* He thrust again, and yet again.

"Am I a fool to trust you, Saer?" Isleen asked him. He was the most exciting man she had ever known. There was something dangerous about him that thrilled her. *"Mmmmmmmm,"* she murmured as he drove them to a pinnacle. *"Ahhhhhhhhh!"*

"You must decide that for yourself, my pretty," he taunted her, withdrawing from her body and setting her down again on shaky legs.

"You are the devil himself, I am sure of it," she said low.

Saer de Bude laughed. "Perhaps I am, Isleen. After all, who but the devil would get such supreme pleasure violating a nun?" Then he was gone into the darkness of the garden, leaving Isleen alone.

She shivered. She was only just beginning to realize how treacherous and wicked Saer really was. At this moment she sensed he would betray her as easily as anyone. She did not doubt that he loved her. Of that she was sure, but of late she had noticed a certain evil aura about him that came close to frightening her. If Eleanore de Montfort gave him a son, would he be satisfied? Or would he want other legitimate children of her body? Would he fall out of love with Isleen, and in love with Eleanore? Had her mother not always said a man would love and forgive any woman as long as she gave him children? But that was one thing she could not do, Isleen thought. She must either prevent her father from finding her another husband, or she must kill off her bridegroom as quickly as possible so she could go to Saer and make certain he rid himself of his pious little nun. She would not be cheated of her lover. *Not this time!*

The Bishop of Worcester received Baron Hugh's communication, read it with raised brow, and sent a messenger off to St.

Frideswide's Convent posthaste with a letter for the abbess that forbade Eleanore de Montfort to take her final vows until the charges
leveled by Baron Hugh and his nephew, Saer de Bude, could be
reconciled or disproved.

Reading the bishop's message, the abbess angrily threw down
the parchment scroll. "Hellfire and damnation!" she swore softly,
then crossed herself in a gesture of penance. Poor Eleanore! She
was only just beginning to recover from the unpleasantness she had
encountered. The abbess was no fool, and she knew immediately
that it was the manor of Ashlin that was at the center of this devil-
ment. According to Eleanore, her attacker was a landless knight.
His attack on the girl had been to ruin her so she would be unfit
for the convent. She would have had to wed him, and the manor
would have been his. Now he and his uncle were attempting to
gain by slander what they had been unable to gain by violence.
"They should have their tongues cut out," the abbess muttered.

Calling a novice to her, the abbess sent for Sister Columba. She
and Isabeaux St. Simon had been Eleanore's best friends since they
were little girls. Isabeaux, however, had left St. Frideswide's two
weeks ago to return home for her long-planned marriage. Sister
Columba would have to do.

The young nun arrived quickly, and bowed to her superior.
"Yes, Reverend Mother? How may I serve you?"

"Sit down, my daughter," the abbess said, and then explained
the situation.

"Oh, how wicked!" Sister Columba cried. "This will break
Elf's heart, Reverend Mother!"

"That is why I have told you, my daughter. You must help to
convince Eleanore that everything that happens, happens for a purpose. I shall speak to her first, but you will remain while I do."

Elf was sent for, and when she came and was told of the charges
leveled by Baron Hugh and his nephew, she burst into tears. "But I
am a virgin, Reverend Mother! *I am!* To lie about such a thing under the circumstances would place my immortal soul in jeopardy!"

"I believe you, my child," the abbess said, "but the bishop does not know you, and he will want more than just your word to prove your innocence. Sister Winifred will have to examine you. Once that is done, there can be no doubt as to the truth of the matter."

"Examine me?" Elf's voice quavered. *"How?"*

"She will insert a finger within your female sheath to determine that your maidenhead is still there intact. It will not hurt, and will take but a minute or so," the abbess said, her face devoid of any emotion.

Elf paled, and Sister Columba gasped.

"We will do it now so you have no time to worry yourself into a swoon awaiting this terrible examination," the abbess said gently. She arose from her seat of office where she had been sitting. "Come," she said. "You, too, Sister Columba. You will hold your friend's hand to give her courage."

The trio departed the chapter house and walked across the cloister to the infirmary. Entering it, the abbess explained the situation to Sister Winifred, who nodded serenely and instructed Elf to lie upon her examining table. The infirmarian brought a basin of water, and washed her hands carefully. Then looking at Sister Columba, she said, "Draw up her skirts, and you, Eleanore de Montfort, raise your legs and open them, keeping your feet upon the table."

"I am afraid," Elf said.

"There is nothing to fear," Sister Winifred said briskly. "Mind carefully what I do, child, for one day you are going to take my place, and may need to conduct just such an examination. Now then, let us begin." The nun dipped her finger in a pot of heavy oil, and gently began to insert it into the girl's body.

With a little cry, Elf fainted.

" 'Tis better this way," Sister Winifred said. "She is more relaxed now." Her brow furrowed in concentration, then she withdrew her finger, washing her hands again. "Pull down her skirts, Sister Columba, and burn a feather beneath her nose to revive her." The infirmarian turned to the abbess. "She is a virgin without any doubt, Reverend Mother. My finger is the first thing to ever penetrate the child. Her maidenhead is intact and most tightly lodged. She has not been tampered with in any way. Her accusers lie. I swear it on the body of our dear Lord himself."

"Thank you," the abbess said. "I had no doubts myself, but the bishop would want more than just the girl's word. He cannot doubt the veracity of this convent's infirmarian, however."

Elf had been revived and helped off the examining table by her friend. "What will happen now?" she asked.

"I will send a letter to the bishop attesting to our findings, but until he gives you his permission, you cannot take your final vows," the abbess said. "I will also send the testimony of Arthur in your behalf, explaining he is in sanctuary here because of the incident, and he will swear on his soul that Saer de Bude, while attempting to rape you, did not succeed. It will be enough. Perhaps by Martinmas you will be able to take your final vows, my child."

"I must be content with that, then," Elf replied.

Several weeks later the bishop sent a message to the abbess of St. Frideswide's Convent. The testimony of Sister Winifred, and the sworn denial of Eleanore de Montfort that no sexual encounter had taken place, were now enough to satisfy him. However, he had been instructed by the king to command Eleanore de Montfort and the abbess of St. Frideswide's to come to Worcester on St. Andrew's Day. The king would be visiting the bishop, and wished to decide the matter of Eleanore de Montfort himself.

For the first time in her life, Elf seriously lost her temper. "Is there no end to this man's perfidy? Does he think the king can force me into marriage with him? I would rather die before I would wed any man! It is impossible! I hope he will grow a wart on the very end of his nose that will spoil his handsome face!"

The abbess bit her lip to restrain her laughter. "My child," she said, "you must not wish evil on any man, especially Saer de Bude. It is obvious God created him without any sense, and surely that is enough of a burden for the man." She patted Elf's hand. "We shall go to Worcester on St. Andrew's Day, and straighten this matter out. You can ask the king to pardon Arthur so he may go home to Ashlin."

Elf nodded. "I am ashamed at my outburst."

"My daughter," the abbess said, "you seek to become a nun, but you are a human being. Mayhap someday you can aspire to saint-hood, but the majority of us are just simple women. We are sub-ject to the same human frailties as are any women. It is not wrong to experience righteous anger, Eleanore. Just do not hold a grudge. I worry that you strive too hard for mortal perfection, when it is the perfection of your immortal soul that is more important."

They departed St. Frideswide's several days before the thirtieth of November, for it would take them a few days to reach the town of Worcester. They were a party of four nuns and half a dozen men-at-arms, although it was unlikely anyone would attack such a religious group. The abbess had asked Sister Winifred, the con-vent's infirmarian, to accompany them because she felt her per-sonal testimony, if necessary, would be valuable. She had also asked young Sister Columba, Elf's best friend. The two girls would keep each other amused on the long ride. Sister Winifred, being elderly, could not ride, and was transported in a small cart that slowed them down. The usual three-day journey took them four.

The skies were slate gray, the countryside bleak in the late au-tumn. Here and there sheep and cattle browsed in the gray green meadows. They stopped the first night at the manor of a baron who was related to the abbess. The next two nights were spent in convent guest quarters, and finally late on the fourth day they ar-rived in the town of Worcester, lodging in the cathedral guest house, which was empty but for them. The king's standard flew from the bishop's castle. They sent word that they had arrived.

The king was eating with the bishop and their retainers in the great hall when the message arrived. "So the abbess has come with her chick," he noted. He was a sad-faced man with sandy hair and a beard with flecks of silver. His mild blue eyes were thoughtful. "Now, we must resolve the matter for once and for all."

"Do you know what you will do, my lord?" his friend, Geoffrey de Bohun, asked him.

"It is an unpleasant situation," the king replied. "Hugh de Warenne wants guardianship over the girl. His youngest daughter was the late lord's wife, and the girl, the lord's sister. If I give him that guardianship, he will undoubtedly take the girl from her convent and marry her to his nephew, Saer de Bude, in order to keep the manor in his family. De Bude claims to have had relations with the girl, but she says he lies, and the infirmarian at the convent has sworn the girl tells the truth and is a virgin."

"Has Baron Hugh supported you, my lord? Is he deserving of such a reward?" Geoffrey de Bohun inquired.

"Baron Hugh has done what is expedient for himself in the years of my reign. He has supported me when it was to his advantage; and he has supported my cousin, the Empress Matilda, when it was advisable to do so," the king said with a wry smile. It was rare he smiled these days, for he had recently lost his wife. The queen had been the stronger of the pair, and he very much missed her wise counsel. He tried to imagine what his wife would do in such a situation as he now faced.

"Was Richard de Montfort your man?" de Bohun wanted to know.

Now the bishop spoke up. "Richard de Montfort obeyed the laws of this land, and gave loyalty to its king."

"But did I not hear that his father was the empress's man, and died in her cause? How important is this manor to you, my lord?"

"It is true Lord Richard's father fought for Matilda, but so did many here at one time or another. Richard de Montfort was yet a child when his father perished, and his sister still a babe at her mother's breast. He never took sides, but obeyed the law and gave fealty to this land's ruler. His sister has been in her convent since she was five years of age. I doubt Eleanore de Montfort has any worldly opinions, and certainly not political ones," the bishop defended the de Montforts heatedly. This whole situation was vexing, but he understood. Land was a man's first base of power, and the de Warennes and their nephew knew it.

"Tell me, my lord bishop, about this manor of Ashlin," the king said quietly. He wanted to make a fair decision.

"It sits near Wales, my lord. It is small, and supports itself, but it is not a rich holding by any means. There is not much else to recommend it. Saer de Bude is landless, and the only way he can obtain Ashlin, for he has not the coin to purchase it, is to marry its heiress."

"The girl has not yet taken her final vows?" the king asked.

"Nay, my lord. She was to have done so in June, but was at Ashlin caring for her dying brother. The date was reset for the feast of St. Frideswide's on October nineteenth, but then there was this claim from the de Warennes and their nephew that he had had carnal relations with Eleanore de Montfort. The lady denied it, and the infirmarian of the convent confirms that Eleanore de Montfort is a virgin. I would have given permission for the girl to take her final vows, but that Baron Hugh complained to you, and you requested to see the girl before you made a decision. Have you made one, my lord?"

"I believe I have," the king said, "but I shall reserve it for the hearing. Have all the parties involved in this matter brought before me after Mass in the morning."

The bishop turned to the messenger who wore his badge of service. "Go to the guest house, and tell the abbess that she and the lady Eleanore are to join us after the Mass in the great hall tomorrow morning."

The messenger bowed, and hurried out.

The three nuns and their novice entered the great hall, and were announced by the bishop's steward. They came forward, gliding like a trio of black swans with one gray cygnet across the stone floor. The abbess made her obeisance first to King Stephen, and then kissed their bishop's ring. Her companions followed suit. The king looked at Eleanore de Montfort, and thought her a beautiful young girl with her heart-shaped face framed neatly by her white wimple, and her large gray eyes with their hint of blue that looked swiftly at him, then lowered modestly. He could not help but smile at the girl. No wonder young de Bude coveted her.

Baron Hugh de Warenne and his nephew, Saer de Bude, were now called into the hall, and they came, the younger man swaggering, sure of his certain victory. His uncle had drunk many cups of wine the previous night with the king's friend, Geoffrey de Bohun, and put certain thoughts into his head, which de Bohun had passed on to the king. Having heard them, and considered well, the king could not help but give Eleanore de Montfort to the de Warennes, which meant she would be his wife very shortly. With his uncle he bowed before Stephen, and then his eyes touched on his fair prize. She glared at him so fiercely he almost laughed. No. She was not meant for a convent. Such passion should be reserved for him, and not some invisible God.

The king spoke. "Baron Hugh, your nephew claims intimate knowledge of the novice, Eleanore de Montfort. She denies any such congress between them. She has been examined by the infirmarian of her convent, who insists the girl is untouched and as pure as the day she was born. Has your nephew lied in this matter?"

"He but confessed it to me this morning, my lord," Hugh de Warenne said contritely. "When I demanded an explanation for his slander, he claimed it was because he loved the lady Eleanore, and could think of no other way to obtain her. He is young, my lord, and impetuous. I beg you forgive him."

"Forgiveness is not my province, Baron, it is the lady's," the king said quietly. He turned to Elf. "Do you forgive him, lady?"

"For his slander of me, my lord, or the lie that he has told his uncle to excuse his slander?" Elf said sweetly.

"You do not believe he loves you, lady?" The king's lips twitched.

"How could he love me, my lord, and behave as he did toward me? How could he love me when he did not know me? I am not such a fool that I do not realize the attraction I hold. It is my manor at Ashlin, of course! This man is landless, and hopes to gain stature through me, but he most certainly does not love me, and I absolutely do not love him! I can say it no more plainly. I belong to God."

"Your manor, lady," the king began, "is in a vulnerable spot. I need a man on that land who is totally loyal to me, to my son, and to our cause. I need a man the people of Ashlin will cleave to and obey. In order to attain such a goal, you must also be on your land. I have discussed this matter thoroughly with the bishop, and we are of one mind. You will not take your final vows, Eleanore de Montfort. You must marry."

"No!" Elf gasped, looking desperately to the abbess. She could hear Matti, now Sister Columba, beginning to weep behind her.

"Now, my child, the only question is, who is to be your husband?" the king continued smoothly, ignoring her small outburst. "You are certain you will not have Saer de Bude for your husband?"

"Never!" Elf hissed. "The man is an adulterer who lay with my brother's wife! I would not have him if he were the last man on earth, my lord, but I beg you, do not force me to the marriage altar. I will give you Ashlin if you desire it, but let me continue on with my life as I have always planned it. In my heart and mind I am a nun."

"Then, if you will not have this man who covets you, lady, I must choose a husband for you," the king said firmly. "Anticipating this, I have already made my choice. You will wed one of my own knights: a man raised in my Uncle Henry's court, a man who has served us with loyalty and devotion for many years. He, like Saer de Bude, is landless. It is time I rewarded him for his many years of service. He is a good man, Eleanore de Montfort. A godly man who will treat you with respect. You and your people will be safe in his hands, as will your manor of Ashlin," Stephen said calmly, ignoring her desperate plea. "Come forward, Sir Ranulf de Glandeville, and greet your bride."

The abbess moved to Elf's side, and gently removed her wimple revealing her hair, unpinning her single thick braid. The girl turned frightened eyes to her. *"Please, Reverend Mother,"* she whispered. When the abbess did not answer, too stricken herself with emotion, Elf turned to the king again. "Why are you doing this to me, my lord? *Why?"*

"Have you learned no obedience, Eleanore de Montfort, in your years at St. Frideswide's?" the bishop scolded her.

"Nay, my lord bishop, the girl is certainly entitled to an explanation of why I am so drastically changing her life." King Stephen held out his hand to Elf. "Come here, my child, and I will explain," he said gently, and when she had hesitantly taken the royal hand, he drew her to his side, speaking quietly. "This decision is not one I have made arbitrarily, or without prayerful thought. The de Montforts, I have learned, fought for my grandfather, the Conqueror, both in Normandy and England, coming with him to take part in his great victory at Hastings. Your great-grandfather then wed Ashlin's Saxon heiress. I suspect it is from her you gained your pale red-gold hair." He smiled encouragingly, then continued. "The blood of Ashlin's original family continued to flow through the veins of Ashlin's de Montfort lords because of that alliance. You have serfs, do you not, my lady Eleanore? How many?"

"Seventy-three, and ten freedmen are part of the manor," she answered the king softly.

"Have they ever rebelled against their lords?" the king inquired.

"Oh, no, my lord! Ashlin folk are peaceful folk," Elf quickly reassured him.

"If called upon to defend Ashlin, would they?" he probed further.

"Of course! Ashlin folk have always been loyal to us," she said.

"*Loyal to us*. To whom, my lady? To your family because they are related by blood to Ashlin's original lords. And this is the reason you must wed. I cannot allow the continuity that Ashlin's blood lords have to their land and to their serfs to be disrupted. It would but confuse your folk and make them resentful of a new lord, unless, of course, that lord was married to the de Montfort heiress. You, my lady Eleanore, are she. Your husband will be able to peacefully oversee the land and defend it for me, because the transition that is to be made from your late brother, Richard, may God assoil his good soul, will be made through you. You seem to be an intelligent girl, and so I am certain that you understand the importance of this transit from the de Montforts to the de Glandevilles."

"Yes, my lord," Elf said low.

"But yet you are resistant," the king noted. "Speak to me truthfully, my lady, and I will try to allay your fears."

Elf moved closer to the king, still clutching his hand nervously. "My lord, I do not know how to be a wife," she whispered. "Even if I were, in my heart, willing, I have been schooled to be a nun. I can read, and I can write. I speak French, English, and Latin. I have become in my short lifetime a skilled herbalist and infirmarian. I can chant plainsong. But, alas, I know nothing about keeping a house, or cooking, or preserving, or making jams, or any other of the valued skills of a good wife. I cannot play upon any instrument. Worst of all"—and here Elf blushed deeply—"I know naught of men or their desires. I would be a most dreadful wife, but I shall be a very good nun."

The king listened gravely to the girl's litany, then he said, "All this may be true, my dear, but as you have learned how to be a good nun, I am certain there are those among your folk who will teach you how to be a good chatelaine. As for the rest, it has been my experience that a bridegroom enjoys schooling his bride in those *other* matters."

"But, my lord," Elf attempted to plead her case once more, but was interrupted by the bishop.

"My daughter, you have been told what you are to do. Now, cease your complaints, and tell the king you will obey him," the Bishop of Worcester snapped angrily. This stubborn little chit was behaving far above her station.

Elf, however, was not about to admit defeat quite yet. There was a light of battle in her gray eyes; she opened her mouth to speak, only to be arrested by a look from the abbess. Elf's mouth shut with an almost audible snap.

"My daughter," Reverend Mother Eunice said, "when you came to us, I believed it God's will that you remain with us forever. However, it is now plain to me that God's will for you has changed, and you must obey it, Eleanore de Montfort. You will be a wife, not a nun. You will give obedience and respect to this good knight who is to be your husband. Perhaps one day you will send us one of your daughters to join our ranks, and that will be God's will. But if you continue to argue with both the king and the bishop, you will shame us, for it will be said that we do not properly bring up the girls sent to us. Surely you would not shame us, child."

Elf sighed deeply, then she looked up at the king. "I am not happy in my heart, my lord, but I will obey you," she said reluctantly.

King Stephen patted the small white hand in his. "Sometimes God's will is difficult to both obey and understand, Eleanore de Montfort. Nonetheless obey we must, my dear. Do not fear. This is a good man to whom I have given you." He turned his head briefly. "Come to my side, Ranulf de Glandeville," he called, and when the knight had joined them, the king put the girl's little soft hand into the large hand of the knight. "In my capacity as guardian of this maiden, Ranulf de Glandeville, I give her to you as a wife with all her goods and chattels. Will you treat her with love and respect, and defend her lands in my name?"

The big hand closed about her hand. It was warm, and there was strength in it. "I will, my liege, as God is my witness," the deep familiar voice said quietly.

Elf's head snapped up, and for the first time since all this had begun, she looked at the man who was to be her husband. *"You!"* she said. "You are the knight who passed through Ashlin before my brother died. You carried Richard's will to both the bishop and the king."

"I am he, lady," Ranulf de Glandeville answered.

"They will be wed tomorrow by the bishop, and in my presence," the king said. "My lady abbess, will you see that the lady Eleanore is suitably dressed for her wedding?"

"I would gladly, my lord, but alas, I have no coin with which to purchase proper garments," the abbess replied, embarrassed.

"The bishop will supply you with all that is needed," the king said, and then a twinkle arose in his blue eyes. "Do not stint in your choices, lady. The bishop, I know, would want to be generous in this particular matter. He must perceive that it will please me to see the lady Eleanore of Ashlin prettily garbed."

"Indeed, yes," the bishop quickly agreed. "Choose what you will for the bride, Reverend Mother."

"My lord," Elf said to the king. "There are two small matters to address before you dismiss us. May I speak?" She gently disengaged her hand from that of Ranulf de Glandeville.

"You may," the king said, noting how deftly she had slipped her fingers from the knight's. Lady Eleanore, he suspected, was going to be just fine despite her disappointment and the suddenness of everything that had happened to her this day.

"The dowry my brother gave to St. Frideswide's, I should like it to remain with them. They have nurtured me since I was five years of age. Then, too, Sister Winifred will now have no one to assist her, and she is not as young as she once was. It will take time to train another girl for her, and that girl must have an aptitude for herbs and caring for the sick. It cannot be just anyone. Now that I am Ashlin's heiress, my lands should be more than enough for Sir Ranulf."

The king looked to the knight. "I agree," he said, "but the final decision is yours, Ranulf. What say you?"

"I agree also, my lord. It is only fair that my lady's dower portion remain with the convent. She was, after all, within days of taking her final vows. I would also add to that two barrels of beer each October in thanks for my good fortune, and my bride."

"Well-spoken!" the king approved. "Now, my lady, what is that other matter on which you would speak to me?"

"It is my serf, Arthur," Elf began.

"He attacked me, causing grievous bodily injury," Saer de Bude spoke up. He had been forced to stand next to his uncle, who did not speak up for him when the king gave Eleanore to his own man. "A serf who attacks a noble is automatically sentenced to death. The low fellow has been in hiding at St. Frideswide's ever since he fled from Ashlin. I demand justice!"

"Do you not know how to speak the truth at all?" Elf demanded fiercely. "Arthur pulled you off me when you sought to violate my innocence. You fell back, and hit your head against my worktable."

"*He hit me!*" Saer de Bude shouted, his reserve gone.

"*I saw no blow,*" Elf boldly lied, glaring directly at the man. She

turned to the king. "Arthur," she explained, "is a year older than I
am, my lord. We were playmates as children, for my brother was
ten years my senior. He had been working in the garden that day.
In fact, he had earlier helped me to light the hearth so I might
make my elixirs. If he had not been nearby in those gardens and
heard my cries for aid, I should have been ruined. His sole concern
was for me. He rushed me from my little workshop to the house,
where my steward, Cedric, and my old nursemaid, Ida, advised me
to return to St. Frideswide's immediately. The steward gave Arthur
leave to accompany me. Only that Cedric sent word that *that* man
was crying for poor Arthur's blood, he would have returned to
Ashlin, and certain death. Instead he asked sanctuary of the abbess,
who graciously gave it. Is that not so, Reverend Mother? Arthur
asked you for sanctuary?"

Reverend Mother Eunice hesitated but a second. "Yes," she
said, "Arthur of Ashlin did indeed ask me for sanctuary, which I
granted." She would not have believed Eleanore de Montfort, so
meek and mild a girl, could lie with such facility. Still, she had not
asked for the abbess's confirmation of her tale, only that the abbess
had been asked for and had given sanctuary. That the rest would be
assumed was not her fault.

And indeed it was assumed. "The serf, Arthur of Ashlin, is hereby
granted my pardon for any wrongdoing that may or may not have
occurred," the king said with finality. "It will be written up for
you to carry with you tomorrow." Then King Stephen swung his
gaze to Saer de Bude. "You are a good knight, Saer de Bude, but
you need more polishing, it is obvious. I am sending you to my
brother's court in Blois. You will remain in the count's service until
you are told otherwise. My brother's court is an elegant and refined
one, and I urge you to learn all you can from being there. You will
leave tonight, and you will carry several messages for me to my
brother. May good fortune go with you."

Saer de Bude bowed to the king. There was no use in arguing
unless he was seeking to have his life shortened considerably. While
he loved Isleen, there was no sense in getting himself killed over

her. There were plenty of other women in the world upon whom he might dote. He bowed low. "I thank you for your kindness, my lord king." Then he stepped back into the crowd in the hall, seeking some male friends with whom he might pass the time until he was summoned to leave. He did not bother to bid farewell to his uncle, who had not been particularly helpful to him this day. If the king had imprisoned him for his attempted assault he was quite certain that his uncle would have remained silent.

"Now, Baron Hugh," the king spoke again, "there is the matter of your daughter. It has come to my ears that Richard de Montfort sickened suspiciously and died. While nothing can be proven against your daughter, there are suspicions, particularly given her carnal liaison with her cousin. Do not deny it, my lord, for there were many who saw them, though they either did not know, or care; yet it is suspected that your late son-in-law, Richard de Montfort, was poisoned by person or persons unknown. But as your daughter and her cousin were the only ones close to Richard de Montfort—as no servant had a grievance against the lord—it is possible that it is your daughter who poisoned her husband. This being the case, I forbid you to make any match for Isleen de Warenne. Incarcerate her in a cloister, and keep her there for the rest of her days, Baron Hugh. She is a dangerous woman."

"My lord," Hugh de Warenne protested, "you have no proof that my daughter would do such a terrible thing. What reason would she have? She loved Richard."

"Your daughter was barren after nine years of marriage. Richard de Montfort had at least three bastards born to female serfs belonging to him. Your daughter may have known and become angry and embittered. She loved her cousin. She might think to kill her husband, have her cousin debauch his sister, the rightful heiress, so the girl would have to marry her rapist. Then, when the time was right, Lady Isleen might kill off the innocent so she could marry her cousin, and together they would share Ashlin."

Hugh de Warenne blustered, "My lord, that is a preposterous tale! You have not one shred of proof against my daughter and Saer de Bude."

"I have enough proof, my lord," the king said icily. "Cedric of Ashlin, come forward and give your testimony."

Ashlin's steward came slowly forward, awed to be in such grand company, but determined to make certain his mistress was safe from Saer de Bude and his family. "I am here, my lord king," the old man said, and he bowed low to King Stephen.

"Shall the steward give his testimony, Hugh de Warenne, or will you cease your carping and do as I have commanded?" the king asked.

"I will obey, my lord," Baron Hugh said, silently damning his daughter to hell. He was going to find the most remote and harshest cloister and see Isleen put away forever! His family had come close to ruin today, and all because of the lewd, murderous bitch.

"Go, then," the king said, "and carry out my will."

Hugh de Warenne bowed, and backed from the king's sight.

"Now," the king said to the steward, "will you pledge for yourself, and all of Ashlin's folk, that you will be loyal to Lord Ranulf, Cedric of Ashlin? Will you accept him as your new master?"

"Right gladly, my lord, as long as he takes care of our lady Eleanore," the steward replied boldly.

"I will take great care of her," Ranulf de Glandeville said.

"Then, we will serve you loyally and with devotion, my lord," Cedric replied, and he bowed to his master.

"It is settled, then," the king said. "The marriage will take place tomorrow immediately preceding the morning Mass."

When they had departed the bishop's hall, Elf turned to her steward. "How did you come to be here, Cedric? I did not give you permission to leave Ashlin."

"I had to come, my lady, and I hope you will forgive me, but your old Ida would not rest easy unless we could all be certain that Saer de Bude did not slander you further or force you into a marriage you didn't desire. We could not serve such a man, although for love of you we would have. Forgive me, my lady."

"But how did you gain the king's ear?" Elf asked him.

"I simply told the bishop's porter that I had important information for the king regarding a case to be heard today. The porter passed me on to the bishop's seneschal, who gained the king's ear for me. I told him everything we had seen and heard in Lord Richard's last months. *She* never noticed us as she pursued her evil desires. There was nothing we could do to stop her, for we are serfs. We would have been punished for uttering our suspicions. Ida thinks it was the sugared almonds she was always feeding the lord. But we heard enough to be certain that she killed our dear lord. I thought the king should know before making any decision in this matter. I am glad, my lady, that you will be coming home to Ashlin, where you truly belong," Cedric finished.

"You will stay with me tonight, steward," Ranulf de Glandeville said to Cedric. "Your mistress must go now to prepare for our wedding." He turned to Elf, taking her hand again. "Lady, you need have no fear of me. You have been gently bred. I will respect your wishes in all matters, for I would that ours be a happy union."

Elf looked shyly up at him. "You are so big."

"And you so petite, lady," he responded with a small smile.

"I fear I shall not be a good wife."

"You were a most gracious hostess that night I stayed at Ashlin, my lady Eleanore. While your sister-in-law looked to her lover, you saw to my meal and to my sleeping accommodation. I think you will be a very good wife."

"But I do not know how to do so many things. It is a simple task to say, bring the lord a plate of food. But what happens when I must decide what food the cook is to prepare?"

"Cedric will help you, will you not, steward?" Ranulf de Glandeville said, his gaze going to the older man.

"Indeed, my lord, and cook will help the lady, and we all will aid her, for we are so glad she is coming home again," Cedric said.

"So, my lady Eleanore," her husband-to-be said, kissing her small hand and causing her to blush before he released it, "you will in due time become an excellent chatelaine."

They had reached the door of the bishop's guest house.

"We will leave you now, my lord," the abbess said. "If Eleanore is to be a bride tomorrow, we must go into the market and the shops to see what garments we can obtain for her."

"The lady Eleanore, Reverend Mother, will be beautiful in whatever she is clothed, I am certain." Then he flushed. "I am no courtier with words, I fear." He bowed to the four women, and with Cedric in tow hurried off.

"For a man who is no courtier, he does quite well with words," the abbess said with a small smile. "I like him."

PART II

THE BRIDE

England 1152–1153

CHAPTER SIX

"You honor my shop, Reverend Mother," the clothier said as he ushered the nuns onto his premises. "How may I be of service to you? I have some fine black wool just in from France."

"Do you have a gown that might serve for a bride, Master Albert?" the abbess asked. "My young novice recently became an heiress on her brother's death. The king and the bishop prefer that she wed one of King Stephen's knights, rather than take her final vows. The king and the bishop desire the wedding be celebrated on the morrow. As you will understand, the lady has nothing but her habit. She cannot be wed in that now, can she?" Mother Eunice smiled hopefully.

"Oh, dear," the clothier replied, his brow furrowing in distress. Then he brightened. "My daughter is being wed in two months' time. Let me call my wife and see if we might not take something from among Cecily's wardrobe that might suit your young lady." He went to the stairs of his shop, and called up, "Martha, come down, for I need your help."

The lady in question descended and, when told of the problem, was immediately sympathetic. "Of course we can help," she noted. "No lady should be wed looking like a little gray dove."

"I have funds from the bishop to pay you," the abbess said.

Mistress Martha smiled. Coin in hand, and not a year trying to obtain the monies owed. Excellent! Her mood brightened even more. "Come here, child, and let me look at you," she said to

Eleanore. "Well, you're shorter than our Cecily, but there is little to raising a hem. The top of you looks about the same size." She turned to the abbess. "We can make good use of both her tunica and her skirts by matching them to the other, more colorful pieces. A nice yellow tunica for the gray skirts," she considered thought-fully. "It will complement her pretty hair. Now, what to put with that gray tunica." She thought carefully. "Ah, yes, rose-and-light-blue-striped skirts. That will give the lass two changes of clothing. Now, for her marriage day gown. A particolored bliaut in forest green, the front embroidered in gold, to be worn with green skirts. It will be perfect on you, my dear, but my daughter hated it on sight, so it is certainly no loss to her. I do not understand, for I think it beautiful, but I believe she found it too fine a gown for a clothier's daughter who is marrying a member of the carpenter's guild—although I believe Peter will one day be a Master in his guild," the clothier's wife said proudly. "Still, there is no arguing with a lass with bridal nerves. Come upstairs with me now, child, and we will see what needs to be done to make your clothing fit."

"Go with Eleanore, Sister Columba," the abbess said. "Sister Winifred and I will remain down here."

The two girls followed the clothier's wife up the staircase, and into a large, bright room. Going to a wooden chest, Mistress Martha opened it and lifted out a yellow tunica. Instructing Elf to remove her own gray garment, she slipped the top over the girl's head. Next she fastened a pretty girdle of deeper yellow with cop-per threads about Elf's hips. She stepped back, then nodded.

"Our Cecily is taller and a bit broader, but you are both slender."

Elf let her fingers touch the soft silk fabric. Since her arrival at the convent, she had never worn anything but cotton or wool. "How do I look?" she asked Sister Columba shyly.

"Perfect. Oh, Elf, I wish you could see yourself. That yellow tu-nica makes your lovely hair even lovelier."

"The tunica is just right but for a nip or two in the shoulders. Cecily's height is in her legs." The clothier's wife smiled at Elf. "The young sister is right. The yellow is a good color for you. Now, child, off with both your tunica and skirts. We shall try the rose-and-blue-striped skirt, and see how much must be taken up."

When Elf had done as she was bid, Mistress Martha knelt, first pinning up the skirts, then pinning the waist to make it smaller. Then she suggested Elf put her gray tunica back on, and when she had, Mistress Martha fastened another girdle, rose silk with silver threads, about the garment. Elf looked to her friend, and Sister Columba nodded with a smile. Now it was time to try on the wedding finery. Mistress Martha lifted the garment from the chest.

"You will wear a camisa with an embroidered neckline, my dear, beneath this," she explained. "I just want you to try it for size." She held the bliaut out for Elf to put her arms into. The bliaut had a corsetlike bodice with long sleeves that were both wide and embroidered. The waistline was low, and attached to a pleated skirt. The low and slit ornamented neckline would allow the decorated neckline of the camisa to show. Mistress Martha laced the garment tightly up the back, clucking as she realized the bliaut would have to be taken in. The tunica tops had been loose, and belted with their own girdles, but the fitted bliaut was too wide for the petite Elf. "It can be done," she muttered beneath her breath. "A seam tightened here, another there. What do you think of the color on your friend, good sister?"

"You are beautiful, Elf," the young nun said. "The dark green and gold of the fabric sets off your delicate coloring, and your hair, perfectly. I wish Isa could see you now. She would be so jealous!"

Elf could not help but giggle. "Shame on you," she scolded her friend. She fingered the beautiful fabric. "I do like the color, but must it be laced so tightly? I find the outline of my body very immodest."

"All the fine ladies are wearing the bliaut, my lady," Mistress Martha said. "Surely if you are being wed by the bishop before King Stephen, you will want to look your best. It will do honor to your new husband as well that you are so fashionable."

"Isa's mother sent her one to wear home," Elf's best friend said. "It certainly wasn't as fine as this one."

Mistress Martha knelt, and pinned the hem of the pleated skirt as well as the waist. "You will be a lovely bride, my dear," she said when she had finished. "Now, get dressed in your own clothing again. We shall return downstairs to the abbess. I shall be up all night sewing to get your garments ready."

"We can help," Elf said.

Her companion nodded. "I am certain the Reverend Mother will agree. We are skilled needlewomen. Your kindness should not be taken advantage of, Mistress Martha."

They returned to the shop, where the clothier's wife explained everything to the abbess, concluding, "And the yellow tunica can also be matched with the green skirt, giving the lady a fourth costume."

"Excellent," the abbess said. "The lady Eleanore will have a suitable wardrobe without too great an extravagance." She turned to Elf. "I have purchased a few bolts of fabric for you, my daughter. You will want to make yourself several more gowns when you return home to Ashlin. And I have taken the liberty of obtaining some veils for your head, as well as ribbons you can use as fillets, since you will no longer wear your wimple."

"I shall need a small bolt of linen, Reverend Mother, for undergarments," Elf said softly. "I have but one camisa as you will recall. I shall want to make others when I return to Ashlin."

The abbess nodded in agreement. Then, turning to the clothier, she said, "What will we owe you for all of this, bearing in mind that the lady and Sister Columba will remain with your wife to do the alterations?"

Master Albert named a sum as his wife nodded in agreement.

The abbess smiled. "You are too generous, I think," she told him, counting out the required coin, and adding two additional silver marks. "One for you, Master Albert, and one for your goodwife for her great kindness toward the lady Eleanore."

The clothier bowed, nodding his thanks, and the abbess in the company of Sister Winifred departed the shop leaving the two younger women behind. Mistress Martha pocketed her silver mark with a pleased smile, then signaled to Eleanore and her companion to follow along back up the stairs. The three settled themselves to begin the task of making the alterations. Elf was silent as she sewed, carefully keeping her eye on her work, but Sister Columba chattered away with the clothier's wife as they hemmed and stitched. Soon Mistress Martha knew a very great deal about the two young women. She was quite fascinated that a novice, within days of her final vows, had been plucked from the convent to marry a knight.

"I do not wish to seem rude," the older woman whispered to the young nun, in whom she recognized a friendly soul, "but does the young lady know about men's *needs*? I hope I do not shock you."

"You are a mother," Sister Columba said. "Mayhap you should attempt to enlighten Elf."

She looked up at the sound of her name. "What is it?"

"Mistress Martha, realizing your ignorance in matters of the flesh, was asking me if she should speak to you as your own mother would were she alive to do so. I think it a good idea, Elf. You would never come with us when we went to the barn, and that was all right then, but tomorrow you are to be married, and as the goodwife says, men expect certain favors of their wives. You must know what will be required of you."

Elf blushed deeply. "I know . . . but I am frankly fearful."

"The natural reaction of a proper virgin," Mistress Martha said, "but, my child, there is really nothing to fear. While a woman's body is a pretty thing, a man's while not ugly, is quite ordinary. While a woman has titties to be stroked and a bottom to be fondled, men have naught but one item of interest. Their manhood. They put a great deal of store by it, however. Boys compare them for size. Men brag on them, and the amorous conquests they have made with them. It's all quite silly considering a manhood is naught but a length of limp flesh most of the time." And then the good woman proceeded to explain as if Elf were her own dear daughter, Cecily. At length Mistress Martha finished, asking, "Now, is there anything you would ask me?"

Elf shook her head.

"You are free, you realize, to ask your husband questions. Oh, yes! Men like to be petted, too. Do not feel shy of touching your husband. And do you know, although of course you must, about preventing conception?"

"But that is wrong."

"Not always," Mistress Martha replied, "leastwise, not to my mind. Not if a woman has had too many babes in a row and her body needs to rest, or if a woman imperils her life by being with child. These dangers must be addressed. Oh, I know the church says that under such circumstances a man and his wife must cease marital relations, but more often than not they do not want to do so. Then, too, if they do, the man's natural lusts will lead him to other women, and no wife wants that. The church, God bless it, does not comprehend these things, and asks too much of us in these cases. Better a wife take a spoonful of wild carrot seeds daily to prevent conception. That way she may keep her husband content in her bed and free from the greater sin of adultery," the goodwife concluded happily.

"I see," Elf said. Although it went against all she had been taught, there was a practical logic to it. "Thank you, Mistress Martha."

It was well past dark when the trio finished the alterations for Elf's clothing. Two men-at-arms from the bishop's staff had arrived to escort the young women back to the guest house. Master Albert accompanied them, drawing a small cart. It held a small wooden chest that had arrived during the afternoon from the furniture maker, whose shop was located just a few doors down from the clothier. Mistress Martha herself had packed Elf's clothes, and she would not let them leave until she had fed them a hot supper of rabbit stew, fresh bread, and newly pressed cider.

They left the clothier's shop, two of Master Albert's own apprentices going ahead with torches, the clothier himself following his lads with the cart, the women behind him followed by the two men-at-arms. They had almost reached the bishop's guest house when a door opened onto the narrow street, light breaking out to brighten the cobbles as some half-a-dozen men spilled from the building. It was obvious they were well filled with wine.

"Aha!" one of the men said, stepping forward to block Elf's path. " 'Tis the lady Eleanore de Montfort, who might have been my bride, but instead is to marry an old man tomorrow." Saer de Bude's face, now dissolute with too much wine and other debauchery, leered down into hers. His breath was foul with sour drink.

"Let me pass!" Elf snapped. It was this man, she decided, who was responsible for all that had happened. Had there been no dispute over Ashlin, the king would never have known of her, and her life would have gone on as she had planned. Angry, she stamped her shoe down upon his booted foot as hard as she could.

With a surprised yelp he fell backward. "Bitch!" he snarled as Elf pushed past him, and the bishop's men-at-arms now stepped quickly into his path to prevent any further encounter between the two.

The porter at the guest house gate greeted them as they arrived, letting Master Albert carry Elf's new chest into the building, where a servant accepted it. Both Elf and Sister Columba thanked the clothier for his kindness before he left. They quickly found their pallets in the dormitory and lay down. Elf was so exhausted by the day's events that she never even heard the nuns arise before midnight to go to the adjoining church to say Matins and Lauds. They did, however, awaken her for Prime, and afterward a bath was brought for the bride while she broke her fast with hot oat stirabout, and bread with honey.

Then it was time for Elf to be dressed for her wedding. As there were no other visitors to the guest house now, they had privacy in which to attire the bride. The abbess admired the beautiful deep green and gold silk brocade bliaut. First Elf was given a clean camisa to put on, and over it a somewhat more elegant camisa, called a sherte, with a neckline embroidered in a band of gold, and long sleeves that had been dyed a green to match the rest of the costume. The abbess laced the bliaut tightly while Sister Winifred attached wide, pleated green sleeves to the brocade sleeves that extended to the elbow. Sister Columba fastened the long, pleated

green skirt to the bliaut, then fixed a green and gold brocade girdle with a polished brass clasp about Elf's hips. The bride had previously put on her stockings, and gartered them at the knee; and
then put on her leather shoes, which Sister Columba had carefully
cleaned.

The abbess took up a small hairbrush, and began to brush Elf's
long hair, which had never been cut, and now extended to her
knees. When the lovely pale red-gold hair was shining, it was left
loose in tribute to her virtue. A sheer golden silk veil was set atop
her head, and held in place with a green ribbon. "There," the
abbess said with a small smile. "You are ready, my daughter."

"Oh, Elf, you are really beautiful!" her best friend said.

"I feel so strange. I have never worn anything but my simple
convent garb. This garment is so rich. I fear I am most out of place
in it."

"Nay," the abbess responded. "It is a costume for a special occa-
sion. For a wedding, or a festival, or if you should go to court. It is
perfectly suitable for your station. But come, now. We are expected
in the bishop's private chapel before the Mass. It is almost time, and
we must hurry."

Escorted by the three nuns, the bride was brought to the place
of worship where the Bishop of Worcester made his personal de-
votions. It was a small chamber. A simple oak altar, a fine white
linen cloth covering it, bore a beautiful gold cross with matching
candlesticks burning pure beeswax candles. There were no windows in the room, but hung about the walls were the stations of
the cross, represented in simple paintings in arched frames. The
bishop in his fine robes was awaiting them, as was the bridegroom.

For the first time since they had met, Elf studied this man she
was about to wed. He was at least a foot taller than she was. His
chestnut brown hair was cropped short in defiance of fashion, and
he was clean-shaven unlike many of his peers. His face was long
rather than round, and he had a squared chin. His nose was prominent, although not out of proportion with the rest of his face; his
hazel eyes oval in shape; his mouth big; his cheekbones chiseled.

His brows were thick and dark, and Elf could not help but notice he had very long eyelashes. His skin tone seemed fair, but weathered. He did not appear too old.

Ranulf de Glandeville was aware of Lady Eleanore's close scrutiny. He was garbed in his finest dalmatica, a rather extravagant scarlet silk with bands of embroidery on the sleeves, and about the neckline. His dark blue chausses—long, tight-fitting hose—showed in the area between the hem of his dalmatica, and his cuffed, soft leather boots. An embroidered blue and gold girdle encased his body. He wore no sword within the holy place, and his head was bare.

The bishop looked for a moment on the couple before him. How suited to marriage was the girl, he decided. Her face, even surrounded by the simple wimple of a nun, was so lovely it would tempt a man far more chivalrous than Saer de Bude. Aye, the girl was not meant for the cloister. This faithful knight of the king's, Ranulf de Glandeville, would master her, and keep both her and her lands safe. His conscience quite clear, he began the marriage ceremony.

Elf listened to the drone of the bishop's Latin. Her fate was sealed. She had been taught all these years to be obedient, yet she felt the flames of rebellion within her heart. She almost jumped with surprise as Ranulf de Grandeville reached out to take her little hand in his big paw. She glanced quickly up at him, but his eyes were focused straight ahead upon the bishop even as he gave her fingers a little squeeze. A terrifying thought leapt into her brain. Could he read her mind? Did he know what she had been thinking? No! He could not have known—*or could he?*

Gently prompted by the abbess, who stood by her side, Elf made her responses, agreeing to her marriage vows before God and this small company of witnesses. To her surprise her bridegroom placed a small, delicately made gold ring studded with rubies upon her finger . . . and it fit perfectly! When the bishop finally pronounced them husband and wife, she turned with Ranulf de Glandeville to find that King Stephen had slipped quietly into the bishop's chapel to observe the ceremony. Now he came forward, and Elf knelt before him, placing her hand in his to give him her fealty, for she had not previously done so.

The king raised the bride up, and smilingly claimed his right as monarch to kiss the bride on both her blushing cheeks.

"I have brought you a wedding gift, Lady Eleanore," the king said. Then he handed her a lovely brooch with a fine green stone in its center. "This belonged to my late wife, Queen Matilda, who like you was the heiress to her family's lands. If she were with us now, may God assoil her good soul, she would give you this gift herself, for my Tilda loved nothing better than giving presents. Wear it in memory of her." He pinned the brooch to the neckline of Elf's dress, and she kissed his hand.

"I am honored, my liege, by your kindness. Mine is not an important family, and yet you have treated me as if I were one of your own. I shall remember both you and the queen, may God assoil her good soul, always in my prayers," Elf said sincerely.

King Stephen nodded. "We will be late for the Mass if we do not go now, eh, Bishop?" He moved off.

"That was well done, Eleanore," Ranulf said.

"I am not without manners, my lord," she told him a trifle sharply.

"I did not think you were, lady."

As Ranulf led Elf out of the bishop's chapel, she saw her steward, Cedric, at the very rear of the holy chamber. "Were you here for the ceremony?" she asked him.

"I was, lady," he told her with a broad smile. "Your old Ida would not forgive me if I could not tell her every detail when we return home." He bowed to the man by her side. "Everything stands in readiness for our departure, my lord," Cedric said. It was obvious he already accepted his new master.

"Good!" Ranulf said. "Attend us at the Mass, Cedric." He turned to Elf. "I realize you will not wish to travel in your wedding garments, and neither do I. After the Mass, we will change and depart immediately for Ashlin. We will travel in the company of the good sisters, and their men-at-arms, as far as St. Frideswide's."

"You have no squire?" she asked.

He shook his head. "I could not afford one, Eleanore. While my bloodline is good, I have naught but my horse, my armor, my weapons, my clothing, and a few coins I have managed to set aside over the years. Our marriage is a blessing for me in many ways. I have been given a virtuous woman to wife. I now possess a manor, which means I may have legitimate sons and daughters. I will have a home in which to grow old."

"How old are you?" she ventured, remembering Saer de Bude's nasty words of the previous evening.

"I am thirty," he said. "It is not too old, I promise you, to father children, lady. How old are you?"

"Fourteen and a half, my lord," Elf answered. Mary's blood! *He was old!*

They entered the church following in the wake of the bishop and the king. The Mass was sung. Afterward they bid the king farewell, and Ranulf de Glandeville escorted his wife back to the bishop's guest house, where she changed from her bridal finery into her gray skirts and yellow tunica, packing up the green bliaut and its skirts with the rest of her garments in the wooden chest. The bishop's servants carried the chest to the cart where Sister Winifred was already seated, her hands firmly in control of the reins harnessed to Sister Joseph's favorite mule.

The little party set off, leaving the town of Worcester quickly behind. The day was cold, for it was December first, but at least it was clear and bright. Ranulf set a quicker pace than the one that had brought them to Worcester. He and Cedric led the way, followed by the two nuns and Elf, the cart, and the four men-at-arms. Even the mule, sensing its direction was toward home, trotted briskly along to the women's astonishment. Whereas it had taken four days to reach Worcester, it took just three to reach St. Frideswide's, and half the day was yet remaining for their journey to Ashlin.

The first night they had stayed at an abbey guest house, with the men in quarters segregated from the women. The second night they sheltered at a convent, again in separate quarters. When they finally reached St. Frideswide's, Elf found it both difficult and

strange to part from the nuns who had been her family since she
was five.

"You are welcome to visit whenever you can," the abbess said,
and she hugged Elf warmly. "God bless you, my daughter."

"It will not be easy to find another assistant like you, my child,"
old Sister Winifred said, "but God obviously had other plans for
you. I could have wished he had let me know sooner." She, too,
hugged Elf. "Come, and visit me, my child."

As Sister Columba looked at her friend, her big blue eyes filled
with tears that spilled down her rosy cheeks. "Oh, Elf, I thought
we would always be together! I shall miss you so very much."

Elf put comforting arms about her. "Don't weep. I'll visit often,
I promise." She hugged the young nun.

"Come now, my sisters," the abbess said, "we must go in, and
give God His thanks for a safe journey." She turned to the knight.
"Return the mare your lady is riding when you can, sir."

"You may have her now," Ranulf said, and reaching out he lifted
his startled wife up onto his saddle. "It is not far, and my lady can
ride with me," he told them.

"Go with God, then, Sir Ranulf," the abbess said, and she gave
them her blessing. Then she led her little party and the riderless
horse through the gates of the convent.

"The mare could have been returned tomorrow," Elf said, somewhat irritated by his actions.

"There is a storm coming, lady," he told her. "Surely you can
feel it in the air. It is December. If you are truly that uncomfortable
riding with me, Cedric can walk, and you may have his mount."

"I would certainly not ask a man of Cedric's years to walk the
distance from here back to Ashlin on a cold day," Elf spat at him.
"How can you even consider such a thing?"

"Then, you are content to ride with me?"

"It would seem I have no other choice," she grumbled.

"You could walk," he suggested. Unable to stop himself, he
chuckled at the outraged look upon her face. "It would seem, my
lady wife, that your convent modesty is fast wearing away, and you

are quickly becoming a mere woman. I can see you have a red-haired temper," he teased.

Ave Maria, gratia plenia, Elf began silently. She had indeed allowed her temper to get the best of her. She would silence her voice, and pray all the way back to Ashlin. While no longer a member of a religious order, she nonetheless must behave with gentle decorum. There was no excuse for shrewish behavior, but were all men so irritating? Did all behave in such wretchedly superior fashion? Elf was suddenly very aware of his great masculine presence. His heavy woolen cloak was the same one he had worn when he had first come to Ashlin. It looked as if it had not been properly brushed since then. It felt rough against her cheek. His arm encircled her, provoking an odd feeling in her.

She sneaked a look up at his face. His was a pleasant face, a very masculine face. There were tiny lines at the edges of his eyes. And in his favor was the fact that he smelled quite clean. A snowflake caught in his thick, dark eyelashes, and Elf realized her husband had been right. There was a storm brewing, and it had already begun. "You were correct about my temper," she told him. "How far do you think we are from Ashlin?"

Cedric, riding next to them, replied, "We are halfway there, my lady. May I ride ahead, my lord, and tell them we are coming? The cook will need to know you are arriving."

"Go," Ranulf instructed. "The path is clearly marked for me to see. Have a hot bath ready for my lady. She is cold and will need its warmth."

Cedric rode off.

"How did you know I was cold?" Elf asked him. "I have not complained, my lord."

"Nay, you have not, but I can feel you trembling against me, Eleanore."

Here was another side of his character, she thought. He was observant of her needs. Interesting. Her brother had loved her as a brother should, but he had given no thought to her at all once she was safely at St. Frideswide's. Father Anselm, while a good priest, was nonetheless a lustful man eager for a quick tumble with the more-than-willing dairymaid, or any other servant girl, if Matti and Isa were to be believed. She had never had any reason to doubt either of them. Her serfs were deferential and kind to her as Cedric, Arthur, and his father, John, had demonstrated, but they belonged to her as lady of Ashlin. The king and the bishop, both figures of power and authority, had rearranged her life without so much as a by your leave, but that was their right, she realized.

So that was all she knew of men until Ranulf de Glandeville. *Her husband. Her lord.* She remembered back to several months ago when he passed through Ashlin and stayed the night. He had been quiet-spoken and grateful for her hospitality, unlike others who had come, accepted the best bed space as their right and gone on their way without so much as a *merci*. On their wedding day he had been aware that she would not want to travel in her best clothing, and had given her time to change without impatience. On the road he had been thoughtful of the nuns, hurrying them, while not driving them, for he knew that winter weather could turn dangerous on a moment's notice even as it was doing now. And she had yet to hear him raise his voice in anger, although she thought him capable of it.

She had heard the girls at the convent speak of the men they knew. Men were figures of authority, sometimes kind, mostly to be feared, they had always said. One girl they knew had voiced the opinion that she would rather be a simple free woman who might be apprenticed, and follow a trade, or craft, than be the daughter of a baron. Several of the guilds were female dominated: the spinners, the weavers, and the brewers, in particular. At least, the girl, had continued, an apprenticed girl was able to follow her trade after serving seven years and could hope to become a master craftswoman. Most of the other girls had laughed, saying that even the female guilds were headed by men. There was no escaping male authority and domination. Even the final authority in certain convent matters had to be referred to the bishop for his decision. Men ruled. Women obeyed.

She was the heiress to Ashlin, but it was now her husband who was in charge. But did she still have any control, or influence, over her lands and her people? Or had her value been only in her lands? How was she to learn these things? Who could tell her? *Mary's blood!*

She felt so terribly ill prepared in every way to be a wife and chatelaine. Did the king not consider this when he made his decision? *No. He did not.* Elf sighed deeply and instinctively snuggled closer to her husband's warmth. Opening his cloak on one side, he wrapped it about her gently, surprising her. *Who is this man I have married?* she considered once again. *What was he?* She would spend the rest of her life finding out.

CHAPTER SEVEN

The snow was falling heavily as darkness descended. The track would have been impossible to find had not men come from the manor, torches in hand, to guide them home. He had paid little attention to the design of the manor when he had passed through last summer. Now he noted the stone wall about the demesne. It would need to be built higher if the house was to be seriously protected from the Welsh. When they stopped before the house, Ranulf slipped easily from his saddle, turned, and lifted Elf down. Turning again, he walked directly through the open door of the house with her in his arms.

"Cedric has told me," he said to her, "that it is an old custom to carry the bride across the threshold of her home."

"It is?" She had not known, but then what would she know of such things? She shivered.

"Where is the solar?" he asked.

"Follow me, my lord, my lady, and welcome home," Cedric said.

"Put me down," Elf said softly. The solar? Why was he taking her to the solar? Did he mean to immediately consummate their marriage? He had certainly not been able to do so before due to the sleeping arrangements in the religious guest houses.

"You are cold, and tired," he said quietly. "Do you have a woman to take care of you, Eleanore?" God's blood! She was the sweetest armful he had ever carried. Lighter than a feather and so precious. From the moment he had seen her, he had been attracted to her, but never in his wildest dreams had he thought to possess her. The king, he knew, had considered giving her to Jean de Burgonne, another of his loyal knights, but Geoffrey de Bohun had noted that de Burgonne was not really a man with a need for a wife. De Burgonne had laughed heartily and agreed.

"An almost nun?" he said with a rough chortle. "God save me, my liege, but I should rather not, given the choice. I like my women saucier than sweeter, and very experienced. Give me a wicked wench who knows how to please a man, and the saints protect me from a shrinking virgin."

King Stephen looked to Ranulf. "And do you feel the same way, Ranulf?"

"Nay, my lord, I should be happy for a wife, especially a proper-tied one as the lady Eleanore of Ashlin. I have reached the age where I am beginning to feel my old wounds each time the rain threatens, my liege. A snug home and a wife will suit me well."

"She probably has a face like a horse," de Burgonne teased. "All these nuns in training do, it has been my experience."

Ranulf had said nothing.

A tiny smile touched King Stephen's lips, for he knew that his knight had passed through Ashlin only recently. The girl was surely pretty. He realized in retrospect that she was probably better off with the quieter knight than she would have been with the rowdy Jean de Burgonne. "Very well, Ranulf de Glandeville, you shall have Eleanore of Ashlin for your wife, with all her property and possessions. You will, of course, renew your oath of fealty to me as the new lord of Ashlin. I am relieved to have a man of your abilities on the border."

"God's mercy!" A voice cut into his thoughts, and he focused his eyes to see an old lady hurrying forward. "My baby! Is she hurt?"

"She is cold and tired," Ranulf answered.

"This is Ida, my lord," Cedric said. "She is the lady Eleanore's old nursemaid."

"Put me down, my lord, I can stand, I assure you," Elf told him. Again she noted his concern for her and was touched.

Ida pulled Elf's gloves from her hands. "Your fingers are like ice!" she said, then glared at her new master. "Could you not have kept her warmer?" Without waiting for an answer, she took Elf's cloak and drew her to the fireplace. "Come, my child, and let me warm you. Cedric, why do you stand there? Bring my lady some mulled wine. We must heat her blood."

"I will leave you, lady," the new lord of Ashlin said, and after bowing, departed the solar with the steward.

"The old woman is too protective," Cedric grumbled. "She thinks my lady still a child, for she lost care of her when the lady Eleanore was only five. Now she will be in her glory again."

"Is there a young woman among the serfs who would suit my lady as a maid? I can see Ida's heart is good, but the work of caring for my wife may prove too great for her. She does not appear to be the sort of female who would ask for aid," Ranulf said.

"You mark the old woman well," Cedric noted. "Aye, I will seek among the girls to see who will best suit Ida's temperament. I will tell her now that my lady is grown and wed, she must have at least two servants, Ida having the senior rank. That will please her vanity."

"The hall is well kept," the lord noted. His gaze swept about the polished stone floors, the blazing fireplace, the shining candlesticks upon the high board.

"The servents know their duty, my lord," Cedric answered, "but they will be better for the lady's fine hand now that she is home."

Ranulf drew a bench near the roaring fire and, taking a cup of mulled wine from the steward, cradled the silver goblet between his big hands. He sipped the hot brew. The storm outside the house was a fierce one, and he would be confined indoors until it was over. Only then could he inspect his new holding. He had seen the shadowed buildings as they had ridden into the demesne. Barns, a church, huts. The livestock would surely be safe and sheltered. He was not the only one who sensed the storm. The serfs were men of the earth and would have known. Still. "Cedric," he called, and then he asked his questions.

The steward smiled reassuringly. "The cattle and the sheep were brought in from their pasturage yesterday, my lord. All is well."

He nodded, relieved, and concentrated upon his cup, looking into the dancing flames, feeling warm again for the first time in days.

Cedric came to him some time later. "The food is served, my lord. The lady has asked to be excused tonight as she is quite exhausted. Old Ida brought her a small meal on a tray."

"Of course," he said, and went to sit at the high board. The trestles below were empty but for Fulk, the manor's sergeant at arms and his few men. Coming forward before sitting down, Fulk introduced himself, bowing to his new lord, and promising a report on the manor's defenses in the morning.

"Are you free, or serf?" Ranulf asked.

"Free, my lord, although I was born a serf here. The lord Robert set me free when he saw where my talents lay. He said I would fight better if I was free. That was over thirty years ago, my lord."

"The lord Robert was obviously correct, Fulk, as I am told the Welsh have never distressed this manor as they have others."

"The nearby Welsh and I have an agreement, my lord. I don't take liberties with their daughters, leaving them with half-English babes, and they don't attack Ashlin, forcing me to kill them, thus leaving their wives and daughters helpless to me." He grinned in a congenial manner.

Ranulf chuckled appreciatively. "Sit down, Fulk of Ashlin, and do not give these young men of yours bad ideas. From the look of them, they have enough of their own."

The men-at-arms laughed, and raised their cups to the new lord of Ashlin, wishing him a long life and many sons.

The younger of the serving girls in the hall wondered if Ranulf de Glandeville would be a kind master, or if he would rampage among them as Saer de Bude had done. The serfs were mostly Saxon and old English. They did not like these Normans in general, but the de Montforts had been good masters. Hopefully the de Glandevilles would also be.

After the meal Ranulf joined Fulk and his men by the fire. They drank and spoke on the things men are wont to speak of when they are without women. The new lord told them that they must build the wall surrounding the demesne higher. That they must train more men to protect Ashlin, as the Welsh were growing restless again. They must be able to resist any attack come the spring, for the king desired that Ashlin be kept safe. The men nodded, pleased.

"We would have done this long ago, my lord, except that poor lord Richard had but one interest from the day he wed with his wife. She consumed him, and then when he grew ill, he could not be bothered. We were fortunate not to look prosperous. Raiding parties have passed us by many times, but taken only a few sheep or cattle. We have let them, and they have left us in peace."

"We will not let them steal from us in the future, Fulk," Ranulf said. "Nor will we allow them to succeed in any attack they make, for attack they will in time."

The hour grew late. Outside the snow fell silently, for there was no wind. Fulk and his men wrapped themselves in their blankets upon their pallets. Ranulf arose from his place by the fire, and made his way into the solar. A fire burned low in the fireplace. The old woman, Ida, was snoring loudly on her pallet by the hearth. He walked past her and into the small bedchamber, closed the door, and gazed about. The fire here was also the only light. He added a few more sticks of wood to the hearth, and the flame sprang up again.

The curtained oak bedstead took up most of the room, he noted. There was a small square table with a basin upon it, and a three-legged stool near the fireplace. He washed his face and hands, drying them on the little square of linen by the brass ewer. Then sitting upon the stool, Ranulf drew off his boots and set them neatly beneath the table. Standing, he pulled off his tunic first, then his two undertunics, his drawers, and his chausses. He laid his clothing upon the stool, and stretched his big frame. Finally walking across the room, he drew back the curtains on one side of the bed.

Elf lay sleeping. He dropped the curtain and walked about to the other side of the big bed, climbing in, and settling himself.

She had heard him come into the chamber, and could not believe he would dare to get into bed with her. He would surely sleep upon the trundle. She had wanted to, but had been embarrassed to let Ida know she would do such a thing. Then she had been so sleepy she had dozed off until she heard him come into the chamber. Now Elf heard Ranulf making his small noises as he prepared for bed. She had almost shrieked aloud when he had pulled the curtain back on her side of the bed, but he had let the curtain drop. She was about to heave a great sigh of relief when she felt the draft from the open curtain on the other side of the bed, and his great weight caused the bed to sag. "W-what are you d-doing?" she squeaked nervously.

"I am coming to bed," his deep voice answered her.

"Then, I shall sleep upon the trundle," she said, moving to exit the bed.

His hand caught at her arm. "You will not sleep upon the trundle, my Eleanore, nor will I. It is too cold a night."

She gasped. "We cannot share a bed!"

"Why not?" he asked her. "We are husband and wife, Eleanore."

"But . . . but . . ." she struggled to answer him.

"Turn about and face me," he said, and pulled her over when she proved reluctant.

Now they were suddenly face-to-face, and Elf blushed a beet red as her heart beat a wild tattoo.

"Now, listen to me, my young wife. You are no longer a nun. As virgins go you are surely the most innocent of the innocent, and so you shall remain for a short time longer. I realize you know nothing of men except what you have heard in gossip from others, and God knows what that was. I am not some ravening beast, drooling lust, who must violate your virtue. How little you must think of me that you believe I would force you."

"I don't know what to believe, or even who you really are, my lord," Elf managed to say. "I am apprehensive."

His glance softened. "You need not be, Eleanore. I pride myself upon my self-control. I will not have to amuse myself among the serf women to slack my burning desires, I promise you. We will learn to know one another. And eventually we will conjoin our bodies for the pure pleasure of it, and also in order to gain heirs. My destiny is to serve the king by watching over Ashlin and managing it well. Your duty is to be a good chatelaine and a good mother. *You are no longer a nun.*"

"How long will you give me?" she whispered.

"We will know when the time is right," he reassured her. "Now, go to sleep, wife. God give you a good rest."

"And you also, my lord," Elf told him, turning onto her side again. Her heart was still beating furiously. It was so odd being in bed with someone, let alone a man. She vaguely recalled sleeping with her mother. Was it in this bed? But in all her days at St. Frideswide's, she had slept alone upon her cot. She was used to sleeping alone. Unconsciously she edged away from him. Then his foot touched her in an innocent gesture. She moved farther toward the edge of the bed. "Wh-what are you doing?"

His arm had reached out, wrapping itself about her, and drawing her back against him. The heat of his body through his knee-length chemise was very disconcerting. "You will never get to know me, Eleanore, if you insist upon running away from me," he told her, and she could have sworn there was a hint of laughter in his deep voice. "Good night, again, petite."

She lay stiffly against him at first, but then the warmth of him seemed to coax her into relaxation. He was already asleep, and his breath ruffled the hairs on the nape of her neck as his rhythmic breathing rose and fell. She thought of Isa and Matti, and all their ribald speech. She thought of Mistress Martha, the clothier's wife in Worcester, and the careful, practical talk she had given Elf explaining the activity between a husband and a wife. It had been very enlightening, but she was not quite ready to put into practice what she had been told. However, she had to admit this man now holding her was not at all what she had expected. He could have had by force what he desired, and consummated their marriage.

He chose to wait. To give her time to become used to this great change in her life. Perhaps, Elf thought, marriage will not be so bad after all.

When she awoke in the morning, he was gone. It was daylight, and therefore late. Elf jumped from the bed, wincing at the cold stone beneath her feet. On the table by the blazing fire was a fresh basin of water. She bathed, and then pulled on her clothing and house shoes. Hurrying from the bedchamber and through the solar, she entered into the hall. Ranulf was at the high board eating his morning meal.

"You should have awakened me," she gently scolded him, crossing herself as she sat to be served. A small trencher of oat stirabout was put before her. She began to spoon it down.

"I thought you needed the sleep, Eleanore, and your old Ida agreed," he said. "We traveled quickly from Worcester, and you are not used to such journeying, petite." He reached out and took her free hand in his. "Did you sleep well?"

"Aye," she said, her cheeks growing warm.

He raised the little hand to his lips, kissing each fingertip in its turn. "I am glad," he replied, then released the hand.

Her breath had caught in her chest, and she couldn't breathe, but she kept on doggedly eating her cereal. Eventually she would be able to draw the breath he had just taken away. She felt so awkward, for she didn't know what to do when he behaved so toward her.

"Drink some cider," he said, shoving the cup into her hand.

Elf drew a gulp of air into her lungs, and swallowed down the cider, coughing when it went down too far.

Ranulf patted her on the back. He so desperately wanted to gather her into his arms, and tell her that everything was going to be all right. She was the most fascinating mixture of shyness and competence. And how feisty she had been before the king. She had spirit, Eleanore of Ashlin, but she had, by nature of her calling, held that spirit in check until recently. Even now she struggled to restrain it; he didn't want her to restrain herself in any manner.

She had finally stopped coughing, looking up at him with watery eyes. "I don't know what happened."

"You ceased to breathe when I kissed your fingers," he replied bluntly. "You must not flatter me so, Eleanore. While I will admit to having a reputation as a good knight, I have but little reputation where the ladies are concerned. You will turn my head if you behave so each time I approach you tenderly, petite." His hazel eyes twinkled at her.

"I am, as you are well aware, not used to being addressed *tenderly,* my lord," she said. "You did indeed take my breath away, but not unpleasantly so." His hazel eyes were like forest pools in autumn. Was it possible to drown in another's eyes? she wondered.

"Would you swoon if I touched you again?" he asked.

"Nay, my lord."

"Nay, *Ranulf.*" His knuckles gently grazed her cheekbone. "It would give me pleasure to hear you call me by name."

"Ranulf," she whispered breathily. *"My lord Ranulf."*

His head spun at the sound of her voice speaking his name. "Now it is you, petite, who quite take my breath away," he murmured low.

A discreet cough ended their interlude. "Good morrow, my lord, my lady," Cedric said. "If you have finished your meal, we have certain manor business to attend to that I would have settled today."

Ranulf took Elf's hand in his, his thick fingers closing over her dainty fingers. "Speak, Cedric," he said. "My lady and I will hear you out."

"We are in need of a bailiff, my lord. We have not had one since the last bailiff died. Lord Richard was so involved with his lady wife, your pardon, my lady, he had no time to decide upon another man to fill the position. John, Ida's son, was the previous bailiff's nephew. He has overseen his uncle's duties since his death, although he has not the true authority. He is a good man, my lord. Honest and diligent in his duties. I would recommend him to you."

"Can he read or write?" Ranulf asked.

"Lord Robert saw that those who sought knowledge were given

it, my lord," Cedric said. "John, like myself, can both read and write. We were taught by old Father Martin, who has since died."

"Is John in the hall?" Ranulf asked.

"I am here, my lord," John said, coming forward.

"You are hereby appointed to the post of bailiff of Ashlin. Bring your records to the lady so she may see them," Ranulf said.

"Thank you, my lord," John said, bowing and stepping back.

"What is next?" the lord of the manor asked.

"The miller and his wife have no children, nor the hope of any, for they are growing old. They ask your lordship for permission to take an apprentice from among the serfs."

Elf touched her husband's sleeve. "Appoint Arthur," she said low. "He is deserving, and will work hard for the miller."

"The lady suggests that Arthur be apprenticed to the miller," Ranulf said. "Is Arthur in the hall?"

Arthur stepped forward. "Aye, my lord." While Elf had been in Worcester, he had slipped home from his sanctuary at the convent. Learning that Saer de Bude also was to be in Worcester, he knew he was safe. He bowed.

"Will you be apprenticed to the miller, Arthur?"

He was being asked what he wanted. Arthur was astounded. This new lord was like none he had ever known. "Aye, my lord, I should not be unhappy to be apprenticed to the miller. It is a good trade, and perhaps one day I may earn enough to obtain my freedom," Arthur said enthusiastically.

"You obtained it the day I became Ashlin's lord, Arthur," Ranulf said. "When you saved my wife from the lecherous advances of Saer de Bude, heedless of the danger to your own life, you proved you were worthy of your freedom. The papers will be drawn up."

"My lord!" Arthur fell to his knees, took Ranulf's hand, and kissed it. "I can never thank you enough!" he exclaimed.

"Ah, my young friend, your seven years' apprenticeship to the miller will make serfdom seem easy," the lord said. "But when those seven years are up, if you have done well . . ." He shrugged. "The miller cannot live forever. See you are a worthy successor to him."

"Thank you, my lord," Arthur said rising. He moved back into the hall among his envious friends. In these last few minutes his status had been raised, his entire life changed.

"Is there any other business we need attend to, Cedric?" Ranulf asked.

"Nay, my lord, that is all this day." He bowed.

Ranulf spoke again. "We will need stone to build the demesne walls higher. Can it be easily found?"

"Yes, my lord. The stone was quarried nearby on the manor lands. More can be obtained. Shall I instruct the bailiff to assign workers to that task?"

"Aye. They are not to work in the snow, however," Ranulf said. "When the storm stops, I will want to inspect the manor."

"Very good, my lord," the steward replied, bowing again.

Ranulf turned to Elf. "You must inspect the bailiff's records this morning, petite. A good chatelaine knows everything about her manor. Should I have to go to war for the king, you will have to manage all of it. So it is wise that you familiarize yourself with all aspects of Ashlin's life, and not just those things that usually concern a woman."

"Can you read?" she asked him. She knew many men, including knights, could not. It was not considered important for a man.

"I was raised at the court of King Henry, a most educated man, petite. Like your father, he gave any who wished to learn the means of doing so. Most of my companions thought learning to read and to write was a waste of time. What need for a simple knight, they would say to me, but one never knows where fate will take us. I thought it worth the time to sit with one of the king's chaplains, and learn my letters, and how to write them. My hand is not fine, but I can do it. Are you surprised? Would you have thought less of me had I not been able to read and to write?"

"Had you been ill educated, my lord Ranulf, I should have taught you myself," she said, surprising him. "I should not have thought any the less of you. Many men have not the time, but the abbess always said it was a great pity, for an ill-educated lord but tempted his servants to steal from him. We will go over John's records together so he can see that you know how to read and to write, too. He will tell the others, and thus prevent anyone foolish enough from believing they might gull you. Now, on another matter, my lord Ranulf, if you are quarrying stone for the walls, then quarry some for the church. It lays half ruined. Until it is repaired, I cannot petition the bishop for another priest."

"Have you any idea of how absolutely adorable you are, my Eleanore?"

She blushed. "My lord!" she scolded him. "What of my stone?"

"You have the sweetest mouth. I should give you the moon and the stars were they mine to give," he murmured.

"But they are not yours to give," she said, "and I just want some stone." He was so outrageous. Her heart had begun to beat faster.

He laughed softly. "The stone is yours, petite."

Fulk came up to them, and almost immediately he and Ranulf became engaged in deep conversation about the manor's defenses. Elf arose and returned to the solar where Ida was awaiting her with a young girl.

"This is Willa. That Cedric," Ida grumbled, "says the lady of a manor needs two serving women. He seems to think I need help taking care of you, my lady."

"I think Cedric was concerned for you, rather than me," Elf soothed her old nursemaid. "You are not young, dearest Ida. It cannot harm you to have a strong young helper." Elf smiled at Willa, a pretty girl with long flaxen braids and bright blue eyes.

"Well, I suppose I can find a use for the girl," Ida admitted. "We've unpacked your trunk, lady. What wonderful materials you have brought back with you. There is even a bolt of fine linen for your undergarments."

"The king and the bishop were most kind to me," Elf said. "Now that I am no longer a nun, I must have some new clothing."

"Lady," Willa said, "what is that beautiful green and gold garment? I have never seen its like before."

"It is called a bliaut, and is very fashionable," Elf told her. "I have not the courage to attempt to make one, however. We shall make just simple tunic tops and skirts. One bliaut is more than enough for a country wife, I think."

The women worked together the rest of the day cutting and sewing in the cozy warmth of the solar. The cook came and made suggestions for dinner. Venison stew, he told Elf, for men liked a good hearty meal on a cold day. And he had several plump ducks, well hung now, that would be perfect with a sweet fruit sauce, a Mortrew—a meat dish made with eggs and bread crumbs—a Colcannon made with cabbage, turnips, and carrots, and a nice Frumenty pudding of wheat and milk with honey.

"Is it enough?" Elf asked the cook.

"Aye, lady, there will be cheese, bread, and butter, too," the cook answered her, and she nodded her approval.

Cedric came and suggested she add several young girls to the staff for cleaning and polishing. "Now that you are home, lady, and a married woman, it is meet that you keep a proper household."

"Do you have any girls in mind?" she asked.

He nodded, and she told him to make it so.

The day waned, and the snow finally stopped. It had not been a hard storm, just a long one. Elf ordered a bath, for she had not had one since her wedding day. On the previous night she had been too exhausted.

"The lord should have a bath, too," Ida said. "He will go first, and you will wash him."

"Me?" Elf looked horrified.

"Of course, lady. It is a wife's duty to wash her husband. Who else would do it?" Ida demanded to know.

"But I have never washed a man, or anyone else but myself, for that matter," Elf protested nervously. "Why can he not wash himself?"

"Lady!" Ida was scandalized.

"I have never seen a naked man," Elf said frankly.

Willa giggled, and Ida turned on her fiercely. "Speak a word, *any word,* that is ever spoken in this chamber, and I will personally cut out your gossiping tongue, girl! Do you understand me?"

Willa paled and nodded.

"Good!" Ida snapped.

"I never knew a wife had to bathe her husband," Elf said.

"And her guests, too, sometimes," Ida told her.

"*Ohh!*" Elf paled.

"Willa," Ida said, "go and tell Cedric that the lady would like the tub taken from its storage place, and filled with hot water. Then go to the linen cupboard, and bring drying cloths and soap." And when the girl had gone, Ida turned to her mistress. "I know you've never seen a naked man, but you're a married woman now. There is nothing terrible about a naked man. I'll help you, my chick. I'll tell you just what you need to do, my little lady, and your lord will be pleased. Now go and tell Cedric to serve up the evening meal. The bath won't be ready until after you have eaten. We'll set it right up here in the solar by the fireplace, and clear it away directly afterward."

Elf did as old Ida suggested, ordering Cedric to have the evening meal served. The men ate with unfeigned and vigorous appetites. The cook had been right, and this was something she would remember. In cold weather the appetite increased. She ate a bit of venison stew, mopping up the winey brown gravy with her bread. Afterward she told her husband that there was a bath prepared for him in the solar.

His face lit in a smile. "Good! I stink of the road. Unlike some, I like to bathe." Then his hazel eyes twinkled. "Will you bathe me, my lady wife?"

Elf nodded. "I don't know how, but Ida will be there to instruct me, my lord. I have not before had the opportunity to bathe a man. It is not a duty called upon in the convent, I fear." She was nervous, but she teased him back nonetheless. "I hope I shall be able to master the technique as quickly as possible."

In response he took up her hand, and began to nibble upon her fingertips. "So do I, petite," he said.

"What is this fascination you seem to have with my fingers, my lord Ranulf?" she asked, but this time she did not draw away.

"It is because you are so delicious, and I knew it the first time I saw you, Eleanore."

"I wore robes of a religious when you first saw me," she said, slightly scandalized.

"It did not prevent me from thinking you were the loveliest maid I had ever seen," he said honestly. "I thought it sad that one so fair should spend the rest of her days a virgin."

"I thought my fate no hardship," Elf told him, equally candid.

He bent his chestnut brown head close to hers, and said low, "There will come a night, Eleanore, when I shall make love to you. Only then will you understand that I was right. You were not meant for the convent. You were meant for my bed and my heart." He kissed her palm.

She arose, wondering if anyone noticed the heat in her cheeks. "Come, Ranulf, and let me bathe you." Her fingers wrapped about his, and she led him from the hall into the solar where the bath awaited them, the great tub steaming with the heat of the water that filled it.

Ida awaited them, an apron about her stout figure. "Come, lord," she beckoned him. "Sit down, and I will have your boots. The mistress has undoubtedly explained to you that I will instruct her in the art of bathing, as it was not something taught her at her convent." She pulled his boots from his feet with an expert twist, then quickly rolled down his chausses.

He stood, and Ida took his tunic, and his two undertunics, his drawers. He stood in his knee-length chemise, which was cut to his waist on either side of the garment. He looked searchingly at the old woman.

She nodded her understanding and turned to Willa, handing her the garments already removed. "Here, girl, see the lord's boots are cleaned, his tunic's brushed, and his chausses and drawers washed and dried for the morning. You're much too young for such a fine sight yet," she cackled wickedly. "Go along, now! Lady, please take your husband's chemise, and lay it aside. Then we will take up our brushes," Ida instructed Elf. She whisked the chemise from her master, handing it to Elf while Ranulf descended into the tub quickly so that his wife got no more than a glimpse of his bare buttocks.

"Hellfire! 'Tis hot," he yelped as his naked body made contact with the water. "Do you mean to boil me, then, old woman?"

"The lady must have her bath after you," Ida explained. "If the water is not hot to begin with, it will be cold when she enters it. Besides, men have tougher hides than we women. Come, lady, and take up your brush. The jar with the soap is there."

He stood in the water while the two women plied their brushes, and scrubbed him clean. Elf delicately averted her eyes as he stepped upon a stool within the tub so he might lift a leg up for washing. He smiled at Ida. There would come a time when Elf would not be shy of him, and indeed, the tub was big enough for two. He longed for the day when they would bathe together, and in doing so aroused himself to an upstanding state. The old lady chuckled conspiratorily at him, her eyes dancing with mirth. Gritting his teeth, Ranulf thought of his last jousting tournament before King Stephen, who had brought the sport to England despite the objections of the clergy. In remembering, his shoulder began to ache where he had been bruised by his opponent—and his immediate purpose was served: his lust was defused.

"Lady," Ida said, "wash your husband's hair, being certain to pick out the nits first."

"I have no lice," he said indignantly. "I keep myself clean, old woman."

Ida ruffled her stubby fingers through his head, pushing the hair aside here and there. Finally she said, "He does not lie, lady."

Elf giggled. Looking at her, Ranulf laughed, too. "The king need not have bothered to send me to Ashlin, Eleanore," he said. "You already have a dragon to guard it."

"If he hadn't sent you," Ida snapped quickly, "this fair maid would have pledged herself to God. We are all lucky, but especially you, my lord."

Smiling, Elf lathered his hair with the thick soap, scrubbing it clean—for this was something she had done with the younger girls at the convent to help Sister Cuthbert—and then ducked his head beneath the water to rinse it. "You're done," she told him.

"Hold up his toweling, lady, and wrap him in it," Ida instructed as Ranulf arose up from the tub. "That's right, now sit him by the fire, and dry him off while I get him a clean chemise. Then it is into bed with you, my lord, before you catch an ague!"

Shyly, Elf knelt and dried her husband's legs and feet. Standing, she dried his back, his arms, his shoulders, his chest, his torso. He was such a big man; his muscled body scarred here and there.

"I'll do the hard part," he murmured to her, and she smiled up at him gratefully as he stood up and walked toward the bedchamber, where Ida was fetching the chemise for him. A moment later the old lady bustled out.

"You did well, lady," she said. "Now, let me help you."

Elf undressed slowly, handing Ida her garments until she wore nothing but her chemise. Boldly she pulled it off, pinning her braid up, and climbed into the tub. The water came up to her neck and shoulders. She sighed with pleasure, for it was still quite warm. After a few minutes of pure bliss, Ida broke into her reverie, telling her to stand upon the bath stool, and handing her a washing cloth and the soap.

"What of your hair?" her nursemaid asked when she saw Elf had finished washing herself.

"It was washed before my wedding," Elf said. "It will do for a few more days, Ida. Besides, it is late, and I cannot go to bed with long wet hair, can I?"

The old woman let out a rough laugh. "If I were wife to that big, warm-eyed man, I should want to hurry to my bed, too. Heh! Heh!"

"Fetch me a clean chemise," Elf said, feeling the heat come into her face with Ida's ribald remark.

"What? You would sleep in a chemise next to that fine husband?" She sighed. "Well, I suppose it will take awhile to breed that convent prudery out of you, lady." She shuffled off into the bedchamber to fetch the requested garment. By the time she returned, Elf had exited the tub and was drying herself vigorously, for the air in the solar was cold after the warmth of the water in the tub.

Elf slipped her chemise on. "God give you a good rest, Ida," she told her old servant. "Tell Willa she may sleep here with you." Then she went into the bedchamber, closing the door behind her. Seating herself on the stool by the fire, Elf unpinned her hair and undid her thick plait. She took up the boar's bristle brush Ida had placed upon the little table, and then his hand closed over hers.

"Let me," Ranulf said.

"I thought you asleep," Elf said softly.

"I was just keeping warm in the bed waiting for you," he said. Then he drew the brush through her long hair over and over and over again until the thick tresses were free of tangles and as smooth as a length of Byzantine silk. His hand followed each sweep of the brush into a rhythmic movement that she found very relaxing. "Your hair is so beautiful," he said. "You are beautiful, petite."

Turning slightly, she moved to take the brush from him. Their lips were so very close, and Elf's heart beat a wild tattoo. For a moment their eyes locked, and she thought in that moment that she would melt, for the heat of his gaze was that strong. Then her fingers closed about the pear-wood handle of the brush, and she took it from him, looking away as she did so. "I must braid my hair now," she said low.

"Yes," he said, standing up. Outside the sounds of the serfs struggling to empty the tub and return it to its place could be heard. "I have had a thought," Ranulf began. "What if we cut a drain into the stone of the solar floor, and installed a spigot at the bottom of the tub? The tub can be placed, when in use, with its spigot over the drain, effortlessly emptied, and easily restored to its storage place."

"That's a wonderful idea!" Elf said. She had finished restoring her hair to an orderly state. "How clever you are, Ranulf!" Going to her side of the bed, she knelt down. To her delight he joined her on his side of the bed, and together they said their prayers. Then they climbed into bed.

Immediately he took her hand in his, but tonight she was neither fearful nor afraid of him. She was beginning to believe that perhaps the abbess had been correct when she said God's plans for Eleanore de Montfort had changed. It was obvious that God had sent her a good man and she must do her best to be a good wife to him. "I know nothing about you, Ranulf," she said to him, "while you know all there is to know of me. Will you tell me of yourself?"

"There is little to tell," he said. "My father, Simon de Glandeville, had lands in Normandy. He was killed in the Holy Land. My mother sent me to King Henry's court to be raised. Then she remarried. My lands in Normandy were somehow absorbed into my stepfather's holdings. When I was old enough to understand what had happened, I went to Normandy with the intent of reclaiming what was mine. I was sixteen at the time. My stepfather claimed that my mother's marriage to my father had not been a legal union. As there were no other male heirs among the de Glandevilles, the lands dissolved upon my mother, and then to him upon their marriage. I had no power to refute his claim."

"But what did your mother say?" Elf wanted to know. "By saying such a thing, he defamed her character and that of her family."

"My mother had been the only child of elderly parents who were now dead. She had no one to defend her, and begged me to keep silent. Her husband, she promised, had sworn to keep her shame and my ill-born status a secret if I would simply accept what had happened. None of it was true, of course.

"My maternal grandmother had been alive before I was sent to King Henry's court at the age of seven. My mother's family was an ancient one, but poor. My father had been honored to have my mother as his wife. He took her without a dower just for her name, my grandmother always told me with pride. Our neighbors, the church, all treated my parents with great respect. This would not have happened had my mother been only my father's leman and I born on the wrong side of the blanket. As a child my father had carried me on his saddle, introducing me to his villagers as *le petit monseigneur,* the little lord. They would always cheer. I was just five, and it was before my father departed for the Holy Land, but I remember it well.

"Still, I was only sixteen, and newly knighted by the king. I had neither wealth nor power with which to challenge my mother's husband. If I allowed him to destroy my good name, I should have had nothing. What little I had would have been stripped from me, Eleanore. I told my mother that I should leave her in peace, but that I would pray for her. I thanked her husband for his *generosity* in protecting my mother's reputation and my good name. He blustered and blew of how much he loved her, that she had been a good wife, that she had given him heirs, that she was deserving of his generosity. I had been raised well by King Henry's court, he pompously told me, and, should anyone ever ask, he would be proud to call me his stepson.

"It was all I could do not to slay him where he stood, but I did not. I departed Normandy, returned to England, and pledged myself to the king's service. I did tell King Henry the truth of my adventure. He complimented me on my wisdom, and advised me to make my home in England. When he died, and the quarrel between King Stephen and the Empress Matilda erupted, I did what any knight in my position would do. I chose a side, and I stuck with it. Men of power have, of course, changed sides in this dispute as frequently as the wind has changed directions, but knights like me cannot afford to do so unless the odds are so overwhelming that to stay with one's choice would be foolish."

"I do not think you foolish," Elf said. "I think you are quick-witted and resourceful, Ranulf. You did the right thing to protect your mother from a husband who would steal from her child, and then threaten to destroy both her good name and his to keep the ill-gotten gains. He must be a very wicked man, for your mother is the mother of his own heirs, and her shame would reflect on them as well."

"Greed, my innocent little wife, does not know shame," he told her. "Your brother's wife was surely proof of that. Our people have little good to say of her. Fulk tells me before her cousin arrived, she would often flirt with the men-at-arms. The king was right to order her put away where she can do no harm."

"I do not see Isleen going meekly into the confinement of a convent for the rest of her life," Elf said. "But let us not speak of her, Ranulf. It pains me to think she poisoned my poor brother. He was a good and gentle man."

"Good men are often the unfortunate prey of evil women," he answered her. "These are things you cannot have known, petite, but they are lessons you must learn. If the king should call me back into his service, I must go without question, and you must look over Ashlin. You must be aware that there is much wickedness in the world, and guard yourself against being deceived by it. Evil often wears a pretty face." He had turned onto his side now, and was looking down upon her.

Elf felt breathless. His was a strong face, and she had already come to love his hazel eyes. "You will guide me, my lord Ranulf," she said in whispery tones, "will you not?"

"Aye, petite," he answered, then dropped a quick kiss upon her forehead before turning away from her. "God give you good rest, Eleanore," he told her, then was silent.

It had been but a swift brush of his lips, but the kiss seemed to burn like a brand upon her skin. She realized she was possibly a little disappointed that he had not kissed her lips. She knew instinctively that his kiss would be sweet, and not filled with violence as Saer de Bude's had been several months back. Was she ready to be a wife in the fullest sense? She was not certain. *I will pray on it,* Elf thought as she drifted off into sleep.

CHAPTER EIGHT

The weather remained cold, but relatively dry. Stones were cut and brought from the quarry to increase the height of the walls surrounding the demesne. The days took on a comfortable cadence. Ranulf oversaw the walls and trained the young men to properly defend Ashlin. Elf spent her days learning those things necessary to being a good chatelaine. She was surprised by how many of them she already knew. How to clean a house, for at the convent they had learned to clean. Now she worked with and oversaw her maidservants. She had learned at the convent how to make soaps. Come the summer she would learn how to make preserves and candied fruits, how to salt meats and fish. Even now she was learning the rudiments of cooking, although Ashlin had an excellent cook. Still, she should know what he did if she was to oversee the ordering of those supplies that they could not grow or harvest themselves.

Once each week Elf was brought the scrolls containing the steward and bailiff's reports. She would go over them carefully, returning them afterward, sometimes with questions. January passed, then February. March was almost gone when one day Elf walked out-of-doors and suddenly realized she was happy. She liked her life here at Ashlin. And her husband . . . a good man . . . a just lord as their people were discovering . . . but . . . but he had not yet consummated their marriage, and surely it was up to him! Did he find her unattractive? She was not a nun any longer as he so often teased her. Then what was the matter?

Rambling, she suddenly discovered that she was at the manor church. True to his word, Ranulf had had stones brought to make the repairs, but the walls came first, of course. She stepped inside the church. The roof would need re-thatching. That could be done this summer. Actually she coveted a slate roof for her church, but there was no hope of that. One day, however, she would have glass for the windows, she promised herself. Nothing fancy like the bishop's church in Worcester, but glass. She walked up the single aisle. The stone altar was bare. She wondered where the candlesticks and crucifix were, or if there had ever been any. The church had been in ill repair since before her birth, although the priest had remained until his death. Turning about, she sighed. There was so much to be done before the church could be reconsecrated, but she would do it.

She walked back to the open door and stood there for a moment surveying the manor. Ashlin was a good place, she thought. Then her eye caught a small clump of bright daffodils by the edge of the wide church steps. She smiled. It was as if she were being told where there is life, there is the hope of better days to come. She started at the sound of Ranulf's voice.

"We will get it done," he said as if reading her thoughts. He put his arm about her, giving her a small squeeze.

"I know the walls must come first," she said. "Look, spring is coming, my lord. The lambs are being born, and there have been no wolves this year so far. We are fortunate."

He followed the line of her finger to the daffodils, and smiled down at her as she looked up at him. Her mouth tempted him. He swallowed hard, and closed his eyes a brief moment, but when he opened them again, her lips were dangerously near his. Helpless to stem the passion surging through his veins, Ranulf kissed Elf, a fierce yet tender embrace. Then, breaking away, he gulped an apology. "Eleanore, forgive me!"

"As you so frequently remind me, Ranulf, I am no longer a

nun," Elf murmured, her glance melting. She held her head up in a very clear indication that she expected him to kiss her again.

"*Eleanore!*" His arms wrapped tightly about her, his mouth found hers.

Her head was spinning. Her heart was pounding. Her belly knotted and unknotted itself in a repetitive rhythm. She slipped her arms about his neck, and for the first time felt the length of him as he lifted her up. His lips were sending her a dozen messages. He was tender, yet savage. She could sense a deeper longing that he sought to mask. *He doesn't want to frighten me,* she thought, but he wasn't frightening her. There was a feeling, deep within her, that was beginning to bubble and well up. The feeling grew with the incredible touch of his mouth on her mouth. *Pressure. Sweetness. A sudden longing she could not understand.*

Finally he broke away, setting her down upon the stone steps. "The serfs will talk," he said softly, but the reality was that if he did not release her, he was going to carry her into the house to their little bedchamber, and ravish her. He had never imagined that this innocent little girl could arouse him so deeply. There was a new hunger gnawing at him, and only her fair body could satisfy that hunger. *But was she ready?* The one thing he feared above all was that he should harm her, or cause her to hate him. *He loved her.* He had almost since the beginning, but until this moment he had not been able to admit it to himself. *He loved her!*

"The serfs will talk anyhow," Elf said, a hint of mischief in her voice. "I have discovered, Ranulf, that I like kissing. Do you like kissing? Or is it boring to you as I imagine you have been kissing women for many years?"

"It is not boring with you, petite," he reassured her.

"I am glad, for I should like to do a great deal more kissing, Ranulf. May we tonight, when we lie abed?"

Again he closed his eyes for a long moment, and then opening them he looked directly at her. "Eleanore, it is said that women are weak, but I do not believe it is so. It is men who are weak, for they cannot control their baser natures. As long as we have lain together, only holding hands until sleep has overtaken us, I have been able to retain a mastery over myself. I swear to you, however, that if you climb into our bed tonight and want to play kissing games, I will lose my vaunted control! You are a sweet innocent, who having finally been kissed, desires to be kissed more. *But I am a man.* I will want more!" His voice was anguished, and he kept clenching and unclenching his fists.

"You will want to touch me," she said softly. She reached up and stroked his face with her slim fingers.

"Yes!" he said, catching her hand and kissing first the palm, then the wrist. He clasped her fingers and stayed them over his heart.

"And it is surely past time we consummated our union, Ranulf. Would you like it if we did?" she said ingenuously. She felt his heart leap beneath her palm, and knew the answer before he even spoke it.

"Aye," he murmured, "it is past time, but I wanted you to be the one to say it, petite. I do not want us to hate each other."

"Give me back my hand, my lord," she said softly.

Smiling at her, he released her, but not before kissing the palm of it once again. "You are sure?"

"I am told the first time hurts," she replied. "It will hurt no less if the first time is months from now, I am thinking, my lord Ranulf."

"I will be as gentle as I can," he promised her.

"I know," she said, before turning to leave him standing upon the church steps, his mind awhirl, his heart thumping with anticipation.

On the high board at dinnertime was a slender silver holder containing two bright yellow daffodils. It was a secret signal between them, a reminder of the night to come. She smiled at him, and, he believed, there was something seductive in her smile. Something he had never seen before. He felt a tightness in his nether region, and recognized the stirrings of serious lust. By the holy rood, he wanted her! How sweet her lips had been this afternoon. She was fresh and innocent, yet alluring. Aye! He wanted her very much!

What had she done, Elf asked herself, in the brief madness that had enveloped her when he kissed her? She had committed herself quite boldly to an irreversible course of action. Was she really ready? Would she ever be ready? She was a wife by a twist of fate. A wife in all ways but one. *And tomorrow?* Tomorrow she would be a wife in every sense of the word. She sneaked a look at this man to whom she would be so irrevocably bound. Though he was twice her age, he did not really seem old. Certainly he could father children on her.

What was she thinking, Ranulf wondered, knowing he was being perused. Would she ever love him? Should he tell her that he loved her? Nay, that would not be wise. What if she did not believe him? They had, after all, been married for only four months. Besides, love was not necessary to a good Christian marriage. She should respect him, and how could she if he admitted to such a weakness as love? He had been patient and kind with her, and she had responded by not keeping him waiting forever. That indicated that she respected him. Best not to ruin a good relationship. He picked up the haunch of a broiled rabbit and began to eat it.

Elf cudgled her brain. What had the clothier's wife said? Ranulf would kiss her, and caress her breasts and other body parts. *What body parts?* He seemed to enjoy kissing her hand and fingers, Elf thought. Was there anything else? Well, she would certainly know soon enough. And the touching, Mistress Martha had said, would arouse his manhood, and then . . . She couldn't believe what she had said to him this afternoon. How brazen she had been. What on earth had possessed her?

He leaned his head, his mouth close to her ear. "If you have changed your mind, Eleanore, I will understand," he said so only she might hear him.

"*No!*" Dear heaven! She had just given up the only opportunity she would get to stop this madness. Why had she said no?

A minstrel had asked shelter of them this night. Now he took up his small harp and began to play for the small company in the hall. The firelight played brightly against the stone walls. The flames of the candles flickered and danced. Ranulf took her hand in his as the bard sang of unrequited love and passion. When he had finished and been shown appreciation by the clapping of his small audience, Elf rose and slipped from the hall.

The tub had been set up that night, and she quickly bathed before Ranulf might come into the solar. "Leave the tub for my lord if he so desires," she told Willa. "Go into the hall and ask him."

When Willa returned she told her mistress, "The lord says he will bathe himself this night, lady. He says he will not be long."

Elf went into the bedchamber, where old Ida was plumping the pillows upon the bed. "Go and find your pallet," Elf said. "The sun has long ago set, and you are not as young as you once were."

"I've put a knife beneath the bed to cut the pain," Ida told her mistress.

"What?" Elf looked puzzled.

"Lady, I am not so old that I do not know what has been going on these few months. You are still a virgin, but you decided today to remedy that sad state tonight. The knife will cut your pain when he enters into you the first time. It is a well-known fact."

Elf flushed. "Is it?"

"Well, lady, you would not be knowing such things being in the convent since you were scarce little more than a babe, but it is so. You are not afraid, are you? There is no need to be afraid."

"I am not afraid," Elf said calmly, but she would be if she didn't get her old nursemaid to leave the bedchamber. This was certainly not a subject she was comfortable discussing with Ida.

"Good," the old woman said. "Then, I shall leave you. Willa and I will sleep in the hall tonight, and every night from now on, lady. You will want your privacy, and that door scarce allows it." She shuffled from the bedchamber, leaving Elf quite astounded.

Did everyone at Ashlin know the state of her marriage, Elf wondered as she unbraided her hair and brushed it out? Was nothing a secret? But she did realize that in any small community, there were no real secrets. There had certainly been none at St. Frideswide's. Slowly she brushed her long red-gold hair, rebraiding it into a single plait, then climbing into bed. Where was Ranulf? Ah, she realized, Ranulf might not know that everyone at Ashlin was aware of their marital matters, and so he had probably remained in the hall with Fulk and his men, as was his custom each evening. Elf smiled and stretched her limbs beneath the coverlet. The room was dim, not overly cold this night. Her eyes grew heavy, and soon she fell asleep.

Looking down on her, Ranulf thought Elf was surely the most beautiful girl he had ever seen. Her thick dark lashes grazed her pale cheeks. Her sensuous little mouth was the most tempting mouth he had known. He had bathed and entered their chamber as quietly as he could. Now he raised the coverlet to slip into bed. Should he awaken her . . . or should he allow nature to take its course when she finally awoke? Unable to help himself, he leaned over and lightly kissed her mouth.

Elf opened her gray-blue eyes and looked into his hazel ones. "You need not have stayed so long in the hall, my lord. It seems the entire manor knows of our private matters," she told him. "Did you not see that Ida and Willa have gone to sleep in the hall? Ida says the door does not give us the privacy we need."

He laughed softly. "So, we are the talk of Ashlin, petite. How did all this come about?" Pulling up his pillows so he might sit, he drew her onto his lap.

Her heart had jumped when he moved her into his arms, but Elf managed not to show any nerves. "Ida told me she put a knife beneath the bed to cut the pain of my defloration," Elf told him.

"Why do women who should know better believe that old wives' tale?" He chuckled. "Mary's honor, petite, you are not fearful, are you? I will not allow you to be afraid of making love!"

"Why does everyone ask me if I am afraid?" Her heart-shaped face was the picture of annoyance, and he almost laughed aloud. "If a husband and wife's coming together in carnal fashion is pleasant, then why should I be afraid? Oh, I know, the first time will be strange, and yes, I know it will hurt when you pierce my maidenhead, but frankly I am more curious as to where everything goes than I am concerned about a brief pain. No, Ranulf, I am not afraid!"

"You are adorable," he said with a sigh. "Now I know why no

woman has ever attracted me enough to induce me into offering marriage. It was obviously God's plan that you be my wife, Eleanore."

To his surprise and delight, she gave him a quick kiss upon his lips. "Are you wooing me, my lord Ranulf? If you are, I like it very much." She snuggled against his chest.

"Dear Lord, help me not to hurry her," he prayed silently. Then his hand reached out to stroke her head. "Your hair is the most beautiful color. It is not a fiery red-gold, but rather a soft red-gold. Have you ever cut it, Eleanore?" His fingers pulled the ribbon holding her plait, and undid it. Then they began to unbraid her long hair. "I want to see you naked with only your lovely tresses for adornment, petite." He took up a thick handful of the hair, and pressed it to his lips. "Ummm, you smell of lavender."

Naked? He wanted to see her naked? Now, here was something she hadn't considered. "Is it fitting that you see me . . . *naked*? I did not know that husbands saw their wives naked, Ranulf."

"But they do," he assured her. "Did not God send you into this world unclothed, Eleanore? We are taught to be ashamed of our bodies, but why should we? God gave us those bodies."

"Oh." Her voice had gotten very small.

Ranulf tipped her face up to his. "You are beautiful, petite, and I want to see you as God fashioned you. I am pleased you are so chaste, but there is little need for modesty with your husband."

Her cheeks were warm with her blushes at his frankness, but she did not look away from him. "There is so much I do not know, Ranulf. I must rely upon you to guide me."

His arm cradled her. Now the fingers of the hand of his other arm began to unlace the ribbons that closed the front of her chemise. Elf's eyes grew wide as her bosom was slowly revealed. She wasn't certain at all that she was even breathing, but she seemed to be. The long fingers pushed aside the fabric slowly, slowly, until the chemise slid from her shoulders, pooling just below her waist to rest upon her hips.

Ranulf let his eye roam deliberately and carefully over her perfect form. Round little breasts, no bigger than small apples, and a waist he could span with his two big hands. *"Mon Dieu,"* he said breathlessly. "You are without flaw, petite."

Never taking her eyes from him, Elf unfastened the laces on his chemise, pulling it open and pushing it down to rest below his waist. Breaking the glance between them, she just as exactingly examined him. She remembered the first time she had seen him in the bath, but this was different. Her two small hands smoothed themselves over the broad expanse of his chest, then his shoulders. Running down his muscled arms, her fingers touched and stopped on a short, but thick scar upon his upper arm.

"The bite of a lance during a jousting tournament," he told her, catching her hand up to kiss the palm.

"Did you win?" she asked, taking her hand back.

"Aye," he said softly.

"And this one?" The pad of her forefinger rested at the crest of a longer, narrower scar upon his shoulder. "How did you come by this wound, my lord?"

"In a battle between the king's and the empress's forces, petite."

"You need more practice," she told him. "Both wounds are on the same side. You leave yourself open there. If you do not change your habits, you could lose your life through such carelessness one day."

"And how, Eleanore, has my little nun divined such an opinion?" he asked, quite amazed by her astuteness.

"It is not obvious, my lord?" was her quick reply.

"Your eye is sharp, lady," he said softly. His loins were beginning to burn with his longing for her.

"You have an improper look in your eyes, Ranulf. I think you should kiss me." Elf realized he was beginning to lust after her. Just looking at her was stirring his desires. His arm wrapped about her again, and his mouth came fiercely down on hers. *He was dangerous!* Then she gasped, quite unprepared for the feel of the hand that cupped her breast, fondled it gently, the rough pad of his thumb rubbing against her nipple until it was stiff and hard.

"Ranulf!" she squeaked, trembling.

"Eleanore."

"Oh!" But Mistress Martha had said men like to touch women's breasts. She had not said, however, that when they did you would feel both hot and cold at the same time, and that your heart would threaten to burst through your chest. No. She had not said that!

"You are exquisite, petite," Ranulf said, his voice thick with an emotion she couldn't fathom. His hand moved to her other breast.

Fascinated, she watched the big hand cup her, the very repetitive motion of his thumb as it rubbed, and rubbed, and rubbed until it achieved the required result, and her nipple stood rigid. His fingers tenderly brushed her flesh until it was so sensitive that she actually moaned with his touch. "Stop," she finally whispered. "I shall die! I know I will!"

In response he kissed her again, his mouth playing over hers like a wildfire, brushing, lightly touching, nibbling upon her lips. She sighed with unfeigned pleasure, and he laughed softly. His hands encircled her waist, and he lifted her up, pressing his face into the shadowed valley between her delightful little breasts.

Elf reached out, using her hands to brace herself upon his shoulders as he held her up. It seemed to her that she was but a feather to him. The feel of his face against her flesh was exciting. Then suddenly she gasped as his tongue swept slowly up between her breasts. *"Ohhhhhh!"* The tongue moved on to lick at her nipples. Ripples of pure excitement raced up and down her spine. But he had not yet finished. His lips had closed over one of her nipples, and he began tugging hard upon it. *"Ohhhhhh!"* Elf closed her eyes with the utter pleasure that was sweeping over her. His mouth moved to the other nipple, and she shuddered with the exquisite thrill of it.

Now he slowly lowered her again into his lap, cradling her in his arms. "You are not frightened," he said. It was a statement more than a question.

"No," she said. " 'Tis lovely. I never dreamed . . ."

He laughed softly. "Of course you didn't, my innocent petite. Little nuns don't know of carnal love, nor should they."

"Matti and Isa used to watch the priest with the dairymaid," Elf told him.

"But you did not, I am certain."

"No, I didn't," Elf answered him. She turned slightly in his arms so that she might touch him again, bending her head and licking at his broad chest. She heard his sharp intake of breath, but he said nothing that would indicate he was displeased by her actions. Indeed his arms fell away from her so she might move freely. The taste of him on her tongue was faintly salty, but the scent of him was more elusive. Soap, and . . . musk? Yes, there was a muskiness about him, and it excited her greatly.

He watched her innocent exploration of his body. Her head moved lower, then lower still, sweeping over his belly, which was knotting in excitement. He knew he had to stop her now, but it was with great effort he raised her back up so he might kiss her. She melted against him, her warm naked skin pressed to his. Their arms wrapped tightly about each other, their mouths fused in a long kiss. Then Elf pulled away and sighed deeply.

The time was almost right. He slowly drew her chemise off, dropping it by the side of their bed. His lips brushed over her face, her eyelids, her straining throat. One hand grasped her shoulder. The other moved over her body tenderly, exploring loveliness such as he had never known . . . or even imagined. She writhed like a flame in his arms. Her skin was as soft as the finest silk, and he could feel her quivering ever so slightly beneath his big palm. She was pure perfection with her sweetly rounded hips and her slender legs.

His fingers brushed over the warm, plump mound of her Venus mont, smooth and devoid of hair as a proper lady's should be. The tightness in his groin was greater than he had ever known. He ceased exploration of her for a moment to pull his own chemise off. Then he began stroking her again. A single finger ran down the shadowed slit dividing her delicate nether lips. He saw the instinctive tightening of her thighs.

To be touched so intimately. She had never imagined she would be touched in such a manner. Only now did she realize how naked being naked was. She felt almost threatened, and yet he was not threatening her. The finger began to push into her flesh. She tensed, and he stopped, kissing her lips softly as if he were reassuring her. The finger moved again, deeper, deeper. Elf struggled not to cry out.

She did not need a knife beneath the bed to cut the pain, Ranulf thought. She needed to be well prepared to receive his manhood. His finger sought carefully for the tiny jewel of her womanhood. Finding it, he began to play with it, teasing it with an extremely delicate touch. His mouth kissed her lips, her face. His arm held her tightly. The relentless finger flicked back and forth over the sensitive little nub of flesh, and it began to swell and tingle with its new sensitivity.

What was happening? Elf felt her heart begin to beat faster. The hidden spot between her legs that he was even now taunting was growing tight, and it felt as if it might burst. She gasped for air as a wave of heat washed over her, and then suddenly she seemed to explode with intense feeling. *"Ranulf!"* she cried his name as she felt the finger leave its place, and push slowly into her. Her lithe body arched against him. The finger was gentle, but a distinct invasion.

Her little jewel had responded quickly to him, Ranulf thought, well pleased. Her body had released a flow of her juices, and his finger was sliding easily into her tight sheath. She winced when it touched her maidenhead, which was tightly lodged, but she did not struggle or beg him to stop. He moved the long finger back and forth within her love channel, and she began to whimper. "Are you ready to be a woman, Eleanore?" he asked her, looking deep into her silvery eyes.

"Yes!" she nodded. *Relief!* She wanted relief from this burning, overwhelming feeling that was threatening to kill her. Instinctively she knew that only Ranulf could offer her that surcease.

"You are dainty, and I am large," he told her. "I could crush you with my size. We must be extremely careful this first time." He

lifted her from his lap, and laid her upon their bed. Then he knelt
before her, leaning back upon his haunches.

Elf's eyes widened with a mixture of surprise and shock as she
viewed her husband's manhood for the first time. This was no boy's
lance, but the full-grown weapon of a man. "You cannot put that
in me," she gasped. "It is too big! You will kill me with it!"

"Nay, petite, it will fit nicely, I promise you," he said. "Now,
open yourself to me, Eleanore, and trust me not to harm you."

Reluctantly she spread herself before him. Taking her gently by
the ankles, he drew her forward until his manhood met her nether
lips. He rubbed himself up and down her slit until it began to pout,
and give off a moistness of its very own. The head of his lance
slipped between those humid lips. He drew her even closer, and
she felt him beginning to delve into her love channel. Elf shuddered, not from fear, but rather from anticipation of what was
to come.

He felt the head of his manhood penetrate her gently, entering
her, moving slowly forward. It was all he could do not to violate
her and take his own pleasure, so great was his lust for her now.
"When I press deep, petite, wrap your legs about me," he instructed her in a tight voice. He began to push forward into her,
and to his delight her slender legs folded themselves about him. She
was tight. She was hot and, oh, so very wet! He groaned with the
pleasure of her. Her body filled his senses, setting his head awhirl.

Elf gasped as his thick and lengthy manhood thrust into her. She
had never felt so invaded—*and yet so complete.* She understood now
the need for their position. By coming to him rather than his coming to her, his large body did not crush her delicate one. She gasped
again. The manhood was moving back and forth within her. The
friction was exciting, and her head spun with excitement as she
realized she was actually enjoying his amorous attentions. Suddenly
he stopped. His mouth came down hard on hers. Then he drove
himself deep into her, shattering her maidenhead as he went. Her
cry was lost in his own mouth, but tears pearled her cheeks as the
pain of her violation overwhelmed her.

Lifting his mouth from hers, he murmured, "Forgive me, petite. There was no other way, for your maidenhead was very tightly entrenched." He kissed the tears upon her cheeks as he began a rhythmic movement within her that set her senses quickly reeling. Faster and faster, and deeper and deeper he pumped his loins against hers.

The pain was gone. It was as if it had never existed. Pleasure, sweet, hot pleasure was beginning to flood her entire being. She struggled to open herself more to him. Little cries were emitted from her throat. "Ranulf! Ranulf! *Ohhh, holy Mother, I never knew! It is wonderful! It is wonderful! Ohhhhhh! Ohhhhhh! Ohhhhhhhhhh!"* Her body tensed, shuddered, exploded in a burst of delicious feelings. "*Nooooo! I want more! Ohhhhhhhh!"* Then she swooned, sliding away into a warm darkness.

He groaned as his love juices erupted to flood her secret garden. He pulsed with pleasure, until finally and reluctantly he withdrew from her and rested on his side.

How many women had he had in a lifetime? Enough to realize that what he had with this girl, this woman, was truly miraculous and special. How he loved her! And she, his sweet Eleanore, could not know. This was her first experience with passion. What if that passion died quickly? Then they would be like so many other married couples, living together with naught but children and hopefully respect in common. He realized he could not bear it if she rejected him. Better she never know he had lost his heart to her. He didn't want her telling him she loved him from pity or duty. If one day she admitted those feelings for him, then, and only then, would he admit his love for her.

Ranulf rose over the still unconscious girl and gathered her into his arms again. He saw the blood upon their sheets, staining her slim thighs. He smoothed her hair and held her tightly, kissing her brow. She stirred faintly, then opened her eyes. "Are you all right, petite?" he asked her.

She nodded, touching his face in a tender gesture. Was this feeling she felt *love*? Or was it merely lust? How could she tell? How could she know? She couldn't ask Ranulf. He would surely be em-

barrassed by her girlishness and naïveté. Besides, he certainly did
not love her, and any declaration upon her part would only discomfit him. They seemed compatible, and they liked each other. If
she gushed of love, he would only be put off. Better she say nothing at all. He was older, sophisticated. Battle-hardened knights
such as Ranulf de Glandeville did not feel emotions like love. Best
she remain silent, and keep his respect and friendship.

"You were very brave," he told her admiringly.

"You were very kind," she answered him. "When can we do it
again, my lord? I must admit, I enjoyed making love with you."

He smiled, surprised, yet delighted. "Ahh, petite, I will need
time to recover from your passion, but perhaps before the dawn we
may join our bodies again if it would please you."

"Would it please you also?" she demanded.

"Aye, lady. You are a delicious and most satisfying armful. The
king has done me a greater kindness than he can ever know," Ranulf said honestly.

"Let us not tell him," Elf said mischievously. Then she let her
eyes wander to his groin. "Ah, it is as Mistress Martha said," she
noted. "In verity her words have proved truth all around."

"Who is Mistress Martha?"

"The clothier's wife in Worcester. While we altered the garments the bishop purchased for me, she explained the intricacies of
lovemaking and the male body to me. I should not have known
otherwise."

Ranulf laughed. "I am relieved you were well instructed, petite."

"Well, the abbess made no attempt to enlighten me, and I could
not be certain of my friends and their prattling gossip."

He laughed again. She was so delightfully practical. He kissed
her lips lightly. "Let us get some rest now, petite," he said, and he
drew the coverlet over them.

When Elf awoke again the fire was low, but there was the faint
light of the day just before the dawn beyond the cracks in the shutters. Looking down upon her husband, she was overwhelmed by a
sudden and great desire to pleasure and to be pleasured. This was
surely lust. She drew the coverlet back, silently examining him.

Her hand smoothed lightly over his flat belly. Then boldly she bent down, and began to lick him. He moaned low, stirring. Elf lifted her head as a tiny movement caught her eye. It was his manhood, and it had stirred ever so slightly. Reaching out with brazen fingers, she touched the thick peg of flesh, brushing over it, and then as it began to truly awaken and elongate, she trailed her little fingers up and own its great length.

"Shameless wench," Ranulf murmured, not even opening his eyes. Reaching out, he lifted her up over his belly, then slowly lowered her until her sheath had fully encased his manhood.

"Ohhhhhh, yes!" Elf breathed. "Oh, yes, my Ranulf!" She clasped him between her thighs strongly.

"Ride me, petite," he instructed her, his voice tight.

Blushing at her own shamelessness, she moved on him, slowly at first, then faster and faster. He pulled her forward so that her small breasts were crushed against his chest. His mouth found hers, and he kissed her hungrily as they loved with fury until the pleasure was so great that it consumed them both as she collapsed atop him, sighing lustily. *"Ahhhhh,* Ranulf! That was wonderful!"

His heart felt as if it would burst with his delight. He laughed aloud. "Nay, Eleanore, you are wonderful! I adore you, petite! There is no other woman like you—and you are indeed every bit a woman now—my sweet wife." His arms wrapped about her.

She was damp with exertions, and so was he. There was something marvelous about lying atop him. She could feel his very strength pulsing beneath her. And he had said he adored her. She had pleased him. *He had pleased her.* Now that she knew what marital relations were all about, she understood the sacrifice she would have made had she taken her final vows. But without Ranulf, she would have known nothing. She would have gone through life innocent of the miraculous and astonishing passions a man and his wife could share. She began to cry.

Immediately he was concerned. He rolled her over into his arms, crooning at her. "Petite, do not weep. What is it? Have I harmed you in any way? Tell me, Eleanore, for you are breaking my heart!"

"I . . . I . . . *I am so happy!*" she sobbed.

"Then, why are you crying?"

"*Because I am happy!* It is all right, Ranulf." She snuggled against him, and patted his cheek.

He was totally confused, but she did not seem in any pain. Was this, then, what men meant when they said that they did not understand women? Kissing the top of her head softly, he thought it must.

CHAPTER NINE

The walls around the demesne now stood twelve feet in height. Inside of the walls, four feet below their top, ran a platform, three feet in width, and well braced. There the men-at-arms might stand on their patrol, having a good view of the surrounding countryside. A staircase was built at each corner of the walls to give quick access to its parapet in case of attack. Hefty new oaken doors, reinforced with iron, were hung on strong iron hinges. The shallow moat surrounding the walls was dug deeper. An earthen rim surrounded it, and its earthen crossover was replaced with a heavy oak drawbridge.

"It's fine enough to withstand a siege," Fulk noted.

"Nay," Ranulf said. "The walls enclose too big a space. It's breachable. Not easily, but breachable by a strong army, though not the Welsh rabble. We need a castle to make Ashlin stronger, but we have not the power, the wealth, or the king's permission to build one. So, Fulk, we will consider how best to defend the manor house itself in the event of an attack. But first the church, lest my lady say I am not a man of my word."

" 'Tis time to plow the fields, my lord," Fulk pointed out.

"The serfs must give us three days a week of work. Those who give me a fourth day's labor to rebuild the church will be paid in coin when the job is done," the lord of Ashlin said.

John, the bailiff, who had been walking with them, nodded. "I will tell all of your offer, my lord."

"I will expect one strong man from each household," Ranulf said sternly. "Tell them no permissions for marriages will be given until the church is repaired, and its roof thatched. The lady desires that a priest be called to Ashlin again. It cannot be done until the church is ready to receive the bishop's man."

The fields were plowed, and the winter crops harvested. Every third field was left fallow in rotation. Of the two remaining fields, one was planted. The other arable field would not be planted until the late summer for harvest the following spring. The ewe sheep had birthed a bountiful number of lambs. They would have wool to sell at Hereford town come the summer fair. There were three new calves. Next to her herbarium Elf recultivated her garden, enlarging it so she would have plenty of medications for her store, with which to dose her people when necessary.

She was happy. Happier, she had to admit, than she had ever been. She had expected to feel a trifle guilty over her happiness, but she could muster no guilt. She liked her life, and she loved her husband, even if he should never know that. Now, she realized, she wanted a child of her love.

"You are too anxious," Ida told her. "Children come when they come, and not before. It is God's way."

"Have you ever had any bastards, Ranulf?" she asked her husband one night as they lay abed. She trailed mischievous fingers over his belly.

The hazel eyes, closed with the pleasure her fingers wrought and anticipation of the delights to come, flew open. *"What?"* Surely he had not heard her aright.

"Have you ever had any bastards?" she repeated. The wicked little fingers tangled themselves in his thick dark bush.

"Why would you ask me such a question?" he demanded, pulling her hand away from his groin, and gently pinioning her beneath him so he might see her face.

"I want a baby," she said, "and I do not seem to conceive. I just wondered if you had ever had any bastards. Perhaps I am like Isleen and cannot have babes. What a tragedy for Ashlin."

"No offspring have been placed at my feet, Eleanore," he told

her, struggling to hold his laughter in check. She was such an outrageous little minx. "I have been careful, however, not to allow my
cock to outweigh my common sense. The women I enjoyed were
wise enough to know how to prevent conception, for children
would have been a burden to them, and they could never be certain of the fathers."

"Do you mean whores?" she asked him.

"What can my little convent-bred wife know of whores?" he
responded, fascinated.

"The girls at the convent knew all manner of things, Ranulf.
We were not all meant for the church. Bad women are rather intriguing when girls are young. The forbidden always has a certain
appeal." She smiled seductively into his face. "Do you want to f—"

"Aye," he interrupted her, "I do, petite." Then a rather wicked
light came into his eyes. "Do you still find the forbidden appealing,
Eleanore? A lovely and skilled whore I knew long ago taught me a
very naughty trick to please both a man and a woman. Are you
brave enough? Or is it just the talk that you find pleasing?"

"Is it very wicked?" she asked him. Her gray eyes shown with
interest. She contemplated his dare.

"There are some who say it is wicked, and others who say it is
not wicked," he answered her. His little nun was becoming quite
the delightful sybarite, he thought. The gray eyes locked onto his
hazel ones. Taking her legs he drew them up, up, up, until they
were well over his muscled shoulders.

Mesmerized Elf watched as her Venus mont was drawn within
easy reach of his mouth. She started just slightly as his lips pressed a
deep kiss upon her nether lips, and then his thumbs slowly opened
her to his gaze. She felt her cheeks flush with the terrible intimacy
of his action. Should she forbid him? Unable to tear her eyes away,
however, she watched him as his tongue slipped from between his
lips and touched her jewel, gently at first, and then with fierce
vigor.

"Ohhhhhh, Ranulf!" The tongue flicked back and forth relentlessly
over her sentient flesh. She gasped with undisguised pleasure as

strong ripples of wonderfully wild sensations began to engulf her. She couldn't watch any longer. *"Ohhhhhh, Ranulf!"* She abandoned herself to the erotic delights his marauding tongue was creating, mewling with her gratification. *"Ohhhhhh, Ranulf! Oh! Oh! Ohhhhhh!"* Her body stiffened, and relaxed as the intensity drained away.

He was hard as iron with her open desire. Lowering her legs just enough, he impaled her with his manhood, and she sighed so gustily that he could not help but laugh. "You are shameless," he said, groaning as he pistoned her writhing body. "Utterly shameless, petite!" By the rood, he could not get enough of her this night! She was hot, and despite the fact she was no longer a virgin, yet tight. He pushed himself as far as he could go, and then pulled her legs up higher to thrust farther. He needed to be deeper within her.

She clung to him. Her senses were completely awhirl. Her fingers clawed his back desperately as she sought the delicious and perfect bliss that the conjoining of their bodies brought her. *I am greedy and selfish,* she thought muzzily. *I think only of my own pleasure.* "I want to pleasure you, too," she gasped as he fiercely used her.

"You are!" he groaned through gritted teeth. "By Christ's blood, you are!" Then together they found paradise, shuddering with mutual release; collapsing in happy contentment in each other's arms.

"You would have been a terrible nun," he finally said when his heart had stopped hammering wildly.

"Nay," she protested. "Had I remained in ignorance of how sweet lovemaking can be, I should have been a very good nun."

Then they both laughed at the familiar badinage with which they always teased each other.

Ranulf declared a full day's holiday on Mary's Day, which was also Elf's fifteenth birthday. A Maypole was raised, and the lord and lady danced about it with their people. Tables were set up in the near sunny meadow, and a feast served at the expense of the master and mistress. Barrels of cider and ale were rolled out for drinking. There were footraces and an archery contest with the winners receiving a young cock and two hens. The church had been finished, its walls repaired, its roof newly thatched. Ranulf gave his permission for half-a-dozen marriages to take place as soon as the priest was sent. Two of the brides-to-be were already with child, but there was no shame in it as it but proved their fertility, and their young men were true.

"There be a rider approaching," one of the girls cried out, pointing and excited, for visitors were a rarity at isolated manors like Ashlin.

The sun glinted off the rider's sword hilt, Ranulf noted. A knight. Was he alone? A member of an advance party? But no. He would not come alone to scout for a larger, menacing group. Besides, the knight rode slowly, which meant his destination was in sight, and that destination could only be Ashlin. Ranulf stood up, and called to one of the house serfs. "Go inside, and bring me my sword. Hurry!" The man ran off, returning quickly with his lord's sword and belt, which Ranulf buckled swiftly about him. Then he began to walk forward, distancing himself from the revelers, distinguishing himself so the strange knight would understand that Ranulf was lord of this manor.

Silently, Elf came and stood by her husband's side. He looked down at her with a small smile.

The rider drew his great warhorse to a halt. "You are the lord of Ashlin manor?" he queried politely.

"I am. Ranulf de Glandeville is my name. How may I be of service to you, Sir Knight?"

The knight dismounted, and held out the hand of friendship to Ranulf, who accepted it. "I am Garrick Taliferro, and I have been sent by Duke Henry to speak with you, my lord."

"Duke Henry?" Ranulf was momentarily puzzled.

"The lord of Normandy, Anjou, Maine, Tourraine, and Aquitaine," Sir Garrick said quietly.

"Empress Matilda's eldest son? I am King Stephen's man, sir. I have always been, and will be until the king is no more," Ranulf replied.

"Sir Garrick," Elf interrupted. "You will be thirsty with your ride. Come, and let us bring you some wine. Rolph, take the knight's horse, and see it is stabled properly, fed, and watered."

"This is my wife, the lady Eleanore," Ranulf said, "and she is correct. I have forgotten my manners. Come, sir. The manor is celebrating Mary's Day as well as my wife's natal day. Please join us, after which we will talk."

Sir Garrick was seated at the main trestle. A cup of wine was placed in his hand by Cedric himself, who had hurried into the house to bring out a decanter. A plate of food was set before the knight, who ate with gusto, quickly emptying the plate twice, and the goblet three times before he finally pushed himself away from the table, a smile of satisfaction upon his face. "Your hospitality is more than welcome," he told them, "and I thank you."

"You will remain the night with us, of course," Elf said.

"Gladly, lady."

"Will you tell us why you have come from Duke Henry?" Ranulf asked. "As I have said, I am King Stephen's man."

"Duke Henry knows this, my lord. That is why I have been sent to you, and to many others like you. I am not here to suborn your loyalty to King Stephen. It is that very loyalty which attracts my master, the duke. Being so off the beaten track, you may not be aware of the events of recent months."

"I was wed to my wife last December first by the Bishop of Worcester, and in the king's presence. Until then I was naught but a knight in the king's service. We departed that same day to return to Ashlin, and have had no visitors at all since we arrived. What has happened? Is the king well?"

"King Stephen is well, and there is a truce now throughout all of the land. Duke Henry arrived in England in January."

"He crossed from Normandy in wintertime?" Ranulf was astounded. The channel in the best of weather was a rough passage, but in the depth of winter could be a raging tumult of a sea. The duke was either very brave, or a fortunate fool, Ranulf thought to himself.

"During his own lifetime King Stephen wishes to crown his

eldest son, Eustace, as England's king," Sir Garrick began. "As you know this is a custom practiced by the French kings. The Archbishop of Canterbury, however, on Pope Adrien's command, refused. Prince Eustace is frankly as unpleasant a fellow as the Empress Matilda is an unpleasant lady."

"Yes," Ranulf said. "I have heard that he is nothing like either of his gentle parents."

"The church now attempts to mediate a solution to this long and dark crisis that has plagued England these many years. The church has suggested that King Stephen rule for his lifetime, but that when he dies, the crown go to Duke Henry, the empress's eldest son." The knight paused, and took a swallow of his wine. "The king," he continued, "of course, resists this solution, but in the end he must come to accept it. Eustace is unfit to rule, and his young brother, William, has assured Duke Henry that he is content as Count of Bologne. William has no designs upon the English throne."

"But Duke Henry does," Ranulf said quietly.

"It is his by right, my lord," Sir Garrick replied. "My master wishes to know if you will support him over Prince Eustace once King Stephen is dead. Your manor, small as it may be, sits in a strategic area, near to the Welsh border." Sir Garrick gazed about him. "Are your walls new?"

"Nay," Ranulf responded. "We have simply strengthened them. Come, and I will show you, Sir Garrick."

The two men rose and walked toward the demesne.

Elf signaled to Willa and Ida. "Come," she said, "we must prepare the best bed space for this knight." The three women hurried into the house.

As they lay abed later, Elf asked her husband, "What will you do, Ranulf? Will you support Eustace or Duke Henry?"

"Duke Henry," her husband replied without hesitation.

"Why?"

"For several reasons, petite. Eustace, whom I have known all of his life, is a very unpleasant man lacking completely in his father's charm or chivalry. I began my career when I was just seven at King Henry's court. That king died when I was almost thirteen. I was Stephen of Blois's page, whenever he was in England. He was his uncle, the king's, favorite. I learned to love him, although if the truth be known, he is not the best of kings, petite. He has charm, and he is a brave fighter, but he has not the other skills needed to be successful. Only the fact that the Empress Matilda is so arrogant, over-proud, and nasty a lady—coupled with the fact it suited the more powerful lords and barons to keep the country in chaos without a strong central government—has kept Stephen king in power. When he became king, I was made one of his squires, then knighted when I was sixteen. He was always kind to me, and generous as well. Had I been a boastful man, I should have been resented by those whose sons were of higher rank. My loyalty was always and openly to King Stephen. You understand why, don't you, Elf?"

She nodded.

He continued. "I knew his queen, the heiress of Eustace, the Count of Bologne, and his wife, Mary of Scotland, King Malcolm's youngest child. She was called Matilda, and she loved King Stephen with all her heart as he loved her. There were three sons of the union. Baldwin, who died when he was nine. Eustace, and William, who is the Count of Bologne today. There were two daughters. The first died before she was two. The second, Mary, is unwed. Count William and his sister, Mary, are courteous and pleasant people. Eustace is violent, haughty, disdainful, and overbearing. Even his own wife, Constance of Toulouse, does not like him, and they have no children. She is the French king's sister, and he hoped to regain Normandy through her. He did not, of course, for France didn't wish to engage the lords of Anjou over the matter. They had taken Normandy while Stephen and Matilda fought over England."

He paused, contemplative.

"I believe I understand, Ranulf, except perhaps for the particulars about Eustace."

"There is a slyness about him that troubles me, Elf. He is too quick-tempered. Frankly, petite, I do not trust him. While I love his father, I cannot support the son."

"But what do you know of Duke Henry?"

"Surprisingly, a great deal, for he has been considered Stephen's rival for several years now since his mother gave up the fight. He is married to your namesake, Alienor, the great heiress of Aquitaine, whose marriage to King Louis VII was annulled on the basis of their consanguinity. She is ten years Duke Henry's senior, but he is mad for her. His household is constantly on the move. He, himself, seems to need little sleep. It is said he can travel the day long and still remain up half the night drinking. His secretaries complain constantly of overwork. He exhausts everyone around him. He is educated and scholarly like his late grandfather, King Henry I. He loves hunting, feasting, and is said to enjoy the ladies prodigiously. He will be a young king, for he is but twenty, and wed only a year, but sired a son three months after his marriage to Alienor of Aquitaine. Some say she seduced him into marriage.

"Duke Henry is a good soldier. While his temper is said to be fierce—'tis said one of his ancestors wed with a daughter of the devil—he is a fair man, evenhanded in his rule. His kingdom is huge, yet well run. Other than his appetite for women, which has not, despite his love for his wife, abated, I can find no fault in him. He is more kingly than Prince Eustace will ever be. That is why I will support Duke Henry. England will be in better hands, certainly stronger hands, with Duke Henry."

"Perhaps the king will agree to the church's compromise," Elf suggested hopefully.

Ranulf shook his head. "I doubt it," he said. "King Stephen is a stubborn man, and every bit as ambitious for his son as the Empress Matilda is for hers. At least when the time comes, my good lord will be dead and not know I cannot support his weakling offspring."

In the morning Ranulf de Glandeville and his guest walked out in the near meadow where the sheep grazed placidly. Elf watched them go, wishing she might hear the conversation, although she knew what her husband would say.

"You may tell your master, Duke Henry," Ranulf began, "that I will support his claim to England's throne upon the death of King Stephen, *but not before*. I cannot afford to make enemies of Prince Eustace and his friends. None of them is above setting the Welsh upon me in revenge. Ashlin has had a bounteous crop of lambs and calves this season. My fields are green with healthy new growth. I want to be able to harvest those fields, and take a fine large load of wool to the fair in Hereford come Lammastide. If my manor is attacked in an effort to redress what Eustace considers a wrong done to him by me, I will not be able to feed my people this winter next, and Duke Henry certainly will not."

"Your walls look strong," Sir Garrick noted with a small smile.

"My walls enclose the demesne only. My fields and my meadows are all open and not defendable, particularly with the crop half grown. The Welsh have left Ashlin in peace because they do not believe it to be worth their time and effort. I prefer they continue to believe that. I prefer that no one offer them coin to come here and ravage my lands. Your duke with his vast lands and his castles already lives like a king. There are only great estates on the other side of the channel. Here in England, however, while we have some great lords, there are many more small manors like mine, with little lordlings like me who work side by side with their people in the fields. If we can raise enough wheat, barley, and oats, enough food from our kitchen gardens, a bountiful crop in the orchards, enough livestock and poultry to keep us through a long winter, we consider ourselves blessed. Your duke must understand this is the way in England.

"I wonder if he does? He is surrounded by those who would please him, who say what he would have them say. They have power and wealth, and they seek to gain even more. I am a simple knight with a small manor. It is all I desire. Duke Henry will have my undying loyalty when he comes into power. I give you my bond, Sir Garrick, and my word has always been known to be good."

"Your reputation precedes you, Ranulf de Glandeville. I will tell Duke Henry what you have told me. They are truly the first honest words I have heard in months. The lords in this land blow with the wind. Few are as pure of heart as you have shown me you are. Neither you and your fair wife, nor your people will suffer for your words. Continue in your loyalty to King Stephen until the day he dies. After that you will be expected to come to Westminster to swear your fealty to your new king, Henry of Anjou."

"It is agreed," Ranulf said, and the two men clasped forearms in acknowledgment of the pledge given by Ashlin's lord, and accepted by Duke Henry's representative.

Several days later, given directions to Baron Hugh de Warenne and supplied with a few provisions, Sir Garrick Taliferro departed Ashlin.

"What will happen to the king's son?" Elf asked Ranulf. "Surely he will not simply give way to Duke Henry."

"Nay, he will not," Ranulf said. "He will fight, but he is no soldier as his father is. The duke will overcome him by force of arms. Then and only then will England have a king who has no rivals to breed up strife and warfare. Henry of Anjou will rule with an iron hand, petite, but we will finally have peace again in this land."

Shortly after Michaelmas came word that Prince Eustace had died suddenly—and quite unexpectedly. The word was brought to them by Hugh de Warenne himself, who rode over from his manor to tell Ranulf. Baron Hugh, a gossipy man, had heard the news from a passing peddler and hurried to inform his daughter's former in-laws. The peddler didn't know the date, but Eustace had died in August. The king, preparing to fight Duke Henry at that time, was a broken man. He agreed to the church's compromise. Henry of Anjou would be England's next king.

"And how is Isleen?" Elf asked sweetly.

"The bitch has run off," Baron Hugh said sourly. "We were hard-pressed to find a convent for her, but we finally had located one in York that would take her, although the fee was outrageous. Still, the king had commanded it. We told her it would not be for-ever, that when Duke Henry became king she would be released, but you know how impetuous Isleen can be. The day we were to leave for York, she was found to be missing."

"Poor Isleen," Elf said with false sweetness.

Baron Hugh ignored the remark and turned to Ranulf. "Sir Garrick visited you first, he said. You have, of course, pledged yourself to Duke Henry."

"My loyalty is always with England's king," Ranulf answered.

"But which king?" Hugh de Warenne pressed.

"God's own anointed king, my lord," Ranulf replied.

Annoyed he would get nothing of value or interest from the lord of Ashlin, Baron Hugh's gaze swung back to Elf. "You are not with child yet?" he asked boldly.

"I am young," Elf told him. "My children will come as God wills it, not a moment before."

"Still pious, I see," the baron said sneeringly.

"You will remember us to your good wife," Elf responded.

Dismissed, and with no further excuse to remain, Hugh de Warenne left.

"He is the most hateful man!" Elf said angrily the moment he rode through the gate.

Ranulf took her in his arms comfortingly. "The children will come, petite, and as you said, in God's own time. We have not even been wed a full year yet." He smoothed her hair. "And we are cer-tainly trying hard to fulfill God's will of us, eh?"

She laughed weakly, looking up at him with tear-filled eyes. "I never thought of children while I was in the convent. There was no point to such thoughts, but now I am a wife, and it is a wife's duty to conceive and bear young. Our pleasure in each other is so great that I sometimes feel guilty there is no fruit of our efforts. What if I am like Isleen, barren stock?"

"You are nothing like your brother's selfish wife, Eleanore," he soothed her.

"Do you want a son, Ranulf?"

"Every man wants a son . . . and a daughter just like her sweet mother, petite," he said honestly. "But if God does not bless us, then I am content to spend the rest of my life with you alone."

Elf burst into tears. "Living with you is a thousand times better than living as a nun!" She sobbed, then turned and fled him.

What had he said to make her cry, he wondered, puzzled. He shrugged with his inability to solve the conundrum and took himself out into the fields to help with the threshing.

Their harvest had been good. The grain storehouses were filled to capacity. The entire manor picked the orchard clean of apples and pears to be put away for the winter. The serfs' huts were all repaired where needed, and fresh thatch put upon the roofs. Arthur and his master, the miller, were kept busy grinding flour for several weeks. The slaughtering was done, the meat salted for future use. Wood was chopped and piled high. Ranulf declared that twice a month, on a day to be named, his serfs could hunt for rabbits and fish in his streams. A deer hunt was planned, and everyone on the estate anticipated the merry feast it would provide Christmastide.

In the manor court over which both the lord and lady presided each month, disputes were settled, fines levied, justice served. Ashlin prospered as it had never prospered before. There was even a stack of coins hidden in a sack behind a stone in the solar wall, for the Lammastide fair in Hereford had indeed proved profitable. The wool crop had been an excellent one.

Elf spent a good deal of time in her little herbarium making salves, lotions, ointments, and unguents for her infirmary. She dried flowers, bark, leaves, and roots that could later be brewed into healing teas, physics, and remedies for coughs and complaints of every nature. She harvested moss to dry and store for dressing wounds. Of late she had not felt particularly well herself. Everything the cook prepared seemed to disagree with her. She gained relief only by brewing up a mint tea, which she would sometimes sweeten with honey. She had six fine hives next to her herbarium, for honey was a wonderful healer when used in certain poultices and remedies.

Finally one rainy afternoon in October as Elf sat in the hall at her tapestry loom, Ida said sharply, "And just when do you intend to tell the master, lady?"

Elf looked up, her needle poised in midair. "Tell my lord what, old Ida?"

"Lady!" Ida was exasperated. "You are with child!"

"*I am with child?* Ida, how do you know this?" Her hand holding the needle fell on the tapestry.

"You have had no show of blood for two cycles now, lady. Have you not realized that? Certainly you are with child. A June baby, if I am not mistaken." The old woman cackled, delighted.

"Are you certain? This was not something that was spoken of at St. Frideswide's. The girls who were to wed were naturally instructed by their mothers before marriage. Ouch!" Elf popped a finger into her mouth, and sucked it for a moment. Innocence had its place in this world certainly, but hers was becoming a distinct and great disadvantage. How long would it have taken her to figure it out, she wondered, irritated. "Is there any other reason for my moon link to be unbroken?"

"Nay" came the answer. "Not until you are an old woman like me, and your flow ceases to be because you are no longer fertile. Such things do not happen to young girls like yourself, lady. Now, when will you tell the lord of this happy fortune?"

"Let us wait until a third cycle has passed me by," Elf said thoughtfully. "You will say nothing, old Ida. No broad hints, or knowing suggestive looks, either. I need more education in the matter."

"Then, speak with John's wife, Orva, lady. She is a mother, and a grandmother several times over. It is she who delivers all the babies born on the manor. She will deliver yours."

The very next day Elf carried a basket of apples and pears to her bailiff's cottage, which was a larger and better-built dwelling than an ordinary serf's. Seated outside her cottage sewing, Orva arose and curtsied.

"Good day, Orva," Elf said. "I have brought you a basket of fruit. I would speak with you."

"Come in, lady," the bailiff's wife invited, and when her guest had entered the cottage, Orva led her to a stool by the fire. "How may I help you, lady?"

"Having spent most of my life at St. Frideswide's, I know very little of the things ordinary women know," Elf began.

"You think you are with child," Orva said quietly.

"I thought nothing," Elf admitted. "It was old Ida who brought it to my attention. I feel very foolish, I must tell you."

"Nay, lady, you must not. Your upbringing, and the vocation planned for you would hardly include knowledge of this kind. Besides, most young women are never certain the first time they bear young," Orva said in motherly tones. "Now, tell me, lady, when was your last flow of blood?"

"Two weeks after Lammastide," Elf said. "There has been nothing at all since."

"Has your flow ever ceased since you began having a moon link?"

Elf shook her head in the negative.

"Have you noticed that perhaps your breasts are growing larger? Or that you suffer from nausea of late? Do certain foods repel you?"

"Yes! I noticed my breasts because when I wore my bliaut at Michaelmas, it was tight in the chest! I can hardly eat a thing these days. Only the mint tea I brew will bring me a measure of peace. And my nipples!" Here Elf blushed. "They have, of a sudden, become very, *very* sensitive."

Orva smiled wisely. "You are with child, lady. From the dates you give me, I would say the child is due at the very end of May, or in the first week of June. Your complaint of the belly will cease shortly, but your breasts will continue to grow larger as they prepare to nourish your child. Your belly will also swell as the child grows."

"What must I do?"

"Eat simply," Orva advised. "Avoid sauces and too much salt. And, lady, do not drink wine. Better you have beer to help enrich your milk, but only if it tastes good to you. I shall come to the manor house each morning, lady, to see how you are doing. Ask me any questions you desire, and do not fear to feel foolish. Only when you are my age with five living children, and seven grandchildren, can you claim to know a great deal, and even then"—she chuckled—"you discover each day how much you have left to learn."

"You will help me when my time comes?" Elf asked nervously.

"Lady, that is my responsibility here at Ashlin, to deliver the babies, but you would not know that having been away so long. I have delivered every child born here for the past twenty years, and before me, my mother did likewise. I delivered you, my lady."

"You did?" Elf's gray eyes grew wide with the knowledge. It was, she realized, extremely comforting to know this fact. Orva had brought her into the world, and Orva would bring her baby into it.

"Aye, I did," Orva said. "You are much like your mother, you know, but far prettier. She had an easy time with her confinements and her births. She looked delicate, but she was strong."

"Yet she had but two children, and Dickon and I were separated by ten years," Elf noted.

"Nay, lady," Orva corrected her. "Your mother bore six children, with you, the youngest. The first was Robert, named for your father. He died of a chill within the year of his birth. Then came the lord Richard. He was followed by two wee laddies, stillbirths both, born in the years your father was at war. How his going frightened your mother. She was not a wife who could send her man off bravely. Your sister, Adela, was born two years before you were. She was just beginning to walk when she was struck down by a spring epidemic of spotting sickness. Your mother was heartbroken, but by autumn that same year she was with child again, and that child was you!"

"I never knew Mama bore all those babies," Elf said thoughtfully. And what else had she missed? "How sad she lost them."

" 'Tis the way of the world, lady," Orva said pragmatically. "She wept as we all weep when we lose a child. It happens."

"It frightens me to think I might lose my child."

"You must not be frightened, lady," Orva advised. "Your mother had bad luck, that is all. Look at me. I have birthed five, and all five are grown and healthy, praise God! You do what I tell you, lady, and you will have a strong babe come next summer."

"Shall I tell my husband, or shall I wait until I have passed my next moon cycle?"

"That is your decision, lady. Sometimes with the first a woman likes to hoard the wonderful secret to herself for a time and not share it," Orva told her.

"One thing," Elf ventured, and she blushed. "Must we cease lovemaking until after the babe is born?"

"He is a big man, the lord, and you are a dainty lady; but if he is very careful, and you are not uncomfortable, I see no reason why you cannot continue on together. Tell the lord to come to me, and I will instruct him in certain ways that are safe as your belly grows larger and more unwieldy," Orva said.

Elf arose, smiling at the older woman. "I thank you, Orva. I was frightened, but now I am not."

"You should not be, lady. Bearing a child is the most wonderful and the most natural thing in the world for a woman to do. You are a wholesome and healthy girl. You will be fine. Do not, however, and I mean no disrespect, listen to my husband's mother. Old Ida means well, but her knowledge is not always sound."

Elf laughed. "She is very dour, filled with dire predictions, even if she doesn't utter most of them."

"How is Willa doing?" Orva asked. "She is my daughter, you know. Just a year younger than Arthur."

"Nay, I did not realize she was your daughter," Elf answered the older woman. "She is a good girl, and serves me well."

"I am glad of it, lady," Orva said, escorting her mistress outside again. "Oh, dear," she exclaimed, for about her cottage were a crowd of women, all anxiously looking toward them. "I should not have asked you inside, lady. We should have walked together in private. All these busybodies will have divined why you have come to see me. The manor will be rife with gossip by tonight, and there is nothing you can do to stop it. I think if you wish to tell your husband of his good fortune, you had best do it today. Do not be angry, lady, for these women mean well. They will rejoice with you that Ashlin is to have an heir of your body, that the line of Harold Strongbow, Rowena Strongbowsdatter, and her de Montfort lord continues through you."

Elf looked at all the anxious faces. They were kind faces, faces she knew. She began to laugh. "In June," she said, "but for sweet Mary's sake, do not gossip until I have had the opportunity to tell my husband."

"But when will you tell him?" the miller's wife asked boldly.

"I think it must be soon," Orva answered for Elf, "for here is the lord now, coming on the run. Someone has told him you were with me."

"Petite, are you all right?" Ranulf ran up to his wife, breathless.

"I am fine, my lord," Elf said calmly.

"But I was told you had come to see John's wife," he said nervously.

"Who else would I come to see but the midwife when I am expecting our child," Elf replied sweetly. "And just who told you I was here? As if I don't already know!" She feigned outrage.

"You are having a baby? *You are having a baby!*" he shouted, a wide grin splitting his face. Then he picked her up in his arms. "You must put no strain upon yourself, petite."

The women about them burst out into unrestrained laughter.

"Put me down, Ranulf," Elf said, laughing herself. "I am having a baby, the most natural of female talents. I am not ill, nor am I injured. Put me down this instant!"

Reluctantly he complied. "But should you not rest, Eleanore?"

"When she is tired, my lord, absolutely," Orva said with a reassuring smile. "She may live her life as normally as if she were not with child. At least for now. And as you are here, my lord, will you come into my cottage, for I would speak with you privately."

Elf grinned, and the women about them hooted with laughter

again, for their men had all received Orva's lectures and instructions when they were first with child.

Still chuckling—and feeling infinitely better—Elf walked back to the house whistling happily. She was not barren stock. She was not like her brother's wife. At the thought of Isleen de Warenne, a shiver ran down her spine. Elf shook it off quickly. Nothing could spoil her happiness. She was going to have a baby!

CHAPTER TEN

Clud, the whoremonger, raised his hand and hit the woman a third blow. "You will do as you are told, you English bitch!" he snarled.

Isleen de Warenne struggled to her feet, and hit her attacker so hard with both fists that the lame man staggered. "I am no common whore," she screamed at him.

"Perhaps not a *common* whore," Clud said, grabbing the woman by her long blond braid, "but a whore nonetheless. I bought you fairly, and now I will have a return on my investment."

"I am the daughter of Baron Hugh de Warenne! I am the widow of the lord of Ashlin," Isleen shrieked furiously. "I was only traveling with that peddler for protection. He had no right to sell me to you!"

"But he did, and now I will have my own, plus a goodly interest back from you. You will make me a fine profit before your looks go, you nasty-tempered bitch. Now you will do as I tell you, or I shall have you tied down and offered to whoever wants you. Do you know what that means, bitch? Plowboys and wanderers passing through will labor over your fair white body without ceasing until your sheath is so wide an army could march through it. Now, get on your back, bitch. The lord Merin ap Owen and his men are here for an evening's entertainment."

"*Never!*" Isleen shouted at Clud.

He raised his hand to her once again, but a voice stopped him.

"Nay, Clud, do not beat her senseless. You will spoil our enjoyment. We like a woman with spirit. Leave us now, and we will have our pleasure of the wench." The speaker was a tall, dark-haired man with a scar that ran from the corner of his left eye down to his chin. It spoiled his otherwise flawless features.

He smiled, and Isleen shivered. This, she sensed, was a very wicked man. "I am a nobleman's daughter," she said defiantly.

"How long do you want her?" the whoremonger asked.

Merin ap Owen handed Clud a heavy silver coin. "We will keep her for the whole night," he said, "and do not argue with me, for I will wager I have just given you double what you paid for her. You already have your profit, Clud."

"Do you mean to kill her then?" the whoremonger wondered aloud.

Merin ap Owen laughed heartily. "Only with our kindness, Clud. Only with our kindness. Now, get out, but send some wine in here."

"Yes, my lord! At once!" Clud said, and he limped out.

Merin ap Owen looked Isleen up and down in a leisurely fashion. "So you say you are a nobleman's daughter, wench. On the wrong side of the blanket, of course. Some serf's get, eh?"

"I am rightfully born," Isleen responded. "What serf's bastard would have my fine features, or my beautiful golden hair?"

"Remove your chemise," Merin ap Owen said.

"No!"

His hand shot out swiftly, hooking into the neckline of the garment and rending it quickly to the hem.

"It is my only chemise," she shouted.

"If you did not wish it destroyed, you should have obeyed me," he said quietly. "You can repair it, provided you remove it now before my men and I rip it to pieces entirely."

Isleen's blue eyes were wide with shock. Looking into his face, she knew he would do exactly as he had said, and so without further argument, she eased carefully from the chemise, setting it aside in a corner of the room. She was totally naked now, for all of her clothing except the chemise had been previously taken from her.

"She has fine big tits, my lord," one of his companions said admiringly.

"That she does," Merin ap Owen agreed, and his hand closed about Isleen's right breast, squeezing it hard. Then he looked directly at her. "But I am being discourteous, lady. I have not introduced myself. I am Merin ap Owen, the lord of this small region. These are three of my best men. Badan, whose name means *boar*. Gwyr, whose name means *pure*, and he is purely wicked, aren't you, Gwyr? And, last, but certainly not least, as you will soon discover, Siarl, whose name means *manly*. These three have pleased me greatly, and so we have come for a night's entertainment, which you will provide, my pretty bitch."

"My name is Isleen de Warenne," she told him in an even voice. Her blue eyes locked onto Merin ap Owen's darker blue eyes. Her first reaction was to be terrified, but these men, she sensed, would enjoy that. She would show no fear before them. What they wanted of her was nothing unusual, and she wasn't a virgin. Four men in a single evening. She had never imagined she would do such a thing, but why not? "If you squeeze my breast much harder, Merin ap Owen, my nipple will pop off. Release it. I can already feel the bruise starting," she said coldly.

"Ah," he said, now more interested in the woman than he had been before, "you are not afraid, my pretty bitch. That is good. We will have far more fun if you are willing, than unwilling. There is too much difficulty in restraining a woman while you're having at her."

At that point a frightened-looking girl lifted the curtain of the alcove and scurried in with a full skin of wine, which she hung on a nail protruding from the wall. Then she scampered out.

"I've never had more than one man," Isleen said bluntly.

"*At a time,* you mean," Merin ap Owen corrected her. She might indeed be a nobleman's daughter, for all he knew, but she was also a born whore. Of that he was quite certain. She had

the look. Lush and lewd. Releasing her breast he took the wineskin, and squirted the sour brew down his parched throat. "Who
wants her first?" he asked, handing off the skin. "Can you agree, or
shall you dice for her? I will have her last." He pulled Isleen into
their midst. "Come on, my pretty bitch, and show my men what a
good time they're going to have. Go on, laddies, she's yours for the
taking."

Caught between the three men Isleen swallowed back a moment of panic. Hands began to roam over her body. Her blond
head was drawn back, and a mouth came down on hers; a tongue
pushed between her lips. She felt fingers exploring her mont,
pushing between her nether lips, and into her sheath. Isleen sighed
with undisguised pleasure, and wiggled hard against the invading
hand. If she could keep them all in check, and from being too
rough with her, this could prove as diverting for her as it was going
to be for them. Two hands slid about to fondle her breasts. Isleen
pushed her rounded bottom back onto the groin belonging to the
hands. *"Ooooooo,"* she murmured pulling away from the kisser, "that's
a nice big one. Do you want to put it in me?"

"Aye," a voice growled in her ear. "Let's dice, boys, before I explode. The bitch is hot, and so am I!"

A pair of dice and a cup dropped on the dirt floor, and the three
men fell to their knees to play. Isleen smiled, and looked directly
into the eyes of Merin ap Owen. He nodded slightly, a faint smile
playing about his mouth. Isleen smiled back, her little pink tongue
licking her lips slowly in a deliberate provocation. He laughed.

"I win!" came the shout, and Siarl scrambled to his feet only to
be pulled back again.

"Not until we see who goes second, and then third," Badan said.
"The bitch got me so hard, I'm all an ache with my lust."

The dice rattled in their cup again. The decision was finally
made. Siarl would go first. Badan second, and Gwyr third. The men
stood up, their hands loosening their clothing as they did. Isleen lay
down upon the pallet on the floor, spreading herself wide.

"All right," she said bluntly, "let's get to it, *manly one,* although I
shall certainly be the judge of that."

"You'll not find me wanting," Siarl said, falling to his knees between her outstretched thighs, and he pulled out his manhood to show her.

"It's a respectable cock," Isleen said in a slightly bored tone, "but 'tis how you use it, Siarl. Now, stuff me full, and make me sing!" she told him with unladylike indelicacy.

Siarl fell upon Isleen, ramming himself into her with a groan, and pumping her over, and over, and over again.

The other three men watched, Merin ap Owen impassively, Gwyr and Badan with increasing excitement, their manhoods exposed, hard, and throbbing. The lord caught the eye of his two men. "She can take two," he said softly. "You are second, Badan, are you not? Go on."

Badan needed no further encouragement. Kneeling behind Isleen's head, he rubbed his cock over her lips. Sloe-eyed, Isleen gazed up at him, then opening her mouth took him in and began to suck even as her hips met each downward thrust by Siarl. The two men sweated and groaned as their lusts rose, and rose, finally bursting almost simultaneously. Each man rolled away from her, panting with exhaustion as Gwyr fell upon the inviting woman. He was a small man, but he had boundless energy, and within minutes he had Isleen howling with pleasure. And when he had taken his own pleasure, Gwyr bounded up with a grin.

"Well, she is as good a mount as I ever rode, my lord. I wish you even better joy of her!"

"Give me some wine, you pigs," Isleen groaned, and they complied with her request. After all, the night was young yet, she thought, and it would be hours before the dawn. Isleen greedily swallowed the bitter brew. Then to their surprise she squirted the wine between her nether lips, put the skin snout into her sheath, and flushed out their seed. The three men watched her wide-eyed. "Well," she snapped at them, "I don't intend getting diseased, or having one of your bastards." Her gaze swung to Merin ap Owen. "Are you ready now?" she demanded boldly of him.

He nodded, unsmiling. "Bend over," he commanded, and then to his men, "Hold her down."

"What are you doing?" Isleen shrieked, struggling to conceal the terror that suddenly arose in her breast. With difficulty she turned her head to see him. He had in his hands a leather strap.

"Legs wide apart, Isleen," he commanded.

She quickly obeyed, realizing resistance in this case was futile and could bring out the coldness in him even further. *This was a man,* she thought, awed, and already half in love with him. The leather strap cracked and made contact with her buttocks. Isleen shrieked.

Merin ap Owen made a disparaging noise. "Come, now, my pretty bitch, you are stronger than that. I gave you but a love tap on your prettily rounded rump. Certainly you've been beaten before."

"Never!" she said. *"Never!"*

"Not your father, or your husband, or your lovers beat you?" he asked, disbelieving. "Well, my pretty bitch, I am going to beat you. Not to punish you, or break your will, but so you may better learn to enjoy pleasure through pain." He raised his arm, and brought it down again.

Isleen grit her teeth, stifling her cry. The strap didn't hurt so much as it burned. As he delivered blow after blow to her buttocks, she began to feel as if they were afire, and then the fire was banked, leaving just a wickedly delicious warmth to her bottom, but a raging inferno of lust elsewhere. She moaned, yet the sound was not one of pain. It was one of desire.

Merin ap Owen smiled, satisfied. "Release her. On your hands and knees, Isleen," he commanded her, and as she obeyed, he slid to his own knees directly behind her, his cock at the ready. He rubbed it between her nether lips, moistening it, then he placed it against the rosy aperture between her buttocks.

"Wh-what are you doing?" Isleen squeaked as his hands tightened about her hips.

"Has no man ever gone this way, Isleen?" he demanded. "Are you a virgin in your bottom hole?"

"Yes!" she gasped, feeling him pushing himself slowly into her body. *"Yes, damn you!"*

"How perfect," Merin ap Owen said, and then he thrust himself deep into her, smiling as she screeched her outrage. "*Ahhh, you are delicious,*" he complimented, drawing himself out, then driving back in once again. "Cease your caterwauling, my pretty bitch, and let your body speak to your mind. There," he complimented her as she stopped her struggles. Then he began a rhythmic motion against her, and was pleased when within moments her bottom was pushing back against his groin. "Good! Good, my pretty bitch! You are enjoying this, aren't you, Isleen? This is wicked, and this is forbidden, and you like it!"

"*Yes!*" she half sobbed.

He laughed aloud, his cock flashing back and forth until his lust erupted, and he flooded her body. "You'll get no brats from me, Isleen," he said into her ear.

"You bastard!" she snarled at him angrily as he moved away from her, and she collapsed facedown upon the straw pallet. Her back channel ached with his unaccustomed invasion, but damn him, it had been exciting! Yet she was still boiling with a hunger that was going to consume her. She rolled over to glare up at him, and Badan fell upon her once again. She wrapped her legs about him, and encouraged him onward to his best efforts. He did not disappoint her.

"How fortuitous," Merin ap Owen purred as he watched the pair. "A bitch who cannot get enough cock, but the night is yet young, my friends."

Still, when the long night was over, Isleen had not been broken, nor was she apt to be, the lord of the region thought. While she slept surrounded by his three men, Merin ap Owen rearranged his clothing so that it had a semblance of order, and left the small chamber to seek Clud, the whoremonger. He found him seated outside of his house upon a bench, drinking, while he fondled a young whore who sat on his knee. Reaching into the purse that hung from his girdle, Merin ap Owen drew out two silver coins. He was not of a mind to argue or haggle with Clud. He held out the coins, and Clud's grimy hand opened greedily.

Still retaining possession of the coins, Merin ap Owen said, "I am taking Isleen with me when I leave this morning." It was a statement of fact. He then dropped the two coins into Clud's outstretched hand.

The whoremonger's fingers closed swiftly about the silver. "She's yours, lord. She would have been trouble for me. You, however, know how to tame a bitch."

"She is not tamed, nor ever likely to be," Merin ap Owen said. "That is why I want her. She's greedy, venal, I suspect, and as dangerous as a mad dog. Yet she suits my fancy for now. Fetch a tub of hot water into her chamber, and bring her her own clothing and a new chemise. First tell my men to return to the castle, and then see to her."

Clud got to his feet, dumping the girl in his lap to the ground. "Aye, my lord, at once!"

"I'll be back at noon," Merin ap Owen said. "Let her sleep for a time, but see she is ready and waiting for me when I come."

"Yes, my lord!" Clud bowed obsequiously several times.

With a sardonic smile upon his lips, Merin ap Owen turned from the whoremonger and walked away. "At noon," he repeated.

"At noon, my lord," Clud called after him.

Isleen awoke as the tub was dragged into the chamber where she slept. She groaned, tired and sore. Lifting her head, she rolled over. The men were gone now, and only the frightened-looking little wench who was the servant girl in the brothel was there. "What is the hour?" she demanded of the girl.

"Almost two hours past Terce," the servant replied. "Master says you are to bathe. Lord Merin will return for you at noon. He bought you from the master. Your clothing is there. I repaired your chemise. Hurry, lady! You dare not keep the lord waiting."

Isleen smiled a feline smile. So the bastard had bought her from the whoremonger. Why? To be the castle whore for his men? That would be just like him, for Isleen had quickly learned Merin ap Owen was a cruel man. Or did he want her for himself? Pray God that was it. She had not given quarter last night. She would not give any now. The Welsh lordling was her chance to have her revenge upon her meek little sister-in-law, the holy Eleanore. If it hadn't been for the little nun, Saer de Bude would now be lord of Ashlin and she, waiting in the wings, would have soon again been Ashlin's lady. She had wanted to be her cousin's wife since she was a child. It was Eleanore de Montfort's fault she was not, nor was ever likely to be now. So she would revenge herself upon the little bitch, and she would use this Merin ap Owen to accomplish her goal.

Isleen bathed herself carefully with the primitive accoutrements provided by Clud. She washed her long golden hair, drying it by the charcoal brazier the servant had brought her to warm the room. Slowly she combed through her hair, freeing it of tangles, combing, combing, combing until it was almost dry. Parting her hair in the center, she wound it into a thick coil at the base of her neck and affixed it with her hairpins. "Find me some scented oil," she told the servant.

"There is no such stuff in this place," the girl said.

"Your master does not know how to run a proper brothel," Isleen said irritably.

" 'Tis the finest brothel in Gwynfr."

" 'Tis the *only* brothel in Gwynfr," Isleen sneered. Then she dressed herself in her sky blue skirts and blue and gold tunic top.

"Ahhh," the girl said admiringly, "I have never seen anything so fine, lady. May I touch it?"

Isleen nodded, amused by the girl's naïveté.

The girl fingered the fine material, then she said, "You are surely the most beautiful lady I have ever seen. If you go with Lord Merin, you will need a serving woman. There are none at Gwynfr Castle, I swear it! I can sew, and do your hair." Her plain face was hopeful.

"Are you a whore?" Isleen asked.

"Nay!" the girl denied vehemently. "Clud is my uncle, and when my mother died, he took me in to serve, but I am no whore. I will swear it on the Blessed Virgin's name!"

Isleen was thoughtful. The girl was plain enough to attract no attention. She was clever enough to want to advance herself, yet meek enough to be controlled easily. She was familiar with the region and all the people. She could prove a useful ally. "Are you freeborn or serf?" she asked the girl. If she was a serf, Isleen would have to wheedle Merin into purchasing her.

"I am freeborn," the girl said, "for all the good it has ever done me, lady. I will serve you well."

"What is your name?"

"Arwydd."

Isleen laughed. The wench was a sly thing. "Gather your things, Arwydd," she told the girl.

"I'm wearing them," Arwydd said wryly.

Isleen looked scornfully at the girl's soiled and sweat-stained garments. "This will not do," she said. "Go and fetch your uncle."

Arwydd ran out, returning a few minutes later with Clud.

The whoremonger looked Isleen over appreciatively, licking his lips as he did so. "Perhaps I am selling you too cheap," he said.

"Whatever Merin ap Owen paid you was too much," Isleen said dryly. "Now, I am taking Arwydd with me, for I must have a servant. Get her some clean clothing, you tightfisted old bastard. She stinks of a year's worth of slave labor, labor you have undoubtedly not paid her for at Michaelmas. Now you don't have to pay her. Just clothe her decently, and I will take her with me. It cannot hurt you to have your niece in service at Gwynfr Castle."

"I have fed her and housed her," Clud whined.

"Indeed. Now, do as I say. I shall also do something else for you, Clud, but first Arwydd's garments. Hurry!" She turned to her servant as Clud hurried out. "Take those stinking rags off and get into the tub, girl. If you are going to serve me, you must be clean."

Arwydd didn't argue. She stripped off her filthy gown, and climbed into the tub to wash herself and her hair. Clud returned with a clean chemise, skirt, and tunic top. Isleen looked them over critically. They were lacking in style, but had one advantage. They were clean. The skirt and top were a medium blue. He laid them on the stool by the tub, leering at his niece's naked bosom.

"Come outside with me," Isleen commanded him. "Arwydd, do not dally, or I will leave you behind." The curtain of the room flapped down, and they stood in the narrow hall of the building. "You have absolutely no idea of how to run a brothel," Isleen told him. "Once I have settled myself with Merin ap Owen, and my position is secure, I shall tell you what to do, and if you do what I tell you, you will be a rich man within a year, Clud."

"And what would a nobleman's daughter know about such things?" He snarled at her. "If you are indeed who you say you are."

"Oh, I am," Isleen assured. "As for what I know, I am a woman. I know men. If all you ever hope to serve are serfs and poor freemen, then continue as you are. But if you wish to add the rich, both free and noble, to your clientele, then you will do what I tell you. Men like beautifully adorned women and sweet scents. They like soft beds and fine wine. Save the sour grape and the pallets for your poorer clients, but learn to service the rich, and your fortune is made."

"And what will you gain for your trouble?" he asked her.

"A small remuneration, Clud, but there is no need for us to discuss that now, is there? First you must see that I speak the truth. Then we will talk about what my aid is worth to you." She smiled sweetly.

Instinct told him not to trust her, yet he was intrigued by her words. He heard himself saying, "Very well, *lady*."

"I am ready, mistress." Arwydd lifted the curtain separating the chamber from the hall, and stepped out. She was clean, her black hair braided into two plaits, her blue eyes alive with hope.

Isleen nodded approvingly. "Excellent," she said. "Now, let us go and await Merin ap Owen's return."

They had hardly stepped outside the door when the lord of Gwynfr came down the street upon a large warhorse. Stopping before Clud's house, he reached a hand down to Isleen and pulled her up onto his saddle.

"I am taking the girl, Arwydd, with me as my servant," Isleen told him.

Merin ap Owen looked down at the slight girl. "Go up to the castle, wench. Tell the steward you are her servant, and he will take you to her chamber."

"Yes, my lord." Arwydd curtsied.

Merin ap Owen turned his mount, and rode off with Isleen. "I was not wrong," he said. "You are a very beautiful woman."

"Am I your whore, or the castle whore?" she demanded of him.

The Welshman laughed heartily. "You do not dissemble daintily, Isleen, do you? You are my whore until I decide otherwise. Occasionally, however, I may loan you to an important visitor whom I wish to particularly please. When this happens, Isleen, you will give my guest a night of ecstasy such as he has never known, so that come the morning he will be amenable to whatever it is I desire. Do you understand?"

"Aye," she said. "It is a clear path you have laid out for me, but I want something in return."

"What?" His eyes were curious.

"The man who sold me to Clud had not the right to do so. I am freeborn. You know this to be so, don't you?"

He nodded.

"I will not grow rich in your service, Merin ap Owen, and I must be rich to be independent. I must have a means of earning monies."

He was absolutely fascinated. "Go on," he said, guiding his horse down the narrow street.

"Gwynfr is on the road to Hereford. An invasion road for both the Welsh and the English. Clud has the only brothel in Gwynfr, yet he knows not how to manage it. Only a lord as corrupt and debauched as you would inhabit such a place. But what if Clud's brothel was elegant enough to serve the rich? Not only plowboys and men-at-arms, but men of substance, and lords. I have offered to aid Clud in attaining such a goal. It will not interfere with any of my duties for you, my lord, I promise. I will do all that you tell me, if I can but use my own time to help Clud."

"And what will you gain in return, Isleen?" She was delicious. She was as evil a woman as he had ever known.

"Nothing at first, my lord, for I must make Clud open his tight fist so we may improve his premises in order that important men seek it out. Then, too, we must find the best and most skilled of whores. And you, my lord"—she leaned against him, and purred in his ear—"you will personally examine each of our prospective jades, so we may be certain they are worthy." Her tongue dipped into his ear, and swirled about it for a moment. "Later, when I have proved to Clud that I can deliver on my promises, I shall take half of the brothel and its profits for myself."

"And eventually cheat the unsuspecting Clud out of his half," Merin ap Owen said, chuckling darkly.

"Of course, my lord," Isleen said in a hard voice. "You don't expect me to go to all that trouble just to enrich that creature?"

Merin ap Owen laughed heartily. "Evil!" he chortled. "You are pure evil, my beautiful Isleen. We shall make a perfect couple. I may even marry you someday."

"No, thank you," Isleen said. "I've had a father, a husband, and a lover or two along the way. I don't intend to be any man's possession ever again, my lord! I shall, however, revenge myself upon my late husband's family, and then settle down to being the richest whoremonger in Wales. *And I shall not be unmindful of your help.*"

He laughed harder. Every word out of her mouth pleased him. As a rule he didn't like women. They were sly and deceitful creatures. Until today there had been no woman in his castle since his bitch of a mother had died. His first wife, a girl of fourteen, he had killed with his depravity. His second, seventeen the day she wed him, had fled to a convent a month after their wedding. He was notified that the marriage was legally dissolved by the church. Her family had not asked for her dower portion back. He later learned that his second wife had been pregnant with his child when she ran away. No sooner had she birthed his son, than she drowned him; but fortunately for her family, she killed herself also. No, women were not to be trusted.

And here was Isleen. Every bit as wicked as he was himself. She made no secret of it, either. She was, he decided, the first honest woman he had ever met, although he would not be fool enough to trust her, either.

"Do you like beating women?" she asked him frankly.

"Just enough to increase their pleasure . . . and mine," he admitted.

"Do you always use that strap?"

"I like a nice thin and whippy hazel switch, too," he replied. "It cuts sharply, but if plied carefully doesn't leave scars."

"Can a woman whip a man, my lord?"

"Yes. There are men who enjoy being beaten, but I am not one of them," he answered her.

Isleen nodded. "Could you teach me? That might prove an interesting diversion for my whores. It would give us a uniqueness."

"You have a head for business," he noted.

"I have an instinct for it, it is true, but no real head for it. I cannot read or write."

"Neither can I," he said quietly, "but I think you must learn, for it would not do to have some scribe cheat you. *Or me.*"

"You want a part of my brothel?" she said, surprised.

"Of course, my pretty bitch," he told her. "If I help you, and I will if you continue to please me, then I must certainly have some part of the rewards. It is only fair."

Isleen pouted a moment, and then her common sense overcame her greed. "Very well," she agreed.

They had reached the castle now. The street had wound up a hill to where it was located. It was small and, from the look of it, not in particularly good condition. The drawbridge and the portcullis, however, were in excellent repair. Inside the courtyard he drew the horse to a halt, and dismounted, lifting Isleen down.

"I will take you to your chamber," he said.

Gwynfr Castle had but two towers. They were connected by the great hall. He led her into one of the towers, and up three flights of stairs. Her chamber, she discovered, was at the top of the tower. It was light, but scantily furnished. There was a fireplace for warmth.

"Where do you reside?" she asked him.

"In the apartment below you, my pretty bitch."

She nodded. She must remain faithful to him unless he chose otherwise, for to get to her, a man must go past his chambers. "If you desire me to entertain a favored gust, my lord, am I to bring him here or elsewhere?"

"I house my guests in the other tower. You will always be sent to await the visitor. You may explore tomorrow to your heart's content, Isleen."

"And when you desire me?"

"I will come here, of course," he told her. "My chambers are for me alone, Isleen. No one enters them but me."

"Who cleans and changes the linen for you?" she demanded.

"It is taken care of. How, is not your concern."

"And what will my exact position here be? Am I your mistress? If so, what are my duties? Do you desire me to oversee your servants? Your cook? I want no misunderstanding between us."

"I have a steward, an old man, who has been in the castle all of his life. He oversees everything, and is quite capable. His name is Harry. You are to do nothing but keep yourself in readiness for my lust, and be an amusing and charming companion when I so desire you to be. Harry will give you whatever you desire to keep you content."

"I want a promise from you right now," Isleen said. "Arwydd is not to be accosted by you or your men. She is no good to me with a big belly. As Clud's niece, she is invaluable to me in more ways than just that of a serving wench. I need her, my lord. She is a clever girl. Promise me she will be left alone."

"Lift your skirts," he commanded her in reply.

Isleen did not hesitate. She raised her skirts high, revealing her naked body beneath. He knelt before her, and using his fingers to open her, began making love to her with his tongue. Isleen closed her eyes, and breathed a deep sigh of pleasure. When he had brought her to a tingling peak, he stood up and pulled his manhood from his disarranged clothes. Isleen knew what was expected without any command being made. Dropping her skirts she knelt before him and, taking him in her mouth, roused him further with her lips and tongue until he commanded her to stop. Pulling her up, he pushed her back upon the bed and, thrusting her skirts up, drove himself into her. She wrapped her stockinged legs about him, her heels beating a tattoo upon his buttocks as he pistoned her. He was a tireless lover, slowly bringing her to her crisis. Then to her amazement, for he had done so last night to her surprise, though she thought it coincidence, peaking exactly as she did. Immediately, however, he arose from her, pulling her skirts down and offering her a hand to arise.

"Tell your wench not to flirt with my men. Not even to look them in the eye, for they are a randy bunch. If she obeys you, she will be safe from my men. The only man in the castle she may trust unwaveringly is old Harry, the steward. Remember that, my pretty bitch."

"What of the three who were with you last night, my lord?"

"They will never make eye contact with you, Isleen. They know if they do they will be killed. They spent a night in paradise. Now they must forget that paradise ever existed. Did any of them please you? Was there one who stood out among the trio?"

"Only you please me, my lord," Isleen murmured softly.

"Especially when I strapped you, and took your bottom," he said with a wicked smile.

"Yes," she admitted. "It was exciting. Will you do it again?"

"When it pleases me, Isleen. You must learn to give pleasure to a man in as many ways as you can. And you must be completely obedient to your lord's wishes, but I think you already are dutiful in matters of the flesh. Are you not?"

"Aye," she said.

"Raise your skirts up again," he said.

She obeyed.

"Bend over," he commanded, and again she obeyed. Taking her beneath his arm, he spanked her bottom several hard, stinging blows. Then his fingers delved between her nether lips, and he smiled a wicked smile. "You are very dutiful," he murmured as his wet fingers came about and pushed into her fundament.

Isleen squealed, and wiggled her bottom lustfully. "Oh, yes!"

"I have always told myself there is no such thing as a perfect woman, my pretty bitch," Merin ap Owen said as the two fingers thrust back and forth within her narrow channel, "but I think you may actually be perfect, Isleen."

Her body shuddered with its new release, and she sagged against him, panting. "*Ohhh,* that was good, my lord, but tonight I want your hard cock there!" He was a wonderful lover, she thought. Much better than her cousin, Saer de Bude. Still, she would not give up her plans for revenge against Eleanore de Montfort. She would enslave Merin ap Owen with her body. Perhaps he would even fall in love with her. And then she would cajole him into attacking Ashlin, into destroying everything that the little nun and her knightly husband had built up. She knew of Ashlin's prosperity. Her father had pointed it out enough to her.

"Ranulf de Glandeville has managed to make Ashlin thrive. If you had concerned yourself with helping Richard instead of lusting after your cousin, things might have been different," Baron Hugh had grumbled. "Why they actually made a profit on their wool at the Lammas Fair. But no! You could not be bothered to be a good wife. To give your husband children. Perhaps you are barren like Saer says, you useless bitch! Now you have brought shame upon the family, so much so, that the king has ordered you punished. Well, I've finally found a convent that will take you in York. They understand the situation. You will be locked in a chastity belt, you wretched bitch, and you will work and pray without ceasing for the rest of your life! They have brown woolen robes they wear year-round. Without chemises, Isleen, in order that the itching of the wool mortify the wickedness of the flesh. You will be fed but once a day, at noon. The food is simple and wholesome. There is no wine, and little meat or cheese. And once I have left you there, my daughter, I hope never to see you again!"

"But you promised I should only be incarcerated until King Stephen died," Isleen wailed.

"I have changed my mind," Baron Hugh said.

Isleen had escaped from her father's house that night. He probably thought her dead by now, but she was not dead. She was alive, and she intended on having her revenge, even if she had to give up her immortal soul to obtain her victory.

PART III
THE WIFE
England 1154

CHAPTER ELEVEN

The winter passed quietly. There was more than enough food for the people of Ashlin and for their livestock. April flew by, and May first came again. On this birthday Elf was great with her child, and every little thing seemed to aggravate her. No one, even Ranulf, dared to forbid her when she decided to travel to St. Frideswide's one mid-May afternoon.

"Do you think it wise?" the lord of Ashlin ventured in his only attempt to stop her.

Elf glared at him. "I have been cooped up here all winter, my lord. I have no one to talk to but Willa and old Ida, who fills my ears with dire predictions with every breath I draw. I will take Orva and Willa with me in case of any emergency, but there will be no emergency. I want to see my friends again!"

"The cart must be well padded," he insisted.

"Whatever will relieve your mind, my lord," she snapped.

"And you will have an escort of armed men, petite."

"Naturally."

"I am not happy that you go."

"It is unfortunate that my desire to see friends disturbs you so, my lord," she replied in acid tones.

Willa touched the lord's arm gently and said, "Orva says a woman near her time can become cranky, my lord. The lady means no disrespect, I am certain."

"You will remember me to the abbess, petite," Ranulf said to his wife. "And to Sisters Winifred and Columba, too." He grinned at her.

"Of course," Elf said shortly.

The cart that Elf traveled in was well padded in thick wool upholstered with blue silk. It had a red-and-blue-striped silk awning over it with side curtains that would roll down in the event of a heavy rainstorm. The awning was waxed to prevent the rain's penetration. Elf was most comfortable sitting with her legs up now. Orva and Willa rode next to the cart, which was surrounded by half-a-dozen men-at-arms. They departed Ashlin in the morning, arriving at the convent in late afternoon. The men-at-arms left them at St. Frideswide's gate, returning home. A nun hurried forth to lead the cart horse into the cloister, its driver having departed in the company of the men-at-arms.

The cart came to a stop, its back gate was lowered, and Elf was helped down by her two women.

"Elf!" Sister Columba came running toward her friend, her dark robes flying. "Oh, Elf! It is so good to see you again!" the young nun exclaimed. She set Elf back, and looked at her. "Mary have mercy! You are huge! He'll be every bit as big as his father, I vow!"

"How I'm going to birth him, I do not know," Elf grumbled. Then she laughed. "It is good to be back," she said happily.

"Come along, and I'll take you to the guest house," Sister Columba said. "You will have it all to yourself."

"Most guests visiting St. Frideswide's usually do." Elf chuckled. "These are my servants, Willa and Orva. Orva is the manor midwife. I thought it better I travel with her."

"Are you that near your time?" Sister Columba said, eyes wide.

"Aye," Elf told her. "I probably shouldn't have come, but I couldn't stand being boxed up at Ashlin one more moment. Then Ranulf attempted to play the lord and master. It was simply too much! Besides, I needed to see you and the others. I have not been back to St. Frideswide's since we returned to Worcester. It's been a year and a half!"

They reached the guest house, and Sister Columba ushered them inside. "What is it like being married, Elf?"

"Very nice," Elf told her, then turned to her servants. "Orva, Willa. Unpack my things, if you please. We will sleep in the dormitory through that door." She pointed. "Sister Columba and I are going to walk in the cloister garden. The bell will sound for the meal shortly. Listen for it." Then Elf hooked her arm through Sister Columba's, and the two young women walked outside of the guest house.

"You have grown so authoritative," the nun noted.

Elf laughed. "I have to be. I am the lady of the manor," she told her friend. "Now, let me tell you about being married. My husband is a kind man with a good heart. He is a fine lord, and our people respect him greatly. My life is a round of daily duties, very much like living here at St. Frideswide's. There is a time for planting and harvesting; for slaughtering and threshing; for making soaps and preserving foods. We have done much at Ashlin since I returned, not the least of which was restoring the manor church. We appealed to the bishop of a new priest, and Father Oswin was sent us in late autumn."

"Then, you are happy," Sister Columba said quietly.

"Aye," Elf told her best friend. "I am very happy, Matti. When I was torn from this life I believed I was to lead, and given to be Ranulf's wife, I thought I should never be happy again, but I am. I am happier than I have ever been in my whole life."

"Do you love him?"

"Aye, I do, though I have never said it to him."

"Why in heaven's name not?"

"Ranulf is a battle-hardened warrior, Matti. Sweet sentiment does not reside in his breast. I should embarrass him if I said I loved him," Elf said with a small smile. "What could he possibly say to me in return? We like each other, and I respect him. We have a good marriage."

"If you said you loved him, he might just return the sentiment," Sister Columba said hopefully.

"But what if he does not? I would discomfit him, and he would be abashed, for he would not harm me knowingly. Nay, it is better things remain as they are."

"I would want my husband to know I loved him," Sister Columba said firmly. "I tell our dear Lord each day of my love for him."

"But it is God you love, Matti. My love is all too human, and my husband would be quite confounded to hear me whispering sweet nothings into his ear." She chuckled.

"Eleanore."

The two young women looked up to see the abbess approaching, her hands outstretched in greeting. Elf took the Reverend Mother Eunice's hands in hers. The abbess looked her former charge over carefully, and then she smiled warmly.

"It is as I said to you that day in Worcester, Eleanore. God has changed your fate. That you bloom with new life, and are so filled with smiles is proof in itself, although I never doubted."

"I'm afraid I did for a time," Elf replied with a wry grin, "but my fine husband won me over."

"The king, while not a wise man, is a good one. I knew he would not give you into rough hands," Reverend Mother Eunice said. "But, surely, my daughter, you are near your time."

"I am," Elf responded, "but I needed to come home again before my girlhood disappears entirely, and I find myself someone's mother."

The two nuns laughed. "Isa did the same thing, although she was not near as far gone as you."

"Has Isa had her baby?" Elf asked. "I did not know."

"A little girl, last year, and she is again with child," Sister Columba replied.

Elf smiled.

For the next several days, Elf picked up her old life, attending the various religious services and helping old Sister Winifred. Her former mentor was teaching a young novice the duties of an infirmarian and herbalist.

"You have your own garden?" the elderly nun queried Elf.

"I do. I have been fortunate in that I have had only minor complaints, simple wounds, and a few broken bones to care for at Ash-lin. I dread a full-blown epidemic."

"You are up to it," Sister Winifred said. "Ahh, child, how it does my heart good to see you again!"

Elf remained at St. Frideswide's for over a week. The morning she was to depart for Ashlin, she arose, and no sooner had she done so when a sudden gush of water poured down her legs. Elf stared, shocked. *"Orva!"* she called in a strangely weak voice. *"Orva!"*

"Mary, Mother of God, protect us all," Orva said, coming and seeing her mistress standing stock-still amid a puddle of fluid. Then her common sense took hold. "Well, lady, there is no help for it. Your child will be born today, and here at St. Frideswide's, it would seem." She held up her hand, seeing the question in Elf's eyes. "Nay, there is no time to return to Ashlin. Traveling when a woman is in labor is too dangerous. The lord would kill us all if anything happened to you or the child. This place is every bit as good as Ash-lin for birthing your babe, perhaps even better. Willa! Come and help the mistress while I go and tell the abbess."

Orva trotted out of the convent guest house, and made her way across the cloister to the chapter house, where she knew the abbess could be found conducting convent business. The morning meet-ing was just coming to an end when she hurried to the abbess's seat of office. She curtsied.

"Yes, Orva?" the abbess said.

" 'Tis my lady, Reverend Mother. She is going to have her baby. I should appreciate some assistance."

"Oh, dear," the abbess said, momentarily disconcerted. But then she smiled a broad smile that few within her world had ever seen. "My sisters," she called out to them. "A baby is to be born here within our convent this day. Sister Winifred, please give all aid and assistance to Orva. The rest of you pray for the safe delivery of Eleanore's child, and her safety through the travails of childbirth as well. You are all dismissed now."

"Mother?" Sister Columba spoke hesitantly.

The abbess looked at the young nun, then patted her arm. "Go and be with your friend," she said in kindly tones. "Keep us informed, Columba."

"Yes, Reverend Mother."

"I will come to the guest house with what you need," old Sister Winifred said to Orva, and she moved off.

"I'll come back with you now," Elf's best friend said.

"Birthing is bloody work," Orva said to the nun. "You don't go faint at the sight of blood, do you, sister?"

"I don't know. I've never seen a lot of blood."

Orva shrugged. "If you think you're going to faint, just get out of the way, sister. It's not likely I'd have time for you if my mistress is in difficult straits."

"How long will it take for the baby to be born?"

"Some come quick. Others seem to take forever. We'll need your prayers, sister."

"The others are praying," Sister Columba said quickly. "I can do more than that surely. I want to help, not stand about wringing my hands at Elf's every cry."

"Praise be to Mary," Orva said, pleased. "I can use all the help I can get, sister. Willa, my lady's serving wench, is young, and while she's seen two of her brothers and her baby sister born, I need more help than she can offer."

The two women entered the guest house. Willa had not been idle. She had gotten her mistress out of her wet chemise, and put a dry one on her. Elf was now back in her bed in the dormitory while Willa struggled to pull and push the refectory table in the guest hall over by the fireplace. It would be used as a birthing table, for the convent had no birthing chair, never having needed one. Sister Columba, seeing what Willa was doing, hurried to help.

" 'Twould be better if we had a birthing chair," Orva said despairingly, "but we'll take what we can and do as best as we can. Where is the lady, girl?"

"She is resting, Ma."

Orva cuffed her daughter lightly. "You know better than to let her lie down!" She stamped into the dormitory, where Elf lay pale and nervous. "Up with you, my lady," she said briskly, and helped

Elf to her feet. "Lying about will not help your child to be born. Have you any pains yet?"

"Nay," Elf said low.

"Well, they'll come soon enough now that your waters have broken," Orva said matter-of-factly. "You must walk, lady. The sooner this child is born, the better you'll be." Putting Elf's cloak about her, she walked her out into the hall, through the door, and into the cloister. "We'll walk together, lady, about the quadrangle. Your pains will soon begin."

"Ranulf," Elf said. "We must send for my husband."

"A man's no use, lady, at a time like this," Orva said in practical tones. "When the child is born, then we'll send for him."

"But what if I die?" Elf voiced her greatest fear.

"It happens," Orva said, "but I don't see it happening to you, lady. You are small, but you are very strong."

They walked . . . and they walked. The damask rosebushes about them were coming into full, profuse bloom. The air was spicy sweet with their fragrance. It was a sunny day, and a light breeze carried the perfume of the rose to them as they traveled about the cloister. Finally Orva allowed them a rest. They sat together upon a small stone bench.

"Have you any pain, lady?"

"Not real pain," Elf said, "but I suddenly feel very, very uncomfortable in my nether regions. I feel heavy there, as if something were about to burst forth from within me."

"Let us walk back to the guest house," Orva suggested. From Elf's words she ascertained the baby's birth might be sooner than later.

Elf stood up. *"Owwwwwww!"* She doubled over.

Orva put an arm about her mistress, and half forced her to move forward toward the guest house. Once inside she signaled to Willa, and together they helped Elf to get upon the birthing table.

"Sister, come, and stand behind your friend. Brace her so she is sitting up," Orva instructed the nun. "Lady, put your legs up, and open them for me. I must examine you now." Orva bent down, and peered hard at her patient. It was exactly as she had thought.

This child was going to come quickly, and be a very easy birth. The lady was fortunate. The child's head was just barely visible. "Put my apron on, Willa," she told her daughter, "and then bring me a basin of water and a carafe of wine. You know what I will need." Orva looked at Elf. "Lady, the heaviness you sense is your child pushing its way from your body. It is coming quickly. Do not push yourself no matter how desperately you want to until I tell you to do so." Orva stood still a moment while Willa tied a large apron about her. Then she washed her hands thoroughly first with wine, and then soap and water. "Do you have a knife to cut the cord and swaddling for the child?" she inquired of Willa.

"Aye, Ma," the girl replied.

"I have brought Eleanore herbs to dull her pain during her travail," Sister Winifred said, bustling into the hall.

"We are not going to need the herbs, good sister," Orva told the elderly nun. "This child will be born quickly. Will you remain, and help me?"

Elf moaned.

Sister Winifred took up a clean cloth, and dipped it in the bucket of cool water. She wiped Elf's beaded brow. "There, child, you are but suffering what our Blessed Mother suffered, and is that not true glory?"

Sister Joseph, the faint aroma of the stables about her, arrived lugging a small manger. "I have brought the smallest of the feeding troughs for the child," she said. "It is thoroughly scrubbed, and lined with clean straw strewn with sweet clover and grass. There is a linen cloth over it all. The baby will be quite safe in it as we have no cradle." She plunked the wooden manger down. "If it was good enough for the Christ Child, it is good enough for this child," she finished pithily. "How is she doing?"

"Very well," Orva said.

"*I will never do this again!*" Elf said piteously. "Why did no one tell me it hurt so much to have a baby? Ohhhhhh!"

"Hush, lady, you are having a very easy time of it," Orva scolded her.

"I want to push!" Elf cried.

"Wait!" Orva told her. "*Now!* Push now, lady, as hard as you can! Brace her well, Sister Columba!"

Elf screamed, pushing hard, struggling to rid her body of this bulk that threatened to tear her asunder.

"Come on, Eleanore de Montfort, you can do it!" Sister Joseph encouraged the straining woman.

Sister Winifred slipped a small leaf into Elf's mouth. "Chew on it, dear," she said. "It will give you strength."

"Ohhhhhh!" Elf wailed again. Then she looked back at her friend. "Be glad you are a nun, Matti!" she half sobbed. She could feel the mass inside her propelling itself forward. The pressure was fierce. She groaned again.

"Wait!" Orva commanded sternly. Then, "*Now!* Push, lady!"

"Ahhhhhhhhhhhh!" Elf's beautiful face was concentrated in her great effort.

"The head! I see the head!" Orva said excitedly. "Just a few more pushes, and we will have the child, lady. Be brave! When the next pain comes bear down with all of your might."

"Ahhhhhhhhhhhhhh!" Elf screamed, her face squeezing itself tightly again. "Ahhhhhhhhhhh!"

Orva's face was now a mask of total attention as she went about her duties. The child's shoulders and partial upper body slid forth. Gently she turned it, wiping its little face. Two blue eyes glared at her. The small mouth opened to draw its first breath.

"Ahhhhhhhhhhhh!" Elf moaned, pushing again as hard as she might. She was so tired. She had never been so tired in all her life.

"Just one more time, lady!" Orva said.

"I don't think I can," Elf protested.

"You must. It is almost born. Just one big push, lady!"

Elf bore down with every bit of strength she had. She was rewarded by a blessed feeling of relief as the child slipped completely from her body, and howled mightily.

"It is a boy!" Orva crowed. "Ashlin has its next lord, praise be to God, our Father, His blessed son, Lord Jesu, and our Mother Mary!"

"Amen! Amen!" the nuns with them echoed, their faces wreathed in smiles of delight. Surely this child was a special child, having been born in their convent.

"This is a fine day for a boy to be born," Sister Joseph announced. "May thirtieth is St. Hubert's feast day, and he is the patron of hunters. Eleanore de Montfort, your son must have Hubert as part of his name, eh? What will you call him?"

"Simon," Elf said. "Ranulf and I discussed it, and we decided to call our son Simon, after his father. He will be baptized Simon Hubert. Is Father Anselm here? Simon must be baptized immediately. Someone send for my husband. Ranulf must know he has a son. Ah! Orva, I yet have pain. What is it?"

"Just the afterbirth, lady. Willa, hand me that basin!"

About them everyone worked busily. Sister Winifred had cut the baby's cord, and neatly knotted it. She and Sister Joseph gently bathed the infant first in wine, then warm water, and finally olive oil. She handed him off to Sister Columba, who swaddled the baby in soft linen cloth. Willa had taken the younger nun's place, bracing Elf up while her mother saw to the afterbirth, which was set aside in its basin to be buried beneath an oak tree later. Elf was cleaned up, put into yet another clean chemise, and carried by the strong Orva to her bed. Sister Winifred brought the new mother a cup of strong wine with a raw egg beaten into it, and laced with herbs to help her sleep.

"I want to see Simon," Elf said. "Everyone has seen my son but me. Has Ranulf been sent for yet?" She gratefully sipped the wine.

"Willa will ride home," Orva said as she placed Elf's son in her arms. The child, howling lustily, immediately ceased his wailing in the comfort of his mother's arms. "It will be light enough for her to reach the manor before dark."

"Will she be safe?" Elf was concerned even as she turned her attention to her son. "He is beautiful," she said softly.

"Did I hear the cry of a child?" The abbess entered the hall.

"Elf has had a son, Reverend Mother," Sister Columba said excitedly.

"He must be baptized," Elf said sleepily. The herbs were beginning to do their job.

The abbess looked down at Simon Hubert de Glandeville. "He seems a healthy lad, praise God. I think tomorrow is soon enough, Eleanore. Besides, you will want his father here with you. Who are his godparents to be, my daughter?"

As tired as she was, Elf looked distressed at the question. "I want you all to be his godmothers," she said. "It seems appropriate, as you are all my family and Simon was born here."

"I do not believe little lord Simon can have that many god-mothers, Eleanore," the abbess said. "I think Sister Columba should act for all of us. That will satisfy the church, and should satisfy you as well. But who will be his godfather?"

"That is my lord's right," Elf told the abbess. "I like your idea, Reverend Mother. My son shall be a benefactor to St. Frideswide's because of the many kindnesses you have rendered his mother, and because I shall teach him it is the right thing to do." This last speech took the remainder of Elf's strength, and her eyes closed almost immediately thereafter, her arm still cradling her newborn son.

"Put him in his makeshift cradle," the abbess said with a small smile. "Then we must go and give thanks in the church for the safe delivery of this child, and for the well-being of his good mother." She turned and glided out, followed by Sister Joseph and Sister Winifred.

"But if Willa is to go for Lord Ranulf, who will watch over Elf?" Sister Columba said aloud.

"I will watch over my mistress, sister. You need have no fear," Orva assured her.

"But you must clean all of this up. . . ."

"Go with your sisters and the abbess," Orva said in kindly tones, understanding the nun's concern. After all, the lady was her oldest and dearest friend. "When you have completed your prayers, you can return and help me. I will be glad of your aid, good sister."

Sister Columba nodded. "You are right," she said, and hurried off to catch up with the others.

"You are capable of saddling a horse," Orva said to Willa. "Go now to the stables and do so. Tell the lord that his lady is well, and his son, praise God, is healthy. Return with him, for I will need your help—and do not let old Ida come along, Willa. Time enough for her to see this child when we return to Ashlin in a few days. Besides, I do not know that the lady should not choose a younger woman to care for her son. Old Ida is over seventy now. Why she will not simply accept her many years and sit in the sun, I do not know."

"Perhaps she feels that when she is dead is time enough to sit in the sun, Ma," Willa, sympathetic to her grandparent, dared to say. "She wants to be useful. If you were her age, would you give up all that is lively and of interest to you, and . . . and just sit?"

Orva stared hard at her daughter. Willa was usually a foolish creature. How surprising that she made such a clever observation. "Hurry along, girl," she answered her daughter, ignoring Willa's astute question. No, she thought, she certainly wouldn't accept or be defeated by old age, but she was far different from her mother-in-law, old Ida.

As if she could read her mother's thoughts, Willa gave her parent a saucy grin before running out of the guest house and across the cloister to the stable. Since Sister Joseph was nowhere to be found, Willa saddled her own horse, mounted, and with a wave to Sister Perpetua at the gate, cantered off toward Ashlin. Arriving, she called to Cedric, "Where is the lord? I bring news." She was swiftly led into the hall, barely curtsying as she hurried up to the high board. "My lord, you have a fine son, born this day at the convent of St. Frideswide's! The lady is also well. Oh!" It was then Willa saw the other lord. The man had visited the manor only a few weeks past. He was a grand one, he was. "Forgive me, my lord," she said, blushing. "I was so excited to bring you the lady's news, I did not notice your guest."

Ranulf was grinning broadly. "You are forgiven, Willa. Tell me, girl, the boy is healthy? And my sweet wife as well?"

"Aye, my lord," Willa replied, and then went on to tell her master of the day's events. "Will you come back to the convent with me, for I was sent to fetch you. The lady is eager to see you."

"Go to the kitchens and get something to eat, girl," Ranulf said.

"You will return to the convent with me. Be prepared to leave within the hour."

"Yes, my lord," Willa answered. Then she curtsied again and went off to be fed. She had not eaten this day, and she was starving.

"Congratulations, Ranulf," Sir Garrick Taliferro said. "A son is a good thing, and now you have an heir for your manor."

"The first of several, I hope." Ranulf could not stop smiling. Suddenly he sobered. "We will go on to Worcester from the convent. You say you do not know why it is Duke Henry wishes to see me?"

"Nay. All I can tell you is he came secretly, then sent me to fetch you. I know not what it is he wishes you to do. The sooner we get there, the sooner you will know."

"We will have to remain the night at the convent," Ranulf said. "We will reach it just before dark, but we can go no farther until the morning."

"I did not expect us to reach Worcester for at least a week," Sir Garrick said. "The duke will be pleased to see us so quickly."

The two knights and the serving girl departed shortly thereafter for St. Frideswide's. The sun had dipped behind the hills separating England from Wales when they arrived. Sister Perpetua opened the gates for them, smiling as they rode through. Dismounting before the stables, they gave their horses into Sister Joseph's care.

"Praise God you have come, my lord," the abbess said, hurrying forward. "Eleanore is most eager to see you, and I imagine you are most eager to see your son, eh?" She smiled at him.

Everybody was smiling, it seemed, Ranulf thought. The introduction of his companion accomplished, the new father said, "Sir Garrick and I must beg a night's hospitality of you, my lady abbess."

"It is granted, gladly."

"Where is Eleanore?" he asked.

"Willa will take you to the guest house, my lord," the abbess replied.

"We have few men as guests," the abbess told Sir Garrick. "The lady Eleanore's serving woman will show you where you may lodge, sir. Food will be brought to you both." Then with a nod she left him.

The two men followed Willa into the guest house. Willa showed Sir Garrett where men guests were housed, as Orva had hurried forward to curtsy and claim Ranulf's attention.

"Welcome, my lord. The mistress is eager for you to come to her and for you to see young lord Simon Hubert," she said.

"Was it difficult for her?" Ranulf asked the midwife.

Orva shook her head. "I would have thought such a little girl birthing such a fine strapping infant would have had a far harder time than she had, my lord. Her labor was but a few short hours, and she bore her child easily. It is rare to see such a simple birth. It was as if the angels were on her side, my lord."

"They surely were," he said softly, "for my Eleanore is the best of women, Orva."

"She is in there, my lord." Orva pointed to the door into the women's dormitory, and her master hurried through it.

"Petite!" Ranulf knelt by Elf's bedside, kissing her forehead.

Elf smiled up at her husband. Dear God, how she loved him! "You are here at last," she said. "I wanted them to send for you when I went into labor, Ranulf, but they said birthing was no place for a man. Look by the fire in the little manger. It is your son."

"You are all right, petite?"

She nodded. "Go, and see Simon Hubert! He is the most beautiful child, my lord."

He arose from her side and went over to the makeshift cradle. Kneeling, he gazed in rapt admiration at his son, lying upon his stomach, his perfectly round little head turned to one side. The head was topped with reddish fuzz. "He has your hair," Ranulf said softly as his finger gently touched the infant's head. "He is beautiful." Standing again, he came back to her side, drawing up a stool so he might sit next to her. "Simon we agreed upon. Why Hubert?"

"It is St. Hubert's feast day, Ranulf," she explained, "and St. Hubert is the patron saint of hunters. I thought it a manly name, but he cannot be baptized until the morrow, so if you do not like it, we do not have to call him so."

"Nay, I think it a fine name, Eleanore."

"You were right, my lord," Elf said. "I should not have come visiting at St. Frideswide's so near my time, but I never thought for a moment that I would have my child here."

He took her hand in his and kissed each finger in a now well-loved gesture. "While I would have preferred our firstborn birthed at Ashlin, petite, you were as safe here as you would have been there. I know your travail was made easier surrounded by the good nuns, whom you love so well and who love you. I am not angry at you."

"They were so sweet, Ranulf. The abbess was as calm as ever. Sister Winifred brought herbs to help my pains and relax me. Sister Joseph scoured a small manger, then filled it with sweet grasses, and covered it with a fine linen cloth so Simon would have a cradle. Matti stayed with me throughout it all. Whatever fears I harbored secretly, I lost encircled by their love and prayers."

"We shall make them a fine gift, Eleanore, to show our gratitude," Ranulf said quietly.

"Can we go home tomorrow?" She smiled hopefully up at him. How very handsome he was! How strong and yet tender, and she loved him even if she did not dare to say it. Her gaze strayed to their son. What a marvel the babe was! His voice cut into her thoughts.

"I believe you should rest for a few days before we attempt to bring you home," Ranulf said. "I am on my way to Worcester in the morning. When I return, I shall stop here, and we shall journey home together, petite. Orva says it was an easy birth, but it cannot harm you to rest for a few days. I have given orders that a dozen of our men-at-arms come here in a week's time to act as our escort. You are not to attempt to leave without me, petite. Do I have your word on it?"

"Aye." She was puzzled. "Why are you going to Worcester?"

"I have been sent for by Duke Henry, who is there secretly. Do not ask me why, because I do not know myself the reasons behind it all. As Duke Henry knows, my allegiance is to King Stephen, but I am certain there is no plot afoot. Sir Garrick was sent to me, and

I hold him to be an honorable man. If I can render our future king some small service without infringing upon my loyalty to King Stephen, then it cannot harm us, petite. Duke Henry's reputation is also one of honor, so I doubt he has asked me to come to Worcester for any nefarious purpose."

"I wonder what he wants," Elf said slowly. "If it is something that no one else can do, and you do it well, Duke Henry will undoubtedly be grateful. That could bode well for our son." She had begun to think like an ambitious mother. "Do not the duke and his wife have a son who is but an infant? Maybe one day Simon could serve him at court! If they grew up together, they might become friends. *Good friends.* What an advantage for our heir, Ranulf. Our fortunes could be made if you serve Duke Henry well!"

Ranulf de Glandeville looked at his wife in amazement. Now, here was a side of Eleanore he would have never expected existed. She had but birthed their son a few hours ago, and already she was aspiring and envisioning a grand future for him. He did not know whether to be pleased or fearful of this new woman to whom he was wed. "Simple knights rarely, if ever, do great lords such great a service that they are rewarded so magnanimously, petite. My name is not so proud that our son would become a playmate of Prince William's." He smiled at her, and patted her hand.

"You cannot know that for certain, my lord," Elf said to him.

Ranulf chuckled. His wife was not about to give up her dreams simply at his say-so. "Duke Henry, being unfamiliar with the country, has probably been asking the men with holdings in the various regions who live upon those holdings, all about the areas. I was sent to Ashlin because it is on the border between England and Wales. Duke Henry is a great warlord, Eleanore. He may be deciding if he wants to attack the Welsh once England is his by inheritance. I can think of no other reason he might send for me, petite." He arose and, bending, kissed her lips lightly. "You have had a hard day, Eleanore. You must sleep now, and grow stronger. Tomorrow you will need to nurse our son."

"Will you come and see me before you depart in the morning?"

she asked him anxiously. "Do not leave without saying adieu to us, Ranulf, and Simon must be baptized before you go."

"I won't leave beforehand," he promised, and then he left her.

Willa reentered the room softly and went to the makeshift cradle, picking up Simon and bringing him to his mother. "Ma says you must attempt to feed him now, lady. Your milk is not yet ready to flow, but the liquid that will come from your breasts is nourishing for the little lord."

Elf struggled to sit up in her cot. Finally comfortable, she unloosed the laces on her chemise and reached out for her son. "How do I do it?" she asked Willa as Simon began rooting about her breasts.

"Just put a teat in his mouth, lady. He'll do the rest," Willa told her mistress. "I seen Ma do it plenty of times."

Cradling her son with an arm, Elf rubbed her nipple against Simon's small mouth. The mouth opened, and then clamped with surprising strength down upon the flesh. She gasped. "Holy Mother!" she exclaimed. "He is just like his father." Then Elf flushed, realizing what she had said aloud, but Willa just giggled. Fascinated, Elf watched as the infant suckled furiously and with great determination upon her. His blue eyes looked up at her, interested. "Aye," she told him. "I'm your mother, Simon Hubert. I never thought to be a mother, but here we are, my son."

Orva came into the dormitory chamber. "Ahh, you have begun to feed him. Good! He's a big boy, lady. Move him to the other breast to encourage your milk to flow. Another day, two at the most, and you will be feeding him royally."

Elf switched the protesting baby from her right breast to her left. Simon suckled as strongly upon the second breast as he had upon the first, but eventually his eyes began to close. Suddenly his little head fell to one side, and he was sound asleep. Orva took the baby and restored him to his cradle, instructing her daughter to watch over the child until she was relieved by another.

"There are three postulants, and two novices within the convent now," Orva told her mistress. "The abbess says they will take turns watching over the baby during the nighttime hours so we may sleep. Are you hungry, lady?"

"I am tired," Elf said.

"Then, sleep," Orva instructed her. "You have done well, lady, and the world is at peace around us, praise be to God and His blessed Mother!"

CHAPTER TWELVE

Sir Garrick Taliferro and Ranulf de Glandeville reached the town of Worcester two days later. Situated on the east bank of the Severn, Worcester was a beautiful little town with a long and proud history. To Ranulf's surprise Duke Henry was staying with the bishop. Worcester had suffered at the Empress Matilda's hand when her troops had fired the town fifteen years earlier. It had not been destroyed, however, and even when King Stephen's men had attacked it five years ago, Worcester survived. Leveled buildings were rebuilt; the cathedral was restored, but for a fallen tower left to be repaired later.

As the duke's visit was a secret one, there was no pomp or show, of course. Ranulf was led into a small, paneled room with a fireplace that burned brightly, taking the chill off the wet early June afternoon. Henry of Anjou greeted him with a small smile upon his lips.

"Welcome, Sir Ranulf."

Ranulf bowed low, becoming acutely aware as he arose of how he towered over the duke. Unconsciously he attempted to shrink himself, but the duke, seeing his efforts, just laughed.

"There is no way, my lord," he rasped in his strangely rough voice, "that you can make yourself any smaller. You are bigger than most men in length. While I am tall enough, I am cleverer than most men. If I were insulted by every man who was taller than I am, I should have no friends at all. Sit down, and we will talk."

The two men sat in high-backed wooden chairs with cushioned seats, facing each other.

"I need your help, Ranulf de Glandeville," the duke said. "King Stephen is not well at all. Losing his beloved wife and my wretched cousin, Eustace, in so short a period of time has made him disconsolate, dispirited. His interest in England, in the things about him have waned. He has lost his joy for living. It is unlikely that he will ever regain it. I am informed he is not expected to live for too much longer. I will be England's king by year's end, I am told. I believe it to be so.

"The line of descent is now clear, settled, established, and approved of by the church. Still, I worry the unruly English barons may seek to foment troubles, for they have very much had their own way during the years my mother and her cousin fought for supremacy here. I must return immediately to Normandy to oversee my estates, and those of my wife; to put in place the government that will rule in my name once I am England's king, and must make my progress back and forth across the channel. When I return in the autumn, I would bring my wife and my son with me to show England my queen and my heir. I hope the sight of them will help prevent trouble. I want you to return to Normandy with me. No one is to know that Alienor and William will come to England when I return. This is a secret that you must keep, for it is you I have chosen to escort my wife and son."

"*Me?*" Ranulf was astounded. "My lord, should not this great honor go to a great lord? I am naught but a simple knight with a small holding. No matter Ashlin's strategic location, I am still not an important man, and you already have my pledge of loyalty, my liege."

The bright gray eyes looked directly at Ranulf. "It is precisely for the reasons you think yourself unworthy for this task that I chose you, Ranulf de Glandeville. I want the queen and my son brought quietly to England without any fanfare. A great lord could not do that. A great lord might consider that by holding my wife and my son in their charge, that they would have power over me. I will not allow that to happen, and it will not with you. You are an honest man. I know that I can trust you, Ranulf de Glandeville. The queen must appear by my side. Once she and my son are here, I can protect them. It is the journey that is dangerous. You will travel in my train of knights when I return to Normandy in a few days' time. You will be one knight among many, and no one will think anything of it except that you are making your peace with me now that King Stephen is so obviously failing." Then the duke saw the stricken look upon Ranulf's face. "What is it, my lord?" he asked, concerned.

"My wife, who is also Eleanore, has just two days ago delivered our first son. She was visiting friends at the convent of St. Frideswide's when her time came upon her. I stopped there on my way to you, my liege, to see her, and our child. I promised her I would return to take them home to Ashlin. If I must go with you when you leave Worcester, how can I keep my promise to my wife?"

"Have you no squire or other knight on your estate who might escort the lady and child?" the duke, slightly annoyed, asked.

"My lord, I have told you, we are a small holding. I suppose I should have a squire, but until I married, I had not the means to support a squire. Would I not be less conspicuous if I came to Normandy alone, with no one to notice me? I should be just another knight, as you have said, coming to make my peace with you now that the lay of the land is clear."

"It is your first child?"

"Aye." Ranulf could not help but smile. "His name is Simon Hubert. He was born on St. Hubert's feast day the good nuns informed my wife. Eleanore thought the name manly."

Duke Henry chuckled. "And do you love your wife, Ranulf de Glandeville? I am mad with love for my Alienor! She was France's queen, but Louis, and his monkish ways, could get but two daughters on her. He had the marriage dissolved on the grounds of consanguinity, the fool! Not only did I gain my wife's vast holdings, poor Louis's second wife, Constance of Castile, has delivered him a third daughter, while Alienor has delivered a son to me! I adore her! Do you love your Eleanore?"

"I do, my lord," Ranulf said quietly, admitting aloud, albeit to the wrong person, what was in his heart. "She was to have been a nun, but that her brother died. She is everything that is good, my lord. I never thought a battle-scarred old warrior such as myself might have a wife, let alone such a sweet wife."

"Stephen will last the summer, I am assured," Duke Henry said. "Take a month to settle your affairs, but be on the road for Normandy by St. Swithen's. Take passage for Barfleur, and come to Rouen. I will be taking my wife and son to meet my mother for the first time. You will join the court there. It is a good thing that you love your wife, Ranulf. You will, therefore, be careful with mine and get her to England in safety. Once you are in Normandy, we will discuss my plans for her passage."

Ranulf de Glandeville arose from his seat, and bowed low to the king. "I am yours to command, my liege."

"You will speak with no one about this, except perhaps your wife, if she can be counted upon not to gossip," Duke Henry warned.

"I understand," Ranulf replied, and backed from the small chamber out into the corridor. There was no one waiting for him. He made his way to the courtyard and into the stables, where he found his horse in a wide stall. After unfastening his sword belt, Ranulf put the weapon aside and lay down on a large pile of fresh straw in the rear of the stall. He was awakened by a narrow beam of light coming in through a crack in the wall. Arising, he peed in a corner, then buckled his sword back on, and left.

"Have my beast saddled in half an hour's time," he told a stable-boy mucking out the stall opposite his. He went outside, splashed water from the horse trough on his face, and slicked back his hair. Following a group of priests into the bishop's palace, he found the great hall, where breakfast was already being served. Baskets of bread were placed on the trestles, and wooden cups for ale were filled by passing servants. There was a small wheel of cheese on each table. Ranulf reached into the basket, and pulled out a small cottage loaf. With his knife he cut a wedge of cheese.

He ate in silence as he did not recognize anyone at the tables around him. Garrick Taliferro was nowhere to be seen, but that was to the good. He did not have to explain what the duke wanted with him. He ate half the bread and cheese, stuffing the remainder in his purse for the road, for he couldn't be certain when he would have the opportunity to eat again. After draining his cup of ale, he arose and left the hall. His horse was saddled and tied outside the stable, but the stable lad was not in sight. Ranulf mounted and rode out.

The sun was just coming up as he passed through the gates of the town onto the road back to Ashlin. He rode until the sun was at its midday zenith, stopping beside a swiftly flowing stream to water his horse. He let the animal graze nearby while he sat beneath a tree and finished the remainder of his bread and cheese, slaking his thirst with the icy water. Refreshed, he remounted his horse and rode onward. It was June, and the daylight remained well into the early evening. Ranulf was relieved when the monastery he had stayed at on his ride into Worcester appeared over the crest of the hill. Reaching it, he begged shelter from the porter at the gate.

He was just in time for a small meal served to guests. He was given a little loaf of bread and a haunch of broiled rabbit with a small cup of ale. The monk in charge of the guest quarters, however, took pity on Ranulf, bringing him another piece of the rabbit, for he could see the knight was hungry, and he was, after all, a big man.

"Where are you bound for, lord?" he asked curiously.

"St. Frideswide's," Ranulf answered, bobbing his dark head in thanks for the additional food. "My wife was visiting when she delivered our son there." He chewed for a moment as he thought about his words, then lied. "I was in Worcester when word was brought me by a passing traveler. I am now going to fetch her and take her home to Ashlin."

"Ashlin? You are the lord of Ashlin?" the monk said.

"I am."

"You are very near the Welsh, and they are, I am told, growing restless of late."

"The manor is well defended, good brother. Our walls are high, and my men-at-arms well trained."

"That will not help if they burn your crops and steal your livestock," the monk replied. "They do it for the pure joy of destruction. The Welsh are godless creatures, my lord."

"Then, I will ask you to pray for Ashlin and its people." Ranulf grew concerned. "Have you heard something of late, good brother?"

"They are raiding again. Just little forays over the border, here and then there. One bandit in particular is known by name. He is called Merin ap Owen, and it is said he rides with a golden-haired witch who is as bloodthirsty as he. No one is safe from them. Several weeks ago they burned a small convent, St. Bride's, murdering the elder nuns and violating the younger women before they killed them. The carnage, it is said, was terrible, my lord." The monk shook his head sadly. "You should not travel alone."

"I am well armed," Ranulf said. "Besides, I do not look like a man worth robbing, good brother."

"There is your horse, my lord."

"True, but Shadow can outrun any bandit's pony, I assure you."

"I will pray for you, my son," the monk said. "And for Ashlin."

Ranulf was relieved that he was, that night, the only guest at the monastery and did not have to share his pallet with anyone. He arose in the gray of predawn to attend Prime in the monk's austere church. He was then given a surprisingly hearty breakfast of oat stirabout in a trencher of warm bread. He ate the cereal and half the bread, putting the other half into his purse for later. After draining his cup of cider, he arose, leaving a coin on the table and thanking the guest-house monk, then went to the stables to fetch his horse. The beast had been treated as well as he himself had, and so in a burst of generosity, he gave another coin to the monk who managed the stables.

He rode again until midday, stopping to water and graze his mount while he devoured the remaining trencher of bread he had carried with him. He would be at St. Frideswide's tonight, and the meal would be another simple one. He longed for home and a hearty supper of a steamy rabbit stew with a wined gravy, a plate of juicy prawns, and a sweet pudding. *Cheese.* As much as he wanted. *Butter.* A fresh crock of it for his warm bread. Ranulf laughed as he remounted his horse and continued on his journey. He had become quite used to the soft life of a landowner. Having to take to the road again as a simple knight would be quite a hardship.

Was he being disloyal to King Stephen, he questioned himself? Yet Duke Henry had asked no great task of him, and that task certainly did not conflict with his loyalty to his king. He had, after all, pledged his fealty to Duke Henry once he became king, Ranulf reasoned. Bring the future queen to England with her child in safety, and he would have done Henry of Anjou a valuable service. What would Henry do for him? Kings were known to reward their faithful servants. What did he want? The question would be asked of him.

Ranulf considered. Suddenly he knew. He wanted the king's permission to build a castle. To seriously help in protecting the border between England and Wales, Ashlin needed to become a castle. He could not build that castle without the king's express permission. He would ingratiate himself with the future queen in order to gain her support as well. Ranulf smiled a wry smile. His wife would be proud of him, he thought, for he was at last thinking like a husband, a father, a lord of the manor. He chuckled, and his horse's ears twitched back for an instant at the sound.

He rode until almost dusk, finally coming into sight of the convent. With a sigh he kicked his mount into a loping canter and eagerly gained his objective. Sister Perpetua was standing at the gates, one side of which were open and the other closed. He rode through and heard the open gate slam shut behind him with a noisy *thunk*. Sliding from his horse, he helped her lift the heavy wooden bar into place.

"Thank you, my lord," the portress said. "We waited for you. Eleanore was certain you would arrive before dark."

"I did promise her I would not linger in Worcester," Ranulf replied. "Have my men arrived, sister?"

"Late this afternoon, my lord. We have housed them with their animals in the stables. Reverend Mother thought it best."

"Thank you," he said. "Where is the abbess? I would pay her my respects before I go to my wife and child."

"You will find her in the chapter house."

He hurried to the directed spot and found Reverend Mother Eunice in the chamber, where she oversaw the business of the convent. The door to the room was open, and the abbess looked up from behind the long oak table where she was working.

"Come in, Sir Ranulf," she said. "Sit down."

He took the chair that was set before the table. "I have things I would impart to you that must remain a secret, my lady abbess," he began. "It is nothing traitorous, but you will understand the need for secrecy once I have spoken."

"Go on, Sir Ranulf."

"The king is dying," he began. "I have been asked by Duke Henry, who has my loyalty once King Stephen is gone, to go to Normandy in order to bring his wife and son back to England. I have been chosen by the duke to do this deed discreetly and in secrecy. It is unlikely that anyone, particularly the great lords, will ever know how the future queen came to England. The duke is returning to Normandy immediately. I will follow in a month. This should be a simple task, but if anything happens to me, I want you to know in order that you may aid my wife."

"I understand, my lord. Will you tell Eleanore where you are going and why?"

"I will. We do not keep secrets from each other, she and I."

"What will you ask the king in return for your service, Sir Ranulf?" the abbess queried him astutely.

"If I succeed in my mission for the duke, I shall ask his permission to build a castle at Ashlin."

The abbess nodded. "You are wise," she said. "We can use a castle nearby to defend our wee bit of the border."

"That is something else I wish to speak to you about. I am told that the Welsh are raiding again this year. There is a particularly vicious bandit among them called Merin ap Owen. He burned a convent recently and slaughtered the inhabitants of it. He rides with a woman, they say. Be on your guard. Make certain St. Frideswide's is secure both day and night."

"We have generally been left in peace, as we are known to be a simple house with nothing of value. We have no silver or gold candlesticks, no reliquaries."

"You have sheep and cattle."

"That is true," the abbess said thoughtfully, "but if the Welsh come, they will more than likely drive off the animals and leave us in peace, Sir Ranulf."

"This Merin ap Owen is a man of no conscience. The younger nuns at the convent he destroyed were violated, Reverend Mother. He did not simply steal. He murdered, and he ravaged." Ranulf arose. "I will go and see my wife and son now. They continue well?"

"Aye," the abbess replied, her mind more on what he had told her than on her guest. A man who ravaged nuns was to be feared. They must pray that this Merin ap Owen not seek out St. Frideswide's.

Ranulf left the chapter house, and walked across the cloister to the guest house. Entering, he was greeted by Orva and Willa. Then his eyes moved past them to where Eleanore sat by the fireplace, nursing Simon. "Petite!" he called to her, and she looked up, her eyes alight, a smile upon her face.

"You are returned," she said. "Welcome, my lord. Come and see Simon. I swear he has grown already."

He rushed to sit by her. *God,* he thought, *how I love her! Why can I not tell her?* But he knew the answer to his question. Eleanore had wanted to be a nun with every fiber of her being. Their marriage had been forced. While women always had their marriages arranged by guardians, most had the opportunity to meet and know something about their bridegrooms before the wedding—and they had not been raised to be nuns. How could Eleanore love him when she had been made to marry him? When her whole life had been turned upside down? Still, she had been a good wife to him, but she certainly could not love the man who had been forced upon her. And he could not bear it if she rejected his love. It was far better to remain silent.

"When can we go home?" she asked.

"If you are well enough, tomorrow, petite. The men-at-arms arrived today to escort us. The Welsh are raiding again, I have been informed. I want you and Simon safe at Ashlin. I must go away in a month on Duke Henry's business, Eleanore."

She looked puzzled and hurt, and he hastened to explain. Orva and Willa had left the hall to give them privacy. "I have entrusted this knowledge only to the abbess and to you. No one else must know why I have gone. You can say nothing, petite. We will arrange an excuse should anyone ask about my absence, particularly if Baron Hugh comes calling and snooping about while I am gone."

Elf had finished feeding her son. "Here," she said, handing the infant to his startled father. "Hold him a moment while I lace up my chemise." Then she laughed at the horrified look on her husband's face as the baby rested in his two big hands. "Cradle him against your chest, Ranulf. He won't break." Elf laughed.

"He's looking at me," her husband said, awed.

"Of course he is," she answered. "Your voice is new to him. He wants to know who you are. This is your father, Simon," Elf cooed. "When you are bigger, he will teach you how to use a sword and a lance, and to ride your own pony. I will teach you to read, and to write, and to have manners. And we will both love you, Simon Hubert de Glandeville, my adorable little son. And we will give you brothers to play with and sisters to tease," Elf promised.

"You want more children? But you have just had a child!" He was surprised and secretly delighted.

"Certainly I want more children! Ashlin will be a castle one day, and the de Glandevilles an important family in this region, Ranulf. Aye, we need more children. Besides," she purred into his ear, "we had so much fun making this one." Before he dropped their son, she took the baby back, laughing softly.

Ranulf swallowed hard. "Eleanore, you make it difficult for me to leave you," he said softly.

"Then, I have achieved my purpose, my lord, and you will hurry home to us." She chuckled.

Willa reentered the chamber carrying a tray. "My lord, we thought that you might not have eaten," she said, putting the tray upon the trestle in the hall.

Ranulf's nose twitched at the fragrant smells coming from the tray, and his eyes widened at the bounty. There was a bowl of lamb stew in a thick gravy with carrots and leeks, a small broiled trout on a bed of green cress, fresh bread, cheese, and a carafe of wine. "This is convent fare?" he asked, surprised.

"The nuns eat simply, their students more heartily. You are a special guest, however, my lord," Elf said. Rising, she handed the baby to Willa, and began to serve the meal. She heaped the food generously into a bowl and onto a polished wooden plate, setting it in front of Ranulf on a small table she had pulled up.

Ranulf ate vigorously, finishing everything that he had been brought. When Elf placed a little dish of wild strawberries swimming in thick cream before him, he grinned happily. Finally, the food all eaten and the carafe drained, he pushed himself away from the little table with a contented sigh. "I have been dreaming for a week of a good meal such as you have just served me, petite."

"I want to leave after Prime," she said. "The sooner we leave, the sooner we will get home. I have been away from Ashlin for a month, Ranulf. I want to go home!"

"You are certain you are strong enough, petite?"

"I am not some delicate flower, my lord. I am strong, thank God! On the morrow we will take our son and go home," she said firmly.

"I can remember a time when you wept at not being able to remain here at St. Frideswide's," he teased her gently, leaning over to kiss her as she sat by his side. "You are not so much the little nun anymore, Eleanore. You are a woman, Simon's mother, and my good wife."

"I am grateful for my years here. And I should have been happy to remain, devoting my life to God, but I am more than content to be your wife and a mother, Ranulf." *And besides, I love you more than my own life now,* she thought. If only you would love me, but I know that can never be. I must be content that you consider me a good wife and look upon me with favor. I must be satisfied that we are friends.

The women slept in a dormitory assigned, while Ranulf slept in the men's section of the guest house. In the morning Ranulf and Elf attended Prime in the nun's church, joining their servants afterward for breakfast. Elf's cart was packed, and when she was settled in it with her son, the abbess and the other sisters came to bid them a farewell.

"We have made you a gift for your church at Ashlin," the abbess said. She handed Elf a lovely woven willow basket that held a beautiful embroidered altar cloth.

"We will treasure it," Elf told the abbess, but her smile encompassed them all.

"Take good care of our godson," the abbess ordered her with a rare smile. "We expect to see him as often as you can manage to bring him for visits, Eleanore."

"Good-bye, my dear," Sister Winifred said. "Here is a bit of angelica root for your garden."

Elf kissed the withered cheek of the elderly nun. "Thank you, sister." There were tears in her eyes.

"Now, now," Sister Winifred chided her gently. "Young Sister Mary Gabriel is working out, even if she has not your instincts." She stepped away from the cart.

"I will not say good-bye, Elf, but only farewell until we meet again," Sister Columba said. "Having you here these last weeks has been a blessing, and it has made me realize that as much as you belong at Ashlin in your capacity as a wife and mother, I belong here within the convent. God bless you, my dear friend." She hugged Elf.

The little train moved from the cloister courtyard out onto the road. The nuns all clustered at the open gate, surrounding the abbess like ducklings surrounding the mother duck.

"Remember fennel water if he grows colicky," Sister Cuthbert called. Being in charge of the children at St. Frideswide's, she knew all such remedies.

They waved. The abbess, Sister Agnes, Sister Hilda, Sister Mary Gabriel, Sister Phillipa, Sister Mary Basil, Sister Anne, Sister Winifred, Sister Columba, Sister Perpetua, and the others.

"Do not forget to keep the gates secure," Ranulf called to the abbess, and she nodded her understanding of his warning.

Elf had not missed the byplay. "Do you think the Welsh will attack the convent?" she asked. In all her years there St. Frideswide's had been a place of peace and safety.

"It is possible," Ranulf said. "I see no reason why the abbess should take chances, petite. If the Welsh come, there is the possibility they will simply steal the livestock outside the gates and leave the nuns alone. St. Frideswide's is not known to have rich accoutrements or a store of coin. They have a fine flock of sheep and a small herd of cattle, which might prove tempting to marauders. Still, there is the incident of that convent burned recently."

They traveled the whole day along the easy road back to Ashlin. Now and then Ranulf noticed a lone horseman on the hills above them, but the rider never came close, so he was not particularly threatening. The cart caused them to move slowly, and Ranulf wished he had twice the number of men-at-arms that were accompanying them. But he had not known of the Welsh threat before he departed for Worcester. Finally, however, they reached Ashlin in late afternoon. The serfs in the fields waved to their master and mistress, laying aside their farm tools to come and see Ashlin's new heir.

"Show them the little lord, lady," Orva said softly.

Elf ordered the cart stopped, and displayed her son to her serfs. There were cries of joy, and many compliments at the healthy little boy. "Here is the line of Strongbow for yet another generation," Elf told her people. "With God's blessing, he will have brothers and sisters in the years to come."

Father Oswin, the new priest of the manor, came forward. "He has been baptized, of course."

Elf nodded. "By Father Anselm, with Sir Garrick as his god-father and all the nuns his godmothers, represented by my friend, Sister Columba. Simon Hubert de Glandeville will be a patron to St. Frideswide's where he was born," she told the priest.

"Amen!" Father Oswin said enthusiastically. He was a pleasant-faced young man with warm brown eyes and straight brown hair.

The cart moved through the gates of the demesne, and up to the manor house. Old Ida and Cedric were both waiting to greet their lord and lady.

"Let me have my child," the elderly nursemaid said excitedly.

Elf laughed. "Oh, no, Ida," she told the woman, "this child will have another to watch over him. I cannot get along without you. Willa cannot serve me as well as you serve me. She needs you to teach her. I will not let you go, though you may take my son for now."

Old Ida did not know whether to be disappointed or flattered. She thought a moment as she took the baby into her arms, then decided that she was indeed too ancient to begin with another infant. An infant required a much younger woman. She realized that she far preferred serving her mistress. "I will help you choose the right woman to care for the young lord. He will be her life, as you and your brother were mine."

Behind Elf, Orva smiled a secret smile. The lady had heeded her advice, but done so in such a way as not to offend Ida. Indeed she had made her old nursemaid feel important and indispensable. The lady was wise for one so very young.

They entered the house, and Elf was pleased to see that in her absence all had been well cared for by Cedric and the servants. Seating herself by the fireplace, she took her son from old Ida and began to nurse him, while preparations for the evening meal went on about her.

"I must find Fulk and speak with him," Ranulf said.

Elf nodded, her concentration upon Simon.

Outside the hall Ranulf found his sergeant at arms drilling a troop of men in archery. "Fulk," he said, drawing the grizzled soldier aside.

"My lord?"

"I am going to need a squire to serve me. Have you among your men one who is suitable for such a position? You know the duties required of a squire. Is there a lad here worthy of advancement?"

"My nephew, my lord. He is nineteen years of age and very strong. I have taught him myself how to use a sword, a lance, and a battle-ax. When I was a young man, I squired Lord Robert. I will teach the lad how to care for your armor and your horse. His name is Pax, and he will be loyal to you, I vow it, my lord."

"I thought you meant your nephew for your place one day," Ranulf noted.

"There is time for that, my lord," Fulk replied, "and there are others, like Sim, who might replace me one day. Pax will need the experience only being squire to the lord can give him. I have taught him everything I could, my lord. He needs the kind of seasoning that he can only gain being by your side now."

"Which one is he?" Ranulf asked the sergeant at arms.

"Pax, come forward," Fulk called, and a young man stepped from among the cluster of men on the archery green.

"Yes, Uncle?" He was of medium height and stockily built. He had a round head and face, brown hair, brown eyes, and an earnest-looking expression. He bowed nervously to Ranulf. "My lord."

"Fulk says you have the capability to be a squire. Do you want to be one? You know the duties involved, but you will also have to go with me whenever I depart Ashlin. Are you willing?"

Pax smiled a smile that rendered his face almost handsome. "Aye, my lord!" he said enthusiastically.

"You have a month to learn your duties well," Ranulf said. "We leave on a journey for Normandy then."

"I will be ready!" the young man said.

"Can you speak any tongue but your own?" Ranulf asked, and was very surprised by the answer.

"I can speak the Norman tongue some, my lord. Enough to get about, and be of use to you. Actually, I understand it far better than

I speak it," Pax answered. "My uncle taught me," he said, replying to the unasked questions he saw on his master's lips.

Ranulf smiled a slow smile. "Understanding it better than you speak it will be of great use to me, Pax," he told his new squire. "You will, of course, gain a facility for the language when you must speak it daily, but no one need know that."

"Aye, my lord."

"You will serve me in the hall tonight," Ranulf said, then turned and walked away.

"Be loyal and suit him well, and your fortune is made, lad!" the sergeant at arms said, well pleased. "He's a fair master."

"What am I to do in the hall to serve him?" Pax asked.

"You'll stand behind his chair, see that his cup and the cup of his lady is kept filled. In large households a page would do such work, but we are a small manor," Fulk said. "You'll have to eat early. Go to the kitchens, and the cook will feed you when you explain. Ah, lad, Ashlin is becoming a fine place. We'll be a castle someday. I hope I live to see it."

"Ashlin, a castle?" Pax was astounded. "How do you know such a thing, Uncle? Ashlin is just a little place."

"The lord was summoned to Worcester, lad," Fulk began. "He returns, decides he needs a squire, and says he's going to Normandy in a month's time. The lord does not need to go to Normandy on Ashlin's business. He goes on the business of some great lord, and he goes very discreetly, for our master is certainly of no importance. If he is successful, he will be rewarded. If it were I, I would ask permission from the king to build a castle here at Ashlin to help defend the border. Now remember, Pax, I know none of this to be fact; but certain things happen in a certain order. You have but to keep your eyes and your ears wide open, boy, and your mouth shut. Do you understand?"

"Aye, Uncle. I'll not gossip."

"Not even to impress those wenches you're always chasing," Fulk warned him. "Your bright smile and your strong cock will keep the lasses content enough."

"Aye, Uncle," Pax said. His brown eyes twinkled, and Fulk laughed.

Pax served his master and mistress in the hall that night for the first time. His big hands were damp with his nervousness, but Ranulf praised him, and the lady Eleanore looked upon him favorably.

"Send your mother to me tomorrow," she told the young man. "You will need more clothing than I'll warrant you now possess. I will see she has what she needs to fashion what you will need."

"Thank you, lady," Pax replied.

"Serve my husband well," Elf told him, "and I will see your serfdom is lifted from you, Pax."

He knelt and kissed the hem of her gown. "Thank you, lady!"

"He is a good lad, I can see," Elf told her husband as they at last lay in their bed that night. "Fulk dotes on him, for he has no children of his own. He has seen that Pax and his other nephew, Sim, have been raised well."

"I'll want to see an example of his skills," Ranulf replied, nuzzling her neck. She smelled so sweet. It was a pity they could not cohabit until he was almost ready to leave for Normandy, but old Sister Winifred had come to him just before they departed the convent, and told him that Eleanore must have time to heal from the birth.

"Certain men, I am told, do not care if they harm their wives, poor ladies," the gentle nun said. "If you would have Eleanore healthy for many years, my lord, you will temper your lustful appetites." She looked at him with a stern eye, and he had actually felt himself blush. The elderly nun chuckled. "For just three more weeks," she amended.

His wife turned in his arms and kissed him slowly, pressing her body, more lush now than ever, against him. "My dear lord," she murmured in his ear.

"We cannot," he replied.

"*Why not?*" Elf demanded, quite outraged. She had been longing for his passion for several months now, and was eager.

"Sister Winifred says you must heal from the birth," he told her firmly. "I would take her advice and not injure you, petite."

"By the rood!" Elf swore, surprising him. "I am not in the convent any longer!"

He chuckled wickedly. "Do you want me as much as I want you, petite? It is torture knowing I must wait." He caressed her hair.

"But you will be gone in a month's time!" Elf wailed.

"We may cohabit the week before I go."

"And then you will ride off to Normandy, my lord, and I am left behind longing for you," Elf said half angry. "You cannot even say how long you will be gone!"

"Would you rather we did not—"

"*Nay!*" she said furiously.

"Would you prefer that I sleep elsewhere until we may be together again, petite?"

"*Nay!*" She burrowed herself against his broad shoulder.

"I thought you had been taught self-denial as a nun," he teased her, tipping her face up. "It is much easier to be good when you don't know how much fun being bad is, isn't it, petite?"

"I hate you," Elf muttered, smacking him lightly on his cheek.

Ranulf laughed and caught her hand, kissing the palm. "Have you any idea of how jealous I am of our son?"

"Why would you be jealous of Simon?" she asked, then she blushed. "*Ohh!*"

"Go to sleep now, petite," he told her. "And be satisfied in knowing the waiting is no easier for me than it is for you."

"*Good!*" Elf told him, caressing him in a delicate spot before rolling over and turning her back to him.

Ranulf laughed again. "Witch," he said softly, and moving onto his side he drew her back against him, his big hand clamped firmly about one of her breasts.

"That's not fair!" Elf protested.

"What?" He feigned innocence.

In reply Elf ground her buttocks into his groin suggestively.

He groaned as he felt himself beginning to seethe with desire. "*That's not fair!*" he complained.

"Two can play at the same game, my lord," she replied dulcetly.

"Go to sleep, Eleanore," he said through gritted teeth.

"Yes, my lord," Elf replied sweetly. His hand upon her breast was both taunting and comforting. She longed for their bodies to be joined, but she knew Sister Winifred was right. Her body was still weak and sore from Simon's birth. Where was the patience she had always prided herself upon in her convent days? She must surely regain it quickly or she would expire from her own desire. She felt Ranulf's soft kiss upon the nape of her neck and, sighing, closed her eyes.

Chapter Thirteen

During the next few weeks, their lives returned to a semblance of normalcy. Ranulf rode out daily to survey the manor. His great concern was for Ashlin's safety, and in this he became more and more convinced that his lands would not be totally safe until Ashlin possessed a strong castle. The walls that surrounded the demesne were high, but they encompassed too open an area—his own house, the church, the huts of his serfs, and the cottages of his freedmen and upper servants. The assemblage was, in truth, a sprawling village. His walls could be breached by anyone with serious intent to do so, leaving his people wide open to the attackers.

The house offered little more protection for his family. It sat upon the flat earth, and once its door was broken in, its inhabitants were vulnerable. Still, Ashlin was better defended now than it had been. The walls were higher, the men-at-arms better trained. He must trust Fulk and his agreement with the Welsh to leave the manor in peace.

As he considered all of this, Ranulf realized that his mission for Duke Henry was of vast importance to his future, and that of his family. Perhaps he might even foster out Simon one day to the new queen's household, as Elf had suggested when their son was born. The lord of a castle had more social standing than the lord of a simple manor. He laughed, knowing that he was aiming very, very high in his ambitions. First they needed permission for a castle to be built at Ashlin. To that end he would strive.

The growing season was proving to be a good one so far. The rains had been plentiful, but gentle. The days warm, the nights cool, yet not cold. The grain was growing well. They waited eagerly for dry weather during which they could cut the hay that would be used for the next twelve months. Elf's garden of herbs flourished by her herbarium. The sheep and the cattle grew fat on the sweet grass.

Midsummer's Eve was upon them before they knew it. There would be a fine celebration, of course. The lord of the manor declared a holiday, as was customary. Many at Ashlin rose early to view the sunrise. As it was a fair day, the sight was glorious. The sky lightened slowly, the deep blue of night growing to a brighter shade, the horizon warming: lemon at first, then gold, purple, and orange. The birds began to sing and chirp even as the sun pushed itself above the border between earth and sky, blazing fiery and red. It was going to be the perfect summer's day.

Already from the bake house the scent of St. John's bread baking wafted on the soft breeze. Made from locust seedpods, it was a delicacy served only at the Midsummer's Eve feast, which would be hosted for the entire manor by the lord and lady of Ashlin. The sheep selected for the feast were driven from the near meadow close to two pits, dug out of the meadow grass, where they would be roasted. Meat was not an everyday occurrence for the serfs. Piglings, stuffed with cheese, bread, nuts, and spices would be served along with a roe deer. Entrayale, a sheep's stomach filled with eggs, cheese, vegetables, bread, and pork was baking, along with Blackmanger, a dish of chicken, rice, almonds, and sugar. There would be spiced lamprey eels, creamed cod, and salmon. There would be a special Frumenty pudding of apples and spices added to wheat, sugar, and milk. There was cheese and butter and curd cheese. And special Destiny Cakes, shaped like common items such as birds, beasts, houses, ships, and household items. There was mead flavored with honey and mint; Cuckoo-foot ale, a sparkling beverage made with ginger, basil, and anise.

Some wandering musicians had come to the manor the evening before asking for shelter. Now they set themselves up to entertain for the lord and lady. They played upon a rebec, drums, frestelles, which were panpipes, a pibgorn, a reed instrument, bells, and a tambourine. Their tunes were lively, and dancers pranced gaily upon the green. Archery butts were set up for shooting contests. Footraces were run. The young girls played Saint-John's-Wort, using sprigs of the plant and its deep yellow flowers to determine if they would have true love or no love at all. There was a great deal of giggling when Willa's flowers ended with a *loves me,* and glances were cast in the direction of the young squire, Pax, followed by more giggles while Willa blushed red. A hunt was held for St. John's fern, which was said to render its finder invisible at will, but sadly none was found.

"Come to the wet fire ceremony," Arthur cried to them as the early evening came.

The manor's inhabitants hurried to the millpond, where small wooden boats were already prepared, a wish previously carved on each boat by its owner. Lighted candles were carefully placed in the miniature vessels, which were then set afloat upon the waters of the millpond. The mill wheel turned, ruffling the surface of the pond and its adjacent stream. The tiny ships bobbed across their tiny sea, some sinking when they found themselves too near the wheel, others having their candles blown out. But those boats that safely gained the other side of the millpond with their candles still alight guaranteed their owners that their wishes would be fulfilled.

"Both of our boats have arrived safely," Elf said, smiling. "What did you wish for?"

"To come quickly back to you," he said. "What did you wish for, petite?"

"The same thing," she said softly, reaching for his hand.

"The bonfires are being lit!" came a cry, and hand in hand the lord and lady of the manor walked back to the meadow.

The fires sprang up around them as they seated themselves at their trestle again. The long day was finally waning. The last of the feast was consumed along with ale and mead. The sunset blazed pink, purple, orange, green, and gold beyond the western hills. The musicians began to play again, even as Cedric nodded a signal to his lord and lady. Elf and Ranulf stood up. With Ranulf leading, Elf took his hand and that of Willa, who took the hand of Ranulf's squire, Pax, who took another hand which took another, and another. Together they all danced in a line, weaving about and among the several fires in an ancient dance called "Threading the Needle." The sun sank away. The sky above them grew dark. The music grew wilder, more primitive until suddenly without warning it stopped. About them was silence. There was not a single sound. Then the fires were quickly doused, and Ashlin's people moved off silently into the night. Some returned to their homes. Young lovers simply slipped off into the darkness. The lord took his lady's hand, and led her indoors. Midsummer's Eve was over, and tomorrow was a working day.

"Willa has gone off," Ida muttered disapprovingly. "I will see to your needs, my lady."

"Nay, find your bed, old woman," Ranulf said quietly. "I can help my wife undress as well as you can."

"And have more fun doing it, too, lord" came the ribald answer. "Heh! Heh!"

He chuckled, then still hand in hand they entered the solar, leaving the rest of the world behind them.

Elf turned and slipped her arms about her husband's neck, looking up into his face. "Soon you will be gone from me to Normandy," she said softly. "I know not how long you will be gone. I am bold, I know, Ranulf, but I would have you make love to me. It has been so long since our bodies were last joined in passion." Her sweet glance was warm, and her silvery gray eyes shone with her open desire for him.

"I would not hurt you," he replied.

Elf laughed softly. "I vow, my lord, you are the kindest man I have ever known, which, of course, is not saying a great deal as I have known no other but you. If I did not know better, I would be certain that you had a lover among the serfs. But I do know better," she hastily amended seeing his startled look. "Ranulf, my lord, my good husband, I have from the beginning enjoyed the pleasures our bodies give us. We have not had that pleasure in months now, and

you are about to go off in a few days to Normandy for an indeter-
minate length of time. Do you not think we might indulge ourselves until then? I have healed quickly, thanks to my herbs and
teas." She smiled winningly up at him, and her hand caressed his
cheek. "Do you not want to make love to me? Perhaps it is not as
difficult for a man as it is for a woman. I must by my own honor
and nature remain chaste while you are gone; but perhaps that is
not the case with you. Perhaps when you reach Duke Henry's
court, you will indulge your lusts with some beautiful and elegant
woman of the court!" Her eyes suddenly flashed, and Elf stamped
her foot angrily. "By the rood, I will not have it!" She began to
pound upon his chest with her small, balled-up fists.

He laughed aloud. He couldn't help it. She had gone from being
alluring and seductive in one moment to being furiously jealous
the next. Was it possible that she cared for him? Ranulf's heart beat
faster as he caught her wrists in a gentle, but firm grip.

"Petite," he said, "I will never betray you no matter my own
hungers, for there is but one woman I desire in all the world, and
that woman is you, Eleanore." Pulling her against his broad chest,
he nuzzled her soft hair. "You, petite, are my wife. I need no other."
His lips brushed hers.

Somewhat mollified, she kissed him back, her fingers all the
while fumbling to loosen the girdle about his tunic.

His laughter was now lower and more intimate. "You are quite
shameless, petite," he teased her. "I can see you will have your way
with me, Eleanore." He helped her to draw the tunic over his head.
Then, reaching out, he loosed her girdle, his fingers pulling her
tunic off. Her skirt fell quickly to the floor, puddling about her
ankles.

Elf unlaced his chemise, opening it so it might slide over his
shoulders, then his torso, his hips, and finally to the floor. Reaching
out, he returned the favor, then drew her to him, her full, naked
breasts pressing against his bare chest, her sweetly rounded belly
against his belly, her love mound pushing against his burning lance,
still held captive within his remaining clothing.

"*Ohhh!*" Elf gasped as he knelt before her and rolled down her stockings, then removed them from her feet. He kissed each knee as he did so. Then he stood again, drawing his braies off.

Elf went to mimic him, kneeling to roll down his hose. She gasped, startled, upon coming face-to-face as it were, with his burgeoning manhood. She had never before seen it quite that close up. Captivated, she stared at it, fascinated to view the source of her pleasure. Other than its size, it had little to recommend it, she decided, yet, oh, what delights she gained when it fitted itself within her sheath. Hesitantly she broke her gaze and drew his hose off. When she again stood up, he looked questioningly at her. "It is not particularly pretty, my lord, but I enjoy the dance it performs with me," she said.

He pulled her against him again, reveling in the warmth of their bodies. "There is so much I want to teach you, petite, now that we are so well acquainted." His mouth brushed against her brow.

"Could I kiss it?"

"Aye," he said shortly.

"What else?"

"You could nurse upon it as I do your breasts," he replied. Dear God, he was going to burst, she excited him so greatly with her talk. The thought of her mouth against him was almost too much.

"If I swallowed your seed, could I become with child?" she inquired, curious.

"Nay," he told her, "but I should not let my seed loose within your mouth. I would save it for your sweet sheath. I do not wish to waste it, petite."

"Would it give you pleasure?"

"*Aye!*" He squeezed the word out of his throat.

Without a moment's hesitation Elf fell to her knees before him, and taking him in her mouth began to nurse upon him vigorously.

Ranulf thought his head would burst. "Gently, petite," he groaned. By the rood she was such a different woman from the innocent he had married less than two years ago. "*Enough!*" he said sharply.

Elf stood, her cheeks pink, and he kissed her passionately, his manhood pushing against her. Unable to help himself he lifted her up, cupping her buttocks in his big hands as she instinctively wrapped her legs about him, and he slowly pushed himself deep within her eager body. Her arms enclosed him, and she sighed deeply, a sound of complete and utter contentment. *Does she care?* he asked himself again. *Or is it simply that she enjoys the privileges of marriage?* He walked through the solar into their small bedchamber, never allowing their bodies to unlock, and laid her back upon the bed. Gently he pistoned her, anxious for any sign of distress on her part, but Elf was plainly enjoying her husband's tender ardor.

"Ahhhh!" she cried softly. How he filled her! How she had missed his passion! Would he ever love her, or must she be content forever with only these wonderful moments between them? Her nails dug into the muscles of his back as her crisis approached, and when hot pleasure rained down upon her, she heard him cry out, too, as his juices flooded her.

He collapsed atop her, and after a moment she pushed at him. His eyes met hers, and the warm smile she gave him almost broke his heart in its sweetness. *He loved her, and he wanted her to love him!* How did a man go about making a woman *love* him. The emotion was surely a different feeling than passion, for he, himself, felt differently toward her when they were not making love. He wanted to protect her. He wanted to share his thoughts with her, and have her share hers with him. He wanted to tell her how much her approval meant to him, and how just holding her hand in his caused his heart to sing. He felt vaguely embarrassed by these feelings, for, after all, he was a man. Should a man be so very tenderly inclined toward a woman? *Toward a wife?*

And what if he shared these emotions with her, and she did not reciprocate? Would that not spoil the rapport they now had together? But was it possible that she might care? Eleanore was not a woman to feign sentiments she did not feel. She was honest and unspoiled. In that she had not changed. If he told her he loved her and she could not return his love, she would say so. The thought that she might not love him was the one thing that kept him from declaring himself. For the first time in his entire life, Ranulf de Glandeville realized that he was truly afraid. Oh, he had been fearful of going into battle, but that was a different kind of fear altogether.

His own mother had rejected him in favor of her new husband. He had been astounded that she could do such a thing, for he was her son. Her firstborn, and yet she had put him aside with apparent ease. When the pain and the shock had drained away, he had come to realize his mother was only doing what was best for her, and the children she had borne her second mate. Though she had stood by while her husband stole her eldest son's patrimony, she had loved Ranulf in her own way; and she had known that he could forge a new life for himself with King Stephen. He had forgiven her, but he had never quite rid himself of the pain of that rejection. Now he knew that his mother's denial of him would be naught compared to the pain and sorrow he would feel if Eleanore rejected his love. Better to remain silent. *At least for now.*

She lay cradled in his arms, her head upon his chest. *Men are different in so many ways from women,* Elf thought. She remembered the girls at the convent saying that all that men could feel was lust and passion. She had since learned that those qualities were not necessarily a bad thing; yet, how her heart yearned for more! She did not know if this *love* was a particularly good thing. Her brother loved his wife, Isleen, and that turned out badly. For love, Dickon had rejected his own flesh and blood and had put her in St. Frideswide's. He did not come to see her but once in those nine years. How fortunate that she was happy there, for her brother would neither have known nor cared if it were otherwise, just as long as Isleen was content. And in the end she killed him because she loved her cousin, Saer de Bude, and he was willing to abet her in her evil perfidy.

Does love render men foolish and weak? Elf wondered. *How I should like to tell Ranulf that he owns not just my body, but my heart as well.* She wanted to be with him all the time and fretted when he was not with her. She could not bear the thought that he was to go to Normandy, not knowing when he would return. For all those years she slept alone on her convent cot, yet now she could not even bear to think of how awful it would be when his broad back would not be

there for her to cuddle against. That was not lust, she knew. When
he smiled at her, her heart grew tight within her. The sound of his
voice made her happy. *How will I bear it when he is not here for me to
share my day with, and he, his, with me?*

She would tell him of her feelings, but she suspected it would
just embarrass him. He was so much older than she, and wiser. He
would surely think her foolish, and she could not bear it if the respect he seemed to hold for her were damaged by her girlish emotions. Ranulf was a sophisticated man, having been raised at the
court. He might not be a man of great family or wealth, but even
Duke Henry recognized his worth and chose him for this mission.
A man like that would certainly be discomfited and abashed by
love. Better that she remain silent. He was good to her, and what
more could she possibly desire?

July came, and it was time for Ranulf to depart for Normandy.
He did so reluctantly. Although Ashlin had been left in peace, the
Welsh had been raiding. A serf sent to St. Frideswide's with several
baskets of plums, a gift from Simon to his godmothers, returned to
tell them that a small flock of the nuns' sheep had been driven off
from a near meadow. It had happened in the night, which made it
more frightening. The nuns had awakened in the morning and discovered the loss. The sheepdog who stayed with the flock had been
slaughtered, and it was the crows feasting on its carcass that had first
drawn their attention.

"Keep one side of the gates closed even during the day," Ranulf
told Elf. "If the Welsh come, the serfs in the fields can run for the
enclosure, but remember to be certain the gates are firmly barred
before the Welsh ponies even get near the drawbridge. Raise it if
you can in the event of an attack. It will make it more difficult for
the enemy. If anyone mounts a serious full-scale attack, it is possible to breach our walls, for they are still too low. I do not believe,
however, the Welsh have that capability. You should be safe if you
take precautions. Be very careful, petite."

"But what if some of our people are caught in the open?" she
asked.

"They must then take their chances, and God help them," he told her. "The safety of *all* of Ashlin's people rests with your decisions, petite. Fulk will be here to marshal our men, but you are the lady of the manor, and it is your word that is law."

"I do not wish to sound like a child, but I am truly uncomfortable with so great a responsibility."

"If I were killed in battle," he replied, "you would have to hold this manor for our Simon, Eleanore, even as your mother did for your brother. She was, I am told, a gentle soul as you are, but she had strength aplenty for her son's inheritance, unlike my mother who allowed my stepfather to steal my lands for their sons. You have the courage, petite. I will be back as quickly as I can." He put a comforting arm about her, and Elf could feel his strength flowing into her as he embraced her.

"Forgive my lapse," she said softly. "I will do my duty."

"I know you will," Ranulf replied. "Keep a watch on the walls both day and night. Tell the shepherds that if the Welsh come in the night as they did at St. Frideswide's, to take their dogs, and disappear into the gorse. They would be helpless against an armed band, and unable to prevent the sheep from being stolen. The sheep can be replaced. Their lives cannot. I need loyal serfs about us."

"Will you send me word when you can return?"

"I do not think I can, as my mission is to be a discreet one. I will try, however, petite. When you hear that King Stephen has died, know that I will be on my way home," he advised her. "It is then the queen will come to England with her son."

Elf had packed her husband's baggage, which would be transported upon a mule. There were two good tunics for the court, and two for everyday wear. She had made him several fine new linen chemises. There were newly sewn hose and braies, chausses, and undertunics. There was a beautiful surcoat to be worn over his armor at court, a fine girdle studded with garnets and pearls, and a pair of fur-lined gloves as well as a light wool mantle lined in lynx.

"I wonder if it is enough," she fretted.

He laughed. "It will have to be. I am but a simple knight. I do not wish to attract attention, petite. I am to be an English sparrow amid all the fine peacocks of Duke Henry's court. Besides, the mule must carry my armor with him as well. I may be invited to join in a tournament."

She paled. "What if you are injured?!" she exclaimed. "And who will wash your garments for you if you are forced to stay more than a month or two? Did Duke Henry think of that when he ordered you to Normandy? No! Of course not! He is to be a king and is used to ordering others about without a care for their welfare."

Ranulf laughed again at his wife's outrage. "Pax will do the laundry," he told her. "It is part of his duties as my squire. He promises to care for me every bit as well as a wife," he teased her.

"Humph!" Elf snorted derisively.

The day was new, the mule packed. Pax had thanked his uncle for the hundredth time for the opportunity he had been given. He kissed his proud mother farewell, and mounted his new horse. Ranulf smiled at the young man's excitement. He knew that Pax had never been off Ashlin lands in his whole life, and for him a grand adventure awaited.

Elf forced back her tears. She would not behave like a silly fool. Ranulf was not going to war, just to Normandy. "I will pray you have a safe journey, my lord," she told him quietly. "I will pray you are successful, and return home safely to us as quickly as possible."

"The hour of my departure but means I am closer to returning home to you, petite," he told her. Then his arms enfolded her, and he kissed her with tender passion. "Keep Simon and Ashlin safe for me, Eleanore," he said, releasing her from his embrace.

"I will, Ranulf," she promised him. Was there something different in his look than had been there before? She had begun to sense of late that perhaps love was not an emotion foreign to him. If only she could tell him what was in her own heart! She watched him as he mounted his great warhorse. He reached down and lifted her up for a final kiss.

Their eyes met, and for a moment Elf thought she was floating.

"Farewell, petite," he said setting her back upon her feet. By the rood, her look had been more than just responsive! Was it possible she might harbor warmhearted feelings for him? Did he dare to hope? He sighed as he kicked his mount into a walk. It would simply have to wait until he returned. Besides, he wanted to be absolutely certain of his position in her life. If she loved him, he wanted to hear it from her lips. He needed to know for sure else he make a fool of himself. He wanted her love, not her pity.

Elf watched until her husband and his squire were no more than a speck upon the road. Then, with a shake of her head, she returned through the gates of Ashlin to her daily round of duties. She had to speak with Fulk, John, and Cedric this morning. There would be crops to harvest in the coming month, and the fields to be tilled and planted with the winter crops. The sheep needed to be shorn if they were to have new coats for the winter and Ashlin have wool to sell at the Lammas Fair. There was so much to do.

On the edge of a wood bordering Ashlin, Merin ap Owen lurked. He did not trust any of his men to scout a possible target for him. This was something he always did himself. It was the secret of his success as a raider. He looked up the hill and saw Ashlin's walls. They were far higher than Isleen had told him. Had she lied? Was she stupid—or had the walls been rebuilt? He opted for the latter explanation, for Isleen was many things, but she was not stupid. He needed to get closer. Isleen had said there was a shallow moat, but if the walls had been elevated, then surely the moat had been deepened.

He moved from the wood onto the narrow path leading up to the walled enclosure. He was dressed simply in greens and browns, the better to blend in with his surroundings. On his back he carried a knife-sharpener's wheel. It was a disguise he used often. There were always knives to be sharpened on any estate, although one such as this one probably had its own wheel. Still, Merin ap Owen did not appear to be a suspicious character and would be granted a night's lodging if he asked, which he would. It was the best way to gain the lay of the land. Servants gossiped, and a woman servant well pleasured talked the most of all. He smiled wolfishly, his step firm.

He was, as he had expected, welcomed to Ashlin. His sharp eye determined that the moat was indeed deeper. Not only that but the earthen bridge across it had been dug away to be replaced by a thick oak drawbridge. There was a platform around the inner walls where the men-at-arms stood on watch, and there were certainly more armed men than he had anticipated. Further, they seemed well trained. Ashlin would be a far greater challenge than he had thought. It would take careful planning to gain hostile entry here. Was it worth it, he wondered?

As he sat in the hall that evening looking about him, he thoughtfully considered the risks, weighing them against the profits of such a venture. The sheep and the cattle were pastured outside the walls. They would appear to be Ashlin's greatest assets, and they could easily be stolen with probably no loss of life. While the hall was comfortable, there was no silver plate displayed, or anything else of great enough value to warrant taking. Isleen's passion for vengeance was what drove her, but his whore did not ever overrule his common sense.

The lady of the manor had married a good man. He divined that by the well-trained men-at-arms and the additional precautions that had been taken to evade raiders such as himself. He smiled. They were the exact foresights he would have taken under such circumstances. The lord, however, was away, he learned from the chatter about him. It would appear to be as good a time as any to raid Ashlin's livestock.

His eye went to the lady of the manor. The little nun, as Isleen called her, was probably one of the most beautiful women he had ever seen. Her pale red-gold hair was neatly braided, and contained beneath a modest veil. There was a serenity about her that he had never known to encompass a woman. His eyes narrowed. He could see her servants both loved and respected her by the way in which they served her. He realized he was, for the first time in his life, in the presence of a *good* woman. He had not thought such a creature existed. It gave rise to another question. What was a good woman like in bed? Did that cool elegance extend to her lord's bed, or was she both passionate and hot in her husband's arms? He was not likely to know, he considered wryly.

Merin ap Owen was given a sleeping place by the fire, and some bread and cheese when the morning came. As they did not need a knife sharpener's service, he took his leave of Ashlin, making his way for the next few days over the hills back into Wales and to Gwynfr. Arriving at his small castle, he went to Isleen's chambers and sent for her to come to him immediately.

"So, you are back, my lord," she said, entering her private apartment. She was garbed in a blue silk gown that favored her eyes, and her golden hair was loose.

"Get on your back, and raise your skirts," he commanded her. "I have missed your hot and eager sheath, Isleen. When you have pleasured me we will talk, my pretty bitch." He fell upon her immediately and used her lustily. She was not as eager as he, although she pretended to be. He knew then she had been betraying him with one or more of his men. He said nothing. Let her believe she could hoodwink him. While he enjoyed her wantonness, he knew that one day he would send her back to Clud, for he could not allow her to make a fool of him, lest his men believe him weak. Finished with her, he arose and straightened out his clothing. "Get up," he told her. "Now we will talk."

"You will attack Ashlin?" she asked avidly.

"Much has changed since you held sway there as Richard de Montfort's wife, Isleen." He went on to explain to her, then said, "The sheep and the cattle we will steal, but there is nothing in the hall worth risking the lives of my men."

"*What?*" she shrieked angrily. "Did I not make it clear to you before you went on your ridiculous scouting mission that I wanted Eleanore de Montfort dead? I will settle for no less than her life, as she has wronged me! And I want the little nun to suffer as I have suffered. I want her used by each man in your garrison before you kill her for me. If you love me, you will do it."

Merin ap Owen laughed. "But I don't love you, Isleen," he said.

"What ever made you think I did? Because I took you for my whore? You are as dangerous as a rabid cat, my pretty bitch. I reconnoiter my target personally because only I can be the judge of its worth. Cattle and sheep are all Ashlin possesses that interest me. There is no value in anything else there. The lady Eleanore's lord is away right now, and so the time is most auspicious to raid their livestock."

"You fool!" she screamed, and began to pound upon his broad chest. "You thickheaded Welsh fool! Of course there is more to Ashlin than just cattle and sheep. Can you not see it?"

He caught her wrists in a cruel grasp. *"What?"* he demanded of her, and then he cuffed her. "What do I not see at Ashlin that has value, Isleen? What do I overlook?" He gave her a shake.

"Eleanore de Montfort!" Isleen cried. "Let me go, you brute! You are bruising me badly." She rubbed the wrists he released. "Is not the lady worth a ransom, Merin ap Owen? Cattle and sheep that are stolen rarely earn their value when sold, and everyone knows the livestock you take for sale are stolen. Leave Ashlin's beasts in their meadows, and take the lady of the manor instead. Her husband must sell them all if he is to pay the ransom you will ask. You will gain double what you would have if you stole the creatures yourself. Is that not a better plan than yours, Merin ap Owen?"

"Aye, it is," he agreed thoughtfully, "but do not think I don't understand your motives, Isleen. You wish to gain custody of Ashlin's mistress so you may wreak your vengeance upon her while she is in my parole. I will not allow you to do it, Isleen. I want the full measure of gold that Ashlin's lord will bring me in exchange for his wife's safety. If the lady Eleanore is harmed in *any* way, my pretty bitch, not only will I lose a golden ransom, I could quite easily lose my life when her angry husband slays me. You wouldn't want that, Isleen, would you?" He grinned down into her face. "You do want me to love you, don't you? I do not know, but if your facile little mind continues to aid me so well, I might learn to love you one day." He pulled her into his embrace, and kissed her hard.

Isleen reached down as she returned his kiss, and fondled his manhood until it was stiff again. Then she pulled him to the bed and, shedding her gown, cupped her big breasts in her hands to tease him. He lifted her up onto the bed, and, standing above him, she spread her legs so that he could scent her musk. Bending down, she rubbed her nipples across his lips. He licked eagerly at them, and she backed away.

"Bitch!" he growled, reaching out and yanking her by the ankles onto her back. Fumbling with his garments, he loosed his lance and couched it securely within her sheath. *"Bitch!"* he repeated as she attempted to dislodge him.

Isleen pulled him down into an embrace and sunk her teeth into his shoulder, biting until she tasted blood. "Now I have infected you with my rabidity." She laughed.

He slapped her several times, but the blows were not hard, merely a warning. "You are clever," he told her, "but not indispensable, my pretty bitch. I may have to kill you one day."

"Perhaps," Isleen told him, "I will kill you first," and she laughed at the surprised look on his face.

He thrust into her again, using her cruelly, forcing her near the peak, holding her back again and again until she began to scream vile curses at him, and he at last gave her her release, mocking her as he did. "You are only a woman, Isleen, and a weak woman at that." Then he laughed, and withdrew from her. "Remember that, my pretty bitch. I must think on what you have suggested." He pulled his clothes back into order and walked out of her room even as she cursed him again.

Isleen, he considered as he entered his own private apartment, was becoming a very annoying encumbrance. Still, she had the same ferocious appetites that he himself possessed. He had to admit to himself that he gained more satisfaction from her than any other woman he had ever known. Still, she was not to be trusted, he reminded himself. She wanted to be rich, and she wanted to be independent. Perhaps he would help her to attain those goals, provided she behaved herself. She would certainly make a better ally than enemy.

Her proposal to kidnap the lady Eleanore was clever. Isleen was right when she said he could gain double in ransom than he would simply by stealing and selling Ashlin's livestock. But if he was able to get custody of the lady and bring her to Gwynfr Castle, could he keep her safe from his wild whore? A dead or injured mistress of Ashlin would gain him nothing. Isleen's grievance with Eleanore de Montfort was not justified. Isleen herself had told him how she had managed to get Eleanore as a young child banished to the convent before she married Richard, and how she had seen her but once before her dying husband sent for his sister nine years later.

Isleen's partner in crime, her cousin, had obviously been a stupid man. He had chosen both the wrong time, and certainly the wrong place, to attempt his debauchment of the lady Eleanore. He would have been wiser to come in the night with the aid of Isleen and take the girl where her servants could not have heard her cries. It was his fault that Isleen's plan had failed. Eleanore de Montfort could scarcely be blamed for defending herself from the unwanted advances of Saer de Bude, nor could her serf be faulted for protecting his mistress.

Isleen's complaint had no basis, in fact. She was, Merin ap Owen concluded, jealous of her former sister-in-law. Aye, that was the crux of the matter. The lady Eleanore was every bit as beautiful as was Isleen de Warenne. And she was respected and loved by her people, which Isleen certainly had not been. How often his whore had complained to him about Ashlin's people. The lady Eleanore was everything that Isleen was not, and Isleen hated her for it. Not that Isleen would have changed given the opportunity. She wanted everything her way, and when she could not have it, she cried foul.

How to keep his hostage safe from her was the problem. Once he had solved the conundrum, he would move on to the issue of how to kidnap her. The lady Eleanore was not worth the loss of life it would take to battle through Ashlin's walls, although once inside the compound, gaining entry to the house was a simple enough matter, he decided. But if he could not get inside the walls, he would have to get his victim outside, where he might capture her more easily.

Merin ap Owen poured himself a goblet of the fine wine he

kept here in his own private domain. Then he sat down by his fire to consider the matter more carefully. The lady was close to the nuns who had raised her. Could she be lured outside her walls by an attack upon St. Frideswide's? Possibly, but not certainly. There was that grizzled and battle-hardened sergeant at arms who served her. He was in charge of the safety of Ashlin, and would certainly know better than to allow his mistress to go to the convent to help her nuns after an attack. He would send his own men to help. Still, such an attack could prove a successful diversion.

Stroking his chin slowly and thoughtfully, he narrowed his eyes in contemplation. If he could get someone into Ashlin's manor house, someone who could drug the gatekeeper, the men on the walls, the household servants, and then open the gates for him . . . now that was the perfect plan! *But who?* Who would the manor folk take in? Not be suspicious of? He needed some helpless creature he could bully, and whose loyalty was unquestioning. *Who?* Then a slow smile lit his handsome features as he realized the perfect pawn for his endeavor. Isleen's servant. Clud's niece. *Arwydd!*

Arwydd was not a stupid girl. She had been clever enough to gain an exit from her uncle's brothel, where she had been naught but an unpaid slave. Isleen never complained about her, which meant the girl was also clever enough to serve a difficult mistress. Could she also serve her master? Aye! She could, and she would or he would kill her himself. He had no use for disobedient servants. And while he thought on it, he decided he would learn who had been futtering his whore while he had been in England. He had warned his men that she was his personal possession, but obviously someone had succumbed to Isleen's bounteous charms. The man would die for it when he learned his name. He would say nothing to Isleen, but she would understand, and more important, so would his men. No one would ever use Isleen again unless he gave them permission to do so.

He smiled grimly, then considered how to infiltrate Arwydd into Ashlin. She would be a runaway slave, of course, whose master had attempted to sell her as a whore, or some such tale. That was a

story sure to gain sympathy from the gentle lady Eleanore. He
chuckled. It was clever, and Arwydd was just the right lass to carry
it off. He would have to think on a series of signals she could use to
alert him and his men, but with his decision, success was a foregone
conclusion. Merin ap Owen chuckled, well pleased with himself—
and even with Isleen.

CHAPTER FOURTEEN

Pax of Ashlin was astounded by all he had seen of the world so far. What stories he would have to tell Willa! His lord and he had departed home and ridden for over a week before they reached the sea. It seemed that England was quite a large country, Pax decided. Finally they came to a town his master called Portsmouth, where they set about arranging for passage across to Barfleur. Pax had never seen such a big place as Portsmouth, and the salty smell of the sea was strange to his nostrils. Only by listening carefully could he make out what was being said most of the time, for the English spoken here was different from that spoken at Ashlin. Fortunately his Norman-speak improved quickly as his lord spoke it with him every day.

"Remember," Ranulf warned him, "to pretend you understand just basic orders and unimportant phrases. That way the others about you will speak freely, and I may gain information that may be of use to me."

"I will, my lord," Pax replied.

"You have done well so far, boy," Ranulf praised him, and Pax was pleased, for he truly wanted to better himself and be worthy of Willa's hand when he returned. If the lord was satisfied with his service, then he would certainly give permission for Willa and Pax to wed.

They crossed to Normandy on a fair summer's day. The sea was pleasant, the sun warm, the winds brisk without being harsh.

"We are fortunate," Ranulf told him as they debarked the next afternoon at the Norman port of Barfleur. "We have crossed quickly and without difficulty. I take it as a good omen."

"Will we sleep tonight in Rouen, my lord?" Pax asked.

"Nay. Tomorrow, perhaps, but then again mayhap not until the night after depending upon the weather and the roads."

They led their horses and the pack mule from their ship.

"Let us find a market, Pax," Ranulf said. "I would purchase us some food, for I know not if we will espy a safe place to stay, and we may find ourselves in a wilderness without inn or abbey. We had best prepare for it, eh?" He mounted his horse, then turning said, "The animals will need a bit of water before we leave the town."

"Aye, my lord! I will see to it," Pax replied.

They found the market first, and Ranulf purchased two long loaves of bread, a small wheel of cheese, a fat sausage, some peaches, and a heavy skin of wine, which he tasted first to be certain it was not sour.

"You are English?" the wine merchant asked.

"Aye," Ranulf acknowledged. "I am but a humble knight and have come to pledge my loyalty to Duke Henry, for our king lies ill."

The wine merchant nodded with understanding. "Better to do it *before* the fact rather than *after*," he opined. "You are a wise man, my lord. You obviously have a care for your family, and that is good. Duke Henry is a generous lord, and the Duchess Alienor the most beautiful and accomplished of women. I saw her once when I was visiting my sister in Rouen. She is a glorious lady, if I may be forgiven for saying so."

Ranulf thanked the wine merchant for his courtesy and his directions to the public trough. They moved on to water the horses, then they set out on the road to Rouen. As darkness approached, Ranulf realized his precautions had been wise. There was neither a religious house, or any other civilized place to lay their heads. When he saw a small spot near a running stream, and sheltered from the view of the road, he ordered a halt to their journey.

"I want no fire tonight to draw bandits," he said to Pax. "We will eat before the light is gone. There is plenty of water and grazing for our animals."

"Will we not be attacked by wild beasts without a fire?" young Pax ventured.

Ranulf smiled. "We are more likely to be attacked by two-footed wild beasts if we have a fire to lead them to us, lad," he said, dismounting. "Look in yonder field at those fat cattle grazing. They would not be left out the night were there beasts about to menace them. Come, let us eat, and then get a good night's rest. I did not sleep well last night upon the open deck of our vessel, for fear someone would cut our throats for the horses and the mule." He chuckled, noting how pale his squire had become at his words. "You can trust no one here, lad," he said quietly. "I am the only person in whom you may put your faith, Pax."

They unsaddled the horses and left them to graze. The young squire then carefully cut two large chunks of bread, cheese, and sausage, handing a portion to his master. They settled down to eat, passing the wineskin back and forth as they needed it. They decided to save the peaches for the morrow. The day had been long, and they were both tired. The sun had set now, and the twilight was deepening into night. It was clear, and, lying upon his back gazing up at the sky, Pax thought the stars different. A quarter moon rose, faintly brightening the landscape about them as the two men fell into a sound sleep.

Ranulf awoke to the sound of a bird calling. Opening his eyes, he could see the sky lightening beyond the horizon. Arising, he went to pee, then gently kicked his squire. "Wake up, lad, 'tis almost dawn," he said. "I want to eat and be on our way. I'd just as soon sleep in Rouen tonight as in another damp field. My bones are getting too old for it."

Pax scrambled to his feet. "I'm sorry, my lord. I did not mean to oversleep."

"Go relieve yourself, then let us eat," Ranulf said.

They left a third of the bread, the remainder of the sausage, and the peaches for a midday meal, eating only bread and cheese with

their wine. The wine sent a bit of fire through their veins, warming them. The morning was faintly humid, and the day promised
to be hot. When they had finished, they watered the horses, saddled them, and were on their way once again. The countryside
about them was a fairly flat valley enclosed by rolling hills. Their
path ran beside the river Seine. By very late afternoon the roofs of
the town were well in view. The knight and his squire crossed the
large humpbacked stone bridge with its thirteen great arches that
spanned the river.

Rouen was a very old city. It had been a provincial capital in the
time of the great Roman Empire, Ranulf told Pax. Pax nodded,
but he had no idea who the Romans were and would not ask for
fear of appearing ignorant. Normandy had been a part of a province called Gaul, Ranulf concluded. Even England had been a
province of the Romans, who called it Britannia. Pax nodded
again, but his eyes were darting about with curiosity as they traversed the narrow streets, which were lined with tall half-timbered
houses of four and five stories. Pax had never seen anything like
these houses.

"We must find a place to stay," Ranulf said, "and as near to the
castle as possible."

"We are not to stay in the castle?" Pax was surprised.

"Not unless we are invited. Remember that I am here merely
to pay my respects to Duke Henry, who will be our next king.
Greater lords than I are sharing sleeping places, crowded together
with their servants like cattle. Perhaps, though, I might beg a place
for us in the duke's stables. It depends on how many men are with
him right now. Let us go to the castle first, Pax. On reflection an
inn could prove too costly for my small purse." He had not told his
squire the truth about his visit to Normandy. The lad was green
yet, and Ranulf could not be certain if Pax could be relied upon
not to gossip.

The Empress Matilda's castle was easy to find. The largest building in Rouen, it had both a great hall and a donjon. They rode
across the castle's drawbridge and into the bustling courtyard. Ran-

ulf's eyes scanned the area, and at last he spotted the stables. He turned his horse toward it, and Pax followed. He sought out and found the stablemaster, importuning him for shelter.

"I am Sir Ranulf de Glandeville, lord of Ashlin. I have come from England to pay my respects to Duke Henry. Is there a place, perhaps in your lofts, for my squire and myself?"

The stablemaster looked the two men over carefully. Their clothing was respectable and of good quality, if a bit travel stained. Their mounts were good. "Do you know anyone here?" the stablemaster asked.

"Sir Garrick Taliferro, who serves as one of Duke Henry's knights," Ranulf said. "He will vouch for my identity and my honesty."

"You understand," the stablemaster replied, "that I must assure myself you are who you say, my lord. So many of the English, and their great trains of knights are now coming here to make their peace with the duke. Space is tight."

"I understand," Ranulf answered the stablemaster politely.

"I will send one of my men for Sir Garrick, whom I also know. If he approves, then I will give you and your squire shelter for as long as you need it."

"I'm no great lord, and I will be grateful," Ranulf replied.

"Here, you, page!" The stablemaster's hand reached out, grasping the thin neck of a young boy. "Go and find Sir Garrick Taliferro, and tell him that Conan, the stablemaster, would speak with him." Then giving the lad a gentle kick, he sent him off.

They had not bothered to stop upon the road and eat during the day. Now Ranulf ordered Pax to get out the remainder of their food, and the two men sat companionably upon a bench by the stable doors eating, and sharing the remaining wine from the skin. They sat for some time, the day sliding into evening and growing dark about them. Finally a shadow loomed up through the gloaming, and Sir Garrick appeared.

"Ranulf! What are you doing here in Rouen? How is my godson?" The knight held out his hand in a warm greeting.

Ranulf arose, taking the offered hand. "I thought perhaps it was time I came to pay my proper respects to Duke Henry. My lady thought it wise also, and Simon thrives."

"Stephen?"

"Failing, but still alive," Ranulf replied. Then he smiled. "If you can convince Master Conan that we are respectable, he will give us shelter here in his stables, Garrick. Can you do so?"

"Aye! I will gladly. The castle is full to overflowing as the duchess has arrived with all her court to visit her mother-in-law. Come, and I'll take you and your young squire to the great hall. It is time for the evening meal. 'Tis not as substantial as the midday meal, for the empress keeps her household on short rations, but it will be filling." Garrick Taliferro chuckled. Then he turned to the stablemaster and said, "The duke would be grateful if you would give this man and his squire and their animals proper shelter, Master Conan."

" 'Tis done, my lord," the stablemaster answered. "Come, my lord, and I'll show you where you'll sleep. Bring your beasts with you, if you please." He moved into the stable, and they followed him deep into the bowels of the building. At its far end he stopped, and pointed to a group of empty stalls filled with fresh straw. "You can stable your animals there, my lord. You and your squire can sleep in one of the stalls, too. 'Tis out of the way, and no one is likely to notice you there. I will ask you to have your squire care for your horses and the mule himself. That way no one will come back into this section of the stables, and your armor will be safe," he said with a wink.

"Thank you, Master Conan," Ranulf said, pressing a small silver coin into the man's hand. "I am grateful."

The stablemaster nodded, and moved off.

"I've had enough to eat, my lord," Pax said. "I'll remain here, unsaddle the horses, and see to their care. You go along."

"You're certain?"

"Aye, my lord!"

Ranulf walked with Sir Garrick to the great hall of Rouen Castle, where the evening meal was just beginning. They found places at one of the trestles directly below the salt. Flat trenchers were placed on the table, one to every two guests. Sir Garrick cut the trencher with his knife, and passed Ranulf a half. The pewter cups were filled with a passable wine. There was a small wheel of cheese on the table. A platter was passed that held what appeared to be joints of roasted rabbit. Spearing one with his knife, Ranulf laid it on his trencher and cut himself a generous wedge of cheese. The priest at the high board stood and said the blessing, then they began to eat.

When he had filled his stomach, Ranulf looked about him. The hall was huge and well filled, mostly with knights and their retainers, although, near the high board there was a trestle lined with lovely women. At the high board sat Duke Henry, his mother, Empress Matilda on his right, his wife, Alienor of Aquitaine on his left. Ranulf had once seen the Empress Matilda. While she had grown older, she had not changed a great deal. Her expression was still one of arrogance and disdain. She had never forgotten her royal heritage. She was the daughter of King Henry I and his queen, who had been the daughter of Scotland's King Malcolm. The Empress Matilda's mother had been a descendant of the last Saxon kings of England. Her blood was bluer than most.

The young duchess, however, was probably the most beautiful woman Ranulf had ever seen. His own Eleanore was a great beauty, but Alienor of Aquitaine's beauty was incredible. She had truly golden hair, and even from where he was sitting Ranulf could tell her eyes were a bright and vibrant blue. Her features were perfect: flawless skin, a straight nose, and a generous mouth that he saw laughed easily.

"Don't fall in love with her," Garrick Taliferro said softly. "Most men do. She enjoys the attention, but she is loyal to her husband."

"As she should be," Ranulf replied, a trifle shocked that his companion should even say such a thing.

"You have not heard the gossip then about her troubadours?"

"Nay. What is said?" Ranulf was frankly curious.

"The duchess's court is the gayest and brightest in all of the world," Garrick Taliferro began. "She loves music, literature, and poetry, and those who make it. Her court is called the Court of Love. It is the troubadours' habit to choose a noble lady, married, of course, for she must truly be unobtainable, fall in love with her, and then write exquisite poetry and song about his unrequited love for the lady of his choice."

"And what does the *unobtainable* lady do when she is singled out like this?" Ranulf asked, amused by such affectation.

"She alternately encourages her troubadour, then disdains him on other occasions."

"How futile," Ranulf said, "and perhaps a bit ridiculous to my mind. Besides, what right have these gypsies to choose a chaste woman and make her an object of their unrequited desires?"

Garrick Taliferro laughed heartily. "You are too practical, my friend," he said. "The ladies love it, and it does their husbands honor that these great troubadours chose their wives to court. There is no evil intended, although in the case of the duchess, there are some who want to believe these young men are her lovers. It is not so, of course. The duchess is far too clever, and too honorable a lady to indulge herself with troubadours. She adores her duke."

"I would not allow such men about my Eleanore," Ranulf responded darkly. "Such creatures have no place at a humble manor like Ashlin." Then he changed the subject entirely. "When do you think I can pay my compliments to Duke Henry, Garrick? I do not like leaving my wife and child for too long. The Welsh are raiding this year along the border. I have raised my walls higher, and I have a good captain who has trained more men in the arts of defense, but still, I dislike leaving them for too long."

"I will speak with the duke when I have the opportunity," his companion said. "In the meantime I hope you will join me and the other knights in the hunt, and on the jousting field."

"I have my armor with me," Ranulf said. "While I hoped my journey would be a brief one, I have spent enough time in a king's court to know it would probably not be. They say Stephen will not last a good deal longer, so I suppose I can expect to be home sometime before Christmastide. I can only pray the Welsh will keep from my gates."

"You may lose livestock, but little else," Garrick Taliferro said smoothly. "Tell me of my godson."

"He is clever," Ranulf said. "I vow he recognizes my voice when I enter the solar, but my good wife says he is too young yet."

"I suppose I should marry one of these days," Sir Garrick said. "I have a small holding to the west of London. My mother lives upon it, and she is forever importuning me to take a wife. Perhaps when Duke Henry becomes England's king, I shall ask her to find me a nubile young lass to wed, bed, and give me heirs. A man needs sons. The king has one, and it is said the duchess is breeding once again."

"Another reason I am anxious to return home." Ranulf smiled. "Both Eleanore and I want more children, but I cannot get them on her if I am in Normandy, and she is at Ashlin."

The evening was a pleasant one. There were jugglers to entertain the guests in the hall, and the duchess's favorite troubadour of the moment, a slender young man with dark curly locks and melting amber eyes, sang a beautiful song of his unrequited love for the fairest flower in Aquitaine. Ranulf had to admit the music was sweet even if he thought the song insipid. The men at his table began to dice, and, not having the coin to waste, he excused himself.

He found his way back to the stables, joining his squire in a large and comfortable stall that Pax had made quite habitable. The horses had been unsaddled, the pack mule unloaded. The animals had been fed, watered, and brushed. Their saddles were set upon the broad carrier between the stalls. His armor was set neatly in a corner with his small trunk. Pax had added more hay to the stall in order to make two comfortable piles that he had covered with their cloaks to make beds.

"You'll have to wash in the horse trough outside, my lord," the squire told his master.

"In the morning," Ranulf said, laying himself down.

The next few weeks passed surprisingly quickly. They ate in the Empress Matilda's great hall. They hunted with the duke and his companions. They jousted, and here Ranulf began to gain a small reputation among the court, for he was unbeatable and had yet to be unhorsed by any opponent. When he one day unhorsed the Empress Matilda's champion, he accepted the laurel wreath of victory from the duke's hands, then presented it to the empress, bowing graciously.

"Who is that?" the duchess asked one of her ladies.

"I do not know, my lady. He cannot be important," she replied.

Alienor of Aquitaine smiled thoughtfully. "He may not be important, Adela, but he is clever, and he has exquisite manners." She turned to her husband. "Who is he, Henry?"

"Ranulf of Ashlin" came the immediate reply. "He has come to pay me his respects. Perhaps now I shall let him." The duke beckoned the knight forward. "We welcome you to Normandy, Sir Ranulf," he said.

Ranulf knelt before Duke Henry. Placing his hands in those of England's next king, he pledged him his fealty.

"Rise, Sir Ranulf," the duke said when the oath had been given and received. "We are grateful for loyal knights such as yourself. Your honest fidelity and faithfulness to King Stephen throughout his reign has not gone unnoticed."

"I will give you that same allegiance, my liege," Ranulf replied.

"We believe that you will," the duke replied. "Now, we present you to your future queen, my duchess Alienor."

Ranulf bowed low to the beauteous woman who was even lovelier close up. "My lady, I pledge to you my loyalty as well," he said.

"We thank you, Sir Ranulf," the duchess said. Her voice held a hint of music and was very sweet. "We have noticed that you have yet to be unhorsed in the joust. You are a fine knight."

"I am but fortunate, lady," Ranulf replied. Bowing, he backed away.

"We invite you to remain with us awhile, Sir Ranulf," the duke said. "Unless, of course, you are needed at home."

"I am honored, my liege," Ranulf replied. "While the Welsh have been restless this summer, Ashlin is in good hands with my wife and is well fortified."

"You have built a keep?" the duke said, his brow darkening.

"Nay, my liege! It is forbidden except with royal permission,"

Ranulf quickly answered. "I have but raised the height of the walls about my demesne to protect my family and my serfs. I hope I have not offended you in that."

"Nay," the duke replied, mollified, and pleased to see the level of obedience rendered by Ranulf de Glandeville. If only all of England's lords were so amenable, but they were not. They were a greedy, grasping lot, and he would rule them with an iron hand. "Return to your friends, Sir Ranulf, and know that we are pleased with you," the duke told the knight. Their eyes met but for a moment in complete understanding.

Ranulf bowed to the duke, the duchess, and finally to the Empress Matilda. Then he moved away.

"Men like him kept my cousin Stephen in power all these years," the empress said, almost grimly, "but he'll render you the same loyalty, Henry. They are honorable these simple knights. Cultivate as many of them as you can. They will keep you in power when your great lords seek to quarrel with you, my son. When did you meet him?"

"What makes you think I have met him before?"

The empress snorted. "My eyes are not so weak they did not see the look that passed between you," she said low. "This simple knight of yours is here for a purpose. *What purpose?*"

"I promise you we will discuss it, Mother, but not in so public a venue," the duke said, and the empress nodded, pursuing the issue no further. She was her son's chief adviser, and they had no secrets from each other. He had learned the art of governance at her knee, but he had also seen how her arrogance had been her downfall, so he had cultivated a softer manner that, while firm, was less dismissive and overbearing. Such an attitude served him well.

Ranulf, in the meantime, returned to the tents where his squire was waiting. Sir Garrick joined them, and the two men talked as Pax disarmed his master.

"That was a clever move on your part," Sir Garrick said. "You have caused a great deal of envy among the other knights."

"I do not mean any offense."

"None is taken." Garrick laughed. "We are all most admiring of what you did in having unhorsed the empress's champion, present-ing the old dragon with your wreath of honor. It was well-done."

"Better not to make enemies of ladies in high places, I have learned over the years." Ranulf smiled. "The duke recognized me, and I was able to pledge him my fealty. He introduced me to the duchess. She spoke kindly to me. I have been invited to remain with the court, and, of course, I could not refuse the invitation."

"Your wife will understand, I am certain."

"Aye, she is a good wife and chatelaine," Ranulf replied, but se-cretly he worried about his petite. Rouen seemed so far from Ash-lin. A small sea and a great deal of land separated them. He wondered if the Welsh had raided them, or if, as had happened in past years, Ashlin and its folk had been left in peace. There was no way to get a message to his wife. Ashlin was out of the way. No one from this court, even a knight returning to England, which none was at the moment, would go their way. No merchant train would, either. Ashlin saw an occasional peddler, but no great train ever passed by. He had to put his family in God's hands now.

After the tournament in which he had overcome the empress's champion, Ranulf began to realize he was being favored by the Duchess Alienor. That same evening in the hall she beckoned him, asking, "Are you a man of the gentle arts, Sir Ranulf?"

He grinned rather wryly, and replied, "My lady, I am naught but a simple knight. While I read, and I can write, I use these talents only as lord of my manor."

"Do you know Latin?"

"Church Latin, my lady," he answered her.

"No poetry?" She cocked her head to one side.

"Nay, lady. What use would I have for poetry?"

The duchess laughed. "Poetry is very useful for wooing a lady, sir. Are there none among my ladies who might take your fancy, Sir Ranulf? If there are, you must learn poetry."

"I am a married man, my lady," he told her. "I came to Rouen but to pledge my loyalty to your husband, and offer whatever small services he would desire of me. While I find the ladies surrounding

you as fair as summer flowers, they are but pale stars in comparison
to your brilliant and radiant moon, my lady duchess."

Alienor of Aquitaine smiled, both surprised and flattered by his
speech. "I think we may make a poet of you yet, Sir Ranulf. Tell
me, if you did not use poetry, how then did you woo your wife?"

"The lady of Ashlin was chosen by King Stephen to be my wife.
The holding sits near to the Welsh border, and the king sought a
loyal man to hold it. My wife had been in the convent of St. Frideswide's since she was five, lady, and was within just a few weeks of
taking her final vows. Instead she was married to me."

"Ah," the duchess said, understanding perfectly.

"We have a newborn son. His name is Simon, after my father,"
Ranulf said, "and Hubert, for he was born on St. Hubert's Day."

"Perhaps one day your son may come to court to serve my little
William," the duchess said. She liked this simple man with his honest answers. There was nothing at all complex about Ranulf de
Glandeville. He was a refreshing change. She turned the conversation back to the arts.

"Can you sing perhaps, Sir Ranulf?"

"Sing?" He thought it an odd question. Men did not sing. "Nay,
my lady, I do not sing."

One of the duchess's ladies leaned over and whispered in her
mistress's ear. Alienor of Aquitaine smiled mischievously. "The
lady Elise wishes to know, if since you do not write or recite poetry, or sing, how you make your wife happy, Sir Ranulf?"

"By making her sing, my lady," Ranulf answered quickly, elicit-
ing a burst of laughter from the duchess and her ladies.

"You are quick of wit by far, my lord," the duchess said, her
blue eyes twinkling and her musical voice tinkling with mirth.
"There may be hope for you after all."

He bowed. "I am but an honest man." He smiled.

He was included in the royal circle more often than not now,
although the great lords considered him of little import. The
duchess entrusted him with her younger ladies in the evening, and
he chaperoned them, keeping them from the more unruly lords and

knights who might compromise the reputations of the naive maidens. He did not flirt as others might have done, for he considered
how hurt his innocent Eleanore would be if she knew it. The
younger girls in the duchess's train took to calling him Sir Uncle,
which Garrick Taliferro found very amusing.

"What a reputation you are gaining," he teased his friend.

"I should rather be called *uncle* than have my wife learn one day
that I had conducted myself in a lewd and lecherous manner,"
Ranulf replied. "Eleanore still retains an innocence due to her
convent upbringing."

"I believe you love her," Sir Garrick said.

"I do, although I have never said it to her. When I go home,
however, I shall. It is past time Eleanore knew it. I have always been
fearful that she would reject me, for I am older, and I was forced
upon her. Still, before I left I thought perhaps that her manner
toward me was softer, that she might have similar feelings for me. I
can be silent no longer."

"Of course you must tell her," his friend agreed. "Although I do
not understand it, women seem to like to hear the words, *Je t'aime.*"

August passed, and September. In early October the duke
mounted an expedition against one of his vassals, Robert de Torigny,
a troublesome man who had suddenly refused to render the duke
his due. Ranulf was invited to join the siege at the castle of Torigny.
He was glad to go, for the gay life of the court and his duties shep-
herding young ladies was not really to his taste. An invitation to the
siege cheered him immensely, and he fought with vigor, earning
the respect of those great lords who had previously been dismissive
of him. He was quickly considered a good man to have by your side,
or at your back.

At the very end of October, word was brought to the duke that
King Stephen had died on the twenty-fifth day of October at
Dover Castle. King Henry accepted the news calmly, then continued his siege until the castle of Torigny was reduced to rubble,
and its lord chastised, humbled. The new king returned home to
celebrate his elevation with his joyful mother and his wife, who

was great with her second child. Te Deums were sung, Masses of thanksgiving and for the soul of King Stephen were offered in all of Rouen's churches. Though it had an archbishop, Rouen had not yet a cathedral.

Ranulf was roused from his bed in the stables one night by the king's page, and without question followed the boy to Henry's privy chamber, forcing himself awake as they went. The king was a man who needed little sleep, and usually made do with no more than four hours. Ranulf bowed as he was ushered into the royal presence, and the page quickly disappeared. The king sat behind a long table covered in parchment.

"Help yourself to wine if you wish," he said, waving the knight to a chair before the table. "By the rood I have never had so much work! My affairs here in Normandy must be in order before I can cross to England. Besides, I am told between the wind and the rain the damned sea is all a rage right now. I'd go myself, but my wife's belly makes me more cautious. The queen will now travel with me, de Glandeville. There is no longer a need for secrecy, but you will have the care of Prince William. It is a great responsibility, for who knows that the queen does not carry a daughter this time. It is thought that I mean to leave my son behind in Normandy, for such a journey is considered too dangerous for a boy of tender years. What fools they take me for, my *loyal* knights! As if I would leave my only heir here to be preyed upon by that pack of wolves! Still, it will be believed the lad stays behind because his household will remain. You must take the prince, and one of his wet nurses, and travel with them to England. You will appear to be a knight with his wife and son. You will leave for Barfleur two days before we do. The details will be worked out in a few days' time."

"Who will know that I escort the prince besides ourselves, my liege?"

"My mother, my wife, and my confessor only," Henry said.

Ranulf nodded.

"Did we awaken you?" the king suddenly asked.

Flushing, Ranulf nodded. He hadn't been aware his sleepiness was that obvious. "Your pardon, my liege."

Henry chuckled. "We need little sleep. We are sure you have heard the complaints. We called you to us now so our meeting would not be noticed and wondered upon. From now on the queen, my mother, or my confessor will speak with you on this matter. When the day comes for your departure, you will be given a purse for expenses."

"What am I to do when we reach England?"

"You will join my progress to London, and it is then that knowledge of Prince William's presence with us will be made known. We will form an English household for him. There will be plenty of eager souls willing to serve my son," the king said almost grimly. Then he chuckled. "You will have your hands full with Willie, de Glandeville. He is just past two years, and an imp. Don't let the little devil intimidate you, for he already knows his place as a royal prince. Be as tough with him as you would your own son. He must obey you, else he endanger you and himself. Be firm!" the king concluded. "You have our permission to do what must be done to ensure the prince's safety."

"I will, my liege, for I wish to get home safely to my own wife and child. I swear I will guard the prince as I would my own son's life, my liege."

"Good!" the king said. "Now, you may go back to bed." He lowered his head again to the papers on his table.

Ranulf bowed himself from the room. The page was gone, and so he found his own way back to the stables. When the king had first told him why he wanted him in Normandy, Ranulf had assumed he would travel in grand style. To learn only he and Pax would be escorting the prince and his nurse was startling. Still, the road from Rouen to Barfleur was not a dangerous road. The child, however, was young. It would almost have been better if he were an infant. Ranulf did not have a great deal of experience with two-year-olds, but as he remembered, they were mobile. He would have to ride with the boy ahead of his saddle. They could not move swiftly. It would not be a simple trip.

Pax was going to have to know. His young squire had proved himself most trustworthy these past months. Still, he would not tell him until he knew when they were going. He made his way to his bed and lay down again. *He was going home!* Soon he would be with his Eleanore and his son. Simon would be a half year old by the time he returned to Ashlin. He hoped the harvest had gone well, and that the flocks and cattle were safe. Pray God the Welsh had left them in peace. Pray God if they had not, that everyone was safe and the damage slight. With that thought Ranulf de Glandeville finally fell asleep again.

CHAPTER FIFTEEN

The men on the walls at Ashlin manor watched with careful interest, then amazement as the ragged figure stumbled across the fields, scattering the sheep. It clambered its way up the hill to the walled manor, hands outstretched in apparent supplication. As it crossed the lowered drawbridge, it became obvious the creature was a female.

"Help me!" she rasped, and collapsed just short of the raised portcullis.

For a moment the men-at-arms at the entry hesitated. Was this some clever Welsh trick? Realizing, however, that there was absolutely no one else in sight and the men on the walls had a clear view of the surrounding countryside, they ran to help the woman.

"Jesu! Mary!" the first man to reach her said. He looked down at the poor creature, who was scrawny to the point of being starved, and black-and-blue with many a severe beating. The man-at-arms didn't know what to do, and stood helplessly looking down at the woman.

"I'll go for Fulk," his companion said, and ran off leaving the first man with the woman.

"Help me," the woman said piteously, reaching out for the man-at-arms, who jumped back nervously.

"Sim's gone for the captain," he managed to say. "He'll help."

The woman nodded weakly, and laid her head upon the ground. Fulk came running with the other man-at-arms. Looking down at the woman, he shook his head. "An escaped slave," he said wearily. Bending, he lifted the woman's head. "You're a slave?"

"No more," the woman said with distinct meaning.

Fulk shook his head despairingly. "Will they come after you?"

"I don't know," the woman answered. "I think I killed him."

"Well, let's hope you did, lass," Fulk said, "or if they think it's worth their while, they'll be after you soon enough. What's your name?" Reaching down, he helped the frail woman to her feet.

"Arwydd" came the reply.

"Welsh? You speak good English for a Welsh girl," Fulk noted.

"My mother was English, from Hereford" was the answer.

"How did you end up a slave?" Fulk began to walk the girl slowly through the portcullis into the manor enclosure.

"My mother was taken years ago. Her captors raped her, and I was born. The man whose slave she became named me. She be dead many years now. He killed her when she objected to his interest in me. I was eleven when he first used me, the pig!" Arwydd spat weakly.

"Is he the one you killed?"

"Aye," the girl replied. "He thought it would be amusing to share me with his friends. They did everything to me that a man can do to a woman. So when he was drunk several days ago, I slit his throat and ran away. I haven't eaten in three days, sir, but what berries I could find, and I was afraid to eat most of them, for fear I'd get poisoned. Please, help me!"

"I'll take you to my mistress," Fulk said. He didn't know if the girl was to be believed or not. She was battered and bruised enough to be sure. She looked as if she had been starved for years, and she probably had been. Her story had a certain ring of truth to it, yet she worried him. She did not quite meet his eye when he looked at her. Was her sudden arrival some clever Welsh trick? He would advise the lady, and he would watch this wench carefully.

He brought her to the lady Eleanore, where Arwydd told her story again. Fulk took his mistress aside while old Ida and Willa took Arwydd off to bathe her. "I don't entirely trust this wench, my lady," he sad quietly. "There is something about her that doesn't seem quite right. I cannot help but wonder how she ended up here at Ashlin when we are so far off the beaten track."

"Perhaps God directed her to us, Fulk," Elf said quietly. "She is fearfully wounded. God knew I could help her regain her health."

"Perhaps, lady," Fulk answered. He always wanted to shout with despair when the lady spoke so sweetly. She still did not fully realize how cruel and fierce a world it was beyond the boundaries of Ashlin and St. Frideswide's Convent. "Heed my words, however, lady," he pleaded with her. "Listen to all the girl says, but do not trust her, I beg you. It is too dangerous to trust a stranger in these times."

"While I prefer to look on the brighter side of life," Elf told her captain, "I am not quite the simpleton you believe me to be, Fulk." She laughed when he flushed. "I will heed your words, I promise," she attempted to reassure him.

He bowed to her, then went about his duties.

"She's thin as a sapling, lady," Willa said coming back into the hall. "Old Ida has bathed her, gotten the nits from her hair. She's black-and-blue all over, though. How anyone could be so cruel to so frail a lass, I do not know."

"Has she said any more?"

Willa shook her head. "Naught, but to thank us for our kindness."

"We'll keep her with us until she heals," Elf decided.

"I agree," Willa said. "Poor lass has never known kindness."

Arwydd was settled into the household. Within a few weeks she had lost her pallor and showed signs of gaining weight. Her bruises were beginning to heal, fading from black to purple to yellow, brown, and green, to finally just the faintest shadow before they were completely gone. While Arwydd's face was round and plain, there was a certain prettiness to it. Her blue eyes grew lively with her returning health. She was set to doing light tasks after a few days, and she did them well. Her greatest talent, however, seemed to be in the arranging of flowers. She loved them, and filled every container she could with the blooms from garden and field, which she mixed freely. Elf encouraged her, for the truth was, she liked Arwydd's flowers and told her so.

Fulk found it interesting that no one came looking for the wench. Surely her murdered master had someone who cared, yet no one arrived at Ashlin in search of Arwydd. This concerned Fulk greatly. He became convinced she was a spy, probably for the Welsh, yet the girl did nothing that he could deem suspicious. Still, instinct nagged at him, so he kept on his guard. He asked Arwydd once who her mother's people had been in Hereford, but Arwydd claimed not to know, so he couldn't send the wench along to blood kin, and thus be rid of her.

August came, but they did not go to the Lammastide Fair this year, for with the Welsh raiding, it was considered too dangerous. September came, and by month's end the harvest was almost all in, but for the orchards, which would take several weeks of picking. On Michaelmas roast goose was served to everyone on the manor, serf and freeborn alike. The servants were paid their wage for the coming year. Several days afterward, however, a man dressed in servant's garments arrived at Ashlin to tell them that the convent of St. Frideswide's was under siege from the Welsh bandit, Merin ap Owen. The abbess had sent him to Ashlin to beg for their help before they were all killed.

Elf was horrified. "You must take a troupe of men and go at once to help them," she said to Fulk.

"Do you know this fellow?" he demanded of her suspiciously.

Elf shook her head. "But it does not matter," she said. "He wears the abbess's badge, and many of the servants were old at St. Frideswide's. He may have replaced one."

"Aye, lady, I did," the man quickly spoke up. "I am the son of Walter, who tended the pigs."

Elf could not remember the swineherd's name, but he had been an old man and this man could indeed be his son. Besides, the convent was being attacked, and they had to help him. She fixed a challenging look on her captain. "There is no reason for this man to come here and claim the convent is under siege if it isn't. You will take a troupe of men, and go to St. Frideswide's now, Fulk. Drive the Welsh off, and secure the convent for the abbess. If necessary pursue the enemy, and destroy as many of them as possible. May God have mercy on their wicked souls! You have your orders. Go, now!"

Something was wrong. Fulk sensed it strongly, but she was the lady, and he could not defy her. He had to obey. He bowed. "Aye, my lady," he told her, "but keep the gates locked both day and night until I return. You must promise me you will do it, my lady. *You must promise!*"

"I will do it, Fulk. Have no fear, for we will be safe," she reassured him gently. She understood his dilemma, but they had to help St. Frideswide's. There was no choice in the matter.

"You will come with me," Fulk told the messenger.

"Aye," the man agreed calmly, but his demeanor did nothing to restore Fulk's confidence in the matter. *Something was wrong!*

Fulk and his men rode posthaste the miles separating Ashlin from the convent. Reaching St. Frideswide's, they discovered its outbuildings burning, its flocks and cattle gone from its fields. They banged upon the gates, and a voice called to them, "Depart you godless Welsh! In the name of Christ, depart!"

"It is Fulk from Ashlin come to help, Sister Perpetua," the captain called in a strong voice.

A small square of the gate opened like a tiny window, and the nun's face shone in it. "Praise be to God!" she cried. The square closed with a slam, and a few moments later one side of the gate opened to admit him.

"Remain on guard here and chase off any Welsh you find," he told his men, then entered into the convent courtyard. "Where is the abbess?" he asked the portress.

"In the church with the others, praying."

Fulk refrained from a pithy reply, instead nodding and thanking the nun. He headed directly for the convent church, crossing himself reverently as he entered, his boots thumping noisily. "Reverend Mother," he said. "The lady Eleanore has sent me from Ashlin to help you."

The abbess arose from her knees, and turned to face the captain, relief showing plainly on her usually composed features. "Captain

Fulk, you are most welcome," she told him, and together they walked from the church, leaving the others behind to continue with their prayers.

"Tell me what happened?" he asked her as they traversed the cloister slowly, rain just beginning to fall.

"It is the Welsh, of course," the abbess said wearily. "They have been taking our flocks and herds by bits and pieces for the past few weeks. Today, however, they fired the buildings outside our walls and slew whoever of our serfs they could find. Those poor souls who had remained at their posts to see the cows were milked and the harvest brought in on time . . . although I am certain it has gone off with the Welsh, if they didn't burn it, too. What we will feed ourselves, our remaining people, and our animals with this winter, I do not know. Then the Welsh were as suddenly gone as they had come. There isn't a sign of them anywhere, as you can see."

Fulk's mind was contemplating the situation. If the Welsh had been outside the convent's walls for several weeks, why did the abbess wait until today to ask for help? He began to consider if he might connect Arwydd's arrival at Ashlin with the Welsh marauders' arrival at St. Frideswide's. "When did the Welsh come, Reverend Mother?" he asked.

The abbess thought a long moment, and then she said, "It was about six weeks ago. They came over the hills without any warning one afternoon. The gates were open, and several of our maidens and younger nuns were outside the gates. Sister Perpetua saw them first, and rang our alarm bell. Those outside the gates barely made it back into the safety of our walls, but praise be to God, and His blessed Mother, they returned unscathed. The Welsh made no attempt to break in then. They spent their time driving away our livestock in small groups and taking everything that wasn't nailed down. Only in the last few days did they make what to me seemed to be but a halfhearted attempt to batter in our gates, but our gates are extremely strong, being reinforced with iron straps. Today they fired the buildings outside, and departed," the abbess concluded.

Fulk's brain was beginning to throb with apprehension and foreboding. He knew the answer to his question even as he asked it.

"Then, why, my lady abbess, did you send your swineherd to Ashlin asking for the lady Eleanore's aid?"

The abbess looked at him, surprised. "I did not send my swineherd to Ashlin, Captain Fulk. I sent no one to Ashlin. The danger was over, and other than the loss of our livestock, some serfs, and some buildings, the convent and its residents were safe, praise be to God. While I am relieved by your arrival, I did not send for you. Captain! Are you all right?"

The color had drained from his face. "A man came to Ashlin claiming to be the son of Walter, the swineherd here at the convent. He said he had escaped with your contrivance, and the convent needed our help. The lady did not recognize him, but she sent us anyway, against my better judgment. She feared for you all, and now I fear for her, as I know the man who came to Ashlin was a Welsh agent."

"God have mercy!" the nun exclaimed, her distress obvious.

"I must return to Ashlin immediately," Fulk said.

"Night is falling, and there is no moon," the abbess said. "You will need torches by which to light your path, Captain. I will have them prepared right away, but you must wait for them. To go without light could endanger you and your men, and then you will be of no help at all to Eleanore. Be patient. We will hurry."

"I will wait outside the gates with my men," Fulk said. "They will need to know what has happened." He bowed to her, then turned to go.

Fulk explained the situation to his men. "Where is the man who came for us?" he asked his second in command.

"He went to check the pigpens to see if any of his beasts had escaped the conflagration," the second replied.

"How long ago?" Fulk demanded.

The second shrugged helplessly.

"He was one of them for certain, and we will not see him again, for he has surely gone to rejoin his master," Fulk said.

They waited impatiently for almost an hour while the torches were prepared. About them the twilight deepened into night.

Without a moon it would be as black as the inside of an empty wineskin. Finally the abbess came through the open half gate, followed by six or so nuns, their arms filled with torches. They passed them out among the men, lighting them from the torch that the abbess carried. Each man was given two extra unlit torches, which they stowed behind their saddles.

"Thank you," Fulk said. After turning his mount, he led his troupe slowly away from the convent. Above them the sky was a gray-black. The earlier rain had subsided, but the dampness made the night even darker than usual on a moonless night. The flaming torches flickered in the light breeze, dancing eerily as the men moved along. There was no choice but to go slowly, for the track was narrow and the night murky. Fulk was frothing with impatience. He had been gulled as neatly as any country lad in the city for the first time.

If anything happened to the lady Eleanore or the little lordling, what was he to tell his master when he returned from Normandy? He had failed in his duty to protect them, and his heart was sore weary with the knowledge. Instinct had warned him that something was wrong, but he had hesitated to question his mistress. *He should have.* She was young and inexperienced. Her convent upbringing caused her to look at the world with an especially kind eye. She trusted too easily. It could be the death of her, he feared. By the rood! A turtle could move faster than they were going! How far had they come? A mile? Three? He would wager that they weren't even halfway there.

The bell tolling from the manor church alerted them to the fact that they were practically at Ashlin. It was as if they were being guided home. *But why was the bell pealing?* Fulk stopped his troupe to consider a moment. Without the torches, they couldn't see their own hands outstretched before them. That meant that neither could the enemy. No one could be lying in wait for them under these circumstances. Had the Welsh broken into the manor enclosure itself? Anything was possible, but something told him this had not happened. He signaled his men forward. The bell was tolling an alarm, he decided. Now suddenly he could see the lights upon the walls of Ashlin. He hurried his troupe a bit faster. He could see the shadowed outlines of the walls and sheep in the fields and meadows on either side of the track. This was odd. If the Welsh had come, why hadn't they taken the livestock?

Fulk moved his companions up the hill to the manor enclosure. The drawbridge was lowered, and the portcullis raised. He stopped again, cautious and confused. What was going on? Then he heard Sim calling to him. Signaling his men to remain where they were, he moved his mount forward to meet his second in command.

"Captain Fulk! Is that you? They have taken the lady!" Sim cried. *"They have taken the lady!"*

Fulk waved his men forward. "How?" He snapped the question as he rode into the enclosure. "Lower the portcullis, and raise the drawbridge when all have entered," he said. Dismounting, he flung his reins to a young stableboy. *"How?"* he repeated.

"We are not certain." Sim's voice quavered.

"Who was on the gate, and what of the men on the walls?" Fulk asked, manfully keeping his temper in check.

"Alfred was on the gate. He and the men on the walls were drugged, Captain. They slept for no more than an hour, and naught was believed to be amiss. Then old Ida come screeching from the house, crying the lady was gone. Willa had taken the little lordling to Lady Eleanor to be fed, and she was not in her bed. They searched the house, but she could not be found. The women are hysterical, and the little lordling cries for his supper," Sim concluded.

"Go to Orva, and tell her we need a wet nurse immediately for the little lord. Then come to the house. I am going to search it myself," Fulk told the man-at-arms. *By the rood! By the holy rood!* He had known that something was wrong! Why hadn't he listened to his voice within instead of blindly obeying the wishes of a sweet, but very naive, young woman? His search of the house would be futile, he knew, from the raised portcullis, the lowered drawbridge, and the open gates, but he had to satisfy himself that she really was gone. His grizzled features grim, Fulk entered the house and was immediately surrounded by howling women. "Be silent!" he roared at them, and they ceased their wails. His glance lit on Willa, dry-eyed and looking calmer than any. "What happened?" he asked her, "and the rest of you keep your mouths shut!"

"We went to bed shortly after the sun had set as we usually do unless there are guests. Shortly before midnight the little lord became restless, and Alyce, his nurse, brought him to the lady to be fed, but the lady was not there. We searched for her, but could not find her, and it was then we raised the alarm."

"Were you all in the hall tonight?" Fulk asked Willa.

"All but Alyce."

"Arwydd?"

"Nay, Arwydd ate in the kitchens earlier, for she was working in the lady's herbal gardens," Willa replied. "She has spent the last few days carefully digging and covering the plants for winter."

A brief grim smile touched Fulk's lips. They had all been given some sort of mild sleeping draught, all but for Alyce, who had been tending her little charge, and Arwydd, who had probably administered the potion into the food and drink that was served; her presence in the kitchens earlier being the key to the puzzle. "Where is Arwydd?" he asked. "When was the last time you saw her?"

Willa thought hard, and then she said, "I have not seen Arwydd since yesterday afternoon when she told me she was going to work in the gardens, and asked the lady's permission to eat early in the kitchens."

"Christ's bloody bones!" The fierce oath burst forth from Fulk's mouth with such violence that the women jumped back, whimpering. "I knew that wench was false, but I could not prove it, worse luck!" His balled fist drove into his palm. "Jesu! Who would want so badly to kidnap the lady that they would plan so cunningly? *Who? And why?"* His brow was contorted as he struggled for an answer. The lady surely had no enemies. Did the lord? They knew little about his life before he had come to Ashlin, save that he was a loyal knight of King Stephen and had once had family in

Normandy. In Fulk's mind it was unlikely that Ranulf de Glandeville would have an enemy this vengeful. He was simply not that
kind of man. *Who, then?*

"It is that witch that killed our lord Richard," old Ida suddenly said.

"Why do you say that?" Fulk asked her, dismissive of the elderly
woman, but nonetheless curious.

"Has there not been a Welsh bandit riding with a golden-haired
woman these many months?" Ida demanded. "Did not the bitch
escape from her father's custody as she was about to be clapped into
a nunnery? Did she not intend to wed our sweet lady to her cousin
then kill her as she had killed her husband? And all so she could
have the cousin and Ashlin for herself? But our lady was saved from
the bitch's evil plotting, and the lady Isleen"—Ida spat upon the
floor—"given punishment by the king himself. A punishment
which she escaped. She is the only person I can imagine who
would hold such a hard grudge against our sweet lady."

"What you say holds a possibility of truth in it," Fulk replied
thoughtfully. The old woman could have hit upon something, he
considered. "But why take the lady? Why not steal the livestock
instead?"

"The lady will bring a ransom from her husband," Ida replied
scathingly, as if he should have realized that himself. "As for the
rest, how am I expected to know the workings of a bandit's mind?
You are a man. You are the soldier. It is up to you to learn the rest!"

Orva entered the hall just then, bringing with her a young
woman. "Maris can feed the little lordling. Her son is ready to be
weaned. She is healthy, and her milk rich," Orva said.

"Thank God," Alyce said, handing her charge to the wet nurse.
"Poor mite's been whimpering for hours now. I give him a sugar
teat, but he needed milk."

As if to give her words truth, Simon Hubert's mouth clamped
itself about Maris's quickly bared nipple, causing her to start, and
he began sucking noisily, his small hands moving up to knead the
woman's breast. His bright blue eyes slowly closed with his ecstasy,
and he relaxed in Maris's cradling arms. The women all smiled

with relief, and Fulk nodded. At least here was one problem that had been easily solved.

"What are you going to do to find the lady Eleanore?" Willa asked boldly. "She has been gone for several hours now, and you can already see the dawn beginning to stain the skies."

"It is the false dawn," he told her, "but the real one will not be far behind, lass. You women must keep to your daily schedule as if all were well. You will do this for the little lord's sake. It must not be known that Ashlin is without *both* its lord and its lady, lest the child be thought vulnerable by ambitious men like Baron Hugh." Although at this point, Fulk thought to himself, *I'd follow my instincts and fight the king himself to protect the child.* "My men have been riding all night, and without proper nourishment," he told the women clustered about him. "See they are fed as quickly as possible, for we shall have to go after the lady as soon as it is light."

Fulk left the hall then to see to his men and the horses. It was beginning to rain again, he noted with displeasure. He sought out Father Oswin, whom he found praying in the church. The young priest arose from his knees, his brown robes swirling about his bony ankles.

"Good morrow, Father. You pray for the lady, I assume."

"I do, Captain."

"She has been kidnapped, I am certain," Fulk said. "We must keep this occurrence secret for the sake of the little lord. Do you understand me, Father?"

"Aye," the priest agreed. "With the lord away and the lady gone, we need no other difficulties, eh, Fulk? Do you know who has taken the lady? And what will you do about it?"

"I do not know who, but I suspect the Welshman called Merin ap Owen who has been raiding hereabouts. We rode all night using torches to light our path, but it was slow going. As soon as my men are fed, we will take up the pursuit. I shall leave Sim in charge of defense when I am gone, and you in charge of the rest until the lady is brought home or the lord returns."

"Do you expect it, then, to take time?"

Fulk shook his head. "I do not know, Father. I honestly do not know. First I must find out for certain who has the lady. Only then can I move on to the problem of how to get her safely home."

"I know you to be a man of action with little tolerance for fools, my friend. And I know you believe in action more than you do in prayer, but, believe me, I shall be praying for your success and the safety of the lady nonetheless," the priest finished with a small smile at the soldier.

"She would want your prayers," Fulk said quietly, "so therefore I will want them, too." With a nod to the priest he hurried off again.

The dawn came in gray and chill. The rain began in earnest, and grew into a steady downpour by the time Fulk and his men were ready to set forth in search of Elf. Fulk cursed the skies angrily. Whatever trail had been left by the kidnappers would be washed out. It was useless even to consider starting out until the rains stopped. He dismissed the men and stomped into the hall, grumbling beneath his breath and wondering why God was testing his patience in this manner when the lady's very life might be in danger.

With no trail to follow he would have to rely on his instincts. The first thing he must do is learn where Merin ap Owen had his lair. The next step would be to ascertain if the lady Eleanore was actually being held by the bandit. If he had taken her, he would want her for ransom. What kind of a ransom? And how the hell were they supposed to pay a ransom when the lord was away? Fulk rubbed his brow. It hurt with all his cogitation, but without the lord to make these decisions, it was up to him to do so.

He groaned with frustration. He didn't even know where the lord was, or why he had truly gone, for he didn't really believe that tale the lord had told of going to Normandy to render his fealty to Duke Henry. Ashlin was no great holding. Ranulf de Glandeville could have rendered a new king his loyalty when that king came to England, and not a moment before. No offense would have been taken at all by such action. There was something else, but the lady had confided in no one, or else she herself did not know. Being such an innocent, she would accept her husband's word in the matter. So, Fulk realized, he would not be able to send a messenger to his master telling him of what has transpired. They were on their own in this matter. Fulk rubbed his brow again. Being in charge was a very difficult thing, and he would never again envy his betters.

The autumn rains did not let up for three long days and nights. The morning of the fourth day dawned cloudy, but dry. Whatever chance they might have had of following the kidnappers' tracks was long gone, the trail having been washed away over the previous few days. Fulk prepared to go in search of Merin ap Owen's hideyhole, but Sim, his second in command, would not be content unless he himself went.

"You insisted upon leading the troupe to St. Frideswide's," he reminded his captain, "and look what happened in your absence. This time I will go. Besides, I am not as well-known as you are, Fulk."

"I did not insist, the lady sent me," Fulk protested.

"You could have sent me in your stead and remained at Ashlin," Sim rejoined. "You are the lord's chosen man to defend Ashlin and the little lord. If you were lost to us, what would happen? I am at least expendable, although I assure you I intend returning home in one piece."

"It would have made no difference if I were here or not," Fulk said stubbornly. "The food, the drink, something was drugged with a sleeping potion. I would have slept as soundly as you did, Sim. Still, there is merit in your argument. I have the most experience of any here in matters of warfare and defense. When the time comes to rescue the lady, I will lead our men forth, but for now you are better suited than I to seek out Merin ap Owen and to see if it is he who holds the lady his prisoner. If he does not, I do not know where to look. All we can do is wait for a ransom demand."

"Which you could read, but I cannot!" Sim said triumphantly.

"The priest could read it for you," Fulk replied with a small smile. Sim was anxious to prove his mettle, and so he should have the opportunity. "If you think to have my place one day, Sim," he told the young man, "you will have to learn how to read and write. A man advances farther when he is educated and can be of more use to his master. A man without knowledge is but fit to work the fields or die in the first charge, lad."

"I thought you meant for Pax to have your place one day," Sim said bluntly. "Will you forsake him for me?"

"You are both my blood kin," Fulk replied, "but Pax will be the lord's squire, and if, as I hope, he does well, he might even be knighted one day. One does not need to be of noble birth to be knighted. Only brave and freeborn. He will earn his freedom, and then, who knows."

Sim nodded, satisfied. "I had best get going," he said.

"God go with you, lad, and be careful," Fulk cautioned him. "Remember, you are not expected to rescue the lady. Only find Merin ap Owen's place, and ascertain that the lady is in his custody. Then you must return to Ashlin, and tell me all you have learned."

"I understand," Sim said, "and I promise to be cautious." He mounted his horse, and moved out of the stable yard toward the gates.

Fulk watched him go, half regretting he had agreed to Sim's suggestion, but more than aware that the lad was right. His experience was of more value here at Ashlin right now than on the trail in search of Lady Eleanore. He went off to find the priest to tell him of the change of plan. Father Oswin was openly relieved to learn the captain was remaining.

"The men are not as certain of Sim as they are of you, my friend. He needs a bit more seasoning as does any young man," Father Oswin said. "You will be happy to learn I have seen the young lordling, and he is thriving with his new wet nurse. Maris is a good woman. She and Alyce will see the child is well cared for, and old Ida will watch over both of those two young women," he concluded with a chuckle.

"That is one less worry, praise God," Fulk said, relieved. "Now all I must do is wait for Sim to seek the answers we need, and then decide how to go about retrieving the lady."

"With God's help we will succeed," the priest said firmly.

"In the meantime I worry how my lady has fared these past few days," Fulk replied. "It has been so wet."

Wet. She had never been so wet in all her life, even in a bath, Elf thought. Her mind was as clear as a cloudless sky on a summer's day now, but it hadn't been at first. She had been so tired when she had gone to bed that night. *Four days back?* Her dreams, at least she had thought them dreams, had been a jumble of confusion. Whispers in the darkness. She was lifted up. She floated away again, only rousing slightly when she felt the cold air on her face, but it was daylight then. Arwydd brought her a warm drink, and then she slept again, and again, and again.

She realized now that her mind was fresh, that she had been carried through the rain in a litter. Where she was she hadn't the faintest idea, but she knew her captors were Welsh by their language. She also realized that Fulk had been wise in being suspicious of Arwydd. The girl had ingratiated herself into the household at Ashlin for the sole purpose of betraying them. And yet, Arwydd remained kind. Today she had spoken softly to Elf so that no one could hear her, pushing a small bag into her hand.

"Hide this, lady," she whispered, "and for mercy's sake, take it to stop your milk. If my mistress learns you have a child, nothing will suit her but that the child be brought to her. You were good to me, but this is all I can do for you. We will be at Gwynfr Castle in a few hours, and after that I am her obedient servant once again."

Elf sniffed the bag. It was sage. "Have you been feeding me this in my drink?" she asked.

Arwydd nodded. "Like you, lady, I know how to heal," she said simply. "My mother taught me before she died."

"Was she really English?"

"Aye, she was, poor woman," Arwydd said. "She wasn't a captive who was enslaved, though. She ran away with my father against her family's wishes. My English grandfather was a wool merchant, she once told me. I was told to tell you that terrible story, although my life after she died has not been a happy one. My father drank himself into the grave, and then his brother, who is a whoremonger, took me in, but only to be a servant in his whorehouse. My mistress rescued me, and so I owe her my loyalty, but, as you were good to me, I have done what I could for you. From now on, however, we are even, lady," Arwydd finished.

Elf nodded, understanding the girl's reasoning. "Tell me just one thing, Arwydd. Who is my captor?"

"Merin ap Owen, lady" came the answer, and then Arwydd moved away from Elf.

She looked about the encampment for its leader. She spotted him immediately, a tall dark-haired man with a decided air of command. No sooner had she set eyes upon him, then he turned and pierced her with a fierce look. Elf flushed, but she did not look away.

Merin ap Owen crossed his camp to where Elf sat. "How do you feel, lady?"

"How much ransom do you want?" Elf replied quietly, then added, "As to how I feel, *wet*. Could you have not sought shelter during these rains, Merin ap Owen? My husband will not pay you for a corpse."

"Your husband is in Normandy, lady, and until he returns to pay me a fine ransom for you, you will remain my guest," he told her. "Be grateful I dressed you before I stole you away," he said with a leer. Then reaching down he pulled Elf to her feet. "You are well enough to ride with me today," he said brusquely. "Come!"

Elf did not bother resisting him. It would have been an exercise in futility. He brought her over to a large dappled horse and lifted her up onto the saddle, swung himself up behind her, one arm going tightly about her waist, the other gathering the reins into his big hand. The men with him, a scruffy-looking lot, were scrambling to gain their own mounts and follow after their master. Arwydd, she saw, had her own shaggy little Welsh pony to ride. The girl no longer even looked in Elf's direction.

Elf said nothing as they rode. Merin ap Owen was quite conversational for a time. "You may not be as comfortable at Gwynfr as you are in your own home, my lady, but you will not be badly treated. And you will have my whore for company. She says she is a nobleman's daughter, although she is such a deceptive bitch, I cannot be certain she speaks the truth to me all the time. I believe you may know her. She claims she was your sister-in-law at one time." Merin ap Owen felt his captive stiffen within his grip. "Isleen? Isleen de Warenne," he said softly, whispering the name in her ear. "Ah, then, you do know her. So the bitch did not lie to me in this instance. That is good."

Elf could not contain her anger any longer. "That creature killed my brother! She poisoned him. You had best beware, Merin ap Owen."

"Why did she kill him?"

"She was in love with her cousin, a knight, Saer de Bude. They devised a plan between them to kill Richard. Then de Bude was to violate me so I could not take my final vows. He would, of course, do the *honorable* thing then and marry me. After a time, I suspect, I would have been poisoned so that vile creature could have her lover and my family's lands as well, which was what she wanted all along," Elf said angrily. "I could not believe such wickedness existed, but it did. God protected me, however, and her plans were foiled."

"How?" he asked. Having heard Isleen's version of these events, he was eager to hear the lady Eleanore's account, which he suspected would be closer to the truth.

"De Bude moved too quickly. He tried to force me in my herbarium. One of my serfs came to my aid. My brother was dead and buried, so I escaped back to St. Frideswide's."

"But you did not take your vows," Merin ap Owen said.

"Nay. De Bude claimed he had dishonored me before the king. I was brought from my convent. The abbess and others went with me. We were able to prove that de Bude lied. The king, however, felt that Ashlin needed me more than the convent did. He also felt I needed a strong lord to hold the land. He married me to Ranulf de Glandeville. De Bude was sent to the Count of Blois's court, and Isleen de Warenne was to be confined for the rest of her life in a nunnery."

Merin ap Owen burst out laughing. "Isleen in a nunnery? The king obviously did not know the bitch at all."

"Nay," Elf agreed, "he did not. None of us could have conceived the evil nature of that woman. It is hard to believe. And now to learn she may be at the center of this plot to steal and ransom me! It is too much to bear! I was taught to love my neighbor, to be gentle, and to be obedient, but Isleen de Warenne destroys all my good intentions, and I want nothing more than to scratch her eyes out right now!"

Merin ap Owen laughed harder. "Wonderful," he said. "You two should provide me with a constant source of amusement this winter, my lady Eleanore. Ah, look. There is Gwynfr Castle just up ahead. May I bid you welcome to my house, lady?" He mocked her.

"Go to hell!" Elf said, for the first time in her life, swearing a wicked oath, and yet strangely she felt quite good about it.

"A bitch and a firebrand," her captor said with a deep chuckle. "This is far better than I had ever anticipated."

PART IV

THE CAPTIVE

Wales 1154–1155

Chapter Sixteen

"So," Isleen de Warenne said, "you have returned at last, *and* you have the little nun with you. Put her in the deepest and darkest of your dungeons! I have explored them, and they are deliciously rat-infested, my lord. Let her pray to God to keep from being eaten alive."

"Do not be absurd, my pretty bitch," Merin ap Owen said. He slid from his saddle, reached up, and lifted Elf down. "Our captive will be housed in my private apartments until her ransom is paid. That way I can be fairly certain you will not allow your evil nature to harm her and cost me a pretty penny."

"I should rather be in the dungeons," Elf snapped. She was cold. She was hungry. And she had had quite enough of Isleen. Holy Mother of God! Why had her brother not seen the creature for what she was?

"No!" Isleen's voice had an edge to it. "You cannot keep *her* in your own apartments, my lord. You allow no one there, not even me, and I at least am your mistress."

"I cannot trust you, Isleen. Your desire for revenge is greater than your common sense," Merin ap Owen replied.

"Revenge?" Elf's voice was tired, but outraged. "You want revenge upon me? For what cause, you murdering witch?"

Isleen was startled by both Elf's tone and her attitude. This was not the meek and gentle little nun she remembered. "If," she began, "you had married Saer—"

Elf cut her short. "I should be as dead as my brother right now! Do you take me for a complete fool, Isleen, that you think I do not know what you planned in order to have your cousin *and* Ashlin?"

"My ladies, my ladies," Merin ap Owen said, his dark eyes dancing with amusement. They would come to blows if he did not stop them now. While eventually he might allow it for the amusement of those in the hall, this was not the time. "Cease your argument." He turned to Isleen, his fingers caressing her jawline. "I am master here, my pretty bitch. Remember it, or I will make certain that you do in a manner I promise you will not like. Do you understand me?" He smiled, then addressed Elf. "You cannot trust Isleen, my lady Eleanore. She will harm you given the chance, because she is basically ruled by her emotions. Do not allow yourself to be alone with her at any time. Do you understand?" He tipped Elf's face up to his glance.

The silvery eyes glared back at him. "Do you think I do not know what she is, my lord?" Elf said coldly. "You may trust I will not seek her company or bear it willingly unless I must."

He laughed. His little captive was like a wet and spitting kitten, but he was wise enough to realize that the kitten had very sharp claws, and would use them if provoked. "Let us go into the hall," he said. "Are you as hungry as I am, lady?"

Elf nodded.

"Good!" Merin ap Owen said, and taking her hand led her into the room and up to the high board, where he seated her on his right, much to Isleen's outrage. His mistress took the place on his left, not at all pleased, which only increased his amusement. "Food!" the lord of Gwynfr Castle roared, and immediately a line of serving men hurried forth with platters and bowls. A young boy filled the goblets, which were set at each place.

Elf noticed that the goblets were of heavy silver, decorated with black onyx. There were silver plates and spoons at each place. She wondered from whom he had stolen them, for the castle itself was a half ruin. The meal was more than decent. There was fish, game, poultry, and lamb, accompanied with lettuces, bread, butter, and cheese. Elf did not stint herself. She was ravenous, and the food was good. She ate and drank until she was filled. When she had finished, she said bluntly, "I will want a bath, my lord. I am still badly chilled and have been traveling four days. Have someone take me to my apartments."

"By the rood, little nun, you have grown bold," Isleen said scathingly. "A bath? Do you think this is a palace?"

"Unlike some, I have been taught to bathe regularly. I do not cover my body in scents to disguise the odor of being unwashed," Elf said sharply. She was surprised at the fierceness in her breast against Isleen de Warenne, but she realized if she showed the slightest weakness, Isleen would be on her like a beast on its prey.

Merin ap Owen chuckled. "Can you care for yourself, my lady Eleanore? The only women here are you, my pretty bitch, and Arwydd."

"I am not some helpless creature, my lord. Remember, I was raised in a convent to do for myself. I had no servants until I returned home again to Ashlin. I can take care of myself, and I want neither Arwydd, nor *that creature* attending on me."

"Let Arwydd at least help you haul the water for this bath you so desperately desire, my lady Eleanore," he told her.

Surprised that he would expect her to carry her own bathwater, but refusing to give way in the face of Isleen's smug glance, Elf said, "I should appreciate the help, my lord."

"Go along with the lady Eleanore, then, Arwydd. You know where the tub is. Set it up by the fire in my apartments," he instructed the servant calmly. "The lady Eleanore will sleep in the little chamber next to mine. While she is bathing, see the room is prepared."

"Yes, my lord," Arwydd said dutifully. Then she looked to Elf. "Will you come with me, my lady?" Her voice was devoid of any emotion.

Elf arose and followed Arwydd from the hall.

"Do you mean to spoil the bitch, then?" Isleen asked jealously.

"I hardly think making her bring enough water for her bath up two flights of stairs and then having to heat it herself is pampering the lady," he replied dryly. "Besides, it will give me a few moments' entertainment watching her bathe. I have never seen you bathe, my pretty bitch."

"Do you mean to have her, then?" Isleen demanded. Her tone was extremely pettish, and she glared at him.

Merin ap Owen smiled a slow smile, rendering the handsome side of his face even more handsome, but he did not answer her. Instead he said, "Stand up, Isleen, and place your palms flat upon the table, even as you bend your body well over."

Isleen stared at him. "You did not answer my question," she said harshly. "Do you mean to have the little nun?"

Merin ap Owen stood, yanking his mistress up by her long golden hair and forcing her body down into the required position. Leaning over her he said, "Shut your mouth, Isleen. If you refuse to obey me instantly again in front of my men, I will be forced to kill you!"

"Jesu!" she half whispered, "you do not mean to take me here before the entire hall, do you?"

In reply he lifted her skirts up slowly, tucking them into the back of her neckline. He had always thought Isleen had a particularly fine bottom. Now he viewed it at his leisure, running his hands over the smooth, round globes of flesh. When she shivered, he inclined himself again over her body and murmured softly in her ear, "Ah, you have been faithful to me this time, my pretty bitch, haven't you?"

"Did you think any of your men would service my needs after you hung those two fools before your little foray into England, my lord?" she returned scathingly.

"Are you ready for my pleasure?" he demanded.

"Nay," she said softly.

"Then, I must see you are prepared," he told her with a chuckle. He stood again, and raising his hand brought it down hard upon her buttocks.

Isleen squealed sharply, and the men at the trestles below the high board now looked up with interest, several of them grinning and making lewd gestures with their hands.

"For each time you cry out," he told her, "I shall add an additional two strokes. I shall now render you twelve instead of ten, my pretty bitch." His hand descended upon her hapless flesh again, smacking her until the correct number of blows had been properly delivered and her buttocks were a bright pink. "Are you ready for me now?" he said.

"Yes!" Isleen cried out, and then gasped as he thrust himself into her female channel. *"Ahhhh!"* She shuddered, feeling his thick manhood probing her lustily.

He laughed as she ground her hot bottom into his groin. "You are the perfect whore, Isleen," he told her as he eagerly pumped her. His fingers gripped her hips, leaving red marks on the white skin. He used her hard, making her cry aloud again and again as his men watched avidly, their mouths open in admiration, some of them even fondling themselves in their excitement. Finally Merin ap Owen was well satisfied, and he withdrew from her.

For a long moment Isleen lay prone over the table, and then with a deep sigh of satisfaction, she arose. "You are a fine lover, my lord," she told him, pulling her skirts down. "I will wager the little nun will not satisfy you as I can."

He sat back down again and drank deeply from his goblet. "Are you jealous, my pretty bitch?" he asked her mockingly.

"Why will you not imprison her?"

"Because she has done nothing to displease me," he replied. "She is a gentle and good lady. I have no quarrel with her. I simply want a ransom from her husband. It is a business transaction, my pretty bitch. Nothing more."

"Then, why not give her her own rooms?" Isleen persisted.

"Because, as I told you earlier, I do not trust you; and because there are no other rooms fit for a lady such as the lady Eleanore," he said. She was jealous, and it amused him to taunt her.

"Then, give her my apartment, and keep me with you," Isleen half pleaded. "I would be at your complete disposal, my lord, and eager to do whatever you wished me to do." She caught his hand in hers.

"Nay, my pretty bitch. It is better that the lady Eleanore is where I am, and where all know I permit no one else to enter," he replied.

"My prisoner is very beautiful, and I would return her to her husband as I found her. *Or almost,*" he mocked his mistress.

"You think her beautiful?" Isleen felt her temper rising. He had never called her beautiful, but he thought the little nun beautiful? "I never before heard it said that Eleanore de Montfort was beautiful, my lord Merin. It is I who am considered a beauty." Isleen preened at him, smiling winningly.

"You are pretty enough," Merin ap Owen told her, "but you are not as beautiful as the lady Eleanore. I know the English consider golden hair and blue eyes such as yours a standard of beauty, but I do not. I find the lady Eleanore with her silvery eyes and pale red-gold hair, her translucent skin, her sweetness of expression, far more beautiful than your common prettiness. Has no one ever told you that? Or have all the men in your life fallen at your feet in awe of your golden and sapphire coloring? You are as wicked as I am, Isleen. That evil is beginning to show through in your face. The lady Eleanore, however, has a good heart, and that is what shows in her fair face."

"You are falling in love with her," Isleen accused him.

He laughed harshly. "Nay," he said. Then he stood again. "I am going to my apartments now, my pretty bitch. Come, and I will see you to your chamber so I may be certain to know where you are." He pulled her up, and dragged her from the high board.

Isleen swore virulently at him as they went. "You are a dog, Merin ap Owen. I will not play your bitch for much longer if you do not treat me better. Have a care! You are bruising my wrist. Owwww! Do not pull me by my hair, you bastard!"

In the narrow stone hallway of the castle, he pushed her against the hard wall, banging her head as he did. "Listen to me. You belong to *me* and me alone. You are no better than a slave, Isleen. You will do what *I* say, when *I* say it, as long as it pleases *me*. I will tell you when *I* am through with *you,* and not you me." His fingers dug cruelly into the soft flesh of her shoulder. *"Do you understand me, Isleen?"* His dark eyes blazed at her.

Isleen was afraid in that single moment. This man was like no other she had ever known. He terrified her, and yet she adored him with every fiber of her being. She would not let Eleanore de Montfort steal him away and ruin her life yet a second time! She would make Merin ap Owen love her. *She would!* "I understand, my lord," she said low.

"Good," he said. "Very good, my pretty bitch." They ascended the staircase, passing his apartment, then moving into the even narrower staircase leading to her apartment in the tower. He opened the door and pushed her through. "Do not come out until the morning, Isleen. I will send Arwydd to you. Once she is inside, I will loose the mastiffs. They will tear you to pieces if you try to enter my apartments. Good night." He pulled the door shut and descended down to the next level, where his own rooms were located. Entering, he said to Arwydd, "Go to your mistress, and be warned, the mastiffs will be loosed shortly. Remain with your lady until the morning."

"Yes, my lord." Arwydd curtsied, and hurried out.

Merin ap Owen glanced about and saw the tub had already been taken from before the fire. Walking into his bedchamber, he looked through into the tiny interior chamber opposite his bed. "You have not prepared yourself for bed yet," he said to Elf, who was fully dressed. "Are your garments not damp from the rain?"

"There is no door, or curtain to provide me with privacy," Elf told him.

"It is better that you are where I can see you," he said. "Take off your gown, lady. As you so pithily reminded me earlier, your husband will not pay me for a corpse. I am certain your chemise is a modest enough garment, and my baser instincts can be kept in check. Besides, if I wanted your virtue, my lady Eleanore, I could take it no matter you were dressed in armor."

She stared at him, not certain if she was shocked or amused by his words. "Blow out the candles on the candle stand," she said finally.

"Very well," he replied, complying. Then watching her shadow, for the bedchamber fire gave some light, he drew his own garments off and climbed into his bed. "Sleep well, lady," he said.

Elf listened to his breathing; shortly he was snoring. She whispered her prayers and tried to sleep, but sleep would not come at first. Her mind was filled with questions for which she had no answers. How had Isleen de Warenne ended up here at Gwynfr Castle? And Merin ap Owen? What kind of a man was he really? While his tongue was rough with Isleen, he was courteous with her. Was she safe from his advances, if indeed he even made advances toward her? It was all very confusing. She was not worried about her son, for the Ashlin folk would care for Simon with singular devotion. A wet nurse would be easily found among her serfs. While he might miss her face, Simon would be oblivious to her absence, given a warm breast to nurse upon and sturdy arms to cuddle him. Elf, however, could not shake free from her desperate sense of loss of both the infant and Ranulf. Her breasts ached every bit as much as her heart, which she felt was near to breaking. But for Simon's sake she had to mask her emotions. Her enemies must not know of his existence.

Ranulf. She sighed softly. He would be safe in Normandy, but when was he coming home? *When you hear of King Stephen's death,* she reminded herself, but she had heard nothing of the king, and here it was October. But then Ashlin in its remote location was always last to hear any important news, Elf thought. And she was stuck here in Wales until her ransom was paid. It could not even be demanded, surely, until her husband came home, whenever that was.

Elf felt tears pricking against her eyelids, and blinked them back. She would not allow this Welsh bandit and his evil whore to know she was fearful. *Ranulf.* Her heart cried out for him. She could see his face in her mind's eye. The dark bushy brows over his warm hazel eyes. His big mouth that could kiss her both tenderly and fiercely all at once. She could almost feel the softness of his chestnut hair between her fingers. How gently he had wooed her. How very much she loved him, and if she ever saw him again in this life, she intended telling him so even if it would abash him! Had anyone ever loved Ranulf de Glandeville? From what he had told her, the answer was no. Well, it was past time someone who loved Ranulf told him so. He would just have to get used to it, and even if he didn't love her because he didn't know how to love, it would make no difference. She loved him, and that was all there was to it!

When she awoke the following morning, Merin ap Owen had gone from the bedchamber. Elf arose and dressed. She walked into the dayroom of the apartment and tried the door into the hallway, but discovered it was locked. Still, a fire burned in the fireplace, and a tray with a carafe of liquid, a small fresh loaf of bread, an apple, and a honeycomb was set upon the table. She wondered if Isleen had poisoned the food and drink, but then decided she was being foolish. She could hear sounds in the tower apartment above her indicating that Isleen was still there. Besides, Isleen would not have a key to her prison.

Elf sat down and ate, prudently leaving half the food for later. When she had finished, she made up the bed in the lord's chamber and her own little pallet, for lack of anything else to do. She next gazed out the window for a time. Gwynfr was set atop a craggy hillock. Below she could see a village. The hills about them were alive with autumn color. The day was gray and rainy. She had only just sat down by the fire when she heard the key in the lock, and leapt up.

Merin ap Owen came through the door. "Ah, you are awake, my lady Eleanore," he said. "Sit down, and we will speak on the matter that concerns us. Namely, your ransom."

Elf seated herself again. "My husband is in Normandy," she said. "You picked a rather bad time to kidnap me, my lord." He was a handsome man, she thought, but for that terrible thin scar running down the left side of his face. "There is no one at Ashlin who can pay you any ransom you are going to demand. No one has the authority."

"You speak as if you do not know when your husband will return."

"I do not know," Elf told him frankly.

"Why did he go to Normandy?"

"He did not confide in me, my lord, although it may have had something to do with his mother, who lives there with her second husband," Elf replied as naturally as if it were the purest truth.

"Or perhaps he went to make his peace with Duke Henry, for I hear the English king is ill," Merin ap Owen observed.

"Mayhap, but my husband has always been loyal to King Stephen, my lord. It was the king who arranged our marriage to reward Ranulf for his dedication and fealty."

"The *why* does not matter," Merin ap Owen observed. "If I must keep you for a time, I will, my lady Eleanore, but to be frank, I had not anticipated it," he told her. "The lady Isleen is a dangerous enemy to have, as you know. While I realize her grievance against you lacks substance, she nonetheless believes her cause is just and seeks her revenge."

"She is a stupid creature with the wit of a flea," Elf said irritably. "She kills my brother, then blames me because I will not allow myself to be killed by her so she may have my family's lands! I once thought I had great patience, but Isleen de Warenne would try the patience of all the saints and angels in God's heaven!"

He laughed aloud, suddenly realizing that he liked this young woman. Isleen had sneered at her goodness, and the truth was that Merin ap Owen could never remember having met a good woman. He was beginning to suspect that Eleanore de Montfort might really be one. "Isleen is indeed stupid," he agreed, "but do not underestimate her, my lady, for while a dullard and simpleton in most ways, she has incredible guile, which is what makes her a treacherous foe."

"It was her idea to kidnap me?"

His dark head nodded in the affirmative. "Frankly, my lady Eleanore, I would have been content to steal all your sheep and cattle, but as Isleen pointed out, I would gain but half their value as everyone knows that what I sell, I have stolen. By stealing you, I force your husband to sell the livestock himself, and gain twice what I would otherwise."

"She has put you to a great deal of trouble, Merin ap Owen," Elf said. "If you had taken the sheep and the cattle, you would now have your reward. Instead you must wait for my husband to return from Normandy, and while we wait, you must keep me safe from your whore. I wonder if you are up to such a task, my lord. It would seem for a stupid woman, Isleen has outmaneuvered us both."

He laughed again. "You are not at all as Isleen described you to me, lady."

"From the time I was five years old until the day I returned home to nurse my dying brother, I never saw Dickon or his wife, but once, shortly after they were wed. Within a convent you are protected from the realities of the world. It is a simple matter to cultivate holiness in a place where there is little temptation, Merin ap Owen. I probably seemed an innocent ninny to Isleen. She bases her impression of me on that brief acquaintance we shared. While I still surely possess a certain amount of naïveté, I am not quite the sweet and simple girl Isleen thinks I am. If she attempts me any harm, I will defend myself with every means at my disposal. The only thing I cannot prevent her from doing is poisoning me. You had best be certain that she does not, else you lose your ransom, my lord Merin."

He nodded, impressed by her astuteness. By the rood, she was a lovely woman! "I will keep you safe," he promised her.

"I believe that you will," Elf replied softly. Then she said, "Must I remain here, my lord, all the time?"

"Nay," he told her. "You are welcome in the hall, lady."

"I cannot simply sit and do nothing," Elf said. "If you have a tapestry frame, I could begin a tapestry; or if you have clothing that needs mending, I will do it for you. I dislike being idle, you will understand, my lord. If you have someone who could gather certain herbs and plants for me, I will make poultices, teas, and salves for your infirmary. Who cares for your sick and wounded?"

"There is no one," he said.

"No one?" She was surprised.

"This is a place of men, my lady Eleanore. Until I brought Isleen here, there were no women. We have relied upon ourselves for healing when it was necessary."

"Have you no wife?" She was curious as to why, but then considering the place, perhaps it was not surprising.

"I have no wife," he answered. For some reason he did not want to tell her he had had two, and neither could abide him.

"Perhaps there is one among your men whom I could teach my arts of healing. That way," Elf explained, "when I am gone back to Ashlin, you will have someone with the knowledge to cure. If an epidemic ever struck here, or in your village below, it could wipe everyone out, my lord Merin. That would be a great tragedy."

She spoke to him as if she were merely visiting as his guest. She was not judgmental of him, and it actually made Merin ap Owen uncomfortable. She should not be kind to him or offer to aid him, he thought. He was her kidnapper, not her host! Yet there was such a pure sweetness about her that he could not for the life of him be anything but pleased. "I will seek among my men for the proper person," he told her. "In the meantime I will choose someone trustworthy to escort you outside to seek what you need. I cannot give you a female companion. Arwydd belongs to Isleen body and soul. If you trusted her before, lady, do not do so now. She is back in Isleen's power and will do whatever is asked of her. I will warn her, however, not to obey her mistress's directives to harm you. Isleen must be constantly reminded that I am master here at Gwynfr. Come now." He arose and offered her his hand. "I will escort you into the hall, my lady Eleanore."

They descended the stairs and, entering the hall, found it empty but for a single servant.

"Gwyll," the lord of Gwynfr said. "The lady Eleanore is in your charge from now on. You are responsible for seeing no harm comes to her. Only I will give you orders regarding her. No one else, and particularly not the lady Isleen, may do so. I will not send my orders by anyone else. I will come to you face-to-face when necessary."

"I understand, my lord," Gwyll replied.

Merin ap Owen turned to Elf. "I think there is a tapestry frame and a loom in the attics that used to belong to my grandmother. I will go and see if I can find it, my lady Eleanore. Gwyll, is there needle and thread to be had in this castle?"

"I do not think so, my lord," Gwyll said, surprised by such a request. "Perhaps in the attics with the loom?"

"Let Gwyll take me, my lord. Surely you must have more important things to do than seek for women's toys."

"Very well, lady," Merin ap Owen responded. "Besides, I should not know what I was seeking. You will. Gwyll, take her, and remain by her side at all times."

"I understand, my lord," Gwyll said with meaning. He didn't like his master's English mistress. She was a truly evil woman.

Elf had little hope of finding what she needed, but to her surprise she did. There was a loom and a frame both, along with a basket of colored wools. Then Gwyll discovered a smaller woven container with sewing materials.

"I wonder to whom these belonged," she said softly.

Gwyll did not answer her, but shrugged, apparently as mystified as she was, although he was not. The tapestry frame had belonged to the lord's grandmother. The loom and its wools had belonged to his master's first wife, who had come dreamy-eyed and full of hope to Gwynfr, only to discover her bridegroom was a monster. She, poor lass, had been so in love with Merin ap Owen, she could not bring herself to face the truth. She had died for her love; and there had been no one to revenge her, for she had been an orphan. The sewing basket he thought might have belonged to her, too. "If you have what you need, lady, we had best return to the hall," Gwyll said. "I'll set up the loom and the frame for you, if you wish it. Mayhap by the fire?"

"That would be perfect," Elf answered him, placing the sewing accoutrements atop the basket of wools, then stepping carefully down the narrow staircase of the half-ruined tower. Here and there a stone from the walls had fallen into the passageway. Elf was surprised that the roof in the attic had been in such good condition else her treasures would have been ruined. She really did need something to do if she was going to be here for even a short time.

Back in the hall Gwyll set up the equipment next to the fire as he had promised Elf. When he had finished, he set a chair by it, then turning to Elf asked her, "Will you weave now, lady, or would you like to go out-of-doors and seek for plants? There is but a light rain today."

"I think I shall remain indoors today, Gwyll. I am still damp from my long ride," she told him with a small smile.

"Do you think you will be with us long, lady?" he asked her politely as he seated her before the loom, setting the tall basket of wools by her side. "Perhaps I should spread them out on the floor for you to see, and then you can decide which colors to use," Gwyll offered helpfully, tipping the container and separating the hanks for her to view.

"Thank you," Elf answered him. "I don't know. It depends when my husband returns from Normandy." Bending, she began to separate the colors, filling her lap with those she wanted. "Put the others away now, Gwyll," she said as she started to string the loom.

"*Ohhh!* How sweet and how domestic" came a sneering comment.

"Good morning, Isleen," Elf replied dryly. "What do you do with your day? Gwynfr is hardly the most stimulating atmosphere I have ever been in, and I am used to using my time wisely."

"So pious. So good. My lord Merin coddles you. If you were my prisoner, I should chain you in the dungeons to be nibbled at by the rats. Your husband could have whatever was left when he paid the ransom! He'd probably be glad to be rid of you. You cannot be of any interest to him in his bed. Do you pray when he mounts you, and takes what small pleasure he can gain off your skinny body?" Isleen stood directly before Elf's loom, glaring down at her, her bright blue eyes filled with her anger.

"But I am not your prisoner, Isleen, although I have been given to understand I have you to thank for my current predicament," Elf replied. There was, Gwyll noted, just the faintest hint of anger in her voice.

"So he told you it was my idea, did he? Well, it was!" Isleen crowed triumphantly. "If your husband is willing to ransom you, it will cost him everything. I wonder if he is willing to give up all he gained when he wed you just to have you back. I hope he won't pay the ransom. Then, I shall put you in my whorehouse to earn your keep!" She laughed when she saw how Elf paled.

"You make me ashamed of myself," Elf responded. "For the first time in my life, I feel an anger so deep that I want to kill you!" She arose from her chair, and glared furiously at her adversary. Her small fists were clenched into tight little balls. "You are a horrible creature, Isleen de Warenne! *God forgive me, but I hate you!*"

Isleen stepped back, surprised by the rage in Elf's silvery eyes. Those eyes blazed, and Isleen had not a doubt that Elf would, if driven much further, attack her person. "So," she snarled, "you are human after all. Good! A weak enemy would offer me little amusement."

"I will offer you none," Elf said coldly. Then she sat back down again and continued stringing her loom.

Isleen looked to Gwyll. "Leave us!"

"I cannot," he said. "Master's orders, lady. I am to remain with the lady Eleanore at all times and take my orders from no one but the lord hisself." There was a faint smile on Gwyll's lips as he spoke, and a determination in his eyes Isleen knew could not be swayed.

Angrily she slapped him. "Impudent serf!" she shrieked, then fell back, her hands going to her face. Astounded she stared at Elf, who once more stood. *"You . . . You hit me!"* she screamed disbelievingly.

"Do not raise your hand again to the servants," Elf warned her. "Gwyll was but doing his master's bidding. You are not lady here."

"Nor are you!" Isleen shot back. She frantically rubbed her cheek. "If you have marred my beauty, I will find a way to punish you no matter your faithful watchdog! I swear I will!"

"You are not injured fatally," Elf said dryly. "The mark of my hand and fingers will fade in a few hours' time, Isleen. As you warn me, however, I warn you. Do not mistreat the servants. Did your mother teach you no better? My Ashlin folk are well rid of you."

"Servants are servants," Isleen said with emphasis.

"They are God's people even as we are," Elf said. "Even you, Isleen, for all your wickedness, are God's creation."

"I hate you. I hate you!" Isleen shouted, and stamped from the hall.

"You have a bad enemy there, my lady," Gwyll noted.

"She was always my enemy even when she knew me not," Elf told the puzzled man. "Now, however, I am wise enough to be hers."

"I'll defend you," Gwyll said. He was still amazed that the lord's gentle captive had defended him against the unjust anger of the lord's mistress. There were none here at Gwynfr who would do the English bitch a good turn, and so he thought the lady Eleanore relatively safe. Ever since the lord had hanged those two men-at-arms for poaching on his preserve, the men could not be suborned by the whore. Only poor little Arwydd was loyal to her, but Arwydd had not the stomach for murder. Still, Gwyll thought, he saw he must guard his charge most carefully.

From the first Elf had seen that weeping and bemoaning her fate would do no good, so she had settled into life at Gwynfr Castle as best she could. While her thoughts were with Ranulf and their son, those two were safe. And, reassured by such thoughts, she spent hours weaving at the loom by the fire, and going out on the hillsides to search for medicinal plants with which to make a store of medicants.

One day when her gaze wandered to the hills about them and remained too long, she heard Gwyll's voice say gently, "You don't even know which way is England, do you, lady? You are safer here. Do not think of escape."

Elf did not respond to him, pretending she had not heard. Instead, she dug her knife carefully into the soil about the roots of a plant she needed, loosening the earth and drawing the plant slowly forth. Gwyll was right. She didn't know which direction England was, and there was no way in which she could find out without arousing suspicion. She handed Gwyll the knife, and laid the plant in her basket.

Gwynfr provided primitive living quarters at best. Most of the castle was a ruin, and other than Arwydd, Isleen, and herself, there were no women, even servants, who came during the day. The life was even harder than the convent had been when it came to simple everyday things such as washing. In order to do that, she was forced to carry her own water to her chamber. Ever since the first night she had come, Arwydd had been forbidden by her mistress from helping Elf in any way, and Merin ap Owen did not interfere. Her clothing was in need of a good washing.

When he had stolen her, Elf had been in a drug-induced sleep. Merin ap Owen had put a tunic dress and a skirt on her, wrapping her in a cloak, before he had taken her away. She had kept these garments as clean as she could with brushing, and shaking, but she had been wearing the same clothes for two weeks now. Her chemise was filthy and needed to be washed, but she had no other to wear. Since there was no door to her little interior chamber, it presented a problem. Then it dawned on her to bathe as she had once bathed in her convent, wearing her chemise. She would do it in the evening before Merin ap Owen came to his apartments. Then she would wrap herself in her blanket, and dry the chemise by the fire in the dayroom. She would then find her bed, and it was unlikely he would ever realize it.

But when he entered his apartment that night, he saw the delicate little garment spread over a chair back facing the fire. At first he was puzzled, then he realized her predicament. Had she been any other woman he would have taken advantage of the moment, but he could not with her. Never in his life had he encountered such a woman as Eleanore de Montfort. She had accepted her situation with a practical fortitude. She made herself useful without being asked to do so, and, for the first time in memory, his servants appeared actually happy.

Her attitude toward him was equally interesting. Isleen had been so scornful of the lady Eleanore, but the lady of Ashlin was no mealymouthed little saint. Indeed, she was quick of wit and quite able to defend herself from his whore, who took every opportunity to belittle or attack his captive. He was quite certain Eleanore did not approve of his ways, but not once, even subtly did she attempt to reprove him or reform him. Instead she went about his castle making herself useful and attempting to help where she could. She had already dressed several minor wounds among his people and cured his cook, who had had a dreadful cough.

Merin ap Owen, who had little use for the gentler sex but for the pleasure they could provide, had to admit that he was faced with a truly good woman. He felt a trifle guilty for having stolen her, but not so guilty that he would return her without a proper ransom. However, when he saw that fragile little chemise drying before his fire, he realized her predicament and was touched that she had not complained, but rather had attempted to solve her problem herself. This was something he could right.

When Elf awoke in the morning and saw that the lord of the castle was gone from his bedchamber, she crept out into the dayroom to retrieve her chemise. It was nicely dry, and to her surprise upon the chair seat there was a small bolt of fine linen. She was both surprised and touched. After dressing herself, she went down into the hall, where he was already at the high board breaking his fast. Isleen was nowhere in sight as she rarely arose early.

Elf took her usual place. "Thank you," she said quietly.

"I did not realize you would be with us so long," he replied. "If I had, I should have stolen some of your clothing other than what I dressed you in, lady. You must not be shy to tell me when you need something. It is not my plan to mistreat you."

"I am not a woman to complain, my lord, but I shall make myself another chemise, and be glad I have it."

Nothing more was said about the matter until several mornings later when she handed him a portion of neatly folded linen with a smile.

"What is this?" he asked her.

"There was far too much linen for just one little chemise," Elf told him. "I made you one, too. I thought perhaps you could use a new undergarment, my lord. I have had to guess at the size, but I believe I am close. Try it on later, and I will make whatever alterations are necessary for the garment to fit you properly."

"Lady . . ." He was speechless. In his entire life no one had ever done anything gratuitously for him. She was his captive. He had stolen her away from her home and family, and would not allow her to return until her husband beggared himself to ransom her. Yet she had thought of his comfort as if they were old friends.

"I think I shall go out with Gwyll today, my lord, with your permission, of course. Soon it will be too cold to dig up the plants I need. I have managed to find quite a respectable stock of things with which to make my medicines." She had recognized his surprise, and sought to cover it over and make him comfortable again.

"Of course," he said. "Go with Gwyll." He cast a sidewise glance at her. God! She was so lovely. With a terrible sinking feeling Merin ap Owen realized that the impossible had happened. The heart he had firmly believed he did not possess had surfaced from deep inside of him. For the first time in his life, he was in love. *He was in love with Eleanore de Montfort.* How had it happened? Perhaps he should have done what Isleen had wanted to do when he brought his captive to Gwynfr. Perhaps he should have incarcerated her in his dungeons, where he would not have been exposed to her charm, her beauty, her wit, and her genuine goodness. But it was too late now. He was in love with the lady of Ashlin, and if he was to return her safely to her husband, he was going to have to be certain that Isleen never found out his secret.

Oh, God, he prayed silently for the first time in years, *please help me!* He wondered if God would hear the prayers of a man such as Merin ap Owen. For Eleanore de Montfort's sake, he hoped He did.

CHAPTER SEVENTEEN

The weather in the Channel was foul, and had been for days. A hard cold wind blew from the north. The rain came in torrents, and the sea was all afroth, the waves crashing over the seawalls in Barfleur. The king, snugly housed, groused and grumbled with his impatience to begin his journey. He must be crowned soon. England had been without a king for over a month. Henry Plantagenet could only pray that there was peace there, no civil war. The line of succession, he kept reminding himself, was clear and undisputed, but, still, the English were a most unruly people.

Ranulf de Glandeville seethed with impatience, too. All he had wished was to complete his mission for the king, get the little prince to England, and then go home to Ashlin. It had been almost five months since he had seen his wife and child. Eleanore's sweet face haunted his dreams, and he longed to tell her that he loved her. Soon. *Soon.* He could have howled with outrage when he learned his services to escort the little prince to England were not needed at all. He had been brought to Normandy on a fool's errand.

Queen Alienor, heavy with her second child, had insisted she would not be parted from her little son. The court had moved almost immediately following the king's campaign in the Vexin to Barfleur. The empress was to remain behind in Rouen to govern Normandy in her son's absence. She had sided with her daughter-in-law. So the little prince would travel officially with his parents and his own household.

"I am overruled by my womenfolk," the king said by way of apology, with a wry smile, "but my mother points out, and wisely, too, that Alienor must not be upset this far along in her confinement. I cannot help but concur, and my Provençal rose will have her son by her side." He shrugged with apparent helplessness.

"Then, I am free to return home to Ashlin," Ranulf said.

"Nay, my good de Glandeville, I would have you attend our coronation," the king replied. "You will remain with the court and cross over to England with us. I am grateful for your loyalty, and would offer you this small reward."

Ranulf bowed. "I thank you, my liege, but serving you with fidelity is naught worthy of a reward."

"Nonetheless, you shall have it," the king said jovially.

He was dismissed, and he knew it. Ranulf bowed again, and moved back into the crowd of milling courtiers. *He wanted to go home!* He didn't want to travel with Henry Plantagenet's great train from Normandy to England and see him coronated in Westminster. He wanted to go home! He had come here on Henry's whim. His mission had come to nothing because of a woman's whim. His reward was to watch these two high nobles crowned king and queen of England. He had wanted a castle, but he had done nothing to warrant such a reward, nor would his Simon ever serve a prince as companion. Ranulf de Glandeville faced the fact that he was not an important man, although for a few brief months he had dared to dream.

On the morning of December seventh, the weather cleared just slightly. The king ordered their immediate departure, despite the fact the harbor master warned the weather would turn foul again before the sunset, and they would be caught in midchannel.

"We go!" the king said, and personally oversaw the loading of the boats with his knights and horses. The queen and her serving women were the only females with the great train; but Alienor, used to hard travel having gone on the first crusade to Jerusalem when she was France's queen, was not fazed at all. She jollied her frightened servants along, walking up the gangplank of her vessel with her small son at her side, holding his hand.

The skies were gray, and the winds were brisk as they made their way out of Barfleur harbor. The seas grew rougher, and then a fog set in separating the ships of the great fleet from one another. Ranulf, Garrick Taliferro, and their squires had taken passage aboard a small smack with one of the king's chaplains. They had secured the horses and the mule, sheltering them from the waves as best as they could. Then they sat together as the captain and his two sailors sailed their vessel toward England. Night came, and the sound of trumpets echoing in the fog to indicate where the vessels were, was somehow comforting. They shared their wine, bread, cheese, and sausage. The priest was, afterward, lost in his prayers for their safety as the ship bounced and bounded across the choppy waters. Up, up, up went the bow of the boat, and Ranulf could hear the wind rushing past beneath it just before it crashed into the sea again. The two young squires fell into a fitful sleep, their nerves raw.

The two men could not make out one another in the darkness, and so Sir Garrick did not see the look on Ranulf's face when he said, "Why were you really in Normandy, my friend?"

There was surely no need for secrecy now, he thought. So Ranulf told his companion the truth, admitting to his confusion when the plans changed not once, but twice. "It was a fool's errand, but how could I refuse a king?"

"You couldn't," Garrick replied. "Men like Henry Plantagenet are not like the rest of us. It would never have occurred to him that he was badly inconveniencing you. And indeed he meant no harm. You know that I envy you, Ranulf? I envy your manor and wife and child. You will go home now, and not have to depend upon the vagaries of a king's wishes in the future."

"But I will not get my castle."

"Your castle?" Garrick was puzzled.

"I hoped that in doing the king a great service, he would allow me to build a small keep at Ashlin. We are so close to the Welsh, and a little castle would help to better control the king's borders."

"He'll eventually make some kind of arrangement with the Welsh princes," Garrick told his friend. "You may be certain of it."

"But a castle would reinforce that arrangement. I know I'm no great lord, but still I had hoped to better myself by doing this favor for the king. In the end it has come to nothing." Ranulf sighed. Then he asked, "Did you not tell me when the king was crowned, you would go home and find a wife? What is to prevent you from doing that, Garrick? You have land. Take a wife from among the merchant class, preferably one who has a rich father. There is no shame in that, my friend."

"I think I shall," Garrick Taliferro said. "I am growing weary of this single life. My mother is no longer a young woman. She would be happy for a daughter and grandchildren."

In the morning the fog finally lifted, and they found themselves just outside of Southampton harbor. Shortly after landing, they learned the king's vessel had been sighted, coming aground just a few miles down the beach near New Forest. Taking their horses, the two knights hurried to find their master, their squires coming in their wake. Word that the king had ridden on the very back of the storm to reach England with his queen and his heir soon spread. The English were joyous.

The great fleet had been badly scattered in the storm, but no ships had been lost. The boats came ashore up and down the coast, debarking their inhabitants and their horses, all of whom met at the various crossroads from Southampton to Winchester, where the king was to go first to secure the royal treasury. Those men who had been King Stephen's strongest adherents waited fearfully to see what would happen, but none dared to call for a rebellion against Henry Plantagenet, grandson of Henry I, and England's soon-to-be anointed king.

Thibault, the Archbishop of Canterbury, had gathered together all the bishops of importance to await the king's arrival in London. The coronation would take place in Westminster, although the great cathedral was in poor condition from long neglect. Still, it was the traditional crowning place of England's kings, and on the Sunday before Christmas in 1154, Henry Plantagenet and Alienor of Aquitaine were crowned king and queen of England. He was twenty-one, and she thirty.

Afterward the king and queen rode through London, showing themselves to the people, magnificent in their coronation garb. The king's white velvet tunic was embroidered with lions and lilies. He was young, handsome, healthy. His willingness to come to England despite the season and the hard crossing told his people that here was a man who would rule with vigor and enthusiasm. The beautiful queen was garbed also in white velvet, her gold and bejeweled girdle glittering in the rare sunshine on this cold December day, her gold hair caught up in a golden and pearl caul, a bejeweled crown upon her head. She looked no older than her husband.

"*Vivat rex!*" cried the Normans.

"*Waes hael!*" shouted those English of Saxon descent.

The king and queen acknowledged the joyful greetings of their new subjects as they made their way through the city, and from there to Bermondsey, where they had taken up residence. The palace at Westminster, rebuilt on the original Saxon site by the king's great-uncle, William Rufus, and made even more beautiful by his grandfather, Henry I, had, like the great cathedral, been despoiled and given over to neglect in the civil war between Stephen and Matilda. A feast was held that night, and bonfires blazed all over the city and surrounding countryside in celebration of the new king.

The following morning Ranulf took his leave of the court, along with his friend, Sir Garrick Taliferro. Together the two men rode for a time until finally Garrick turned onto the road west into Glouster and Ranulf headed northwest toward Ashlin. With luck, he would be home in time for Christmas. *Home! His Eleanore! Their son!*

"My lord! My lord!" Pax called shortly after Garrick had left them. "We must stop and rest the horses. They are sorely winded. I, too, am anxious to get home, but 'twill take far longer if the horses die under us, and we must walk."

Laughing at himself for his boyish impatience, Ranulf heeded his squire's warning. They slowed their mounts to a walk and finally stopped at a small inn nearby to rest the night. The innkeeper's wife fed them bread and stew. They slept with their animals, however, for the area was remote and poor. They could as easily awaken in the morning to find their beasts gone and Ranulf's armor with them. The following day the lord of Ashlin manor kept a more reasonable pace. The weather, while cold, was at least dry. The next few nights they managed to find shelter at monastery guest houses, where there was at least some element of safety for them and their horses.

Finally on the afternoon of December twenty-fourth, they realized the landscape about them was familiar, and now they unconsciously hurried their horses. Coming over a hill, they saw Ashlin valley below them and the manor with its village just beyond its hill. Even the animals, sensing home, moved more quickly. Ranulf saw the sheep in the meadows and the cattle browsing in the pastures nearby. Relief swept over him. The Welsh had left them in peace despite their active raiding season of the summer past. He noted with pleasure that while the drawbridge was down, one side of the gates were firmly shut. His instructions had been followed to the letter.

There was no one in the fields at this time of day except two cowherds preparing to bring the cattle in for the night; and a few shepherds watching over the sheep. He waved to them. He could see the men-at-arms patrolling the walls, and then he heard the trumpet that was sounded to alert the gate that visitors were coming. He longed to push his mount into a gallop and race through his gates. Instead he held the warhorse to a sedate walk, clopping across the drawbridge and into the village.

"Welcome home, my lord," the man on the gate said, but there was no smile for him.

Ranulf and Pax rode down the village street to the manor house. It was growing dark, and he could barely see the smoke from the chimneys, the flickering light from the tiny windows of the cottages. A sheaf of light poured suddenly onto the ground before his home as the door was flung open. Ranulf dismounted and handed the reins of his mount to Pax.

"Take the horses to the stables," he said, and hurried inside.

"My lord, welcome home!" Cedric came forward, signaling a servant to take the master's cloak.

Ranulf looked about the hall, recognizing the servants and Father Oswin, and saw a cradle by the fireplace that obviously contained his son. He walked over and was amazed at the child who stared back up at him. This could not possibly be his son. "Where is Simon?" he asked to no one in particular.

Alyce giggled, then reached into the cradle and picked up the child. "This is your son, my lord."

"But . . ."

"You have been gone five months, my lord," Alyce explained. "Babies grow quickly. Here." She thrust Simon into Ranulf's arms.

Father and son stared at each other with the same eyes, the same expression. Ranulf was astounded, seeing himself mirrored so clearly in Simon's face. "By the rood!" he exclaimed. "He surely is my spit!"

"He is, my lord," Alyce agreed, taking back her charge.

"Welcome home, my lord," Father Oswin said, coming to his side. "I am well pleased that the lord of the manor will be here to celebrate the first of Christ's Mass tonight."

Ranulf nodded, looking about the hall, searching. "Where is my wife?"

"Come, my lord, and let us sit," the priest said.

He stood stock-still. "Where is Eleanore, good Father?"

"Kidnapped by the Welsh last autumn, my lord," the priest replied bluntly, then added quickly, "but she is alive."

Cedric pushed a goblet of wine into his master's hand.

Ranulf drank deeply. "How do you know? And how did it happen that my wife was vulnerable to such an attack? Where was

Fulk and the rest of you that my lady was stolen away so easily? Why have you not yet recovered her safely?" Ranulf's voice was rising, as was his temper, which few had ever seen, and certainly not here at Ashlin. There was a red mist forming before his eyes as his rage rose.

"*Sit down, my lord*," the priest instructed, drawing his master to a chair by the fire. "I will explain it all if you will but sit."

Ranulf sank heavily into the carved armed chair.

"Shortly after you left, a girl, badly beaten and as thin as a willow wand, came to Ashlin and begged sanctuary. The lady gave it to her. We healed the girl's wounds and fed her, and the lady included her among her women. Some weeks later a swineherd from the convent of St. Frideswide's came to say the convent was under attack. The abbess had sent this man for our help. Nothing would do, my lord, but that the lady must send Fulk and enough men to drive off the Welsh."

"Had there been an attack on the convent?" Ranulf asked.

"Yes, and no," the priest said, and went on to explain the rest, concluding, "When we realized the lady was gone, we were frantic."

Fulk, who had hurried into the hall, took up the tale. "I rode with my men through the night to reach Ashlin when I realized we had been deliberately drawn away, and that the swineherd had been sent by the Welsh themselves to lure us off. It rained for the next three days, my lord, and we could not search because there was no trail to follow. Finally, when the weather cleared a bit, I sent Sim out to find the lair of the bandit, Merin ap Owen, for I was certain it was he who had stolen the lady. Sim was gone for almost three weeks, but when he returned we knew for certain that it was indeed Merin ap Owen who held the lady captive. Sim had seen her, well guarded, walking on a hillside by the bandit's castle. It was much too dangerous for Sim to attempt to steal her back, so he returned to tell us what he had seen."

Ranulf nodded, the red mist was fading slightly, but now there was a fierce, burning anger centered in the middle of his broad chest.

"Soon then, a ransom demand was delivered by one of the Welshmen's men. Merin ap Owen was aware that you were away. He says he will keep the lady safe until your return. You are then to sell all the cattle and the sheep that you possess to ransom her. When you have the monies, you will make a signal by lighting pitch torches all around the perimeter of the walls. Someone will always be watching, and when the signal is received, Merin ap Owen will come in several days' time to make the exchange with you. We were forced to allow his messenger to return to Wales to say that we understood his wishes, my lord."

"It was well thought out," Ranulf said slowly. "I would not have believed a bandit so clever."

"He is of noble blood, my lord, but wicked, rumor has it," Fulk replied. "I am so sorry, my lord! It is my fault! I should not have let the lady send me to St. Frideswide's!"

Ranulf shook his head. "Nay, Fulk. You obeyed your mistress as you should have done. Had the girl, Arwydd, not betrayed my wife, none of this would have happened. Even if you had been here, there would have been no help for it. You know how you like your food and drink, my friend. With your appetite, you might still be sleeping. Praise God you were not, and knew what to do afterward." Ranulf clapped his captain comfortingly on the shoulder.

"What are we to do now, my lord?" Fulk asked him.

"First we will keep Christ's Mass," Ranulf said. "Then I must decide, after speaking with Sim, what our chances are for rescuing my lady wife. The better course might simply be to pay the ransom. I find it interesting that I am instructed to sell all my sheep and cattle in order to ransom my Eleanore. This was well planned, my friends. The Welsh could have stolen my flocks and herds. Instead they stole my wife, for they knew I would get more for my livestock than they would. Aye, this was no spur-of-the-moment decision on the part of Merin ap Owen. It was cleverly conceived and well executed."

"But if you sell the sheep and cattle, my lord," Father Oswin said, "how will the manor survive in the coming year?"

"Merin ap Owen may have set a watch on us," Ranulf said, "but that watch will only be near enough to see the signal on our walls, not near enough for us to discover and catch the watcher. Tomorrow is a feast day, but on the day after, we will move the sheep from the far meadows where they now are to the near meadow. While we are doing that, we will cut the ewes from the flocks that are close to lambing. We will hide them in the barnyards, where they are not easily seen. That way we will have the beginnings of a new flock of sheep. The Welsh will be none the wiser, for their interest in us will disappear with the gaining of the ransom. The harvest should have been good enough for us to feed the sheep over the winter months," Ranulf said.

"There are several cattle with calf," John the bailiff said, for he, too, was now in the hall.

"We'll keep them, too," the lord of the manor decided. "There is a quarter moon tonight. Have the cowherds take them from their pastures and put them in the barns. I will not lose my wife, but neither will I allow this bandit to beggar us, either."

"Will you kill him, my lord?" Fulk asked.

"Eventually, but first we must regain custody of the lady," Ranulf said quietly. "When we do, however, I shall do the king a service by ridding the border of this man and his rabble."

"Amen!" Father Oswin exclaimed.

"Come to the table, my lord," old Ida called. "The meal is here, and you have traveled far. My lady would want you well cared for, I know."

The elderly woman's words pleased him, but Ranulf de Glandeville could not help but wonder if his wife was as snug this night in her captivity as he was. Seating himself at the high board, he thought how lonely it was without her. *Eleanore!* he cried in his heart. *Ma petite, je t'aime avec toute ma coeur.* Outside the hall the wind began to rise.

E lf started in her place by the fire as she wove. She could have sworn she had heard Ranulf's voice. The wind moaned outside the shutters, and she shivered. It was the eve of Christ's Mass, but there was nothing different here at Gwynfr Castle: no priest to celebrate the Mass. She had learned from Gwyll that the priests considered Gwynfr, its inhabitants, and its lord cursed and the devil's own. On the solstice there had been much celebrating and drunkenness. Isleen had brought her whores into the castle to entertain the men.

"You must remain in my apartment," Merin ap Owen said, "and not come out lest you be harmed." Then he had locked Elf inside, pushing the key back beneath the door to her for safekeeping. That way, he had explained to her, no one could take the key off his person when he was drunk. They both knew he meant Isleen. "When I return here, I will be sober, and I will request the key from you," he said. Then he had gone.

Below in the hall she heard the shrieks and shouts of the drunken debacle. There was a tray upon the table with food and drink. Elf ate, then sat by the fire sewing. Once or twice she thought she heard footsteps in the passageway outside the apartments, and once the door handle was rattled strongly. Elf sewed on, a poker by her side. She did not expect anyone to be able to break in, but she would be able to defend herself if they did. Eventually the noise below died away, and fully dressed she lay down in her little chamber, the poker next to her pallet.

In the hall Isleen cajoled her lover. "Let us give her to the men tonight, my lord. I want to see her debauched."

"I shall give you to the men instead," he said. He was drunk, he knew, but not without his wits. Isleen might want revenge, but he wanted the ransom she would bring. Besides, if he could not have her, certainly no other man here would. The thought of anyone despoiling her exquisite beauty or breaking her brave spirit angered him. He stood up, dragging Isleen with him. He tore her gown from her, and hauled her up upon the high board, naked for all to see. "Here, lads, is my own private whore for your pleasure this night, but no other night, for I am a jealous man! Who will be the first to have her right here upon the high board? She'll make you a fine feast!"

"You devil!" Isleen spat at him as the men-at-arms crowded about the high board, leering up at her, their hands pulling her down upon her back so they might fondle her full breasts. They spread her wide, and then Isleen found herself mounted successively by a group of eager men who used her vigorously. She didn't really care. None could arouse her like Merin ap Owen. She responded to please them, and retain her reputation as a passionate woman. Turning her head, she saw Merin ap Owen with a red-haired wench in his lap. The girl was as naked as she was, and riding the lord energetically, her head thrown back, the muscles in her throat straining as she screamed her pleasure. *Bitch,* Isleen thought. Tomorrow she would have every peasant in Gwynfr humping the red-haired whore. She wouldn't enjoy that half as much as she was enjoying Merin ap Owen.

The night wore down, and eventually all in the hall, filled to capacity with food, drink, and pleasure, lay sprawled in sleep. Merin ap Owen looked about him and, standing up, sought for Isleen. She was asleep beneath the high board, two men sprawled over her. He reached down and pulled her out to her feet.

"Come on, my pretty bitch," he growled at her. "You are not done yet; and it would seem my randy cock cannot be truly satisfied until it has visited your hot and wicked sheath."

Fully aware now, Isleen smiled at him. "Bastard! I am used raw by your men thanks to you, and now you are ready for more? What's the matter? Didn't your little red-haired whore please you? Or was it because she was not your little captive?" Then she laughed seeing the look of surprise upon his face. "Did you think I haven't noticed those languishing looks you give her when you think no one is observing you? You are like a cowherd with his first maid!" And she laughed scornfully, but in her heart Isleen was darkly jealous.

She had caught him off guard for a brief moment, but then he slapped her lightly as he drew her up the stairs. "If I treat the lady Eleanore differently than I do you, my pretty bitch, it is because she is a lady and a truly good woman. You are an evil whore with a soul as black as night. I fear you are the perfect match for me."

On Christmas morning, while the snow swirled outside Gwynfr Castle, Elf sat as usual weaving at her loom. After her morning prayers she softly had sung a little carol she remembered from St. Frideswide's. It saddened her that there was no Christmas here in this place. The tapestry was beginning to take shape. As this was no place for a religious theme, she had taken her inspiration from the hills about them, weaving a pattern of green mountains, a blue sky, and a field of flowers. She intended to set a pair of deer in the landscape as well.

Elf shivered with the cold. Her cloak was not enough over her simple tunic and skirts. Despite the fact she huddled by the fire, the chill always came through the stone walls whose mortar was either worn with age or gone entirely. She thought of her own warm hall at Ashlin. How was her little Simon? Had Ranulf returned yet from Normandy? When was she to be released from this terrible captivity? It was Christmastide, and yet there was no Yule log here as there would be at Ashlin. There were no scented beeswax candles, roast boar, or Ashlin folk singing carols in the newly restored church. It was Simon's first Christmas, and she would not be there to see her baby wonder at it all. For a moment a black anger came over her, but she fought it off remembering that the Christ Child had come to bring peace on earth. She let her thoughts return to her home. She missed her querulous old Ida, Willa, faithful Cedric, stalwart Fulk. She missed her bed and the good food her cook prepared. Here at Gwynfr the meals were dull. There was hardly a green to be seen unless she asked.

Outside the wind howled mournfully. Elf shivered again, then started as a heavy fur cloak was dropped over her slender shoulders. Surprised, she looked up and found herself face-to-face with Merin ap Owen. Their lips were almost touching. Startled, she flushed and drew back, unable to speak. The look in his eyes! She had recognized that look. It was the same look that Ranulf had for her, and in a flash she realized what it was. *Ranulf loved her!* Her heart soared with the knowledge, then plummeted as quickly. *Merin ap Owen loved her, too!* He looked away.

"Gwyll has pointed out to me that you have few garments, and now that winter is here, you might be able to use a heavier cloak," he said in a quiet voice.

Elf swallowed hard. "Thank you, my lord," she answered, bending low over her weaving.

"It is wolf. The cloak. I hunted them down myself last winter," he continued.

I must look at him, or he will think something is wrong, Elf thought. She glanced up again. "I am grateful, my lord. I already feel warmer. I shall use it on my pallet at night as well."

"Why did you not say you were cold?" he demanded.

"It is not my habit to complain."

"Ask for what you need in future, my lady Eleanore. Granted our situation is unique, but it is not my intent to make you uncomfortable or harm you in any way. I am an honest man, and give value for the coin I gain. I would return you to your husband in good condition."

Elf giggled. She couldn't help it.

He smiled, for he had never heard the sound of laughter from her throat. "What amuses you, lady?"

"*You are an honest man?* You are a bandit, a thief, Merin ap Owen!" Elf chortled.

He laughed. "Aye, but I am an honest bandit, an honest thief."

"I wonder if the nuns at St. Bride's thought that of you," she said softly.

He flushed at her words. "Blood lust is a difficult thing to control, lady. Never before had I ravished or murdered like that; but that day I was driven to it by a she-devil. I was weak. I am ashamed of it, but it is done and cannot be undone."

"You could pray for those you wronged, Merin ap Owen," Elf told him gently. "A wrong can be undone by a right. If you are truly contrite and ask God's forgiveness, He will give it to you."

He smiled wearily at her. "I am past salvation, my lady Eleanore. Perhaps if I had met you earlier in my life, but I did not." Then with a small bow to her, he turned and walked away.

Elf's hand returned to her loom, but she felt a great sadness for Merin ap Owen. What had he been before Isleen had come into his life? Gwyll said his master was a wicked man from birth, but had he really been wicked, she wondered? Probably yes, she admitted to herself, for Gwyll loved Merin ap Owen and was completely loyal to him. He but spoke the truth, as harsh as it was. What a world this was, Elf considered, and she should have known none of it had she remained in her convent. There would have been no Ranulf or Simon. In the world one had to take the good with the bad, she realized. The good, she thought hopefully, far outweighed the bad. The rising wind rattled the windowpanes.

Snow. This was bad, Ranulf thought irritably. He had wanted to send Sim to Gwynfr to tell Merin ap Owen that he had returned, and would comply with his demands as quickly as a buyer could be found for his livestock. There would be those who would wonder at his selling his flocks and his herd. Some might even take advantage of him. It was a difficult problem, but he would solve it. He wanted his wife home safe.

The storm finally stopped, and as it had not been a hard snow, Sim set out for Gwynfr. He arrived with the first day of January. He rode up the hill to the castle, his eye scornful of the ruin and the neglect he saw.

"What do you want?" the man behind the portcullis demanded.

"To see Merin ap Owen," Sim replied.

"He don't see strangers."

"I have come from Ranulf de Glandeville, the lord of the manor of Ashlin, and your master will indeed see me," Sim snapped.

"Wait." The gatekeeper disappeared, returning several long minutes later. Without a word he raised the portcullis halfway, allowing Sim to duck beneath it as he rode into the courtyard. "Through there," he said, pointing toward one of the two towers that still stood.

Dismounting, Sim did not bother to thank the porter. He headed straight for his destination. He came into an entry and was met by a villainous-looking fellow who signaled him to follow, leading him into the great hall. There at the high board sat Merin ap Owen himself, and on his right was the lady Eleanore, looking pale, but otherwise unharmed. On his left, sweet Jesu, was Isleen de Warenne! Now, Sim thought, there is the real cause of all our troubles. Sim bowed.

"My lord, I have been sent by my master to tell you he has returned to Ashlin. He will follow your instructions, but he would be certain that his lady wife is safe and will indeed be returned."

"You can see your lady for yourself," Merin ap Owen said. "I am an honorable man, even if my ways are a bit unorthodox. When may I expect the ransom for the lady Eleanore?"

"My master must be cautious in selling his livestock," Sim began. "If he appears anxious to do so and sells them all in the same place, there are apt to be questions. He would obtain the best price for his sheep and his cattle, for he holds his wife in the highest regard."

"What is this delay, and why do you prevaricate with us?" Isleen suddenly demanded. "Your mistress has been gently treated to date, but she could find herself in the dungeons if your master should make any attempt to trick us!"

"Be silent!" Merin ap Owen thundered. "You are not mistress here!" He turned his glance back to Sim. "A delay does seem odd to me. What is the reason for it other than what you have told me? Does the lord of Ashlin not want his wife back?"

"My lord, if my master appears to be in need or in distress, the merchants will take advantage of him. He will get no more for his cattle and sheep than you would have gotten if you had simply stolen them in the first place," Sim explained in practical tones. "You took the lady for ransom because she would bring you more, did you not?"

"This serf is too clever by far," Isleen said. "Kill him!"

"If you kill me, who will take your words back to my master?" Sim asked quietly. "Oh, you might bring my lifeless body back to

Ashlin, but is that really the message you wish to deliver to my master, my lord? That will not tell him that his lady is well and safe, will it? Only my voice can speak the words that will reassure him, and keep him from coming down upon you with all the wrath of a wolf on the fold."

Merin ap Owen chuckled. "You are no simple serf, are you?"

"My name is Sim, my lord, and I am next in command after Captain Fulk" was the quiet reply. "My master would show you the respect of sending someone of stature from Ashlin, and not some witless clod. May I speak with my lady, please, my lord? A few words to reassure her husband?"

Merin ap Owen nodded. "But here, for all to hear, Sim."

"I bring you greetings from all at Ashlin, lady. We pray daily for your continued safety and for your return. Father Oswin said I was to tell you that everyone is well and thrives, and all who love you would have me speak their names. Cedric, old Ida, Willa, Simon, Orva, and Fulk. Your husband says he will secure your release as quickly as is humanly possible, my lady Eleanore. Have you a message for him?"

"Tell my lord," Elf said, "that I am safe, and have been well treated by Merin ap Owen. Tell my lord that I send him my love." She smiled broadly at him, nodding.

Sim bowed politely. He was pleased with himself for having been able to tell the lady her child was well without the Welsh lord and his whore understanding. He knew his lady would want to learn that her son was safe, but all at Ashlin believed that her captors did not know of the child, else they might have taken him, too.

"Go back to your master," Merin ap Owen said. "Tell him my patience is not endless, but I understand his caution. Return in a month with the time and place of the exchange. It must be a neutral spot, however. Tell your master that if he should attempt to betray me, or regain custody of his wife without paying the ransom, I shall kill her," Merin ap Owen said with emphasis. "Do you understand, Sim of Ashlin?"

"I do, my lord, but you need have no fear. The lord of Ashlin wants nothing more than the safe return of his wife, for he holds her in high regard and great esteem," Sim said quietly. Then he bowed first to the lord of Gwynfr Castle, then to Elf.

Merin ap Owen nodded. "Go, then," he said.

Sim bowed again, and departed the hall.

"Impudent bastard!" Isleen sniffed. "You should have killed him, and sent him back in pieces to his master."

"You are too quick to rash actions," Merin ap Owen said quietly. "There is no profit in killing an unimportant messenger. When I kill, it is for a good reason, not for the pure joy of it as it is with you, my pretty bitch." He turned to Elf. "You will be home by spring, my lady Eleanore. Will it please you?"

"Aye," she said honestly. How good it had been to see Sim. She had so very much desired to speak to him privately, but how clever he had been in allowing her to know that Simon was well. And Ranulf. He had returned safely. His return would mean that King Stephen was dead, and that England had a second Henry upon the throne. The word had yet to filter into Gwynfr, not that it made any difference.

"You must finish your tapestry before you leave us," Merin ap Owen said. "I shall hang it here in the great hall over the fireplace so all may see it, my lady Eleanore."

"It is a small enough price to pay for my keep, my lord," Elf answered him. How his eyes looked at her. He struggled hard to mask his longing, but she now knew it for what it really was. *Dear God,* she silently prayed, *get me home safely!* It had gotten to the point where she could hardly look at him, and she frankly feared the nights. She made it a point to hurry to bed immediately after the evening meal so that when he entered his bedchamber, she, in her little stone alcove, was long asleep. *Although she really wasn't.* She did not dare to sleep until she heard him snoring. His desire for her frightened Elf. Worse, she was curious of that desire. This was temptation such as no nun at St. Frideswide's had ever faced, and she prayed to resist it daily.

And Isleen. She was no fool. Surely she saw where her lover's interest lay. If she became jealous, and she was easily jealous of Merin ap Owen, what course of action would she take? That thought in itself was frightening. *Oh, Ranulf!* she silently cried. *Please hurry! I want to go home! I want to feel your strong arms about me, and taste your mouth upon mine. I want to hold our son in my arms. Oh, Ranulf! Hurry.* Hurry!

CHAPTER EIGHTEEN

He had a heart as hard as flint, Isleen thought as she sat next to Merin ap Owen at the high board. He didn't love her. She had deluded herself into believing that he might one day, but that day was never going to come, Isleen had finally admitted to herself. Not that he was incapable of love. Oh, no! Where Eleanore de Montfort was concerned, Merin ap Owen had a heart that bloomed like a rose. *The bastard!* And her rival, who had developed a tongue as sharp as any thorn, sat meekly by the lord of Gwynfr Castle's side, sipping delicately from her cup. *I wish it were filled to the brim with poison,* Isleen thought viciously. The pious little bitch!

She was, Isleen decided, going to have to begin to consider herself for a change. While she had to admit that the Welshman was the best damned lover she had ever had—and she knew that she was certainly the best lover he had ever had—it was simply not enough. For the first time in her life, Isleen knew she needed more than just a good lover. She was, it seemed, like other women after all. She needed to be loved, and if she could not be, then she needed to be in complete control of her own fate. Why was it that no man had ever loved her? She was beautiful.

Richard de Montfort had said that he loved her, but the truth of the matter was that he had only lusted after her like all men, and he had been in awe of her beauty. He became quite boring. After they had been married awhile his ardor had cooled. He had expected her to function as a housekeeper, to be someone who dressed the putrid sores, and dosed the disgusting coughs of his serfs. She shuddered with distaste at the memory. She was not that kind of a woman, and she had tried to explain it to him. She needed admiration, and she needed others to wait upon her. To take special care of her. The manor should have had servants to do the menial tasks that Richard expected her to do. Oh, her mother did them, it was true, but her mother was an old-fashioned woman.

And then there had been her cousin, Saer de Bude, who had seduced her first when she was a child; although, if the truth had been known, it had been she who had really seduced him. She well remembered when her father had made the match with Richard de Montfort. Saer had no lands, no home to take her to live in. Then there was that silly matter of consanguinity. At first she had been so upset by the thought of another match. But Saer had calmed her, promising no matter what happened, they would be together again one day. However, until she had taken matters into her own hands and begun to poison her husband, then called him to come, he had quite disappeared from her life.

When he finally came back into it, he claimed to have been off attempting to become more worthy of her. *The liar!* She and she alone had been his only means to gaining an estate and becoming respectable. From the way he had behaved at the end, she strongly suspected he wouldn't have killed Eleanore de Montfort at all, but rather kept her for his lawful wife and Isleen for his mistress. She was glad now their plot had failed. It would have been a terrible betrayal, too great for her to bear.

But it was nothing to the betrayal of Merin ap Owen. *What did he see in Eleanore de Montfort?* By the rood, he was actually pining over her like some lovesick boy. And he hadn't even had her! *Or had he?* Was he really telling Isleen the truth about that, she wondered? How could he be in love with a woman he had not joined his body to yet? She didn't understand it, and was seriously beginning to believe he was lying to her. As for her rival, she was a sly puss, Eleanore de Montfort! She wouldn't want anyone, least of all Isleen, to know of any adultery. She surely had to be Merin ap Owen's lover! Why else did she always look so calm and serene, the little bitch! Well, Isleen would no longer be fooled!

Now, what was she to do about it? Merin ap Owen watched over his precious captive like a mother hen over her chicks. When he wasn't there, that damnable old serf, Gwyll, was at Eleanore's elbow. As much as Isleen wanted to harm Elf, she faced the fact it was unlikely she would ever get the chance. So how was she to revenge herself on those who had hurt her so deeply? She knew very well that Merin ap Owen, while he enjoyed her sensual nature, was becoming bored with her. He would toss her aside as easily as he would any peasant wench. And then what was she to do?

She had only begun to organize and refine Clud's whorehouse; she was in no position yet to push the whoremonger out and take it over. She had not the funds, nor did she think she could obtain the strong support of Merin ap Owen at this juncture. He would very much enjoy throwing her out and leaving her to fend for herself. Bastard! But a woman couldn't fend without gold, she knew.

And then she realized the solution to her problems was right before her very eyes. She would steal the ransom Ranulf de Glandeville was to pay for his wife before it even got to Gwynfr. With that ransom and a good horse, Isleen de Warenne could go wherever she chose, set up the finest whorehouse England had ever seen.

London. She would go to London! Merin ap Owen would never find her. He would think Ranulf de Glandeville had betrayed him. He would rape Eleanore de Montfort before he killed her so that in the end Isleen would indeed be revenged! It was a foolproof and a perfect plan! Isleen's color was high, and her heart beat wildly with excitement as she considered her victory.

"You have the look of a cat that has just cornered its prey," Merin ap Owen said to her. "What are you thinking about, my pretty bitch?"

"Of how Ashlin, and all its people who were unkind to me will suffer and be destroyed when Ranulf de Glandeville must sell off all his livestock to regain custody of his wife," she lied, looking directly into his dark eyes. "They will starve without cattle to sell at the Lammastide Fair. There will be no wool, either, without sheep.

How will they buy what they need for the coming years? How will they afford seed and other supplies that are not manufactured at Ashlin?"

She laughed meanly. "Ranulf de Glandeville will not think he has gotten such a bargain after all, and the serfs will curse his name. It is really quite delicious to contemplate," she finished, and the truth was it was a wonderful thought. A bit of a bonus, Isleen considered. She wondered if Ranulf de Glandeville would come to avenge his wife. Would he kill Merin ap Owen, or the other way around? Her thoughts kept getting better and better.

"You have such a black heart, my pretty bitch," he said. "I think I must have you before too much more time has passed. Your wickedness excites me very much, Isleen." He turned to Eleanore. "It is time for you to seek your chamber, lady. Do not wait up for me," he mocked her, knowing his words would cut into Isleen, "for I shall be very late."

"And should you hear noises coming from my apartments above you, lady," Isleen said, "do not be disturbed. My lord is most vigorous when he is in my bed." She smiled a feline smile.

"All men, I am told, are vigorous in your bed, lady," Elf replied sweetly. She arose and curtsied to them, then left the hall.

Merin ap Owen laughed softly. "She is a true spitfire," he said admiringly. "By the rood, I'd like to get between her legs!"

"Do you expect me to believe that you haven't already?" Isleen snarled, all pretense of civility gone. "Do you think I believe for one moment that you haven't had her again and again since you brought her to Gwynfr, and ensconced her in your chambers? She may look like a little saint, but I doubt she is any longer, and you certainly are not!"

"You know me not at all, my pretty bitch," he said in a soft, deadly voice, "if you think I would dishonor myself by dishonoring my captive. All women are not like you, Isleen. Most may be to a certain extent, but not all. Eleanore de Montfort is a good woman."

"*You love her!*" Isleen accused.

For a long moment his dark eyes bored into hers, then he smiled an inscrutable smile at her. He would admit nothing to this bitch who railed at him. What he felt for Eleanore de Montfort was the purest feeling he had ever had. He would not spoil it by saying aloud what was in his heart to this harridan. He arose. "Come along, my pretty bitch. There are better ways to amuse me than you are now doing. I believe your bottom is in need of some correction. A good strapping to begin with, then I shall burnish you to a fine glow with a bunch of birch twigs. And then, my pretty bitch, you will take me into your hot, wet sheath, so we may truly pleasure each other," he said.

"She cannot give you what I give you," Isleen murmured breathlessly as she followed him from the hall.

"No," Merin ap Owen agreed with a smile. "She cannot."

Elf heard them passing by as they made their way down the narrow corridor and began to climb up to Isleen's chamber. Isleen was giggling, and Merin ap Owen's dark laughter followed her. It was at times like this, Elf realized how truly wicked her captor was. And yet he had never really been unkind to her. Indeed he was just the opposite with her as he was with Isleen. Why was that? Alas, she had no answers because of her inexperience. How much longer would it be before she saw her husband again?

It would not be long now, Ranulf thought, as he counted out the coins that John had brought back from Hereford, where he had sold off half of Ashlin's cattle. The other half had been sold in Worcester. The sheep had gone to the bishop, who had been apprised of the situation and agreed to purchase them. He had been generous, much to Ranulf's relief. A churchman was not above taking advantage of a desperate noble. Now, Ranulf realized, he must decide upon a time and a place for the ransom to be paid. Only when it was delivered would Merin ap Owen free Eleanore. God! It had been so long! Looking across the hall at his son, Simon, crawling about, pulling himself up whenever he could, he realized how much she had missed.

Sim departed for Gwynfr in a heavy winter rain. There was just enough time for him to reach Wales and offer a choice of meeting places. Merin ap Owen greeted him, Isleen de Warenne at his side and looking sour. There was no sign of the lady Eleanore.

"I'm to see the lady is safe still, my lord," Sim said politely.

"Gwyll," Merin ap Owen called. "Go and fetch the lady Eleanore so her man may see she is unscathed."

Gwyll moved quickly off.

"What suggestion does your master have for a meeting place?" the lord of Gwynfr asked.

"He offers you two choices, and if they do not suit, he will accept your choice, my lord. Just over the English side of the border are the ruins of an old hall. We call it Briarmere. Or we could meet atop the verge, on the border itself," Sim said.

Merin ap Owen thought for several minutes on the selection. He knew Briarmere well. The ruined stone hall was a place from which an ambush could easily be set. He had himself attacked hapless prey from there. If he could get there first . . . on the other hand, if the lord of Ashlin got there first . . . no. This time Briarmere would not suit. On the other hand, atop the verge was an excellent site. Out in the open there was no place for anyone to lay in wait. He smiled. Ranulf de Glandeville had thought the same thing, else he would not have offered so obvious a choice. "The verge, in ten days' time," he said.

"Agreed," Sim responded. "I will bring the gold, and you will bring my lady in exchange."

"Nay. You will bring the gold, and then you will wait until the gold has been brought back to me. I must ascertain that your master has been honest, and not filled the ransom bags with small stones topped by gold pieces. When the gold is all in my hands and counted out, then the lady will be brought to you. I will bring her myself to be certain she is delivered safely into your hands. The verge is but a few hours' ride from Gwynfr."

Sim's instinct was to protest the method of exchange, but he knew he had not the authority, nor did he have any real choice in the matter. Merin ap Owen was absolutely in charge.

"In ten days' time my courier will be awaiting you" came the reply. "There will be no one with him. He will be alone as must you."

Sim nodded.

"Sim!"

He turned, and saw the lady Eleanore had entered the hall. "My lady!" He bowed to her, but she took his hand and asked, "How are all at Ashlin? My husband, old Ida, Fulk, Willa, and Simon?"

"They are all well, lady, and eager for your return home," he told her. She looked well, if pale, and perhaps a bit drawn.

"How long?" she said.

"I shall bring the ransom in ten days' time, my lady, and then once the lord Merin has satisfied himself that all is right, you will be brought to me, and I will escort you home."

Elf nodded. Then she sighed. "The end seems so much longer," she said, "now that I know the end."

"As you see, your lady is in good condition," Merin ap Owen said. "Now, go, and tell your master so you may return quickly with the ransom."

"Aye, my lord, I will," Sim replied, bowing. Then he quickly left the hall.

"So," Isleen sneered, "your husband was willing to give up what small wealth Ashlin had for your return. He must be in love, but he will not think so highly of you come next winter when you all starve."

"We will not starve, Isleen, although I will admit with our livestock gone, it will be harder for us; but God will provide," Elf responded. "I cannot help but wonder where you will be next winter."

"What does that mean?" Isleen snapped, her blue eyes blazing.

"I have not the experience, of course, but it does seem lord Merin might be growing bored with you. After all, what can you offer him that other women cannot?" Elf smiled tauntingly. What was it about Isleen that brought out the worst in her?

Isleen flew at Elf, her claws bared, but Merin ap Owen jumped between the two women, laughing.

"You bitch!" Isleen hissed.

"Whore!" Elf returned angrily. "Do you expect me ever to forget my brother, and what you did to him?"

"Had you cured Richard, you should be drying up in your convent now, a perfect fate for you!" Isleen shouted. "Instead you gained a husband who obviously loves you and a fine estate."

"But you murdered Dickon!" Elf shouted back.

"Aye, I did," Isleen said with devastating frankness. "He was a boring man who expected me to be his servant. He had no real manners, or delicacy of refinement in our bed. Not at first, but I will tell you that I soon grew to hate your brother! I enjoyed seeing him suffer! I was glad when he finally breathed his last!"

"God forgives you, I know," Elf said, "but I do not think I can, though it be a black mark on my immortal soul. You are the most evil creature I have ever met, Isleen. God help you."

"Save your pity!" Isleen snapped. "I do not need it. Pity yourself, for I will have succeeded in destroying Ashlin when that ransom is delivered. What will you go back to, *sister*? A ruin, and a host of hungry, whining serfs!" Then she laughed.

"I will go back to a husband who loves me, Isleen," Elf said, knowing that she spoke the truth. "Our love will survive even your wickedness, and Ashlin will survive because we will rebuild it together. I should rather be poor and in want with Ranulf, than be the whore that you have become, *have always been!*" She shook off Merin ap Owen's restraining hand. "I am not afraid of her, my lord, nor can she harm me." Then Elf walked proudly from the hall, her head high.

"I want her dead!" Isleen said low through gritted teeth.

"Harm a hair on her head, my pretty bitch," he replied, "and I will kill you, but it will not be an easy death. You will suffer as no one has ever suffered before."

Now it was Isleen who shook him off. "You are a fool, my lord! You want her. You ache for her. You need to feel her fair white body beneath you to still the burning in your loins, but you will not take her. The ransom is practically yours! You do not mean to return her until it is safely in your hands. Why not have your pleasure, then, of this pale creature that you desire? Who is to know? And can her husband ask for the return of his gold because you have lain with his wife? Do you think she would even choose to tell him what you did to her?"

"You are jealous, my pretty bitch," he purred at her. "You think to tempt me into a dishonorable act to wreak your revenge on the lady Eleanore; but I am not a fool, Isleen. I am not like the other men who have passed through your miserable life. I see you for what you are." His hand stroked her jawline, moving to her throat, his slender fingers tightening just slightly about her neck. "You cannot entice me to injure the lady's body . . . or her soul. You must surely understand by now that I am not a man who can gain pleasure as easily as other men. I need to inflict pain upon my bed partner, Isleen." His fingers tightened as he bent to brush his lips against hers lightly. Lifting his dark head he saw the fear in her eyes. Merin ap Owen smiled. "I think we understand each other, do we not?" He looked down into her face, releasing her, noting the marks of his fingers on her white neck. Brushing the skin lightly, he smiled again. "The lady Eleanore could not bear my passion, Isleen, but you can. You are mine, and I will keep you here with me unless you do something to displease me greatly, in which case I shall not return you to Clud the whoremonger, my pet. I shall give you to my garrison. They will, in a very short and unpleasant time, kill you."

"You are a monster."

"As are you, Isleen," he responded softly, "but I am the stronger of us. Be warned, and do not forget."

"I will not," she said. No. She would not forget. It would cause her to be more careful, but steal the ransom from under his nose she would.

"Lift up your skirts," Isleen heard her lover command.

She complied, laughing as she did so. "You are such a wicked devil, my lord," she told him. "Shall I pretend I am your innocent captive? Oh, help! Help! God and His saints save me from this big, randy cock! No! No! You shall not have me!"

He slapped her, and Isleen laughed the harder. *"Bitch!"*

"Admit it! You wish I were her," she taunted him, "but she could never please you as I will please you, my lord Merin!" Then Isleen pulled his dark head down, and kissed him fiercely.

In her little chamber Elf shuddered as if something had just trod upon her grave. It had become so difficult of late to be with Merin ap Owen, to look at him when she spoke to him. From the moment she had seen the secret in his eyes, and realized he was in love with her, she had been uncomfortable with him. He had, of course, said nothing. He was careful now so that they did not even accidentally touch. But now and again she would glance up from her weaving and see him gazing with heartbreaking longing at her. She sighed sadly. Even had she been free, she could never love him, Elf knew. The darkness that surrounded him was too great for her to overcome. He frightened her.

And she pitied him as well. That, she knew, would be the greater injury, for him to know that he was pitied. She had learned these past weeks from Gwyll of the lord of Gwynfr's two unhappy marriages. Poor man. He really did not know how to love. But now that she realized, was almost certain, that Ranulf loved her, now that she could admit that she loved Ranulf, her world had changed. She longed to be in her husband's arms once more. She instinctively knew that the joy they had shared before would be a thousandfold better once they admitted their love to each other. *Soon, my darling,* she thought happily. *Soon!*

Eleanore. *Ma petite.* His heart called out to her, and he could almost swear that she responded to his cry. *I love you, my darling. I adore you! When I have you safe in my arms again, I shall never let you go.*

Dear God, please bring her back to me.

Sim returned to Ashlin, and reported to his master. "She is well, my lord, if a trifle pale. She has not been mistreated, I would stake my life upon it. Merin ap Owen has chosen the verge for the payment of the ransom and the exchange. First, however, he must have the gold. Only then, when he is satisfied you have not cheated him, will he himself bring the lady to you," Sim explained.

"I do not like it," Fulk said. "He frets to Sim about you cheating him, but how do we know we can trust him to return our lady?"

"We do not, any more than he knows we will bring the gold," Ranulf answered. "There comes a time in such negotiations, Fulk, when one must trust because there is simply no other way. We have reached that point. Sim will deliver the gold, then wait for my wife. We shall, however, be at Briarmere in hiding. It is but several miles from the verge. Once my lady Eleanore is safe, we shall follow after this Merin ap Owen, slay him, and reclaim our gold. Then I shall be able to purchase our flocks back from the bishop, and a new herd of cattle. My wife's safety, however, is paramount."

"If you're going to kill the lord of Gwynfr," Sim said, "then you had best kill his whore as well. The lady Isleen is the major cause of all this misery, and she hates my lady Eleanore. Merin ap Owen would have been content to take our livestock had it not been for the lady Isleen. Still, I will say, he is master in his own house. He has treated our lady well when, I suspect, if the lady Isleen had had her way, our good mistress would be dead or close to it now. If you leave this woman alive, my lord, she will seek again to harm Ashlin and the lady Eleanore. She must die even if it not be chivalrous, for she is very wicked. Baron Hugh does not know where she is, and so he need not know she is dead, not that he would care, I'm thinking."

Ranulf de Glandeville nodded thoughtfully. "I am loath to order the death of a woman," he said, "but I believe you are right, Sim. You and Pax will take care of the matter when we get to Gwynfr. Be merciful, and give her a quick death. I take no pleasure in her suffering. I will see that Father Oswin absolves you both afterward."

The gold was counted and carefully placed into two soft leather pouches. It was a goodly sum for the cattle had brought a particularly high price. Ranulf had to admit to himself, if he admitted to no one else, that he had considered holding back some of the gold. Would the bandit really know? But then he pushed the idea from his head, for he would not endanger his precious Eleanore for a few paltry coins. They had held back sheep and cattle. Not many to be certain, but enough to give them a new beginning.

Ranulf did not know if anyone was still watching, and so Sim set out with only two other men-at-arms to protect him and the ransom he carried. They would remain at Briarmere awaiting their lord while Sim rode on to meet the Welshman's courier at the verge. Ranulf and his party would start out two hours later. Anyone watching would have long gone on to Gwynfr with the news that the English messenger was coming.

The early spring weather was gray and damp. On the morning of the fourth day, after leaving Ashlin, Sim rode up the verge to where a mounted and cloaked horseman was awaiting him. He could not see the fellow's face clearly, but what did it matter, he thought as he handed over the two bags. Merin ap Owen's courier weighed each bag in his gloved hands. Then he growled, "Master will be pleased." Turning, he rode off down the Welsh side of the verge, and disappeared into a thick copse. Sim settled down to wait. It would be anywhere between four and five hours. It began to rain, gently at first, and then hard. Sim cursed his luck, and huddled beneath his cloak next to his horse. He sneezed, feeling the water seeping into his boots, which were already leaking. Soon his feet were soaking wet, and worse, they were cold. He waited, and he waited. Finally the rain stopped. Perhaps they had been delayed by the weather, Sim thought. The sun began to peep from behind the clouds, and Sim smiled to see a small arc of a rainbow spring out between the hills. He thought it a good omen, yet Merin ap Owen still did not appear with his lady.

Then his brother, Pax, hailed him from below the hill. Sim walked halfway down to meet him.

"No one has come?" Pax asked.

"If they had, would I still be here, wet and cold?" Sim snapped.

"But you delivered the gold?"

"Several hours ago to the Welshman's courier. I know it was he for he wore the badge of Gwynfr upon his cloak. After I gave it to him, he said his master would be pleased," Sim reported. "I thought perhaps the rain had delayed the lady."

"I will go back and tell our lord," Pax said, and hurried off on a run.

Sim shrugged, and climbed back up to the top of the verge. Scanning the landscape beyond him into Wales he could see nothing moving. What in the name of heaven could have happened, he wondered? Was Merin ap Owen not satisfied with the amount of the ransom? But it had been a most generous amount, twice what the bandit would have gotten for Ashlin's livestock himself. Yet something was wrong. The sun was now beginning to dip lower on the horizon. Sim sneezed several times. I can't just stand here, he thought. Then going to his horse, he mounted it and rode off into Wales. When Pax found him gone, he would go back to the lord, and they would come after him to Gwynfr. There just wasn't any other choice in the matter, nor, he sensed, did he have much time.

It was just after dark when he finally made his way up the craggy hill into the courtyard of Gwynfr Castle. He was immediately surrounded and pulled from his horse. Then he was dragged into the hall and thrown on his knees before Merin ap Owen. Sim tried to stand, but was shoved to his knees again. He heard murmurs of, "Kill the English bastard!" in the background behind him. Raising his head, he looked questioningly up at the lord of the castle.

"You have nerve, Sim of Ashlin, I will grant you that," Merin ap Owen said. "Where is the ransom?"

"My lord," Sim said in as calm a tone as he could muster, "I met your courier atop the verge, and handed the two bags of gold coins over to him several hours ago. I have been waiting ever since for you to bring my lady Eleanore to me as had been agreed upon. When you did not come, I thought that possibly you had been delayed by the rains, but then when the rains stopped, and you still had not come, I knew something was wrong. So I came to Gwynfr myself. Why have I been treated so badly by your men?"

"You say you met my courier?" The Welsh lord looked down from his place at the high board.

"I did," Sim answered firmly.

"What did he look like?" Merin ap Owen demanded.

"I could not see his face, for it was hidden beneath his hood, but his cloak bore the badge of Gwynfr, my lord. When I had given over the ransom, he said you would be pleased. Then he departed," Sim replied.

"You saw not his face? Was he tall? What did his voice sound like? You say you have delivered the gold, and yet I do not have it," Merin ap Owen told the startled Sim.

"I did not see his face, for the hood," Sim repeated. "The day was dark, and the storm close. The courier never looked directly at me, now that I recall it, but kept his upper body in shadow. His height was shorter than taller. He said but four words to me. *Master will be pleased.* The voice was gruff, and I thought at the time that it was an odd voice, for you Welsh have voices that are usually more mellifluous, but, then, why would I be suspicious of a man wearing your badge who met me at the appointed hour and at the ap-pointed place?" Sim concluded rather sarcastically.

"Why indeed," Merin ap Owen said, and suddenly he was thoughtful. Then he said, "The messenger I sent you was a tall man, and his voice was indeed soft and musical. His body was found a mile from Gwynfr a little while ago, Sim of Ashlin. He did not have the gold. The ground beneath him was dry, though the body itself was soaked with the rain. This tells me that he was killed be-fore your alleged meeting on the verge. Is it possible you lay in wait for my man, murdered him, then returned to the verge to await whoever followed him? Has your master truly paid the ransom, or does he believe you can diddle me?"

"My lord," Sim said, horrified by this turn of events, "I swear to you upon my lady Eleanore's life that I met your courier upon the verge and turned over the ransom payment to him. My master would not endanger his wife for any reason. I am telling you the truth. I murdered no one. I followed your instructions to the letter. If you have been betrayed, you had best look to your own house for the traitor."

Again the lord of Gwynfr was silent, his handsome face deep in concentration as he considered the Englishman's words. He had to be telling the truth. Why else would he have taken his life in his hands to come to Gwynfr? His dark blue eyes narrowed in thought. There was only one person audacious enough to betray him in his own house. She should be by his side right now, but she had sent word by her servant that she was ill with a flux, and begged to be excused this evening.

"Get up," Merin ap Owen said to Sim. Then he turned to his man, Badan. "Go to the lady Isleen's apartment in the top of the tower, and fetch her to me. If her servant girl says she is ill, insist in my name on seeing her yourself. And if she is not there, bring Arwydd to the hall to me. Do not mistreat her, however," he warned.

Badan ran off with a nod. Sim got to his feet and rubbed his knees. The stone had been hard, and he had been thrown none too gently upon it. He stood silent, waiting, wondering.

"Your lady is safe," Merin ap Owen said quietly, then nothing more.

After some minutes Badan returned to the hall, dragging a most reluctant Arwydd with him by her arm. The girl was crying and clearly very frightened.

"Where is your mistress?" Merin ap Owen demanded of her in a cold, hard voice. "Speak up, wench!"

"I . . . I do not know!" Arwydd sobbed.

"She told me the lady was sleeping, but when I pushed past her into the bedchamber, the bed was empty, my lord," Badan said.

"Where is your mistress?" Merin ap Owen asked a second time.

Arwydd sobbed all the harder. "I swear on the Blessed Virgin's name, my lord, that I do not know!"

"You knew enough about it to lie, wench," the lord of Gwynfr said. "You must know something even if you do not know where your mistress is."

"My lady went out early today," Arwydd said. "She did not say where she was going, nor when she would be back. It was not her habit to tell me these things. Usually she said nothing, but today she asked that if anyone sought her out, I was to say she was ill and sleeping. That is all I can tell you, I swear it!"

"Yet when it grew dark, you did not come to me and say she was missing," Merin ap Owen pointed out.

" 'Twere plenty of times she didn't come back until after dark, my lord," Arwydd told him. "If I had come to you and then she had returned, she would have beaten me black-and-blue. I was only her servant. I saw to her clothing and hair. I brought her whatever she asked of me. She never spoke with me but to give me an order or to complain about something. She was not an easy mistress, but it was better than serving in my uncle's whorehouse."

"If I find that you are lying to me, Arwydd," the lord of Gwynfr said softly, "I shall give you to my men for their pleasure."

Arwydd threw herself down before the high board. "My lord! I swear to you that I know nothing more than I have told you! Do not give me to your men, I beg you!" She held out her hands to him, pleading.

"My lord," Sim said quietly, "I believe the girl speaks the truth. The lady Isleen has discarded her because she would have been a liability had she known the lady's plans. Had Arwydd been gone from Gwynfr with her mistress, you would have discovered the lady Isleen's perfidy all the sooner. Now she is long gone on whatever road and it is certain that she has taken the gold."

"And murdered my courier," Merin ap Owen said. "Isleen always liked poison, and there was not a mark of violence upon my man's body. His lips were quite blue, and there was a bit of dried froth about his mouth. His horse was gone, and could not be found in the vicinity. My treacherous leman obviously took it. She planned this well, but I shall find her, and I shall show her no mercy! Get up, wench!" he snapped at Arwydd. "Go back to your mistress's apartment while I consider exactly what I shall do."

Arwydd scrambled to her feet, and dashed out of the hall as if she were being pursued by all the devils in hell.

"My lord," Sim spoke. "What of my mistress? I paid the ransom you required in good faith. It is not the fault of any at Ashlin that the gold has gone astray."

Merin ap Owen looked down on the young Englishman. "I must have the night to reflect on all of this. You may sleep in my stables with your horse, Sim of Ashlin. Come back to the hall one hour after the sun has risen, and I will render my decision on this matter. You could not start back to Ashlin tonight in any event. Have you eaten? No? Then, go the kitchens, and you will be fed. My men will leave you in peace now, for you are as much of a foolish dupe as I have been."

Sim felt relief coursing through his body. He bowed, and hurried out of the hall. Watching him go, Merin ap Owen almost laughed aloud. The lad had shown courage, but his hasty retreat indicated his fear of the situation. Still, he had come to Gwynfr, and he had asked for his mistress's release.

"What will you do, lord?" Badan asked him, and Merin ap Owen saw the curious faces turned up to him.

"I do not know yet," he answered.

"But you will seek out the bitch?" Badan persisted.

"Aye, I will," Merin ap Owen said, "but the rest I do not know. I will think on it, but be prepared to ride come the morning." He arose then and left the hall.

Elf sat by the fireplace, mending one of his tunics. She looked up, her lovely face serious. "What has happened? Was not this the day I was to be released, my lord? Yet it is already night, and I am still here at Gwynfr."

"My courier was murdered, and the gold stolen from him," he said. "Now I must decide what is to be done."

Her face grew paler than it normally was. "How did this happen, my lord?" Elf laid her sewing aside and arose to face him.

He explained to her exactly what he had determined based on the information Sim had brought, on Arwydd's testimony, on the evidence of his own eyes and instincts. Then to his surprise Elf burst into tears, sobbing so piteously that his heart almost broke. He wrapped his arms about her in a gesture of comfort. Surprised, she looked up into his face, and Merin ap Owen was lost in the moment. Unable to restrain himself, his mouth took hers in a burning, fierce kiss.

Startled, Elf was not certain at first what to do. She had never been kissed so skillfully by anyone but her beloved Ranulf. Instinctively her lips softened, and she was only brought to her senses by the sudden realization of his hard body against hers, his lustful member throbbing against her belly. Still, for a brief moment she allowed herself to be swept away before marshaling her forces, her two small hands pushing against his broad chest. *"My lord!"* She pulled her head back. "Please, my lord, this is wrong, and you well know it!" She stepped away from him as if to put a safe distance between herself and his fiery heat of passion.

"How long have you known that I wanted you?" he asked her.

"Since Christmas morning when you put the wolf-skin cape about my shoulders," she answered.

"I love you, Eleanore," he said softly.

"I know, my lord Merin." There were tears in her silvery gray eyes.

"But you do not love me." He sighed sadly. "You love your Ranulf. Does he love you as I do? Totally, completely, and without reservations? Ah, I never knew that to love brought such pain!"

"Aye, he loves me, and I him," Elf said honestly. "And this you did not know. We have a son, my lord Merin. It is not just my land or my husband calling me back, it is my child. If Ranulf paid the ransom and was honest with you, how can you not allow me to return home on the morrow? No matter your reputation, no matter what I have heard said of you, no matter what you have done, I must judge you in light of how you have treated me. You have dealt with me fairly and with honor. That is how I shall always remember Merin ap Owen when I have returned to my husband, to my son, and to Ashlin."

"I could take you now, here, and show you no mercy!" he cried.

"And having tasted your kiss, my lord, I have no doubt that I should respond to your passion, but come the dawn I should be weighed down with a guilt so heavy it would never leave me," Elf told him. "Women are weak, it is said, but they, too, have their honor. If you dishonored me, you should dishonor yourself. I beg you not to do so, my lord Merin. Do not allow your lust to destroy the friendship that has grown between us. I have never known your like, nor will I ever again, I think." Her eyes met his, pleading, yet proud.

He could force this petite woman, so delicate of bone. She could not prevail against his strength, there was scarce a woman born who could. *But he loved her.* A man did not despoil and hurt something so fair, so innocent, so sweet. The Merin ap Owen that Isleen de Warenne knew might do such a thing and not have a care; but the Merin ap Owen that he was for Eleanore de Montfort would not act in so dishonorable a fashion. Reaching out, he took her two hands, raised them up, and kissed them.

"It would seem, Eleanore, that my love for you is stronger than my lust. Tomorrow I will set you free to return home to your most fortunate husband. And this promise I give you: The Welsh will not distress Ashlin again in my time." He released her hands. "Go to bed now, my love, resting safe in your goodness. Only you know the man I might have been. Tomorrow after you have left me, I will begin a hunt for a vixen. I will run her to ground, I promise you, and I will kill her. She will never trouble you again."

"Do not kill her on my account, my lord," Elf begged him.

He smiled. "Her death will not be on your conscience, my love, but on mine with many others; but your God will surely not punish me for ridding the world of the devil's own daughter," Merin ap Owen said. "For that I must certainly be rewarded."

Chapter Nineteen

"Give me Arwydd to take back with me," Elf said to Merin ap Owen the following morning as she prepared to leave his apartments for the last time. "You know what will happen to her if she is left here at Gwynfr or returned to her uncle's establishment."

"You would have her despite what she did?" he asked, surprised.

"She did what she did to survive," Elf responded. "She is a good girl at heart. I cannot forget that she protected my son from Isleen by keeping the secret of his existence from her."

"If she will go with you, you may have her," he replied. "I will send her to you. Then come to the hall, so I may turn you over to the faithful Sim of Ashlin. I want him to take you from Gwynfr before your husband arrives to attack me, and lives are needlessly lost. I have no doubt that Ranulf de Glandeville is near. I know I would be if you were my wife." He smiled a wry smile at her, then made to leave her.

"My lord!" she called after him, and he returned to her side. Elf stood upon her tiptoes, and kissed his scarred cheek. "I would not embarrass you, or endanger my own reputation by doing this publicly in the hall," she told him. "I thank you. I believe there is much good in you, my lord, despite your evil reputation. Seek for that good for the sake of your immortal soul. I will pray for you, Merin ap Owen," she promised him.

"Then, I shall be as near to being saved from the devil's hellfire as I have ever been," he told her softly. Raising her hand to his lips, he caught her gaze a moment. "We would have been magnificent together, my lady of Ashlin," he said. Then he was gone.

She felt the heat in her cheeks. She felt the tears slip down her face, and brushed them impatiently away. She did not love him, and yet the knowledge of his love for her was almost too heavy a burden for her to bear. *Oh, Ranulf,* she thought. *I need your strong arms about me reassuring me that all will be well!*

"Lady."

Elf looked up to see Arwydd standing hesitantly in the doorway. She motioned to the girl to come in, then said, "I believe you are a good girl no matter the bad mistress you served so faithfully. You are a free woman, Arwydd, and so you are free to make your own decisions. I offer you a place in my household if you will come with me. It will not be easy at first. You betrayed the Ashlin folk. They will not allow you to forget it, for they have long memories, especially my Ida. But I will intercede for you with them if you truly give me your loyalty. In time they will forgive you, for they are good folk at heart."

Arwydd fell to her knees and, lifting the hem of Elf's skirt, kissed it fervently. "Lady, oh, lady! Your kindness has saved me! Gladly will I come. I will bear whatever I must, for in truth I did grievous wrong to the Ashlin folk. I will beg their forgiveness upon my knees! I swear upon the Blessed Virgin's name to serve you honorably and faithfully all of my days!"

Elf raised the girl up. "Then it is settled," she said calmly. "Come, for we are due in the hall. The lord of Gwynfr is about to free me, and I am eager to begin our journey home."

They descended into the hall, where the morning meal was already in progress. Seating herself at the high board, Elf ate heartily of the hard-boiled eggs, cheese, butter, and bread she was served. She quenched her thirst with a watered wine. She saw Sim at a trestle below and, smiling, nodded to him. Then Merin ap Owen stood, and spoke.

"I am an honorable man, as you can all attest. The lord of Ashlin manor has delivered the ransom I requested for the return of his wife. The fact the ransom was stolen from me is not his fault. For me to continue to hold the lady Eleanore as my captive would be a dishonorable act. I will therefore release her into the custody of her man-at-arms, Sim of Ashlin. They will leave Gwynfr in peace. And when they have gone, we will depart to seek out the vicious vixen who has stolen my gold. Go, and prepare yourselves to leave. I know not how long we will be away, for I cannot even say in which direction the bitch has gone, but we will run her to the ground, lads. And after . . ." He laughed darkly.

The sound sent a chill up Elf's spine. The man she knew had disappeared once again, even as the man they all feared returned in his place. She arose and, without another word, walked down from the high board to where Sim now stood anxiously waiting for her. "Let us go home, Sim," she said, and he nodded wordlessly.

Without a backward glance they departed the hall and walked out into the courtyard, where Arwydd stood holding the horses.

"*She's* going with us?" a disbelieving Sim asked.

"She is a good girl, Sim," Elf said firmly. "Besides, I will not leave her here. She will serve me loyally. You will see."

Sim thought his mistress mad, but he would not question her, for it was not his place to do so. Besides, the lord would send the deceitful witch packing as soon as he laid eyes on her. He helped the two women to mount their beasts, then climbed atop his own horse, and they were off. They rode slowly down the hill away from Gwynfr and onto the narrow track that led them toward the verge, and England.

The day was unusually beautiful, the sky above them a clear blue, the sun shining brightly, the air warm with a definite feeling of spring. It was the first time in days that Elf could remember the sun shining. She considered it a wonderful omen, although perhaps not for Isleen de Warenne, who was to be hunted down. Where had she gone? Elf wondered. But no matter. If Merin ap Owen did not catch her and kill her, she would still have to face God's judgment for her wickedness. She put Isleen from her mind.

"Merin ap Owen thought my lord might be near, Sim. Do you think it is so?" Elf asked her man.

"Aye, lady, he is. I am surprised we have not come upon him yet," Sim answered her. "I thought surely he would be at Gwynfr's gates by dawn, but, perhaps finding me gone off the verge yesterday, he divined my purpose and is waiting a reasonable time for my return."

They rode on for a short time, and then over a hill they saw a party of riders coming. Elf strained to see, and then with a whoop she kicked her mare into a gallop, riding straight for the oncoming men. Sim immediately recognized his Ashlin companions and smiled. His lord moved out in front, pressing his own mount forward at a faster pace until the two parties came face-to-face, and the mingling horses skidded to a stop.

Ranulf de Glandeville was off his horse in a flash. Reaching up, he pulled his wife from her mare and wrapped her in a hard embrace. "I love you," he whispered fiercely into her ear. *"I love you!"* Then he kissed her hungrily, desperately drinking from her lips like a dying man wasting away from thirst.

Breathless, Elf finally pulled away from the kiss, looking up at him, her face filled with pure joy. "Why did you not tell me this before," she demanded. "I ached to hear you say those words, for I love you so damned desperately, I thought I would die from it!"

"You love me?" Now his look became one of surprise.

"Aye, I love you, you big oaf! How could I not love a man who treated me with such delicacy and gentleness?"

"Then, why did you not say it?"

"Because I thought a sophisticated man of the world such as yourself would scorn such words. I feared you would feel obligated by them, and despise me for a romantic fool. I had gained your respect and your trust. I did not want to lose them by softly prattling of love," Elf told him. "Why did you hesitate to say these words to me until now?"

"I did not think you could love a man who took you from the life you loved and had always thought you would live," he admitted. "But, Eleanore, I think I loved you from the first moment I saw you in the hall at Ashlin, so kind and so thoughtful, seeking so desperately to save your brother's life. I never thought to have a real home or a sweet woman to care for me and bear my children. Then there was the king giving me this incredible gift of you. I feared if I told you of what was in my heart, you would not believe me. I feared you would disdain me, think me a fool who but attempted to gull you so I might more easily have your body. I feared the loss of your friendship, petite." His knuckles lightly grazed her cheek, brushing away the single crystal tear upon it. "Do not cry, petite. We are together once more. I shall never allow you to be in danger again. You will continue on to Ashlin while I go to Gwynfr to destroy it. Merin ap Owen shall not pillage the countryside this year, or in any other year to come."

"Nay," Elf told him, her hand on his arm.

"Have I cause for jealousy, then?"

"Walk with me, my lord, and allow me to explain," Elf said. "I am not certain whether I should be flattered by your jealousy, or offended that you would think me unfaithful to you, Ranulf. Come." She took his hand, and they moved off across the fields while she spoke earnestly to him, explaining that it had been Isleen de Warenne who had been the instigator of the plot to kidnap her. "Make no mistake, my lord, Merin ap Owen is deserving of his reputation, yet he treated me with courtesy, and aye, even kindness while I was in his charge. He protected me from Isleen's attempts to harm me. In his own way he is an honorable man. Isleen, disguised as Merin ap Owen's courier, yesterday took the ransom from Sim and has disappeared. That is why I was not returned to you then. Sim is very brave, Ranulf. As it grew near sunset, he rode on to Gwynfr. It was then the deception was discovered. Yet this morning Merin ap Owen freed me to return to you. He is not all wicked, *and* he has given me his word that Ashlin will not be disturbed again."

"You believe him?"

"Aye, I do," Elf said quietly. "You must trust me in this, Ranulf. I was Merin ap Owen's captive for four months. There is a side to him he does not show to others, except perhaps his longtime servant, Gwyll, who looked after me. There is goodness in him, Ranulf. I slept in an alcove off his bedchamber all those months because he feared that Isleen would hurt me given the chance. His apartments, however, were not open to anyone but Gwyll. I was safe there. Not once did this man attempt to accost me in a lewd manner. I could have been back at St. Frideswide's, for that matter, I was so safe in his charge."

Her words troubled him, but Ranulf knew his wife would not lie to him. It simply was not in Eleanore's nature to lie. "What did you do during the day?" he asked her, curious.

"Gwyll and I found an old loom and a tapestry frame. We put them by the fire, and I kept myself amused in that manner. Before the winter set in, I gathered roots and plants to make a store of salves, lotions, and medicines for the castle. They had none at all. I showed Gwyll what he is to do in the future," Elf finished.

Ranulf laughed. He simply couldn't help it. It was so very typical of his wife's sweet nature and kind heart. "I suppose you mended the Welshman's clothes for him, too," he half teased her.

"Aye, I did," she admitted. Then she giggled. "There are no women, even servants, at Gwynfr Castle, my love; and Isleen was certainly not about to repair the poor man's tunics. I could hardly have my captor going about looking shabby."

He roared with laughter. "Petite," he told her, "I most certainly do love you with all my heart and soul. You are quite unique, my Eleanore."

"The lord Merin has gone after Isleen, Ranulf. He will, I suspect, have a difficult time finding her, for she could have gone in any direction. Gwynfr is already a half ruin. Leave it be, so that when, or if, he ever returns home again, what is left of Gwynfr will be there to shelter him. Let us go home and see our son, my lord. I think it is past time we gave him a brother." She smiled up at him.

Ranulf nodded in agreement. How could he refuse her request? He really could not. Merin ap Owen had almost beggared them, but he had his wife safely back.

They walked back to their horses, where the others awaited. Now the lord of Ashlin noticed Arwydd. "Who is she?" he asked.

"Her name is Arwydd," Elf began.

"The wench who betrayed Ashlin?" he demanded, his brow darkening.

"The very same," Elf replied calmly. "She is to be my new servant, my lord, and I will hear no more about it. Arwydd made a bad mistake. She was compelled to serve a wicked mistress. She repents of her own ill judgment, and she has done us both a great service. Arwydd knew about our son. Yet she helped me to dry up my milk before I reached Gwynfr, and she never told either her mistress or the lord of the castle of our child. What do you think Isleen would have done if she had known we had a baby, Ranulf? All the devils in hell could not have prevented her from going to Ashlin and stealing our son away. Arwydd prevented this tragedy by remaining silent. She deserves a second chance, and I mean to see that she gets it. She is freeborn, and she has a good heart, Ranulf. She served Isleen faithfully, and her reward was to have her mistress desert her. She will be loyal to us, I guarantee it."

"It would seem I can deny you nothing, my lady wife," he answered her.

Elf stood upon her toes, and kissed him lightly upon the lips. "Thank you, my lord," she said as he then lifted her into the saddle.

Ranulf mounted his own horse.

"Are we going after the Welshman, my lord?" Sim asked him.

"Nay," Ranulf replied, and then briefly explained to his men the reason for his decision. "Ap Owen has gone after Isleen de Warenne. He is punished if he catches her, and he is punished if she eludes him, I am thinking," he concluded. "Let us go home!"

By late afternoon they were well over the border and into England again. The day remained fair, and the countryside about them empty but for their party. For the next three days they traveled back to Ashlin, camping at night in the open, for so desolate was the countryside that there was no religious house for them to shelter in, or even the rudest inn or manor house. Each night the horses were staked within a crude enclosure of brush, and a huge fire was built to keep away any predators. They were a large enough party to be safe from bandits. They ate what they could catch, and the bread they carried with them.

Finally in early afternoon of the fourth day, they topped a rise, and there below them was the manor of Ashlin on a near hill. Elf's heart beat faster, and with great happiness, for sometimes in the darkest night she had wondered if ever she would see her home again. At the look upon her beautiful face, Ranulf reached out and took his wife's hand in his for a moment, squeezing it gently. Their eyes met, and she smiled.

"Simon will not recognize me," she said.

"You will not recognize him," he told her. "When I left to go to Normandy, he was not even two months old. When I returned just at Christ's Mass, he was seven months old. I was astounded. It was as if I were being shown a different child. It will affect you the same way, I am thinking, petite. He pulls himself up now, and stands. He crawls, and he says all manner of babble, which his nurses pretend to understand. Although, all I can ever make out clearly is the word *Da,* which he says when he sees me." He chuckled. "He is quite a child, petite. Do not fret if he is strange with you at first, for that is only to be expected. He has not seen you in several months, but he will soon warm to you again, and probably never know or even remember that he was once separated from you." He raised her hand to his lips, and kissed it. "Tonight, petite, we will begin the arduous process of making a brother for Simon. Ashlin must have more than one son." He released her small hand from his, and smiled into her eyes.

"I need a daughter," she said boldly.

"We will do our best to arrange for that, too," he assured her with a broad grin.

Elf laughed, and together, their men behind them, they came down from the hills to Ashlin. Their serfs were plowing in the fields, but once they saw the lady of Ashlin, they cried joyously and came running to greet her. Those who recognized Arwydd, however, glared darkly in her direction. They knew well the part she had played in Elf's abduction, for old Ida's tongue had not been idle, and the elderly woman was respected among her peers. Arwydd shivered at the black looks being sent her way, instinctively pressing her mount closer to Sim's.

"Don't look to me for protection," he said to her. "I agree with them. If I were the lord, I should have sent you packing."

"You know nothing of me," Arwydd snapped at him. "You have lived your whole life safe and secure here at Ashlin. You know little of true evil or wickedness. I do. I will never betray our lady Eleanore again. It broke my heart to do so before, but I was afraid of what they would do to me if I did not obey them. Now I am free of the lady Isleen and the lord Merin. I will endeavor to win the trust of all at Ashlin, even if it takes me a lifetime." Then, straightening her back-bone, Arwydd sat up in her saddle, her eyes focused ahead.

"It may take a lifetime with some," he said. "The lady is beloved of us all."

"I know," Arwydd replied meaningfully.

"I'll be watching you," Sim said, "to make certain you don't deceive us again."

"If you watch me too closely," Arwydd said, not looking at him, "you'll make your wife jealous."

"I have no wife," Sim said.

"Because no girl will have such a rough fellow as yourself, I imagine," Arwydd responded. "Oh, Mary, Mother of God, protect me! There is that old Ida, and she is the one I truly fear."

Sim chuckled. "You're wise, lass, for she'll not hesitate to put a knife between your ribs given the chance. She may be old, but she's as fierce as any warrior in his prime, old Ida."

"My lady! My lady!" Old Ida cried as Elf was lifted down from her mare. She clutched the young woman to her scrawny bosom weeping. "Praise God, His Blessed Mother, and all the angels in heaven, you have come home safe to us!"

Elf comforted her weeping nursemaid as best she could. "I was never really in any danger, Ida. I was well treated, I promise you. Now, I want to see my son."

It was at that moment the old lady, relinquishing her hold on Elf, let out a screech, leaping back like a scalded cat and pointing a bony finger. *What is she doing here?* Ida advanced on a pale-faced Arwydd. "What is this deceitful Welsh bitch doing here? Have you come back then to destroy the whole family this time, wench?

Someone give me a knife! I will kill her now before she can do us any further harm!"

Elf stepped between Arwydd and her outraged nursemaid and explained as she had to Sim and to Ranulf.

"Your heart is too good, lady," Ida said grimly. "I do not trust the Welsh. She will be trouble," the old woman predicted darkly.

"There will be no trouble," Elf said sternly. "Do you all understand me? This girl protected Ashlin's heir. For that I am eternally grateful. She is under my protection. Any who harms her by word or deed will have to answer to me. Remember that I am the lady here!"

Arwydd suddenly knelt before Ida and, looking up at the old woman with tear-filled eyes, pleaded, "Please, Ida, forgive me the wrong I have done the Ashlin folk!"

"Clever baggage," the old woman muttered, glowering down at Arwydd. "You will have to earn my forgiveness, wench, but I will not speak against you to the others. That, at least, your pretty plea has gained you."

Arwydd scrambled to her feet and hurried after Elf, who was already entering her home. Alyce came forward carrying her little charge in her arms. Elf felt the tears sliding down her cheeks as she took her son into her arms. His hair was her own pale red-gold, but Simon de Glandeville looked at his mother with his father's warm hazel eyes. Elf kissed the child passionately until he protested and squirmed away from her, holding out his arms to Alyce.

Elf laughed. "Oh, Simon," she said to him, "you must forgive your mama. I have missed you so very much, and missed so much of you, *bébé.* But they tell me you will never know of this separation, and within a short time you will be used to your mama again." She kissed the top of his head, and handed the little boy off to Alyce. "Thank you," she said to the young serf who had cared so faithfully for her son.

"Maris fed him, lady, and still does," Alyce said blushing with her mistress's praise.

"Tell her she must continue to do so, as my milk has been dried away now," Elf responded.

"My lady! Welcome home!"

"Cedric!" Elf held out her hands to her steward, smiling.

He took her hands, and pressed them to his heart a moment, then stood back to allow John the bailiff and Fulk to come forward. They both greeted her happily. Elf thanked them both for their care of Ashlin in her absence.

"Sim," she told Fulk, "was very brave, and did well in the face of adversity. You may be proud of your kin, Fulk. I promise you that the next time you advise me, I shall listen well."

Fulk's eyes grew visibly misty. "Thank you, my lady," he said, grateful she did not hold him responsible for her captivity.

"I'll want a bath after the meal," Elf announced as they seated themselves at the high board.

The meal was served, and Elf ate with relish, particularly of the roasted meats and the greens, which had been few and far between at Gwynfr, whose cook it seemed boiled everything to mush. There was even a sweet pudding of boiled wheat, milk, sugar, cinnamon, dried apples, and raisins. She practically licked her wooden bowl clean, swallowing down the last of her sweet wine with a sigh.

"It would seem," her husband noted, "that the kitchens of the Welshman left much to be desired. Do you want the rest of my pudding?"

Without a word Elf switched bowls with him, and scooped up the remainder of the pudding with a mischievous grin. "I was hungry for sweets," she said.

"So am I," he replied, his hazel eyes twinkling, and she giggled. It was a wonderful sound, he thought. "Go and bathe, petite."

"Let us bathe together, Ranulf, my dear lord," she invited him, and her glance was warm. "We have both been on the road for several long days . . . and nights. I believe we would find the water salubrious." She arose from the high board and, walking to the door leading to the solar, turned to look seductively at him. Then she was gone.

A feeling, unfamiliar to him these last months, rippled through his large frame. His member actually tingled in anticipation, then began to harden with lust. He drained his cup slowly, making a small attempt to bring himself under control. He had waited for this night for months. He would not spoil it with undue haste. Willa and Arwydd came from the solar, giggling. They had once been friends, and now Elf's approval of Arwydd restored, Willa saw no reason to hold a grudge. The two young women had taken up where they had left off.

"Lady says you are to join her, my lord," Willa said.

"And we're not to return until morning," Arwydd added.

He grinned at them conspiratorially evoking another burst of giggles from the two girls. He walked across the hall to the solar and barred the door behind him. Turning, he caught his breath in surprise. She awaited him as naked as the day she had been born. He closed his eyes briefly as he felt his hunger for her welling up once again.

"My lord," she murmured low. "Let me help you to undress so we may have our lovely bath. The water is perfect, warm and just lightly scented with the fragrance of flowers." She drew him over to a stool. "Sit, please, so I may remove your boots."

He sat, not certain if he should be shocked by her boldness. What had happened to his innocent Eleanore? Was it possible that Merin ap Owen— He pushed the suspicion away. The one thing he could be certain of was that his wife had been faithful to him in her captivity. Had she not, she would either have killed herself or told him of it and begged his forgiveness. Besides, why was he concerned that she was so suddenly deliciously impudent? Was it not for his pleasure? His eyes caressed her round little bottom as she bent to pull off his boots. Then she drew off his stockings.

"Please to rise, my lord," she instructed him. Kneeling she slipped his braies down and slid her hands beneath his tunics and chemise to caress his naked flesh, fondling his bare bottom with kneading fingers. She rolled the fabric of the braies down his legs, smoothing his calves as she did so. "Foot," she said, tapping his left foot so he would lift it. Then the right foot. Sitting back on her haunches, she folded the braies and set them on the stool.

Standing again, Elf smiled teasingly up into his face. Then she went about the business of removing his outer tunic, and the two undertunics he wore. Now Ranulf was clad only in his linen chemise. His raging manhood thrust the soft material forward. Licking her lips with her tongue in a provocative fashion, Elf slowly unlaced the garment, her hands pushing it open, smoothing over his broad chest, sliding the garment off his shoulders so that it fell to the floor. "Now," she said, "we are equal, my lord," and bending her head she stroked his warm flesh with her wet tongue, teasing at his nipples until he thought his head would burst and his loins explode with their raging desire for her.

Ranulf drew her up and wrapped his arms about her. His lips played softly over her lips. *"What,"* he demanded, "has happened to the little innocent I married?" Then, before she might answer him, he kissed her hard as their bodies pressed together heatedly.

Elf knew she was yet in control, but she was half-conscious with the pleasure his lips offered. *Too long!* Too long, she thought muzzily. Her breasts were molded tightly against his chest. The heat from his body was utterly intoxicating. His manhood was like iron against her belly. His thighs were like rock. Her lips softened and parted just slightly beneath his. His tongue played with her tongue, sending shivers of delight and anticipation up and down her spine. Finally she drew her head away from him. "The water will grow cold if we do not bathe soon, but our desire, I think, will continue to remain hot, my love."

His hazel eyes were overflowing with his passion, but he released her and climbed up the steps into the tall oaken tub by the fire. Then reaching out he lifted her in with him. Elf took up the sea sponge and filled it with liquid soap. Then she began to wash him, rubbing the sponge over his back and his chest, down his arms, across his shoulders, around his neck. She took a small soft cloth to wash his face, then his ears. The sponge dipped beneath the water to wash what she could not see. Ranulf gritted his teeth and bore her delicious ministrations. On her command he dipped himself beneath the warm water to rinse. Then it was his turn.

Taking the sponge from her, he renewed the soft soap and rubbed across her back and shoulders, laving water with his big hand to rinse her silken skin. Laying the sponge aside on the ledge of the tub for a moment, he slipped an arm about her and drew her back against him. He kissed the nape of her neck softly, nibbling lightly at the tiny curls springing forth where her long hair was pinned up.

"Delicious," he murmured against her skin, then he nipped the flesh and laughed softly when she squealed, pressing her bottom against his groin.

"Witch," he told her, taking up the sponge again in his free hand. He encircled first one breast, rubbing lightly over the soft mound, slipping the sponge between her two breasts, and then moving on to the other. He could see the effect he was having upon her, for her little nipples thrust themselves forward, peaking hard. His hand moved beneath the water to smooth firmly over her Venus mont, cupping it.

Elf sighed with pleasure. She wanted this to go on forever and ever. Then to her surprise he pushed her firmly against the wall of the tub, pulling her thighs apart and bending her slightly. She felt the head of his manhood seeking her love channel, and then he was filling her full of himself. "Oh, Ranulf!" she murmured.

"I could wait no longer," he whispered in her ear. "Follow my rhythm, petite. There will be more afterward, I promise you!" His loins began to move against her, and Elf instinctively pushed her buttocks back against his strong thrusts. Her head was beginning to spin with delight as she felt the strongly pulsing, pulsing cadence of his manhood within her. His fingers dug into the flesh of her hips as he held her steady, pressing deeper and deeper within her wet and burning softness. Elf could feel her husband growing thicker and more demanding of her. She whimpered her pleasure, needing him so desperately she thought she would die. And then their combined passions exploded in a crescendo of boiling juices that crowned his manhood and flooded her heart and body with joy.

They cried out together, and he slumped for a long moment

against her, his hands moving up to her breasts, teasing the nipples so that she spasmed again and yet again. When he came to himself, he turned her about and kissed her hungrily, his mouth fierce and demanding against hers. "It is a beginning, petite, but not yet enough," he growled in her ear. His hands clamped about her buttocks, and she felt him against her, already eager with his need for her.

"I never knew a man could be so insatiable," she said to him, wrapping her arms about his neck and pressing her breasts against his broad chest. But while he had driven her to an apogee, she could sense it had not been enough for her, either. Her breasts felt hard and quite dissatisfied with a strong longing that was unfamiliar, and yet familiar.

"It has been close to a year since I had you in my arms," he told her, "and all that time I remained faithful to you, petite. At Queen Alienor's court of love, there were many beautiful women who would have gladly filled my bed, but I could only think of you, petite. My precious wife. My only love." His face was sincere with the declaration. There were, she noticed for the first time, small fine lines about his eyes. "My mission for the king came to naught, Eleanore. We shall have no grateful Henry Plantagenet granting us his permission to build a small keep here at Ashlin. We shall remain what we have always been. A simple manor, and worse off for Merin ap Owen."

"We will regain our lost ground, my lord. Did I not see some sheep with their lambs in the enclosure by the barns?" she asked him.

"Aye," he said with a small grin. "We shall speak on it later, my love. For now my lust has just been barely slaked. I want to take you to bed, wife, and bury myself in your sweet body." He climbed from the oak tub, lifting her out after him.

Together they dried each other, leaving the damp drying cloths on the stone floor of the solar as they entered their small bedchamber. Before he might draw her into bed, however, Elf knelt and, taking him in her mouth, pleasured him as she had once done before the separation. Her tongue ran around and around the ruby head of his manhood, teasing him, playing with him until he forbade it further. Picking her up, he placed her carefully upon the bed, her legs over the edge, her feet not quite touching the floor.

"I will show you the same pleasure you have shown me," he said, and then gently parting her nether lips, his head dipped between her thighs.

Elf gasped with delight as she felt the very tip of his tongue in that most secret of places. He licked her slowly. His tongue sought the opening to her passage and pushed in as far as it could go, tasting her renewed juices. She cried out with pleasure as his tongue began to play with her tiny jewel, and she felt it swell and burst with the delectation he offered her. "*Ohhh*, yes, my lord! It is *soooo* good," she mewled.

And when he had seen that she enjoyed this pleasure, he pulled her onto their bed fully, joining her with a smile. "I have wanted to give you that delight for so long," he said, kissing her lips so that she could taste herself upon them. He cupped her mound in one hand. "You are so warm and alive, my love. I do not believe I shall ever gain enough of you." His head dipped, and he fastened upon one of her nipples, suckling eagerly.

She cried out softly, her body arcing as the pleasure coursed through her again. He would surely kill her with his tender loving. Was it indeed possible to die of love? His hand kneaded the breast strongly, and Elf half sobbed. "I need you inside of me, my Ranulf! I am aching with my desire for you!"

Removing his hands from her body, he pinioned her between his thighs, and then he slowly entered her body, groaning with delight as he did so. She was the most perfect lover, he thought happily as his great lance sheathed itself deep inside her. He began to move with deliberate leisure upon her, within her, feeling her body welcoming him.

Elf wrapped her legs about her husband's torso, drawing him as close as she could. She could feel his throbbing and pulsing within her, and with a behavior she hadn't known she possessed but knew was right, she contracted her muscles to squeeze him tightly. When he groaned, she knew she had given him pleasure, and did it again and again until he pleaded with her to cease, for he desired her delight, too. She allowed herself to drift away, engulfed by his love, his strength, his warmth. She was slowly, slowly ascending to a place of incredible pleasure such as she had never known. She clung to him breathlessly, and as the stars burst behind her closed eyes, she cried out his name. *"Ranulf!"* Then she tumbled into a place of incredible sweetness and warm darkness, hearing him cry her name as she fell. *"Eleanore!"*

When she awoke, it was to find herself sprawled half upon his chest, his arms about her. She smiled happily. There would be another child of their shared passion this night, Elf sensed, and she wanted that child and the other children that, God willing, would follow. She did not care that Ashlin would have no castle. She was content with what God had given her. A husband she loved, and who loved her. A healthy son named Simon Hubert. Ashlin with its good grazing and growing land. Her loyal serfs and freedmen and women. A guarantee from Merin ap Owen that he would leave them in peace. She was even grateful for a king she did not know, Henry Plantagenet, who had brought order and rule back to England again. And then there were the nuns, her true family and dearest friends, from St. Frideswide's. She must go and see them soon, to assure them she had come through her ordeal quite unscathed.

"What are you thinking about?" Ranulf suddenly asked her, his voice startling her as it cut into the quiet of her thoughts.

She raised herself off his warm chest so she might look into his eyes. "I am thinking of how fortunate we are," she told him. "I am thinking of how much I love you, my Ranulf."

The happiness that lit up his face at her simple words touched her heart to its very core.

He drew her into the circle of his embrace, turning her so they might still look upon each other. Lifting her hand, he kissed each of her fingers, smiling into her eyes as he did so. "The words, petite, were hard for me to first say, but now I am no longer afraid of them. I loved you yesterday. I love you today. And I will love you tomorrow and always, Eleanore."

She looked into his hazel eyes, which were misty with his admitted emotion. How could she ever have doubted, she wondered? "I will hold you to that promise, my lord husband," she said. "Yesterday, today, tomorrow . . . *always!*"

EPILOGUE

London 1159

The house on Trollops Lane, just outside the Aldersgate, was one of the finest that had ever been built in or about London. It was not wood, like the majority of the homes and shops in the town. It was built of stone, and had a slate roof unlikely to catch fire. It had a garden behind it, and it was rumored that the lady Strumpet, for that was the name the owner of the house went by, owned the fields beyond as well.

The door was kept by two dark-skinned Moors, eunuchs it was said. They wore bright red baggy silk pants, and vests cut from cloth-of-gold that were embroidered and bejeweled. A wide gold sash was wrapped about their waists. From those sashes hung sharp-looking curved scimitars. Inside the house the decor was expensive, elegant, and very lush in the Oriental fashion. It was like no other house in England. The serving girls were all extremely pretty, and the whores full-bodied and very willing, not to mention most beautiful. Beautiful women cost far more to lie with than ordinary wenches. The house on Trollops Lane was the finest whorehouse in the world, or so it was said. Any and every kind of pleasure was offered to the gentlemen who called. They had but to ask.

The house stood a full four stories tall. On the fourth floor the servants lived comfortably. On the third and second floors were the comfortable rooms in which the women entertained their clients. The first floor was used for greeting and entertainments. There was a deep stone cellar, too. It was there fine wine was kept, as were rooms for patrons whose tastes ran to the more exotic, the painful, and the bizzare. Yet so well built was the house that the sounds of such forced pleasure never arose from that cellar.

Entertainments were always unique and daring. My lady Strumpet had a great and colorful imagination. The most popular evening each month was when a virgin was offered up to the house's patrons. The maiden was brought to the hall and placed upon the high board. She was always fully garbed to begin with. Sometimes she was dressed like a lady of the court. Other times a merchant or a farmer's daughter. Sometimes the virgin was gowned as a nun with her beads or as a gypsy girl. The patrons would eagerly pay to have articles of the girl's clothing removed until she was quite naked. Then the bidding would begin in earnest for her maidenhead. The winner would be given his prize for the entire night, but only after the innocent was publicly deflowered by her patron upon the high board. That way all saw that when the lady Strumpet offered a man a virgin, he got a virgin. The virgin was always lightly drugged to assure her cooperation; but some still struggled and shrieked, adding to the evening's amusement.

It was even said that King Henry, whose carnal appetites were well-known, patronized the house on Trollops Lane when he was in London. The queen, while very beautiful and said to be every bit as passionate as her husband, had been kept busy birthing heirs for their vast domains. Alienor of Aquitane had come to England with her firstborn child, Prince William, and a full belly. The little prince had since died, but the queen had given England three more princes, Henry, Richard, and Geoffrey, as well as a princess, Matilda. If she had ever heard of the house on Trollops Lane, she was too well mannered and, at that point in her life, too confident of her husband's love even to mention it.

It was but two hours until the dawn. The house was very quiet now, the patrons having taken their pleasure and gone their way, or having decided to remain for the whole night. The lady Strumpet sat within her locked apartment, counting the many coins taken in that night. She was attired in a diaphanous chamber robe, for the evening was warm and her body was still a good one. It amused her to greet her guests dressed so provocatively. Many of them openly desired her, but it was she who chose her lovers. She never retained them for too long a time, lest they grow complacent and certain of her affections. She wanted no man to have charge over her ever again.

"You are as beautiful as ever, my pretty bitch," a familiar and certainly most unwelcome voice said to her, breaking the soothing silence.

Isleen turned slowly about, feigning surprise. "Who are you?" she said, pretending she had never before seen this man.

Merin ap Owen laughed. "Do not dissemble with me, my pretty bitch. I have come for my monies. You have invested my gold quite nicely, my dear. Two bags, I believe it was. I shall have three off of you, for certainly you did not borrow it from me and expect me not to charge you interest." He was garbed all in black.

"I do not know what you mean," Isleen said loftily, still attempting to pretend she was ignorant of his purpose in coming.

His gloved hand shot out and grasped her by the neck. *"I will have the gold you stole from me, my pretty bitch!"* His fingers tightened about her throat just enough to give pain, but not enough to seriously injure her. "I have tracked you these five years, Isleen. You have been a most wily vixen to bring to ground, but now the game is up. *Give me my gold!"* He released her so she might speak again.

Isleen de Warenne, the lady Strumpet, rubbed her injured flesh, all the while glaring at him furiously. She was alone. Her bodyguards were sleeping on the fourth floor. Her rooms, like all the others in this house, were virtually soundproof. "When I left you, my lord," she said acidly, "I gave you something better than gold. Something you desperately desired, but were too cowardly to take for yourself. I gave you Eleanore de Montfort. Did she weep and scream when you raped her? Did you enjoy her? Or did you learn that she was a very great disappointment before you finally killed her?" Isleen smiled nastily.

He looked at her with distaste now. She had aged, and was no longer quite the young beauty she had been when she was his leman. "I did not rape the lady Eleanore," he told her, smiling. "Did you think me so foolish, I would not divine your plan for revenge? I returned her to her husband as unscathed as the day I took her by force from Ashlin. It was not her fault that you murdered my courier and took his place. It was not her fault that you stole the ransom her husband sent for her release. Now, give me my gold, and I shall be on my way. We will not meet again."

"I will give you nothing!" she snapped at him. "I am a powerful woman, my lord Merin! The greatest lords in the land come to my house to be entertained. The king himself has been in my bed! If you try to take what is mine, I shall ask the king for his help. He will give it to me. He has said he has never known a woman like me," she concluded proudly, looking at him defiantly. "You are naught but bandit scum."

"It is true, Isleen, that I am a bandit lord, but you are a thief, and there are many who will attest to it. The king is a fair man. If he hears your true story, he will clap you in the prison. When Sim of Ashlin came that night to Gwynfr to learn why the lady had not been released, we pieced together what had happened. Under the circumstances I could not retain custody of my captive. I have sought for you ever since. My men left me two years ago to return to Gwynfr, certain you were dead or gone to Normandy. But I knew better, and I persisted. Now I have found you, and I want what is mine. Give it to me willingly, or I will take it by force."

"*You romantic Welsh fool!*" Isleen hissed at him, hearing only one thing. That he had left Eleanore de Montfort untouched. She had been certain her enemy was long dead. "To idolize Eleanore de Montfort, and why? She is like all women, my lord, and all women are whores at heart. *Even your precious lady Eleanore!*"

He hit her with his open palm. The force was such that he actually heard her neck snap, saw the surprise in her blue eyes as she realized she was a dead woman. Then Isleen crumpled to the floor.

Merin ap Owen bent and sought for a pulse, but there was none. Isleen de Warenne was quite dead. With a fatalistic shrug, he stepped over her body and walked to the fireplace. Counting over from the center stone atop the arch, he slowly pulled the heavy gray block from its place. He had been watching Isleen for several nights now to learn her routine, so his visit might be a simple one. He had seen through the window how each night she opened her hidey-hole, and placed the ill-gotten gains of the evening inside.

Now, reaching deep, he drew out half a dozen bags of coins. She probably had a goldsmith with whom she deposited the bulk of her funds. This would be the taking from just the past few nights. There were also several items of fine jewelry. He casually pocketed them. They would not do Isleen any good now. Replacing the stone carefully in its niche, Merin ap Owen gathered up the several bags of coins. Blowing out the candles and snuffing the lamps in the rooms, he went to the window through which he had entered. Opening the shutters, he stepped through. He turned a moment before re-closing the shutters to view Isleen's fallen body a final time. "Farewell, my pretty bitch," he whispered to her. And then he was gone into the night, well pleased with himself.

He had kept his promise to Eleanore de Montfort. She would never again be troubled by Isleen de Warenne. His pretty bitch was now in hell awaiting him, but perhaps he would not join her one day. Did not the lady Eleanore say even he could be delivered from the devil if he would but repent of his sins and wickedness? Had not she believed there was good in him? Five years on the road had taught him that to be alone and filled with evil was not a good thing. He did not know if he could ever be really good; but his mission fulfilled now, he knew he wanted to try. Reaching his horse, he stowed his booty in the saddlebags and set off down the old road called Watling Street, stopping six times along the way over the next few days to lay a bag of gold upon the altar of churches that he chose at random. The jewelry he left at the last church.

He moved northwest for the next several days, finally reaching the town of Shrewsbury. There he sold his horse and gear, pocketing the small profit for the final gift he meant to make. He walked through the town to his destination where he knocked upon the gates that opened to reveal a brown-robed monk.

"I wish to devote the rest of my life to God, good brother," Merin ap Owen said, "but I do not know if God will want so great a sinner as me. I have robbed, and murdered, and violated the fair sex. I am the worst of the worst, and I have escaped punishment for all my wickedness. Now I wish to repent, if the abbey will have me. My name is Merin ap Owen."

"God is always happy to welcome a repentant sinner, Merin ap Owen. Come in! Come in!" the monk cheerfully beckoned him. "We have some as bad as you here already. You are not the only man to offend our Lord. Still, I am certain God has been waiting for you for some time now!" And smiling, he ushered the penitent through the abbey gates.

The thought crept into his head unbidden that the lady Eleanore would be surprised—or would she? *Seek the good in you for the sake of your immortal soul,* she had told him. Well, he was going to try. A smile on his face, Merin ap Owen followed the brown-robed monk into the cloister, and into a new and better life.